INDELIBLE

ALSO BY HEATHER AMES

Brian Swift & Kaylen Roberts Mystery/Suspense series
A Swift Brand of Justice (Book 2)

Suspense
Night Shadows

Romantic Suspense
All That Glitters

Contemporary Romance
The Sweetest Song

Upcoming Books
Swift Retribution (Brian Swift & Kaylen Roberts—Book 3) Fall 2019
Ghost Shop series (mystery/suspense with a paranormal twist—Book 1) 2020

INDELIBLE

Brian Swift & Kaylen Roberts mystery/suspense series

Book 1

HEATHER AMES

Well of Ideas Press

ISBN (paperback) 978-0-9991359-5-2

Some events touch our lives. Others change them forever.

CHAPTER ONE

Kaylen Roberts stirred uneasily and flung one arm across her eyes to shield them from the harsh Miami sunlight.

Carefully turning away from the glare, she licked dry lips. Her mouth felt like it was lined with cotton, no doubt a punishment for drinking too much champagne. Last night she'd celebrated, this morning she was paying for it.

Light streamed through the windows, its reflection bouncing off mirrored closet doors. Confused and sluggish, Kaylen tried to gather her wits, but her mind refused to cooperate and scattered thoughts drifted through her head like radio waves from a badly-tuned station. As she slipped back into a dream state, a memory surfaced of her face bumping rhythmically against a man's back as he mounted stairs, his footsteps echoing on concrete treads. Her hair caught on his jacket buttons as he laid her down, and she remembered pain as he pulled away from her. The image jerked her awake.

She found herself in her own bed, damp hair clinging to her forehead, air conditioning blasting her. Shivering, she pulled the comforter up to her chin. Her clock told her it was 9:00 AM. The photograph of her boyfriend, Tim Madison, smiled at her from its silver frame beside the clock.

"Don't you grin at me like that," she muttered, glaring at his handsome face. "What the hell did you help me do to myself last night?"

When she dragged herself upright, the room spun in sickening circles. Kaylen groaned. Despite a splitting headache, she refused to believe she had a hangover. She'd been so careful not to drink more than two glasses of champagne. None of her backers would have been impressed if she'd gotten drunk.

She clearly remembered the early hours of her supper club's opening night. Drinks flowed freely, champagne corks exploded with the energy of popcorn kernels roasted over an open fire. Jammed wall to wall, her guests and patrons laughed, talked, and even shouted above the Big Band music. Waiters hoisted loaded trays as they ran more than walked between tables; bartenders filled glasses with beer on tap and mixed cocktails with lightning speed, and couples held each other close as they danced on the small wooden floor in front of the stage. Controlled pandemonium, Sam Wilson, her mentor and friend had called it, laughing as he lifted his glass to toast her success.

Kaylen allowed herself to drift with the snapshot memories. She'd been talking to Tim and Sam when intense nausea swept over her. Tim had half-carried her into the bathroom behind her office and held her head while she retched miserably into the toilet bowl. After that, she had only those dim recollections of being carried and then laid down. Otherwise, her memory was as black and fathomless as a moonless night on the ocean.

What had she done, or more importantly, what had been done to her?

Her mouth felt incredibly dry, her throat parched. Advil, she decided. And water. She moved carefully, anxious to avoid aggravating her pounding headache. *What the hell?*

Even her right leg hurt. Either she'd scraped it somewhere, or maybe Tim wasn't as strong as he looked, and he'd dropped her after she passed out. She threw off the covers and discovered she was completely naked. Her black silk cocktail dress lay balled up on the floor several feet from the bed. Her shoes rested in positions that suggested they had been kicked off, one upside down beside the TV stand, the other balanced precariously on one end of the dresser.

Hers weren't the only clothes on the floor. A pair of black jeans and a black t-shirt lay in one corner of the room. Large black sneakers played footsie with her lace panties. Her strapless bra dangled from the door knob, and navy-blue boxers draped the bedpost.

A stifled moan moved her attention from the scattered clothing to a large hump on the other side of the bed. She tried to remember what Tim had been wearing the night before. A tux, she thought. White shirt. Dress shoes. She looked again at the sneakers on her bedroom floor. Tim never wore battered tennis shoes. He always dressed immaculately. And he wore briefs, not boxers. Her heart accelerated into an uncomfortable gallop.

She leaned over and pulled the comforter down a couple of inches. Spiky blond hair peeked out. Kaylen's heart skipped a beat. Tim's hair was black. She didn't even know anyone with a haircut like that.

Oh shit, she was naked in bed with a stranger!

She carefully scooted away, but even the slight motion of the bed disturbed the man. He rolled onto his back, his face still covered with the sheet. Despite a strong urge to jump up and run as far away as possible, Kaylen kept edging slowly toward the side of the bed. She had to get rid of this guy. She'd never had a one-night stand in her life. In fact, until she met Tim, she'd lived the life of a nun since her husband's death. Whoever this man was, she wanted him out of her condo as soon as possible.

But she had to get her bathrobe on before waking him up and telling him to get out. She swung her legs off the bed and tried to stand. Her head swam. She staggered, her feet becoming entangled with the comforter. Powerless to stop herself, she fell. An involuntary scream ripped from her throat, and the hump in her bed shot upright. Frozen by panic, she stared in horrified fascination as her unwanted guest turned his head in her direction. Her own dark gaze met blue eyes deeply flecked with gold, like sun streaks. Blond eyebrows drew together as he stared at her. She discovered her limbs weren't frozen after all and bounded for the door.

Her flight ended in an undignified tackle. Before she knew what had hit her, she was lying on the floor, her nose level with her discarded shoe. She lashed out with her good leg, her foot catching her attacker square in the stomach. He swore and released her. Kaylen grabbed her aching thigh and clenched her teeth.

"Christ," the guy said. "Where am I? And where the hell are my clothes?"

Kaylen drew in a deep breath.

"Don't you *dare* start screaming again," he said.

Out of the corner of her eye, she saw him grab the comforter to cover himself. *Careful*, she told herself as she sat up to face him.

"Sorry I grabbed you," he said. "That was a reflex. Long as you don't make any sudden moves, I won't do it again." He rubbed a hand over his face. "I'd like to stay in one place for the next few minutes. I've got a splitting headache, and thanks to you kicking the crap out of me, a pain in my gut."

Kaylen had expected assault, not sarcasm. Anger overwhelmed fear. "Bastard," she said. She grabbed her cocktail dress and held it against her.

"Hmm." He raised one blond eyebrow. "I don't think you're in any position to start insulting me." He offered her the other end of the comforter. "Here. This'd be a whole lot better than that rag."

Kaylen shook her head. She'd have to move closer to him, and she wasn't going to do that under any circumstances. "This is a designer dress, not a rag," she said. With as much dignity as possible, she pulled her crumpled dress over her head and zipped it up.

"Well, excuse me for not noticing," he snapped, his voice rising. "Damn it…" He stopped and took a deep breath when he saw her recoil. "Look," he continued in a kinder tone. "I told you I'm sorry I tackled you. I don't know what else you want me to say."

"Apologizing's a start," she said. "But that's not nearly enough."

"Okay…what if I tell you that you don't need to be afraid of me?" He watched her intently. "I'm not going to rape you, if that's what's scaring you."

If he thought that was going to make her feel any better, Kaylen decided, then he was an idiot.

"You've got some nerve, telling me not to scream or be frightened," she said, testing his truthfulness by getting up and limping over to a chair. "What do you expect me to do when I wake up in bed with a naked stranger…offer you a cup of coffee?" She glared at him. "Who *are* you, and what are you doing here?"

He glared right back. "Rudeness isn't going to get you anywhere, lady," he assured her. "Neither is firing questions at me that I can't answer. I don't have any damned idea what I'm doing here."

He sat propped against the bed, one hand clutching his stomach while the other gingerly explored the back of his head. Aged somewhere between his mid to late thirties, with a day's growth of stubble covering his hard, angular chin, he didn't look like a deadbeat. His hair was clean and well-cut, and he didn't reek of sweat or alcohol. Despite the battered condition of his tennis shoes right at Kaylen's feet, they didn't smell, either. When she looked at them, she saw her panties again. She tried to slide them under the chair with one foot, but he was watching her, damn him, and she saw the corner of his mouth quirk, as though he thought her fear and embarrassment were amusing.

She glanced surreptitiously at the bathroom door. Ten feet, she thought. She might make it if she could get up fast enough. But Kaylen wondered what advantage she would gain by locking herself in a room without either a window or a phone. The condos were well-built. She doubted anyone had heard her scream or whether they would pay attention even if she pounded on the wall for help.

"I wouldn't try running again if I was you. I might not be such a gentleman the next time." He folded his arms and gave her a slow, lazy, and very annoying smile. "I'm still waiting for you to explain yourself."

"Explain *myself?*" Kaylen pushed strands of tangled chestnut hair out of her eyes and shook her finger at him. "Listen, I'm not the one who needs to do the explaining. I live here. *I'll* ask the questions. Let's start with 'who do you think you are, breaking into my home,' and then we'll move on quickly to you giving me a damned good reason for being in my bed!"

A scowl replaced his smile. "I've already told you I didn't break into your place, and princess, I have no idea why I was in your bed. With a temper like yours, I *sure* wouldn't climb in there by choice." He held up one hand when Kaylen started to protest. "You've got more explaining to do than I have. I bet you were the one who hit me over the head and dragged me into your bed. The last thing I remember about last night was getting out of my car in the parking lot."

CHAPTER TWO

Kaylen stared at him. "You must think I'm really gullible. Hit over the head, huh?" She snorted in disgust. "Even if I *had* hit you, which I can assure you I didn't, how could I possibly have carried you through the parking lot and upstairs? I'm not an Amazon, for God's sake. This condo's on the second floor."

"I wouldn't know *what* floor you live on." His voice rose again, and his eyes turned hard and cold. "I have no goddamned idea what's even outside this *room.*"

He stopped abruptly, his face contorting. Kaylen waited, unsure whether he was going to grab her by the neck or get control of himself. Mercifully, he chose the latter.

"Sorry," he said, his tone clipped but quieter. "Shouting at you isn't going to solve anything, and it's making my headache worse." He gingerly fingered his scalp and winced. "I can prove I was knocked out." He turned away from her and pointed. "See? I've got a knot."

Kaylen *did* see it, and dried blood on his hair, too. "Oh," she said. It seemed he was as much a victim of this bizarre scenario as she. A rude victim, she thought, remembering him calling her "princess." She choked back her irritation. "Why don't we try this again? What's your name?"

"Brian Swift." He settled back and grimaced as his head touched the mattress. "You?"

"Kaylen Roberts." She looked him over again.

Muscular arms and powerful legs poked out beyond the comforter.

Judging by the length of those legs, she guessed he was probably around six feet. Built like a man trained to take care of himself, he also looked like he would be prepared to do so whenever necessary. Kaylen imagined he could defend himself very successfully now he was no longer groggy. She decided to ignore the urge to flee from the room. It was irrational, and it wouldn't get her any answers.

"All right," she said. "What were you doing in the parking lot late at night?"

"Waiting," he said.

"Waiting for what?" She glanced at his scattered clothes. The black shirt, jeans and tennis shoes looked uncomfortably suitable for blending with the night.

"I can't tell you that."

"I bet." She tried to make eye contact, but he avoided her gaze. "You're not going to tell me anything else, are you?"

"No," he said.

"Then you'd better get dressed and go," she told him. "Before I call the police," she added.

That produced a reaction. For the space of a heartbeat he looked startled, and then it was gone. "You think you're in any position to call the cops?" He gave her a disconcerting stare. "What're you gonna tell them? That we woke up in bed together? They'd laugh at you."

Kaylen looked at her hands, clasped so tightly the knuckles had turned white. If only she could remember how she got home. She thought again about being thrown over some man's shoulder and wondered if Tim had carried her in, stripped her and dumped her in her bed, or whether Brian Swift was responsible.

Brian was right about one thing. She didn't need the cops asking her the same questions and concluding she'd had too much to drink followed by casual sex with a stranger. Neither did she want any negative publicity wrecking her club opening. Her mind suddenly produced another disconcerting flashback of her staggering all over the bar as she tried to get to the bathroom.

Uneasily, she admitted that she might not have made it before she vomited. Her memory released another disconcerting tidbit—throwing up on a pair of jeweled shoes. Kaylen shuddered. Apart from the possibility of losing her own money, she felt even more worried that her backers would pull out if they thought she couldn't handle the responsibility of the club. If they did, then she'd be totally screwed, unable to even make payroll, let alone the rest of the monthly overheads.

She shifted position to relieve the pressure on her sore leg and the ripped seam of her dress gaped open, exposing her thigh. She started to pull the ends of the dress back together but stopped, staring in disbelief.

"What's wrong?" Brian leaned forward.

Kaylen barely noticed him, her gaze riveted on her leg. She released the silk, which slid away to reveal the tattoo of a rose in full bloom in the middle of her right thigh. The colors were muted yet vivid to her shocked mind. It was a beautifully drawn rose, its stem filled with minute thorns and entwined with a blue ribbon, which lay artistically coiled next to two pink petals, fashioned so well that they appeared to have fallen only moments before. It might have been beautiful on someone else, she thought, but not on her. On her it was an obscenity.

"Did you do this?" she asked. She pointed to the tattoo. "Did you put this…this *thing* on me?"

"No, I didn't." He held the comforter tightly anchored around him with one hand while he retrieved his clothes with the other. "Even if I knew how to do a tattoo, I'd never put one on a great leg like yours." He pulled his t-shirt over his head. "Besides, that rose was done by an artist, and art's definitely not one of my talents."

Kaylen covered her face with her hands. Tears welled up. If only all this was a nightmare, she thought, but she knew it wasn't as moisture from the tears trickled down her cheeks. Her head still felt thick and heavy, her thoughts jumbled. She heard Brian pulling on the rest of his clothes.

He walked over and squeezed her shoulder. "Sorry about your leg."

Fully dressed, he looked very much in control of himself, whereas Kaylen felt more exposed and vulnerable than she had when she first realized he was in her bed. She brushed the tears away and sniffed.

"You've had a rough night," Brian said. He glanced at her leg again. "Even rougher than mine by the look of it." He leaned over to pick up his shoes, swayed and grabbed the TV stand. "Damn." He shook his head. "I'm dizzy."

Kaylen pulled the tattered ends of her dress together. "I just don't get it," she said. "I was at the opening of my supper club and having a really good time until right out of the blue I started feeling lightheaded. Then I vomited. So much. I couldn't seem to stop." She frowned, trying to push the fog out of her brain. "After that, I must have passed out." Her hair kept falling in her eyes. Annoyed, she brushed it off her face. Her skin felt clammy, her tongue thick and coated. "I can't *think* straight," she said. "I feel so out of it. Like I'm...I'm..." She struggled to find the right words.

"Drugged," Brian said. He walked over to the window, leaned against the wall and peered out.

Kaylen watched him. "You think so?" Her unease grew. "What are you doing? Are you looking for someone?"

His eyes narrowed as they shifted from the window to her face. "Just checking to make sure the press isn't out there or something. In case this is some publicity stunt you or someone you know cooked up." He tilted the blinds and cut the merciless sunlight to a muted golden glow. "Kaylen Roberts. You're that socialite. The philanthropist's widow. What was his name? George something...yeah, George Bannister Roberts."

Kaylen nodded curtly. "Yes."

She was used to that speculative look, and to the comments that usually accompanied it. *A young woman of twenty-eight, marrying a sixty-year-old man.*

What was she thinking? She must be a gold-digger.

It'll never last.

And it didn't, but not for all the jaded reasons brought up by the naysayers and gossipmongers. Cancer had taken George within two years of their marriage.

Kaylen forced those still-painful memories aside. She had more immediate problems to deal with than resurrecting her grief over her deceased husband.

"Do you really think I'd drug myself and then give myself a tattoo, or allow anyone else to do those things to me?" she asked Brian. "What do you think I am, some sort of freak?"

Again with the hair, she thought, as curls flopped in front of her eyes. When she raised her hand, her dress slid off her leg again and exposed her thigh all the way up to her hip. Kaylen's cheeks flamed. She felt more helpless than she had ever felt in her life, even when the tabloids were at their worst. Tears blurred her vision, and she made no attempt to hide them as they coursed down her cheeks.

Brian turned away to look out the window again. Kaylen scooped up her panties and managed to pull them on while his face was averted. At the thought of how he could use this incident to his advantage in the not-too-distant future, she cringed. If he talked to the media, her backers would pull out. She'd fought so hard to win their respect and trust, but they wouldn't want to be connected with a scandal, even if she denied it. Kaylen knew her venture had been considered a high-risk investment, a young, single woman opening a supper club.

Brian might even try to blackmail her. She fought a tightness settling into her chest, making it harder to breathe. George's ex-wife would love that. The dreaded Sylvia and her four adult children had contested the will and kept Kaylen in litigation for more than a year, even though they had already inherited the bulk of George's estate.

Brian's voice broke into her whirling thoughts. "Are you decent now?" he asked.

"Yes. I suppose so." Kaylen didn't know whether to thank him for keeping his face turned away or haul off and give him another lump on his head just on principle. Perhaps if he was unconscious again, she'd be able to drag him downstairs and dump him back in the parking lot, where he belonged. It was still early, and maybe none of her neighbors would notice.

"Some people would do more than tattoo themselves for attention," he said, interrupting her irrational train of thought. "But assuming you're *not* a freak…," he gave her a quick smile, "…then whatever you took was probably put into something you ate or drank."

He was way too big and heavy for her to drag anywhere, Kaylen told herself. She had to get her still-wandering mind back under control and stop these delusions from popping into her head. She watched him pull on his shoes without unlacing them.

"What possible motive would anyone have to drug and tattoo me, let alone put a stranger in bed with me?" she asked.

He shrugged. "Smells like a set-up. I think the whole thing was staged to look like you and I had a great time in here last night. Maybe someone's jealous of you or your club, or wants to ruin your chances of success because they think it's gonna mess up their own business. The tattoo sure doesn't fit the rest of that picture, though." He glanced at his watch, walked over to the door and opened it. "I have to be somewhere in an hour and a half, and I can't cancel. It's business. I can meet you later to compare notes, if you want; see if either of us has remembered anything else."

"I'm going to call the cops and report this," Kaylen said.

"I already told you that'd be a mistake." He paused, started to say something, stopped himself and strode off down the hallway toward the front of the condo.

Kaylen followed. "What are you afraid of?" she asked.

"I should think *you'd* be the one who's afraid." He sounded defensive.

"What are you implying? My conscience is clear." She ran into his back when he suddenly stopped.

Brian turned, his smile sarcastic and annoying. "Ever heard of guilt by association?"

She backed away and tossed her head. "I've got no association with you."

"Maybe, but not all your friends are squeaky clean. If you involve the cops in this, you might very well end up causing a lot of trouble for those friends as well as yourself."

"What are you talking about? I don't have any shady friends. My business is legit, too." She frowned. "I think you're confusing me with someone else."

"Not me, princess. I never confuse anything."

CHAPTER THREE

Brian left her standing where the hallway split two ways, the left side leading to the kitchen, the other to the living room and front door. He chose the right side. Kaylen's fear returned with a vengeance. If he was unconscious when he was brought into her condo, how would he know the way to the front door?

"You said you were waiting in the parking lot," she called, breaking into an uneven jog. "But you never said for whom."

He was in the middle of the living room. He stopped and turned to face her again. "I told you, I…"

"I know." She waved her hand dismissively. "You're not able to tell me. That's not good enough. Neither is walking out of here with some vague promise to see me later. You told me you thought we'd been set up. I want to know why you think that."

"What about that picture on your nightstand?"

"Huh?" She shifted her weight to her sore leg and then decided she'd better sit down when it protested. "That's my boyfriend. Why do you want to know?"

"He's not who he says he is."

Kaylen's headache intensified. She massaged her temples. "And how do you know that?"

"I just do."

"Not good enough. You keep asking more questions than you're giving answers. Do you *know* Tim?"

Brian kicked at the bottom of the couch. "I guess you could say that."

"Is he a friend of yours?" Kaylen tried to remember if Tim had ever mentioned Brian's name. She didn't think so.

Brian laughed mirthlessly. "Hardly."

"A business acquaintance?" she pressed.

"An acquaintance—sometimes. When it's convenient for him." Brian shrugged, the movement jerky and hinting at thinly-disguised animosity.

"Do you know where he went last night, after he took me into the bathroom, I mean?" she asked.

"Do you?"

"I told you—stop answering questions with questions." She balled up her fists. "You're driving me crazy," she said. And the tears started again. "I can't take it."

Brian hesitated, then took a step toward her. "I..."

Someone started pounding on the front door. "Police," a man shouted. "Open up!"

Kaylen looked from Brian to the door. "For God's sake," she said. "Now what?"

CHAPTER FOUR

"Get rid of them," Brian whispered. He pulled her to her feet and turned her toward the door.

Kaylen felt like telling him she didn't *want* to get rid of them, but remembered only too clearly his remark about the whole incident being a set up.

"If you don't get rid of them, you could be in more of a mess than you think you are already," Brian hissed in her ear.

"Don't threaten me," Kaylen said, but she swallowed a lump of fear. If this wasn't a publicity stunt meant to embarrass her and cast a cloud over George's memory, then it had to have more sinister implications.

"Ms. Roberts? Ms. Roberts, open up!" The pounding on the door intensified. "Ms. Roberts, if you don't open the door, we're going to have the manager use his pass key."

Kaylen unlocked the door and partially opened it. On the threshold stood two police officers and Sims, the manager, a big bunch of keys dangling from one hand.

Sims looked at Kaylen and his eyes widened in shock. "Ms. Roberts! Your…your hair. Your…your *dress*…" His voice faltered and ended in a high-pitched squeak.

Kaylen pushed back her unruly hair and smoothed her rumpled skirt. She tugged the ripped edges of material together and leaned against the doorframe as casually as she could, considering her heart was now thumping harder than her headache.

"Can I help you, officers?" Her voice sounded like the piping of a small bird. She cleared her throat. "Is something wrong?"

The officer standing in front looked her up and down. "Busy night?" he asked, belligerence coloring his voice. A large, overweight man with a scowl on his hard, square face, he looked like he had no patience left for a member of Miami's jet set.

"I was out late at my club opening." Annoyance rose inside her. Forget calling the cops for help if they all acted like him.

"Ms. Roberts just opened Bannisters," Sims said into the silence. "The supper club," he added when the police didn't react.

"I see." Officer Belligerence widened his stance.

Kaylen saw his name tag. "Hudson," it read. She repeated it silently. She wanted to remember it in case she needed to make a complaint to the department later. "What are you doing here?" she asked.

"We had two reports of a disturbance," Hudson said. "First an anonymous call, then a few minutes later your downstairs neighbor called, complaining that screaming woke her up."

"I had a nightmare and fell out of bed," Kaylen said.

"Must have been one powerful dream." He pointed toward her leg. "Your dress is ripped."

Kaylen grabbed the slippery silk and held on tight. "It must have happened when I fell." She forced herself to make eye contact. "You said an anonymous caller reported a disturbance before Mrs. Wilkinson called to complain. Do you know what time that was?"

The second officer finally spoke from behind Hudson and Sims. "The dispatcher reported the call at eight-fifty," he said. He sounded a little more sympathetic than his partner, at least. "The caller was male. He didn't identify himself. We were already on our way when the second call came in."

Younger than Hudson by at least 10 years, he leaned against the railing with his hands resting lightly on his belt. Kaylen wasn't fooled by appearances. Despite his youthful face and relaxed posture, she would be willing to bet he was observing everything within his field of vision.

"I can assure you there's been no disturbance here," she said, mentally asking herself if she had lost what remained of her mind. Then she reminded herself the first call about a disturbance had gone to the police dispatcher a full ten minutes before she woke up.

"Are you sure you're okay, ma'am?" the second officer, Turner, asked.

"You can come in and search my condo if you don't believe me," she told them.

Let Brian Swift sweat that one.

"I don't think that's necessary as long as you say you're okay." Turner pushed away from the rail. "Come on, Hudson," he said. "Let's get back to the unit. There's nothing going on here."

Hudson backed slowly away from Kaylen's door. "Listen lady," he said. "The next time you close your club to outsiders, you might want to think about what happens when they turn away people like me. I brought my wife and some friends to have a night out, but we were refused admission."

"I told them not to turn anyone away unless they didn't have money for the cover charge, or they couldn't meet the dress code," Kaylen said. The last thing she wanted was to piss off the local police. Bannisters would always be on their list of places to visit and ticket for anything and everything. "As long as you had thirty dollars each for the cover charge and jackets for all the men, you should have been able to get in, unless the club was already full."

"Yeah, well it wasn't. I saw other people going in after we were told to leave. Friends of yours, no doubt." His hand rested on the black leather holster at his hip. "I bet you had one of your friends make that first call this morning." He gave her a look full of animosity. "Wouldn't hurt your club any to have your name in the news, would it? You society types are all the same. Always looking for publicity."

Kaylen colored up in response. "I did not," she said. "I would never do that."

She wanted to slam the door in his face, but that would be childish. She bit back a retort she knew she would regret once it left her mouth. Yet another man who thought she was playing some sort of twisted prank, she thought. Brian Swift had a decidedly uglier and even ruder clone.

"Thank you for your concern and for investigating those reports," she said instead. She looked at Sims, hopping uncertainly from one foot to the other. "I'm fine," she assured him, then closed the door before he could say anything else.

CHAPTER FIVE

Kaylen smelled coffee. *He wouldn't dare!* She walked into the kitchen, where she found Brian sitting at her breakfast table, two bottles of water and a container of Advil in front of him.

"You certainly make yourself at home fast." She jerked out a chair and sat down.

"Want some?" He pushed one of the water bottles and the Advil toward her. "Coffee'll be ready soon."

"Did you find everything you need?" She drummed her fingers on the table as she fought the desire to start yelling at him again, despite both their headaches. "Or would you like something else—breakfast perhaps?"

Her sarcasm apparently escaped him. "No," he said. "Coffee's fine." He grimaced. "The thought of food makes me ill. I fixed myself an ice pack." He held up one of her dish towels, wrapped into a neat bundle and wet with melting ice.

Kaylen felt her mouth drop open at his audacity. "All right, enough stalling." She pushed the water aside. "I want to know why you're here, what you were doing, and exactly who you are. If you don't give me satisfactory answers, I'm calling the police back." She rapped her knuckles on the butcher block surface of the table. "I didn't like the innuendo you threw out before those cops knocked on the door. That's the only reason I didn't hand you over to them. Why did you say my friends and I could get into trouble?"

"Forget it. I was just trying to talk you out of telling them I was here." Brian got up from the table and took two cups from the cabinet above the coffeemaker.

Kaylen frowned. He seemed to know the layout of her entire home. "How did you know my cups were in that cabinet?" she asked. "Did you search my place before I got home?"

"Nothing that fancy, and I'm not telepathic, either. Common sense would tell anyone the best location for cups would be above the coffeemaker." He flashed her that disarming grin again.

Annoying, she thought. *Really annoying.* "I want the truth," she said.

He sighed, purposely she thought, to make her aware he was getting frustrated with her single-mindedness. "I told you, I got hit over the head in the parking lot."

Kaylen decided she had more reason to sigh than he did. He only had a headache to complain about. "Why won't you tell me who you were waiting for?" she pressed.

"Because it's got nothing to do with this. A more important question is why I was brought upstairs and dumped in your bed."

Kaylen shrugged. "I think you may be right, someone wanted it known we were together. That cop told me the first call about the disturbance came at eight-fifty. That's ten minutes before I woke up. But I can't understand who would benefit from sending the cops over here to find you and me in bed and that tattoo on my thigh, other than a rival club owner. Why not wait to see if the club even succeeded before pulling a stunt like that? It makes no sense." She looked down at the tattoo peeping out from the split in her skirt. "None of it. Least of all this."

Brian set a cup of coffee in front of her. "You'd better drink this, it'll help clear your head. You want cream and sugar?"

Kaylen wrapped her cold hands around the cup and felt the warmth seep into her palms. "Cream."

She watched him open the refrigerator and take out the little jug she kept on the top shelf. She didn't trust him, and he certainly wasn't doing anything to help her overcome her misgivings.

"Brian, who are you?" she asked as he placed the jug in front of her and sat back down. She tried to make eye contact, but he either had his full attention on energetically stirring his black coffee or he was avoiding her gaze.

He tapped the spoon on the edge of his cup and laid it on the table. "I'm a charter boat captain. I've got a motor yacht at the Coconut Grove Marina." He took a sip of his coffee. "Slip ninety-five. A thirty-eight-footer named the *Destiny.*"

"Where do you live?" Kaylen asked.

"On the boat." He put the cup down.

"Then why were you over here in the middle of the night?"

"Visiting a friend." That time he really looked at her, the ghost of a smile playing around his lips.

"Oh." Kaylen realized he might have been waiting for a girlfriend. If he was trying to protect someone's reputation, then she should back off with the questions. Goodness knows she would want that sort of discretion herself if she was in the same position. "Where do you know Tim from?" she asked.

"Your boyfriend?"

"Why do you always answer a question with a question? Can't we have a normal conversation?" Exasperated, she pushed aside her half-finished coffee. It didn't seem to be helping much. Either that or Brian's infuriating presence was wearing her down. "I'm tired, sore and confused," she said. "Would you please stop making things worse by playing stupid games?"

"Sorry. I can't tell you what I don't know, that's all."

"Okay, I get the picture." Kaylen pushed her cup even further away. The smell of the coffee, usually so welcome in the morning, was making her stomach churn. "I think you'd better go. I know where to find you. Slip ninety-five. I want to take a shower and talk to my doctor about getting this tattoo removed."

Brian drained his cup. "Sorry I'm not being more help. Like I said before, we can get together later, when we're both feeling better."

"I don't think you're willing to produce any new information regardless of whether it's now or later. But on the remote chance that you suddenly decide to play things straight…" She watched one of his eyebrows raise, like he was really astonished that she thought he was covering something up, "…then you can get in touch with me at Bannisters this evening. After nine's best, because we're really busy with the dinner rush before that." She stood up.

He took the hint and stood, too. Their faces were level. Kaylen watched to see if he drew himself up straighter, as so many men did when confronted with her 5'11" height, but he only met her gaze steadily.

His eyes were really unusual, she thought, unable to avoid staring at them. They looked like the sun shining in a clear blue sky. If she'd ever seen those eyes before, she bet she would remember them, drugged or not.

"I'll be in touch," he promised, laying his hand on her bare shoulder.

The warmth felt strangely comforting. Kaylen couldn't remember when she'd ever felt so annoyed by anyone, yet reassured by such a simple gesture. Brian felt oddly familiar in a way she couldn't put her finger on.

"See you later." He strode ahead of her to the front door. "Better change your locks," he advised.

"I know." Kaylen felt the unease return with force now Brian was leaving her alone. Strange she should feel that way, instead of being relieved he was going without attacking her and ransacking her condo.

"You'd better be careful with that tat when you shower," he said. "I've got a couple. Use only the mildest soap and don't scrub, even though I know you want it off you. You'll just make yourself really sore. Put a cover over it and then leave it alone until you see your doctor." He closed the door behind him.

CHAPTER SIX

Kaylen slid the chain into place, then put a chair under the doorknob for good measure.

She showered carefully, following Brian's instructions, even though she resented him acting like he was a friend instead of an intruder.

She dressed in a soft cream cotton skirt and red shirt, the latter an attempt to brighten the pallor of her skin. After looking in the mirror, she decided no amount of makeup or bright clothing could bring color to her cheeks. Her chestnut, shoulder-length hair only accentuated her sallow complexion.

The first available appointment with the doctor was at two o'clock. That gave her a couple of hours to talk to someone who might be a whole lot more helpful in figuring out the reasons behind last night's events than Brian "I'm not able to tell you what I don't know" Swift.

Sam Wilson's name came to mind before anyone else's. Since her husband's death, Kaylen had depended on Sam for support and guidance. The savvy restaurant owner, who had been her husband's best friend, had also become hers.

But before going over to see Sam, she had better call Tim. He was notorious for leaving his landline ringing at least eight times before picking it up, his rationale being that only the most determined people would wait that long for him to answer, and therefore, the call would be worthy of his attention. Kaylen didn't need any more frustrations. She called his cell.

But he wasn't answering that, either. "Leave a message at the tone, and I'll get back to you," Tim's cheerful baritone told her. Kaylen resisted the urge to swear and hang up. She told him he'd better call her back ASAP if he wanted to remain on speaking terms with her, much less call her his girlfriend.

She had frequently wondered why she put up with his quirks. There were days when all his charm and insouciance did nothing but grate on her nerves. Today he had no get-out-of-jail-free cards. If he couldn't come up with a really good explanation as to why he'd abandoned her to wake up in bed with a stranger, then they were through.

Come to think of it, she decided, as she dialed his landline and listened to the rhythmic ringing of the unanswered phone, maybe breaking things off with him would be best anyway. She couldn't see herself having any sort of stable future with a man who couldn't even pick up a phone. When the answering machine finally clicked on, she waited for what seemed like a lifetime before it beeped, and then it cut her off halfway through her brief message, the memory apparently full.

She'd better give him a couple of minutes, she thought. If she was unavailable when he called back, she'd never hear the last of it. The red light on her own answering machine was flashing. She punched the button and listened to half a dozen messages from friends concerned about her abrupt departure from the club, checked her cell and heard a dozen more. The time-stamps told her she must have left around midnight. One of the messages, from her best friend, Sandy Cole, confirmed her worst fears about her behavior the previous evening.

"I bet you've got one hell of a headache, girlfriend." Sandy's husky voice held more than a hint of laughter. "You up-chucked all over Angela Crossfield's handmade Italian sandals. I bet she never gets that crap out of those rhinestones."

"Oh, no." Kaylen groaned. Angela's husband was one of her backers. Depression rolled into her life with a vengeance.

A message from Sam told her he had stayed to oversee the closing, for which she would thank him profusely, and also confirmed Tim had planned to take her home. She pulled up the hemline of her skirt, peeled back the dressing she had placed over the tattoo and stared at it again. Why her?

She still couldn't believe she had awakened to this nightmare morning. She called Tim's cell again. The phone buzzed in her ear. Ten rings…twelve…fifteen. Even *he* would never let the phone ring that many times, and what was up with his voicemail? A recorded message suddenly announced the mailbox was full and the cell phone user was unavailable. Kaylen took the cordless with her as she paced up and down in front of the coffee table. She wondered who else she could call to find out Tim's whereabouts.

She noticed the edge of a magazine poking out from under her sofa. She didn't remember leaving anything to fall off the coffee table. She bent over to pick it up and saw something on the cream leather of her couch. Something red, right at the base, next to the floor. She put down the phone and leaned closer. There was a minute spot of what appeared to be blood. When she pulled out the magazine, she found two more, slightly larger spots smeared across the front page of Cosmopolitan's latest issue.

CHAPTER SEVEN

Brian walked briskly down the dock and boarded his boat. He'd named the *Destiny* after losing his job, and that name carried more than a touch of irony. He now depended on charters for a living, and he had one that afternoon. He glanced at his watch. Eleven-thirty. The caterers were due in a half-hour.

He pulled off his clothes in the confines of the cabin, took a speed shower and shaved. Coffee was a must-have. He made a pot before pulling on shorts and a t-shirt. He slipped on sandals, downed more Advil and took a mug of strong black coffee up on deck.

A fresh breeze stirred bright-white sails on the yachts in the crowded marina, and Brian hoped it would help clear his head. The last thing he remembered about the night before was standing beside his car in the parking lot outside Kaylen's condo. Judging by the bruise on his head, someone had hit him from behind, toted him upstairs, stripped him and left him in her bed. Unless she was a terrific actress, she was probably already lying there unconscious.

Where was Tim while all this was going on? Kaylen had said she remembered leaving the club with him, but didn't remember arriving at the condo. Was he with her then, or had someone else taken her upstairs? An uneasy feeling stirred in Brian's stomach. They had both been set up for some reason, and he needed to find out why.

Damn Tim! He threw the remains of his coffee overboard, then threw the mug, too. His younger half-brother was the bane of his life: irresponsible, thrill-seeking and always in trouble. Tim had told him about Kaylen. No exaggeration there, Brian thought, remembering only too clearly her flawless body and her courage.

She was one hell of a woman, Tim had said. Brian had to agree. He felt more than a headache at the thought of her.

"God." He leaned his elbows on the rail in front of him and placed his head in his hands. She was his brother's girlfriend, and he didn't want to cause any more arguments with Tim. They'd had way too many lately. Well, Brian told himself, searching for excuses, he hadn't *tried* to climb in bed with her.

He knew he had to see her again whether he wanted to or not, if he was going to piece together the events of the previous evening. He also had to find and talk to Tim. If he hadn't spent so much time with Kaylen, he could have run over to his brother's apartment before coming back to the *Destiny*.

Someone had called the cops to make sure they were found together. If he hadn't stopped to talk to Kaylen in the hallway, he would have been the one who opened the front door, and they would have recognized him. Funny, he thought, how fate stepped in sometimes and took a hand.

A gust of wind scooped up spray from a passing speedboat and showered him with cold droplets. Swearing, Brian jumped back and shook the water off. He glared at the people waving and yelling "Sorry" from the other boat. One more goddamned thing in a line of them, he decided. Last night was a disaster. Tim had sounded uncharacteristically frantic when he'd called to ask Brian to meet him in the parking lot outside Kaylen's condo. He was in a lot of trouble, he told Brian, and asked him to make sure he wasn't followed.

But despite his best efforts, Brian now knew he *had* been followed, and then knocked unconscious like some stupid amateur. Tim's associates were too damned good. He should have been more careful. Now, instead of answers, all he had was a headache and a shitload of questions. And he'd been unable to reach Tim, either on his cell or his landline.

Brian wondered if Kaylen had reached Tim already to ask his reasons for leaving her unconscious and unprotected. If she had, he expected he wouldn't have to find Tim, Tim would find him. No doubt there'd be another of their classic fights, and Brian knew he'd be the one to back off, as he had always done since their mother, on her deathbed, had made him promise to take care of his brother because he was "different."

Tim was "different" all right. Since the age of ten, Brian had been getting him out of trouble with teachers, neighbors and friends, followed later by cops, drug dealers and anyone else with whom Tim came into contact.

"Shit," Brian said to a seagull sitting at the other end of the rail. The bird regarded him with one bright, beady black eye before flapping its wings and unhurriedly wheeling off to more hospitable parts.

Brian tried Tim's cell and landline again. He'd had no success while driving from Kaylen's condo to the marina, and as the phone buzzed incessantly, he knew his luck hadn't changed after getting back to the boat. He couldn't even get a message into his brother's full voicemail.

Fuck Tim. If his brother wouldn't answer the phone or pick up his messages, Brian thought, then he'd damned well turn up at Kaylen's club that evening, as she had suggested. That way, he could find out more about her involvement with his brother. Was she just Tim's girlfriend, or a business partner, too? If she really didn't know what Tim was up to, then Brian decided he'd have to enlighten her.

He cleaned the head and tidied the galley while he fought his conscience. Grudgingly, he acknowledged that being angry with Tim was no reason to ruin his relationship with his girlfriend. From what Tim had told him, Brian thought that for the first time in his brother's life, he might actually be taking a relationship seriously.

The caterers arrived, their heavy footsteps echoing below deck as they boarded the boat. Impatiently Brian directed and helped them fill the refrigerator with canapés and champagne, stock the freezer with ice and place a white linen cloth on the table in the stern.

He began to think they would never leave. He pushed the signed receipt into the hands of the shocked supervisor and curtly told the waiter remaining on the boat to sit down and not touch anything except to ice the champagne.

He returned to his cabin and closed the door. Finding Kaylen had an unlisted number, he called Bannisters and passed himself off as a reporter doing a story on her phenomenally-successful club opening. The employee who answered was reluctant to give out any information until told he would be prominently featured in the article when Brian came to the club that evening. In little more than three minutes, Brian had both her landline and cell phone numbers.

CHAPTER EIGHT

Kaylen opened her condo door to chaos. Her entire life lay at her feet. Photos pulled from albums littered the floor, bottles lay smashed, their contents soaking into the carpet, slashed clothes were piled in the bedroom. Stuffing ripped from both her couch and mattress covered everything. Her kitchen cabinets stood open, broken dishes and glassware filling the counters, the sink and the floor. Even her refrigerator and freezer had been emptied. Milk and yogurt mingled with pieces of china, open cereal boxes, sliced bread and fruit juice on the tiles below.

Utter fury enveloped her. After the shock of being drugged and left in bed with a stranger, a visit to the doctor had confirmed her fears…the tattoo would require surgery to remove, and even then, due to the colors used, the outcome would be less than optimal. Now someone had violated her home and destroyed her memories.

She dropped her purse on the edge of the deeply scratched teak dining table and bent to retrieve her wedding album. Cottage cheese spattered photos of her leaving the church on George's arm. Kaylen called 911, her mind whirling. Why would anyone do so much damage? They must have been looking for something, but what?

"Are you sure the condo's empty?" the dispatcher asked. "Ma'am you'd better wait outside until the officers arrive."

Kaylen hadn't even considered she might not be alone. The hair on the back of her neck rose, and a ripple of fear iced her back. She grabbed her purse and clutched her album to her chest as she ran back out the door and downstairs to the parking lot, her heart hammering. A pair of officers arrived within10 minutes, thankfully not the ones who had come earlier. Kaylen didn't think she could have taken another visit from Officer Hudson. Her legs still shaking, she agreed to sit in her car while they searched the condo.

Within minutes she was told it was safe to return. Kaylen perched on the only dining chair that had escaped the rivers of milk and juice while the police filled out paperwork and asked her a lot of questions. Other uniformed personnel arrived and took photos of the carnage. Kaylen watched with a numb detachment, still cradling her wedding album as they stepped on and over the remains of her life with George. They dusted unsuccessfully for fingerprints. She was asked to make an inventory of missing items and told to change her locks. Finally, she was given a card with a number to call if she had questions. Then they all left.

Kaylen closed the door after them. Wearily she began picking up her belongings. Who was ruining her life? She wondered if Brian had managed to make an imprint of her key while she had been talking with the police earlier that morning. The thought galvanized her. She called the same locksmith she had used for the club. He promised to come over as soon as he completed his current job. Pressed, he told her he'd try to get there in forty minutes or less.

She took the garbage can from the kitchen and began filling it with pages torn from books, the ruined photo albums and a ripped-up pile of fashion magazines. She belatedly thought about her jewelry, dropped the magazines and ran into the bedroom.

Although her jewelry boxes had been emptied all over the floor, she managed to find everything and gather them onto her stained and ripped comforter. What little amount of cash she kept on hand in a decorative canister in the kitchen still lay inside the open container, resting in a puddle of red wine. The trashing of her home seemed like the work of a madman. She hoped the locksmith would hurry and started piling broken wine bottles and glasses into trash bags.

The phone rang. Kaylen ran back into the living room and found the receiver on the floor behind the couch. She snatched it up, worried the locksmith needed more directions. But as soon as she answered, the caller hung up. Annoyed, she shoved the contents of the cushions back inside their covers and tossed them onto the couch. The phone rang again.

"Yes?" she snapped.

"Hi, Kaylen. It's Brian Swift."

She sat on one cushion that wasn't as badly stained as the others. It was on the tip of her tongue to tell him what had happened to her condo in her absence, but she stopped herself.

"What do you want?" she asked instead. She picked up a couple of books that looked like they might be intact and stacked them on the coffee table.

"I want to take you up on your offer," Brian said. "I thought I'd come to the club at nine tonight. Maybe we could eat dinner together, unless you think that'd cause a problem with Tim." Kaylen picked up another book, found it had only half its cover and tossed it toward a growing pile of trash between the living and dining areas. "I haven't even talked to Tim yet," she said. "He hasn't returned my calls, and his voicemail's full. I'm pretty mad at him, so if you see him, you let him know, okay?"

"I doubt I'll see him before you do," Brian said. "But if I was you, I'd be mad at him, too."

"I can't go out for dinner," she said. "The club only opened yesterday. I need to be on the premises." She sighed. Did she really want to see Brian again, or did she want to keep him away from her? What if he *was* the one who had trashed her place while she was out? He knew she'd be gone for a while.

"I figured we'd eat at your club." Brian's tone was sharp. "I'm not trying to ask you out on a date. I thought you wanted to figure why we were put in bed together as much as I do, and we've both got to eat sometime today."

"How did you get my number?" she asked. "It's unlisted."

"I called the club."

"And they gave it to you just like that? I'll fire all of them!"

"Don't do that," he said. "I'm responsible. I kind of stretched the truth and managed to trick one of your employees into giving me the information."

"I suppose you do that often...stretch the truth, I mean. Did you come back into my condo today?"

"Of course not. I've been busy. I'm going out on a charter in a few minutes."

Kaylen felt not only depressed but very, very tired. "I had a break-in while I was gone this morning. Someone completely trashed my place."

"Christ. Did you call the cops?"

"Yes, but I don't think they found much except a big mess. They said there were no signs of forced entry. They told me to get better locks. I've called a locksmith."

He swore under his breath. "You want help cleaning up? I can come over when I get back to port. We could talk then instead of over dinner."

"I don't know, Brian. I'm very worried about your part in all that's happened to me since midnight."

"I swear to you, I'm as confused by all this as you are. And remember, most of it has happened to you, not me. I think I was just in the wrong place at the right time."

Kaylen chewed her bottom lip while she debated. "Well, okay," she said. "Come to the club tonight. I'll make sure I've got an hour to spend with you. That should be more than enough. I can't do better than that, I have to be able to close up."

"Fair enough."

Kaylen felt overwhelmed. She didn't even know if she had any clothes left to change into that evening.

"Are you sure you don't want me to come over and help you clean up?" he asked. "I get back at six, but I know that may be kind of late."

"No," she said. "I've already had enough of trying to do this myself. I'm going to call my housekeeper. My insurance will have to foot the bill for new furnishings." She looked around her living room and shuddered. "I may even check into a hotel for a couple of days. It's pretty creepy in here."

They said goodbye and Kaylen hung up, still unsure whether she was being a fool for agreeing to see him. She tried Tim's phone again, getting the same frustrating results as before. Her housekeeper, Rosa, said she'd come over right away. Kaylen looked at her watch. Ten minutes to four. She still hadn't talked to Sam, having opted instead to run past Bannisters and check in with her manager after her appointment with the doctor. She decided she'd go to Sam's restaurant and use him as a sounding board while she tried to get something into her stomach.

But first, she had to prioritize tasks for her housekeeper. She took a pen out of her purse and used the back page from one of the torn books to make a list that started with washing what remained of her clothes, then taking her cocktail dresses, currently strewn across the bedroom floor and stained with makeup, over to the dry cleaners.

While she pulled out a bag and searched around for an outfit to wear that night, she tried to come up with names of possible enemies, but failed. George had gone out of his way to donate money to various charities, assist the local community, and endear himself to the citizens of Miami. After his death, Kaylen had done her best to continue the same practices, but on a much smaller scale. She gave time and money to the arts, the homeless shelters and the conservation groups. None of their members would have any reason to terrify her.

Briefly, she again wondered if perhaps one of her competitors was trying to drive her out of business, but she doubted anyone would want to spend time and energy trying to shut her down. The business might fail on its own, although the success of the opening forecasted a bright future. The first night's take had exceeded expectations according to her manager, Rob Diaz.

Kaylen decided the incidents had been directed against her personally, not her club. She found a couple of intact outfits buried under other ruined clothing and packed them into the bag along with her tennis shoes and some underwear that had escaped shredding. Black high-heeled, sling-back sandals lay under the comforter. Relieved, she added them to the bag. She pulled out a blue cocktail dress that had fallen into one corner of her closet and hung it over a dining chair. Rosa arrived as she was gathering toiletries from the bathroom floor and inside the shower stall.

"Whadda mess, Miss Kaylen." Rosa made *tsk tsk* noises while she rolled big dark eyes and pushed strands of wispy brown hair under her red kerchief. "You want I should throw everythin' out, or you wanna try to save this stuff?" She pointed to stained and torn table linens, lying on the floor under the dining table.

"Those were wedding presents from George's children," Kaylen said, more to herself than to Rosa. She had wondered how long she should try to keep all these reminders of her marriage. It looked like fate had taken a hand and made the decision for her. "Throw them out," she said. "I never entertain here, anyway."

When she left, the washer had already been filled with sheets and towels, Rosa was working hard in the kitchen, and the locksmith had arrived. Kaylen paid him in advance and promised Rosa she would return within an hour. She needed to get away from the ruins of her life and put something more substantial into her stomach than a half-cup of coffee. She locked her bag into the trunk of her car, hung her cocktail dress on a hook in the back seat and drove over to Coconut Grove.

CHAPTER NINE

Sam's restaurant, The Hideaway, sat on a quiet side street opposite the marina. A favorite with locals since he'd purchased it ten years before and carried out extensive renovations, he'd never had problems filling the little bar and grill to capacity for breakfast, lunch or dinner. His chef had been with him the entire time, updating the menu periodically to satisfy the changing tastes of diners and always bringing in new dishes from the eclectic Miami community.

Kaylen, arriving slightly before five o'clock in the afternoon, was surprised to find the dining room almost deserted. She knew Sam catered to the older crowd with an early diner's special from 4:00PM to 6:00PM.

As soon as she pushed open the glass door, she entered a tropical oasis. A mural of an Everglades scene covered one entire wall, its riot of green leaves and tropical birds reflected in water that seemed so real, Kaylen had seen small children touch it reverently with one finger, to see if they could produce ripples. Potted palms leaned over the tables like conspirators eavesdropping on the customers' conversations.

Gracing rattan tables, pink cloths bright as nail polish evoked flamingos and welcomed diners. Starched white napkins stood at attention in the center of oversized, cobalt blue plates, and sprays of multicolored freesias trailed from glass bowls in the center of each table. Sunlight streamed through big glass windows, but the air conditioning was cranked up to a comfortable level, augmented by lazily circling bamboo-bladed ceiling fans. Low level piped-in music whispered strains of Vince Gill.

As soon as Lenny, the head waiter seated Kaylen by the window, Sam came out of his little office behind the bar. "Hello, hello," he said, brushing her cheek with his lips. He sat down opposite, easing his ample girth onto the chair. "Coffee?" he asked. "We've got a new roast in, it's exceptional."

"Sounds great. I'd like water and some Advil, too, if you have it."

"Got a headache?" Sam chewed the end of an unlit cigar. "You were really celebrating last night."

"I guess so. I don't remember too much, but I sure paid for whatever I did. Do you know what happened?"

Sam shrugged and took the cigar out of his mouth. "You were ill. Tim told me he was taking you home after you couldn't even stand up without help. He must have used the back door, because I never saw you two go out the front. He was better able to carry you than I was, so I didn't argue with him." Sam's brow furrowed and he leaned back, lacing his fingers over his stomach. The rattan chair creaked in protest. "I wasn't too happy about him taking you out like that, but I figured I'd better stay behind to make sure the place was closed up right and the take deposited. I know your manager seems like he's a good guy, but someone had to look out for your interests." Obvious disapproval added a glint to Sam's small brown eyes, half obscured by drooping lids and the heavy black brows bristling above them.

Kaylen fought a desire to get defensive. Plainly, he thought she'd been irresponsible, and was letting her know without coming right out and saying it. "Thanks so much for taking such good care of Bannisters for me," she said, managing a half-smile. "What would I do without you?"

That was the truth, she thought, giving herself a mental reprimand. Sam had always given her support, guidance and a comforting shoulder to lean on when she felt she couldn't cope with the responsibilities that came from being the widow of an icon.

In response, he sandwiched her hand between both of his, warmth oozing from his pudgy fingers into her cold ones as he squeezed them. "Most of the time, you'd do just fine, K.T," he assured her. "You sure needed help last night, though." He shook his head. "I've never seen you like that. You passed out, you said?" He stared at her. "You look pretty pale right now. When was the last time you ate?"

"I don't remember," Kaylen said. "I've been so busy and nervous, I wasn't hungry." She picked up the menu and opened it.

Sam grunted, and the chair creaked ominously again.

Lenny bustled over with coffee, water and a bottle of generic pain reliever. He whipped a pen and pad of paper out of his pocket. "Did you decide what you'd like, Ms. Kaylen?"

She stared blankly at the long list of choices confronting her. If someone had told her the menu was printed in a foreign language, she couldn't have felt more confused. Her brain, still whirling from everything that had happened to her that day, refused to process one more piece of information.

"I have no idea," she said helplessly. Her stomach did an ugly little flip. "Maybe something light and not too spicy?"

"How about Eggs Benedict?" Lenny suggested, pen poised.

"With that sauce?" She grimaced. "No, I don't think so. Maybe a cheese omelet and whole wheat toast?"

"Coming right up." Lennie scribbled energetically before taking the menu from her. "Mr. Wilson?"

Sam shook his head. "Just coffee."

Lenny scurried away.

Kaylen added a splash of cream to her coffee and sipped.

"Like it?" Sam asked.

Kaylen took another sip. "Not much. It's kind of bitter. Tastes like the old coffee blends with Chicory."

"You want something else?" Sam started to raise his hand for Lenny.

"No. It's okay. It's probably just me." She took another sip and licked her lips.

The warmth of the sun coupled with the hot drink relaxed her knotted muscles. Her eyelids became incredibly heavy, and she felt herself dozing off. Sam's gravelly voice brought her back to reality.

"What's up with you?" He sounded somewhere between annoyed and worried. "I've never seen you act like you did last night, and you still look out of it." His eyes narrowed. "Did you take something other than a couple of glasses of champagne?"

"Not that I know of." She met his gaze. "You should know me better than that."

"You've been damned stressed out lately. If you got a prescription, I wouldn't hold it against you. But you need to own up if you're over-medicating."

"*What?*"

Kaylen's coffee slopped as the cup clattered back onto its saucer. The handful of other diners raised their heads and silence fell across the room. Lenny came running. He whisked away the cup and saucer and wiped up the spill while Kaylen and Sam regarded each other across the table.

"I'll bring you some more, Ms. Kaylen," Lenny said into the charged air, and then he scurried away even faster than he had before.

"You think I took pills and then drank alcohol?" Kaylen's lethargy took off like a helium balloon into the cosmos. "I'm not a complete fool, Sam. I put everything I had into Bannisters. I'd never jeopardize my livelihood on purpose with a stupid stunt like that."

"I thought, because of the stress…," Sam muttered, fixing his gaze on his manicured fingernails.

"Well, think again," she said. "I had nothing but a couple of glasses of champagne."

"And that resulted in you behaving the way you did last night? Come on, K.T."

"I think maybe someone slipped something into one of my drinks, but I can't figure out why. How many people noticed my behavior?"

"After you tossed your cookies in front of the bar, a lot of them."

Kaylen groaned. "Shit," she said.

Sam's eyebrows rose again like twin caterpillars glued to his wrinkled forehead. "What's gotten into you? You never swear in public."

"Yes, well I'm not acting like myself lately. *You* told me that." Kaylen uncapped the pain reliever and shook two pills into her hand. "I'm going to have to apologize, especially to Angela Crossfield." She told him about Sandy's message.

Sam shook his head, but he didn't say anything else. Kaylen figured he was probably expecting another outburst from her and didn't want his diners to leave their meals and bolt out the door.

"You'll have to tell me who was at the bar," she said. She downed the pills with a couple of sips of water. "At least I can do damage control with *them*. Not much I can do about the rest of the patrons, or about the gossip that's going to spread." She found herself eagerly gulping down the rest of the water. She still felt dehydrated and dry-mouthed. "I wonder if I'm going to hear what I did or didn't do in the society column of the *Miami Herald?*"

She couldn't tell Sam she had woken up in bed with Brian. Blurting out the truth was too embarrassing, and after Sam had accused her of taking drugs and reproached her for swearing, she wasn't going to give him another chance to find fault with her. He'd probably love to lecture her about her morals before letting her know she'd made a poor choice of boyfriends, even though he was the one who had introduced her to Tim in the first place.

The arrival of her omelet gave her a momentary distraction while she tried to decide how much more to tell Sam, or even if she was going to keep the tattoo a secret as well. She made a halfhearted attempt at eating, but put down her fork after only a few bites, the cheese tasting like candle wax. She tried nibbling the toast but it stuck in her throat and she had to give up, drinking two cups of the bitter-tasting coffee and another glass of water instead.

Sam watched her in silence. After she pushed the plate away, he slid his chair back and picked up his cigar. "Let's take a walk, so I can smoke this," he said. "The air'll do you good. I think you've got more to tell me, but you're holding back."

"I'm not holding anything back." She crossed her fingers under the table.

"I know you better than that." He stood up and buttoned his double-breasted cream suit jacket.

Kaylen sighed. "Okay, I'll go with you, but not because I want to spill my guts." She opened her purse.

"Forget it. Put your money away. You didn't eat anything," Sam said.

"I'm leaving Lenny a tip at least." She placed some bills beside her plate.

"Fair enough. Come on."

CHAPTER TEN

Kaylen followed Sam's lumbering bulk out of the restaurant. His sparse black hair blew away from his crown as they passed through the swinging front doors. He had developed a slight limp over the last few months, blaming a bum right knee. His face had grown more florid, and Kaylen had wondered if he'd started drinking too much after the restaurant closed.

They fell into step and strolled up a side street to the crosswalk opposite the marina entrance. Sam pushed the button and they walked over after the light changed.

Kaylen breathed deeply. The sea air started to clear her head. Mercifully, after Sam lit his cigar, the smoke blew away from her.

"Are you going to the club tonight?" he asked.

"Yes, and I'm staying the whole evening. I've got to prove I'm a hands-on owner." She pushed her hair away from her face. "I don't want my backers pulling out because they're nervous. You know how much trouble I had getting people to believe I can handle this business."

Sam's eyes lost their accusatory glint. "The way the club took off last night, honey, I very much doubt you have anything more to worry about from your backers," he said. "That 'Forties' theme's a real hit."

A lump rose in Kaylen's throat. "I can't take credit for that idea. George told me what theme to use. He was incredibly gifted, Sam. I know we've both said that countless times before, but the longer he's gone, the more I see what I lost. He managed to do right by Sylvia and the kids and still leave me with the means to take care of myself."

Sam smiled. "When he told me you'd agreed to sign that pre-nup, I thought for sure you'd lost your mind and he wasn't playing fair with you, but it looks like it all worked out for the best."

"I could never have managed his investments. He and I both knew that. I'm pretty savvy as a club owner, thanks to you, but Sylvia was the one who'd make sure George's business ran on oiled wheels until their kids were ready to take on the responsibility."

"What are their names? I don't remember." Sam blew smoke rings. "The amount of years I knew George, you'd think I would." He watched the smoke thin out and blow away. "Pete and Holly are the older ones. But I kind of lost track of the younger two after they went off to college."

"Trisha and Art, the twins." Kaylen turned her face into the wind and felt the sting of salt on her lips.

She watched multicolored flags energetically snapping on top of the numerous masts in the marina. A rhythmic pinging came from ropes tapping against metal. She remembered how appalled George's children were when their father started dating her right after his divorce became final. Kaylen knew their initial protests were because she was barely three years older than Pete, the eldest.

The youngest manager Sam had ever trained, she was far from immature, and had understood their reservations. When introduced to George, she had been instantly attracted, but very hesitant to accept his dinner invitation because of their age difference.

Despite that hesitation, he had wooed her gently but persistently, until she gave in to his charm and discovered his generous nature and abundant capacity to love her. After his death, she thought she'd never find those feelings again.

She had drifted, lost and alone, until the first anniversary of his death had passed and she decided to open a supper club. She presented her plans to the backers George had used for his own ventures and convinced them to invest. Bannisters took shape and life started anew.

Kaylen forced herself to stop reminiscing. Those days with George belonged in the past. Now she was experiencing a very unsettling present. Sam stood quietly beside her, evidently waiting for her to tell him whatever he thought she was holding back. He had a lot of patience and always expected her to cave in. But this time, she decided he was going to be disappointed.

"I want to be able to enjoy my club and its customers tonight," she said. "I need the kudos." *Wasn't that the truth*, she thought. "Last night I felt too ill to appreciate anything." She wondered what the symptoms of food poisoning were. Did they include disorientation as well as vomiting? "Sam." She touched his sleeve. "No one else got ill, did they?"

"No way." He looked shocked. "The companies you use are the same ones who deliver to me. You think I'd risk food poisoning in my place?"

"No, of course not." She hooked her arm through his. "Let's walk," she said.

They continued on in silence while she tried to think about what she had eaten the day before. "You know," she said, drawing a complete blank on breakfast or lunch, "if I've got any memory left at all, I think all I ate yesterday were a couple of the hors d'oeuvres at the club last night, so that couldn't be the reason."

"There you have your answer. No food. Too many drinks. No wonder you puked." He patted her hand. "Take my advice, K.T. Eat *before* you go to the club tonight, even if you don't want anything. Otherwise you could have the same thing happen again."

She shuddered at the thought of even part of last night repeating itself. "I'm only drinking mineral water tonight," she assured him. "Have you heard anything from Tim today? He didn't stay with me last night."

"He didn't?" Sam raised an eyebrow. "I wonder why not. You looked like you needed someone to hold your head while you were worshipping the porcelain god."

"I don't think I threw up anymore after leaving the club. He must have carried me up to my condo and put me in bed. He didn't leave me a note or anything, and when I tried calling him today, he never picked up. That's not like him."

"Maybe you scared him off." Sam laughed, then stopped when he saw Kaylen's expression. "You're taking this too seriously. You got shit-faced, honey. It happens. Don't make a big deal out of it, unless there's something you're not telling me."

Why would he keep asking her that? She told herself she was being paranoid, but she couldn't bring herself to open up and tell him the truth. She'd spent most of the day thinking about confiding in Sam, yet here she was hiding things from him. As they passed a bench, her leg brushed against the edge of it and the tattoo smarted, like a reprimand. The only other people who knew of its existence were Brian, her doctor and the person who had placed it there. Kaylen decided that was already at least two people too many.

Brian's cautionary words about Tim echoed in her brain. "Is Tim who he says he is?" she asked Sam.

His eyebrows drew toward each other again. "That's a strange question to ask after you've been dating the guy for months," he said. "What did he tell you?"

"That he's an entrepreneur, and he's always traveling because he's involved with start-ups," Kaylen said. "He told me he lives in Little Havana because he's keeping an eye on the building for a friend. It's a real dump of a place. He's never invited me over, but I've driven past a few times. I wonder how he even thinks it's safe to park his car on the street outside, much less live there."

"He pretty much told me the same things he's told you, honey," Sam said. "The whole area he lives in is slated for redevelopment. His friend's going to make a pack of money out of a very cheap investment if he keeps that building a while longer."

Kaylen sighed. She'd have to sit Tim down and find out about those start-ups. Talking to him was always like having a conversation with someone who wasn't interested in anything but the immediate present. He brushed off any potential discussions about his frequent absences, and she had to admit she'd enjoyed their dates so much, she'd never pushed for answers.

She'd only been living in the immediate present too, at least regarding emotional relationships. If she wanted more in her life than a successful business, then she was going to have to make some changes. She needed a partner who would be there for her whatever happened, not someone who would leave her to fend for herself.

She needed stability from a partner as well as excitement and good looks. All those wonderful qualities George had possessed. "I have to go back to my condo and pick up new keys," she said, suddenly anxious to get her life back under control as quickly as possible. "I'm having the lock changed," she added when Sam stared at her.

"Why would you want to do that? Change the lock, I mean?" Sam looked at her suspiciously. "See, there *is* something you're not telling me."

"You're wrong," she said. "Just drop it. Please. The lock's been acting up, that's all." She was unwilling to launch into a lengthy explanation or yet another lie to cover up for what she wasn't telling him. She was afraid he would insist on becoming involved with the lock changing, like he wanted to be involved with the rest of her life. "I've had a splitting headache all day, and I still feel spaced out," she said, avoiding direct eye contact. "Will you come to the club later?"

Sam nodded at a middle-aged couple passing the bench with two Afghan Hounds on leashes. The man and woman both smiled, checked Kaylen out and walked away, their heads close together as they whispered to each other. Kaylen pulled oversized sunglasses out of her purse and put them on. She didn't want anyone else recognizing her.

"To answer your question," Sam said. "Yeah, I'll be at Bannisters around eight, after I make sure I greet my own customers. My staff can handle anything, but I still like people to know I'm the owner."

Kaylen checked her watch. "We can talk more later, then. I'd better get going. I have to run a couple of errands before I go over to the club, and it's almost six o'clock. Are you going to walk back with me or stay here for a while?"

"You go ahead. I'll take my time going back. It feels good to be outside." He made for the bench.

Kaylen gave him a quick kiss on the cheek and left. She drove quickly back to her condo. She hadn't planned to spend so much time with Sam. Now it was too late for her to check into a hotel before she went to the club. She would have to make the best of it and get ready at home. Hopefully, Rosa had made the bathroom a priority, she thought as she ran upstairs.

Too late, she realized she didn't have a key to get inside. She knocked on the front door. Silence greeted her. She turned the knob. The door opened and swung back to reveal not order, but the same chaos she had left two hours before.

Kaylen felt really annoyed. She stomped inside and slammed the door.

"Rosa? Rosa!" *Where was the woman? How long did it take to go to the cleaners, for God's sake?*

She kicked aside a spilled rubber plant, threw her purse on the dining table and walked into the bedroom. The carpet squelched beneath her feet, stained dark blue from water seeping out of the bathroom. She heard running water.

"Rosa!"

How could someone she had employed for three years and thought competent leave a bathtub filling with water while she ran an errand? Kaylen walked into the bathroom, grabbed the shower curtain and pulled it back, leaning over to turn off the jet of water cascading from the shower head. And then she staggered back, clinging to the shower curtain, which came away, rod attached, from the wall.

She slipped in the water and fell, striking her head against the vanity. She fought for traction while the plastic curtain wrapped itself around her legs and imprisoned her.

"No!" The word tore from her lips as she disentangled herself and scrambled to her feet.

Floating face down in the tub, Rosa's body looked obscenely, horrifically obese with the bright red, loose housedress billowing around her. Her hair, normally pulled into a thick knot at the base of her neck, waved around her head like seaweed on the surface of the ocean.

Kaylen staggered from the bathroom. Even in her befuddled, terrified state, the scrawled red lipstick message glaring from the mirrored closet door drew and trapped her gaze: THIS IS WHAT HAPPENS WHEN WE DON'T GET WHAT WE WANT.

Despite shaking, clumsy hands, she dialed 911 and reported the murder.

As she sank onto a dining chair to await the arrival of the police, her landline rang. She waited while her answering machine clicked on. Only static was recorded, then an audible click as the phone line disconnected. Kaylen whimpered. For the first time in her life, she knew the meaning of real fear.

CHAPTER ELEVEN

Brian pulled on a beige jacket, pocketed his billfold and grabbed his keys. He walked up on deck and took a moment to appreciate the deepening dusk. The sun had faded below the horizon, leaving an orange glow. The first stars of the evening twinkled over the numerous pleasure craft in the bay.

On nights like this, he felt glad to be on the water. He sighed as he stepped from the boat to the dock. He'd paid a very heavy price for the *Destiny*. If he'd known just *how* heavy, he'd never have signed on the dotted line

He strode up the dock. He'd worked non-stop on charters for the last three weeks, and the incident at Kaylen's had taxed his already frayed temper. That afternoon, blaming a traffic jam from an accident, the driver of the catering truck had arrived late to pick up the trays, dishes and waiter. By the time Brian had showered and dressed, it was close to 7:45PM.

He picked up his pace and pushed his fatigue and irritation aside. He'd arranged to meet Kaylen at 9:00PM, and he wanted to stop by Tim's apartment on the way. Even with the delay in the catering pick-up, he should make it to Bannisters on time.

The shadows had visibly lengthened and the secluded, sheltered spot where he'd parked his car lay in almost total darkness. He swore under his breath. Now he'd have to waste even more time trying to get inside his Camaro. As soon as his hand came into contact with the door, he started to feel around for the lock.

The first blow caught him behind his right ear. He staggered and fell against the car, his head striking the roof. He barely had time to think about defending himself before something hard and unforgiving hit his kidneys.

He let out a howl of pain, whipped around and lashed out, catching his attacker in the face. The man grunted and countered with a jabbing right hook. The salty taste of blood filled Brian's mouth as he kicked out. A grunt assured him he had connected with his opponent, and he moved in on the offensive.

He might have stood a good chance of fending off the attack if a second assailant hadn't used what felt like a baseball bat on his ribs. The excruciating pain sent him to his knees. Brian fought for breath as another vicious punch sent him crashing to the ground. His cheek felt the warmth and roughness of the parking lot's sunbaked surface, and he tried to concentrate on that instead of the blows raining down on his head and shoulders while kicks punished his ribs and back.

He hugged his head and tucked himself into a fetal ball to minimize the damage. No longer able to tolerate the accelerating agony, he willingly tumbled down a long tunnel to oblivion.

CHAPTER TWELVE

It was very dark when Brian became fully conscious. Dark and painful. He dimly remembered waking up a couple of times, trying to get up and passing out again.

He moved very carefully that time and moaned as his body reacted. Whoever had attacked him couldn't have wanted to kill him, he decided. Instead, the expertly-delivered beating must be a graphic warning about something.

Breathing shallowly to avoid aggravating the pain again, he rolled awkwardly from his side to his stomach. Somebody wanted him to either keep out of Tim's business or stay away from Kaylen Roberts. Maybe both.

He managed to get onto all fours and then use his car for support as he struggled to his feet. His ribs ached with every breath, sparks of pain shot through his jaw, and his head pounded. His back felt like a truck had driven over it…several times. Brian crept slowly back to his boat, where he removed all his blood-spattered clothing and showered.

Dabbing himself with a towel, he walked past the full-length mirror on the back of the closet door and stopped at the sight of his reflection. Welts and bruises covered a good portion of his trunk. His swollen jaw gave him the appearance of a chipmunk storing food for winter.

"Fuckin' hell."

He figured a couple of his ribs were cracked, and the split lip probably needed suturing. He could do with something stronger than Tylenol to knock out the pain, but a glance at the clock showed it was 9:30PM.

He didn't have time to feel sorry for himself or spend hours in the ER. He'd missed his appointment with Kaylen, and if she thought he'd stood her up, she'd refuse to talk to him at all. He needed to get to Bannisters, and it would take more than a beating to prevent him.

No stranger to pain, he'd learned to detach himself from the physical sensations. This time would be no different, except it pissed him off that he'd been jumped without realizing he was even being watched. Twice in less than 24 hours, he reminded himself. *Fuck, these guys were good*, or maybe he'd completely lost his edge in only three weeks. The beating had to be connected to last evening's events or they would have stolen his wallet, he told himself as he took it out of his pants pocket.

He suffered through pulling on clean clothing and shoved his feet into loafers. Not wanting to risk a repeat performance with his attackers, he called a cab for his trip to the club.

The cabbie looked shocked when he saw Brian's appearance. No, Brian told the guy, he didn't want to go to the hospital. He'd been in a car accident the day before, and he was late for an appointment. He was willing to double the fare for a fast ride. That got results, but Brian's ribs took another beating as the cab weaved through traffic, shot through yellow lights and turned corners on a dime.

Relieved to get out of his ride in close to one piece outside the club, Brian attached himself to a large group of twenty-somethings who told Bannisters' doorman they had dinner reservations. Keeping his face averted, he linked elbows with a couple of giggling girls who appeared to have already started their partying elsewhere, and they pulled him inside.

The subdued lighting in the club awarded him some anonymity, but also made it more difficult to find Kaylen. The area around the bar was filled with a moving tide of people, the hubbub of conversation and loud music from a live band. Brian stayed at the back of the throng while his eyes adjusted to the gloom. He didn't want to force his way through the crowd until he had a good reason to do so.

He circled the bar and scanned faces until he saw Kaylen talking with people at the far end, where a short set of steps led down to a dining area half-mooned around the edge of the dance floor. She held a glass of what looked like water in one hand while she gestured with the other. She certainly wasn't looking for him, Brian decided, watching her intently. Her attention stayed on her companions: a short, overweight and balding man in a tux, and a woman who slightly resembled Kaylen.

The crowd parted momentarily when names were called and people walked toward the dining room. Brian took the opportunity to reach the bar and order a scotch and soda. He needed a boost before he approached Kaylen looking like a prize fighter who had gone ten rounds and lost every one of them.

Her clientele included many of Miami's rich and famous. Brian recognized faces he had only seen on TV or in newspapers. He watched Kaylen interact easily with all of them. She looked beautiful, poised and very much at home, while he felt like a big fish out of water. She had class and he had none, he told himself as he watched her talking with politicians, news personalities and the CEOs of several local Fortune 500 companies.

The tops of her breasts swelled above the material of her strapless blue dress. Her tanned skin reflected gold and silver beads sparkling on the bodice. Her waist looked so small, Brian thought that if he placed both hands around it, his fingers would meet.

His drink arrived, placed on a coaster and served with a small bowl of mixed nuts. Brian pulled out a twenty-dollar bill and paid while his common sense reminded him that Tim had held Kaylen in his arms. His hands and lips had caressed every square inch of her, from those ripe breasts to her shapely legs and beyond. Brian knew he had no business thinking about her as anything but a potential source of information, but he couldn't get rid of the thoughts, not when she had suddenly noticed him and was walking toward him with her hips swaying in perfect rhythm.

He took a big gulp of his drink and almost spat it back out. The liquor burned his cut lip like the touch of an open flame. He gasped, and the glass slipped from his fingers as his ribs sent an instant reminder that they wouldn't tolerate any sudden moves.

"So you decided to stop by after all," she said, looking at the spilled drink on the otherwise immaculate bar. The bartender hurried over to mop up the mess.

She was so close, Brian felt her warmth. She smelled a whole lot better than anything else he had been around since the sun had set that night. "I told you I'd be here," he said. "I couldn't make nine o'clock, because I got jumped by a couple of guys in the marina parking lot."

Kaylen's eyes widened as she got a better look at his face.

A man reeking of liquor lurched into him. Instinctively, Brian shoved him away. The man staggered, grabbed the metal rail attached to the bar and stopped. "Hey, watch who you're pushing, jackass."

Brian's temper flared. He stood up as straight as he could manage and turned to face the guy. "Fuck off," he said. "Now."

His opponent was built like a Mack truck and had the fists to match. Although Brian avoided a predictable haymaker, he was moving too slowly to protect himself from the body punch that finished the fight before it even got started, connecting with his already much-maligned ribs and sending him, doubled over, into Kaylen's outstretched arms.

Mayhem ensued as Brian tried to get his feet back under him and his adversary moved in for Round Two, but a bouncer took the drunk away. After that, things became fuzzier, and Brian found himself falling slowly to the floor. He lay there on his back, watching a surreal forest of pants and bare legs moving around him.

When Kaylen and the older man she had been standing with, who she called Sam, discovered some of Brian's other injuries, he was loaded into a car with his head in Kaylen's lap and a cold, damp towel on his lip. Her hand rested softly over his as he clutched his chest.

"We're going to the hospital," she told him. "I must have been blind not to see the marks all over your face when I first saw you, but it was pretty dark in the club, and I've had such a horrible day. I was mad at you. I thought you'd stood me up."

"No way," he managed through the cloth.

"Don't try to speak," she said, and he felt those long, slender fingers of hers caressing his forehead.

A bump in the road ruined the moment, and he passed out in response to the sickening jolt. Bright lights brought him back to consciousness, as did a trip onto a gurney, which effectively took his breath away. He stared at the overhead lights as they wheeled him into the ER, but the glare compounded his headache and he was forced to close his eyes again.

"What happened?" A man's voice asked.

Brian made the effort to open his eyes. A doctor was bending over him, or at least he reckoned the guy must be a doctor, judging by the white coat and the stethoscope dangling around his neck.

"He said he got into a fight," Kaylen said.

Brian struggled to sit up.

"Relax." The doctor firmly pushed him back. "Is he allergic to any medications?" he asked Kaylen.

"I don't know," she said.

"No," Brian said. "I'm not, and I don't want you giving me anything. I'll be fine. I need to get out of here and rest."

"Does he have insurance?" A woman with a clipboard entered his peripheral vision.

"No," Brian said. "You can talk to me. I'm not dead or unconscious. I don't have any insurance, and I don't want any treatment." He struggled again, but his determination to ignore the cracked ribs fell apart and he involuntarily moaned.

Kaylen's hand slipped into his. "I'll pay," she said. "Whatever the cost. Please take care of him. He's in so much pain."

"I'll take care of the details for you, K.T.," said a gravelly voice.

Brian turned his head and regretted it as his vision blurred. He blinked and refocused to see Sam standing beside the woman with the clipboard. The gurney started moving again, and he was wheeled from the hallway into a room. The doctor barked rapid-fire orders for tests while a nurse wrapped a blood pressure cuff around Brian's arm. He felt an uncomfortable squeeze as it inflated. Something cold rubbed against his arm, followed by the prick of a needle.

"That'll make you more comfortable," the doctor explained when he tried to protest.

"It's all right, Brian. I'm not going anywhere." Kaylen's hand was on his arm again. "You won't make me leave, will you, doctor?" Her voice sounded husky, concerned.

"You'll have to stay in the waiting room while we take him for X-Rays and suture that lip," the doctor said. "Then you can come back. Based on the results of the tests, we'll decide whether to admit him. He's pretty banged up."

The shot started to take effect, and Brian felt like he was floating above his body. He tried to keep his eyes open but they refused to focus, so he gave up. He wondered if Kaylen had been sent to the waiting room while he was stripped and a gown placed on him.

The X-Rays were painful, even with the shot. By the time he'd been moved around on the table a couple of times, he began to wake up again. They numbed his lip and sutured it, brought Kaylen back from the waiting room and told them he had hairline cracks in two ribs and bruised kidneys, but no other internal injuries. They were informed that if his symptoms worsened, they were to return. When prescriptions had been written for antibiotics and painkillers, they were left alone.

"I'll help you get dressed," Kaylen said. She brought his clothes over from the chair.

"I can manage." He waited and looked pointedly at her.

Kaylen shrugged. "Okay. I'll pull the curtain and give you some privacy, but I think you're going to need me."

"Thanks." He picked up his boxers.

Kaylen left him alone, but he could see her legs and feet on the other side of the curtain. He wiped beads of sweat off his forehead and gritted his teeth as he dragged the boxers over his feet and up his legs. Bending made him dizzy. He leaned back against the plinth and waited for the lightheadedness to pass before pulling his t-shirt over his head. By the time he got halfway into his dress shirt, his breathing had been reduced to shallow panting. Abandoning the buttons, he leaned over to grab his pants. The room swam in lopsided circles, and he clutched a nearby metal gurney for support.

"Kaylen," he said.

She came back immediately. Without saying "I told you so," or reprimanding him in any other way, she helped him into his pants and zipped them up. She finished buttoning his shirt, put on his shoes and took his arm. "Come on, I'm taking you home," she said.

"Your place or mine?" He took a couple of awkward and unsteady steps. His body felt stiff and painful. How was he going to work a charter the following afternoon?

"Your place," Kaylen said. "And I'm staying with you." She bit her bottom lip, her face clouded with worry. "My housekeeper was murdered in my bathtub this afternoon," she said. "While I was out running errands."

"Christ," Brian said. "What the fu…hell?"

Tears glistened on her cheeks. "I don't think I can ever live in my condo again."

Her grip tightened on his arm and he winced.

"Oh, God. I'm sorry." She let him go.

Brian missed the support as well as the contact. He was afraid he was going to fall on his face. "What the hell is going on?"

"I don't know." Her eyes met his. "What I *do* know is that being near me is dangerous. Rosa was murdered, and now look what's happened to you. I'm so scared." She laid her head against his shoulder and started sobbing.

Suddenly, Brian didn't care what Tim thought or what Tim wanted. His brother wasn't around now, when Kaylen so desperately needed comfort and protection. Alien feelings washed over him as he wrapped his arms around her and held her as close as he dared. His face burrowed into her sweet-smelling hair. He felt her soft warmth and knew he was in deep trouble. He'd better find Tim in a hurry and give him back his girlfriend before they were fighting on a very personal level. Brian reminded himself that regret wasn't something he indulged in, and personal relationships were definitely in a category he classed as inaccessible. Sadly, he released her.

"Let's go back to the boat," he said. "I don't know whether it's much safer than your condo, but at least you might be able to get some sleep while I keep watch. I'll be able to hear anyone coming. It'll be okay, I promise."

"I don't think I'll be able to sleep after what's happened today," Kaylen said as they started walking along the corridor toward the front doors of the ER. "But you're right, I really do need to lie down and rest. So do you." She slipped her arm around him after he lost his balance and leaned on the rail running along the wall. "Ooh," she said when he sucked in his breath. "Sorry. I bet that hurts."

Brian moved her arm down a couple of inches. "There, that's better. I'm kind of dizzy. That was one powerful shot they gave me."

"You've got so many cuts and bruises, I'm almost afraid to touch you," she said. Her voice quivered. "Brian, I think you got attacked because you were with me this morning."

"Maybe. Maybe not." He couldn't bring himself to tell her anything more.

CHAPTER THIRTEEN

Sam's driver dropped them off at the marina. Brian refused to let the man help him. He didn't want anyone else to know where the *Destiny* was moored. With Kaylen's support he staggered onto the boat, the effects of the beating and the pain medication making him heavy and lethargic. All he wanted to do was lie down, but Kaylen insisted on undressing him as he stood with his legs braced against the edge of the bunk.

"This is becoming a habit, lady," he said as she unzipped his pants.

Kaylen frowned. "Don't call me that. My name's Kaylen. Use it. Or you can call me K.T." She managed a half-smile. "My husband gave me that nickname. Sam still uses it."

Brian fought off the urge to topple over backwards and forced himself to concentrate on staying awake. "You sound like you haven't really moved on after your husband's death. Why are you dating Tim?"

"I *do* miss George," Kaylen said. "I had two wonderful years with him before he died." She unbuttoned Brian's shirt and slid it off his shoulders.

It seemed she barely touched his chest, but the weight of her hand was enough to make his legs give way.

She pulled off his shoes, her face averted. "I've only felt able to start dating over the last few months." She slid his pants over his feet, took his clothes to the closet and placed them on a hanger, her back to him. "I wish George was here now. He always made me feel safe."

She kept her face turned away from him. He needed to make her understand he could look after her, too, even in his present condition. Maybe he should tell her he had a gun in his nightstand, but that might make her even more worried and doubtful about him and his intentions.

"Tim doesn't make me feel that way," Kaylen said. "He's exciting and fun, but I've got no illusions about any long-term relationship with him." She closed the closet door and turned around, her brow furrowed, her eyes bright with unshed tears. "He certainly doesn't make me feel anything like safe, especially after leaving me alone yesterday evening. Look what happened." She kicked off her shoes with more force than was necessary and they landed on the other side of the room.

"Sorry. I didn't mean to upset you." Brian silently cursed his clumsiness. After fifteen years on the police force, six of them as a detective, he frequently tended to turn normal conversation into some form of interrogation. He tried to think of a question that might bring them back to more neutral ground.

"I know what the K stands for, but what about the T?"

"Theresa." She gave him a wobbly smile. "It's my middle name." She tossed his shoes over to join hers. "Lie down," she commanded. "That's enough talking for tonight."

She had to help him get his legs onto the bunk. The beads on her cocktail dress shimmered with an unearthly glow in the dim light of the cabin. "Kaylen," he said. "There's something you need to know."

"Hush," she said and headed for the door. "I'm going to get some water, so you can take your pills."

She left so abruptly, Brian knew she felt too emotional to hear any more secrets. He pulled the sheet up to his chin and groaned. Lying down felt worse than sitting up. A dull throb in his back reminded him how bruised his kidneys were. He remembered the doctor telling him that if he found blood in his urine, he had to see his own physician or go back to the ER. He didn't have time for either and gave his kidneys a mental command not to malfunction.

He tried to think of something, anything other than his own problems. He thought about Kaylen being married to George Bannister Roberts. The guy had to have been at least 30 years older than her. What the hell was a young woman like Kaylen doing with some old guy?

He figured her marital status explained a few things, including Tim's staying power. Tim had never had a girlfriend for more than three days, let alone the three months he had been telling Brian about her. Tim was a realist. He had expensive tastes and liked money a lot. Who better to find comfort and happiness with than a rich young widow?

Brian admitted he could see how Kaylen had been charmed by Tim. So many women were. But did she really seem capable of being Tim's accomplice in his latest scheme? Was Bannisters a front for some other business?

Training and instinct told Brian no, but someone close to Kaylen had manipulated them both like pawns on a chess board, and he intended to find out who as soon as he could stand upright without help.

Kaylen came back into the cabin. "Take these." She held out a glass of water and a couple of pills.

Brian didn't argue. He swallowed the pills and gave the glass back. Their hands touched. Neither of them drew away. "Stay with me." He entwined his fingers with Kaylen's and pulled her down to sit beside him.

She placed her other hand over his. "I'm not going anywhere," she said. "You'd better move over, because I'm going to share *your* bed tonight. It's the only place I feel safe right now, and don't ask me to explain why, because I can't."

Brian felt lightheaded. *Must be the Vicodin* he thought.

"Kaylen," he said. His brain was getting scrambled, and he knew talking was only going to get him into trouble, but he couldn't stop himself. "I need to say somethin'…"

She must have misunderstood. Or maybe she saw or sensed something he didn't want to reveal, even to himself. "This isn't the time," she whispered. "You're hurt, and I'm with Tim."

He wanted to argue, to tell her she was reading him wrong, but as he attempted to sit up, a knife-sharp pain in his side caused him to change his mind. Reason returned with the pain. If and when she found out about his relationship to Tim, she'd hate him. So would his brother.

He pulled her down and took her in his arms. "You're right…not the time." He clumsily pushed the hair back from her face with a gentleness he hadn't known he was capable of until that moment.

"Brian…"

"Shh." He licked dry lips and tried to get his scrambled thoughts back in order. "I'm not…we're not…*damn it.*"

"It's okay," she said.

"No. Wanna tell you, you're vuln'able an' I'm pumped fulla drugs…"

"I *know,*" she said. "Sleep, Brian."

"I don't wanna wake up an' find I ruined…" His eyes refused to focus. "You're best thing s'ever happened to me," he finished. *Oh, God. Why had he said that?*

Kaylen stared at him and then looked away.

Brian closed his eyes and felt completely and utterly humiliated.

"We'll talk tomorrow," she said, her voice unsteady. "When you're feeling more like yourself."

He grunted in response. There was no way he was going to open his mouth again that night.

"You know, there's something so familiar about you," she said. "You make me feel like I know you already. It's the strangest thing."

Not strange, he thought as he stopped fighting against the drugs and the fatigue. Some of his mannerisms mirrored Tim's, and they both had their mother's smile, although he couldn't remember that he'd had any reason to use it that day.

Kaylen gently pulled her hand out of his, and he mumbled a weak protest. He missed the warmth and intimacy. Something he hadn't experienced for too long. He managed to open his eyes briefly, but they kept wandering around like they had some other place to go and he couldn't follow. He thought he saw Kaylen's dress fall to the floor, but he couldn't swear to it, as he might already have been dreaming.

But it seemed he'd only been asleep a few minutes before she was gently shaking him back to consciousness. "Brian, please wake up," she whispered, her voice urgent and filled with fear. "I hear someone moving around up on deck."

CHAPTER FOURTEEN

Kaylen looked at Brian's face, marred by the livid bruise on his cheek and the swollen, sutured lip. Her first attempt to awaken him didn't seem to have had any effect whatsoever. She wanted to shake him harder, but hesitated. What if he was unconscious instead of asleep? What if she hurt him even more by trying to wake him up?

She leaned close to his ear. "Brian!" She tapped his shoulder. "Someone's on the boat."

His eyes opened slowly. He blinked, and his brow furrowed.

"Listen," Kaylen said. "Somebody's creeping around the deck."

"I hear them." He struggled to turn over and clutched his side.

Kaylen heard him swearing under his breath. He wasn't going to be able to do anything. What was she thinking? She grabbed her cell from the nightstand. "I'll call nine-one-one," she said.

"Like hell." He pushed himself up onto one elbow. "Move," he said through gritted teeth.

Kaylen got up fast. He looked like he meant business.

He swung his legs over the side of the bunk and rolled awkwardly into a sitting position. Cradling his ribcage, he used the nightstand to push himself to his feet. "I'm so goddammed stiff," he complained, wincing as he stretched upright.

Dawn sent fingers of red-gold light threading through the cabin, dimly illuminating the interior. The luminous dial of the clock showed 5:30AM. He took a gun out of the nightstand drawer. "Stay here," he told her. He took an uncertain step and swayed.

Kaylen reached for him.

"I'm all right. Just a bit lightheaded."

He waved her away and walked slowly across the cabin. A pair of shorts hung on the back of the door, and he put them on before leaving the room. Kaylen heard his feet padding almost soundlessly across the wooden floor of the salon toward the steps.

Despite the pain and the drugs, he had managed to gather his wits in a matter of seconds. Kaylen wondered what sort of man could do that. Definitely not the ones she knew. She felt a little uneasy about the gun, but she figured Brian might need protection out on the open waters.

She glanced down at her outfit. Black lace bikini panties and one of his t-shirts. If she needed to get off the boat in a hurry, she wasn't going to run around the marina in that outfit. She changed into her dress and looked disapprovingly at her sandals. High heels. Idiotic, given the turn her life had taken.

What if the intruder overpowered Brian? She felt sure she had heard more than one set of footsteps on the deck above. Gun or no gun, he was alone and weakened from his injuries. As the incident in the club the previous evening had graphically demonstrated, one punch and he would be doubled over.

She looked around for a weapon and found nothing except clothes in his closet. But a baseball bat, casually leaning against the wall next to the nightstand, would work. Brian seemed more than prepared for trouble, she thought, taking a firm grip on the bat and stepping behind the door, he actually seemed to be expecting it. She fought a desire to follow him. The last thing he needed was to worry about her as well as himself.

Footsteps echoed down the steps and came toward the cabin. Kaylen braced herself and raised the bat above her head. The door swung wide, almost hitting her. Startled, she jumped aside, bringing the bat down hard. It swished past Brian's shoulder.

He looked at the bat. "Put that thing down before you kill me." He shook his head. "I figured you'd ignore what I said. Good thing I react quickly or I'd have another lump on my head." He sat carefully on the bunk. "No one up there." He placed the gun on the nightstand. "About last night…"

"Don't say anything. I think we were both acting a little out of character."

She had trouble making eye contact. He looked far too appealing in the early morning, still sleepy-eyed from the effects of the drugs and dressed in a rumpled t-shirt over tattered cut-offs. A light dusting of golden stubble meandered over the cuts and bruises on his face.

"Let's forget it," she said.

"Hard to do." He got up and took a short-sleeved dress shirt and beige chinos out of the closet.

"It would be a lot better for both of us if you made the effort."

She forced herself not to help him as he struggled with the shirt. She needed some distance that morning. Her emotions were way too raw and close to the surface. She really wanted him to hold her, which she told herself was ridiculous.

She had to rely on herself, not seek comfort from others. She knew that from experience: her mother had died. George had died. People who appeared invincible were not. She jammed her feet into her sandals, which pinched her feet…like she needed any more rebukes that morning.

To avoid looking at him, she went into the galley. "Maybe I heard a drunk up on deck, or kids on the wrong boat," she called. She saw dishes in a drying rack and what looked like an inch of day-old coffee in a carafe.

"Maybe." Brian didn't sound convinced.

Kaylen fussed around washing out the carafe and putting away the dishes while he finished dressing.

"How about I take you home?" Brian, wearing a beige jacket over the dress shirt, stood a couple of feet away.

Kaylen hadn't heard him coming, and she jumped.

"I startled you. Sorry." Hands in pockets, he leaned against the counter.

"It doesn't take much since yesterday." Kaylen placed the last dish into the cupboard and closed the cabinet. An audible click announced the door was secured in the event of rough weather.

She weighed her options. She could refuse Brian's offer and walk over to Sam's restaurant. He always arrived before the staff in the morning, and he'd definitely take her home. But she knew she'd get a judgmental look from Sam when she arrived with uncombed hair and smudged makeup, and she wasn't ready to defend her actions to him again.

"I could take a cab or a car service," she said without conviction. She didn't like either option. Whoever had been on deck could be lurking somewhere between the boat and the street. Or she could be picked up by an imposter. She'd heard stories about that. She shuddered, feeling chilled and defenseless in her strapless cocktail dress.

Brian frowned. "Why would you do that when I can drive you?"

She managed to give him a half-smile. "Doesn't make much sense, does it? Okay, I'll go with you. I don't think I could face getting into a stranger's vehicle, anyway. I feel spooked enough right now."

"I'm a stranger," he pointed out. "Almost, anyway. But you've spent the last two nights with me. Last night by choice. So maybe we've moved on to being acquaintances."

Kaylen felt her cheeks flush. "Do you always try hard to make people not like you, or are you singling me out?"

"It's one of my gifts. What can I say?" He shrugged. "I'm not out to impress you."

"I noticed that."

He had more than rough edges, she decided. He was abrasive. "Do you have any coffee?" she asked. "I could really do with some."

"Sorry. I'm fresh out." He picked up her purse, swinging it back and forth by the strap. "Come on. We'll grab some from a drive-through."

"You're in a big hurry to get rid of me suddenly," she said. "You wanted to come over to the club last night to compare notes. We could do that now."

"You're the one who said you needed to get home," he reminded her.

"That's true." She grabbed her purse as it swung toward her and hurried past him.

But Brian stopped her with a hand on her arm as she was about to mount the steep steps. "I'd better go first. In case whoever you heard decided to come back."

"You think they would?" A ripple of fear coursed through her. She stepped aside.

He was wearing the gun in a holster under his jacket. She glimpsed it as she slowly followed him up the stairs. He was definitely prepared for trouble. She waited until he motioned her to join him on deck. He locked the cabin door and they quickly made their way onto the dock.

"You've got to learn to be more careful," he chided. "You could have walked up those stairs into an ambush."

"I'm not used to living in fear," Kaylen said. She wanted to ask him about the gun, but told herself she should keep her questions to herself until she was safely home.

"That's probably true, but you might not live much longer if you don't start thinking before you act." Brian took her hand. "Let's make it fast." He tugged her into a fast trot.

Kaylen's ungainly trot turned into outright running as she tried to keep up with him. He kept her hand in his as they dodged between cars, his grip strong and reassuring. So much for him being stiff and painful, she thought, her feet and ankles registering a strong protest about the level of activity.

"I don't think I was cut out for this," she said when he stopped suddenly. "I'm scared out of my wits while you're acting cool as a cucumber."

"I'm not." Brian pulled her behind an SUV as two men came walking between the cars toward the dock. "I'm sweating." He mopped his brow with his forearm.

Kaylen clutched his other arm as she watched the men pass. They were loudly discussing the weather and its possible effects on their morning fishing. She breathed a sigh of relief. "I'm such a coward," she said. "I'm terrified of everything and everyone right now."

"You're no coward," Brian said.

He brushed her hair back from her face with a touch so unexpectedly gentle, it felt like a caress. Kaylen stared at him.

"You're a welcome surprise," he said, his voice as soft as his touch. "You've made me like you, when I didn't expect to."

She felt puzzled. "Why would you expect not to like me?"

"Because I thought you'd be an empty-headed socialite."

"Wow," she said. "You don't pull any punches, do you? If this is your way of telling someone you like them, then I'd hate to see the way you treat someone you *don't* like."

Brian's attempt to smile ended up looking more like a scowl. "Yeah, you wouldn't wanna be there, that's for sure. Come on." He took her hand again. "My car's right over here."

He led her to a serviceable old bronze Camaro that had seen better days. Kaylen thought his conflicting tastes in boats and cars only revealed yet another facet of his complex character.

"You've got guts, Kaylen," he told her as she settled into the passenger's seat. His lips pulled into a thin line and he winced as he eased behind the wheel. "You make me want to protect you, but I don't know if you'll trust me enough to let me."

Emotion threatened to choke her. Just when she thought she'd been left alone in a frightening new world, an unlikely and unexpected source of comfort had come to her.

"Ready?" Brian asked when she didn't answer, his voice strained, his face averted.

"Yes." She struggled not to start crying again.

No amount of telling herself she was with Tim, or even reminding herself of the way she had met Brian did anything to chase away the wish to stay close to him. But he'd told her she was vulnerable, she reminded herself. She struggled to think of some cool, flippant remark to ease the tension in the car, but failed. No one had offered to take care of her in such a way since George died. Not even Sam. Certainly not Tim.

"Thank you," she said. She hesitantly touched his arm. "I'm so mixed up right now. I don't know what to think or who to trust. But for some reason, I don't feel that way when I'm with you."

"Don't thank me too quickly." He managed a lop-sided smile. "I'm only a gentleman some of the time, and you don't know if I'm reliable or trustworthy yet, either."

"I'll remember that." She smiled back, grateful he had lightened the moment. "But if you were going to hurt me, you would have done so already. You've had plenty of chances."

"That's true. But did you think that maybe I'm trying to get something out of you, too?"

"Don't even go there," Kaylen said, unease flooding her. "And besides, you just offered to protect me. Are you trying to play mind games with me?" Her voice quivered, and she realized she was about to start crying again. "I'd appreciate it if you didn't. I can't take much more."

"No mind games, princess. I promise."

He might have used that horrible name he'd given her, but his voice was low and his gaze steady. Kaylen felt him wipe away the tear rolling from the corner of her eye.

She grabbed his hand. "I'll hold you to that," she said, and they were staring at each other in a very disconcerting way that made her heart speed up. There was tension between them, and it had nothing to do with fear.

Brian turned the key in the ignition while Kaylen wondered what was wrong with her, or maybe with both of them. He was covered in bruises, and she'd been terrorized. The only emotions they should be feeling right then were fear or anger.

They peeled out of the marina at a breakneck pace. She rolled down the window and grabbed the doorframe for support as they tore onto the expressway. "Do you always drive like this?" she asked when she could get her breath. "I told you I was anxious about getting into a car with a stranger. You're not doing anything to reassure me."

He glanced at her. "Sorry. I'm a fast driver, and I'm not used to having…," he hesitated, "…eh, ladies in my car."

"Ladies?" Kaylen pulled her hair out of her mouth and licked dry lips as they weaved from lane to lane, passing cars in rapid succession. "What in the world are you talking about?"

"Hold on." He accelerated and pulled across two lanes to take the ramp they had almost passed, flipped a quick right and cruised through a yellow light.

Kaylen abandoned any further conversation. She wanted him to keep his full attention on the road. As they roared along, she swore it would be the last time she ever got into a car with Brian behind the wheel.

He careened into the condo's parking lot and pulled up in front the steps to her door. He turned to look at her. "You want me to walk you inside?"

Kaylen wondered if she had the strength to get out of the Camaro without help. "No." She grabbed the door handle with a shaky hand. "I don't want to get into the habit of needing a bodyguard. I'll be fine." *Liar*, she thought. She wouldn't be fine at all.

Driving with Brian might not be the scariest thing she had done that day. The thought of walking into that condo made her want to scream and run. She promised herself she would only stay there ten minutes, tops. She had to change out of her cocktail dress and tidy herself up. Nobody was going to see her looking like she had slept in the open on a bench, or worse, in some guy's bed, even if she had.

"We need to talk later," Brian said. "I think Tim's got something to do with what happened yesterday. I'm going over to his apartment right now. I can't get him to answer the phone."

"Me neither," Kaylen said. "And his voicemail's full." She took her purse from the floor, where it had landed after Brian's spectacular exit from the expressway. "I wanted to go over to his apartment myself, to give him a piece of my mind." She hugged the purse to her chest as a chill moved through her, despite the warmth of the morning sun. "But after what happened to Rosa, I needed to be in a crowd, where I felt safer. Do you have a pen? I can give you my cell number."

"I already got that yesterday, when I got your home number from one of your employees." Brian had the grace to look a little sheepish.

"*What?*" She had trouble breathing. "My God, I'm surrounded by idiots. They're going to get me killed."

"I'm pretty persuasive when I want to be," Brian said. "But you'd better meet with your staff and warn them not to let anyone else sweet-talk them into giving out your personal information."

Kaylen sighed. "That's like shutting the door after the horse already bolted. The people who shouldn't have my information probably already do by now."

"Let's hope not." Brian watched her get out of the car. "Remember," he said. "I'm the one who was used as a punching bag. Maybe I'm the real target. Although that wouldn't explain what happened to your housekeeper, would it?"

"No." Kaylen shook her head. "It's me they're after. There was a message on the mirror in my bedroom. It said they want something, and that Rosa was murdered to prove they mean business. I told the detectives I don't know what they're talking about. I don't have anything they could possibly want."

Brian stared at her as though she had lost her mind. "Why the hell didn't you tell me this before?"

"Do you really think you were in any condition to hear about messages on mirrors last night?" Anger rose inside her. He wasn't only abrasive, he was downright bossy. "Why do you think I need to tell you everything? You're not a cop, you're a charter boat captain." She slammed the door.

When he looked at her, a contained rage blasted her like a wall of heat. "Because I'm trying to help you," he said, his lips barely moving. "None of your *friends* seem to be doing that. I guess you think you're too good to accept help from me, princess, otherwise you wouldn't hold back information that might put a stop to all this."

"You're incredibly rude and insensitive," Kaylen told him. "In the past twenty-four hours my whole life's been turned upside down. I'm terrified, you ass, and if that makes me act irrationally, then tough."

Brian's fingers clenched the steering wheel until his knuckles turned white. "Don't start yelling at *me*. I've got a vested interest in what's happening to you. Remember, I'm the one who got beaten up."

"And you won't go to the cops. What's wrong with you? That's their job, solving crimes. They're professionals."

"Some of them." Brian shoved the Camaro into reverse, but kept his foot on the brake. "I'll think about reporting the beating, but I'm wondering if someone doesn't want me around you, and was telling me in a not-so-subtle way. Are you really sure it's not someone you know?"

"Absolutely."

Brian started to rub one hand across his face but stopped, grimacing. "So we're back to square one."

"No one saw you with me yesterday morning," Kaylen said. "Not even those two cops or the manager." She shuddered. The day felt cold despite heat bouncing off the blacktop and shimmering around the luxury cars. "Unless…you don't think those cops hung around and saw you going out of my condo, do you? But even if they did, who would they tell, and why?"

His fingers tapped the steering wheel. "I've got to get going. We can talk more about this later. I'll call you after I go over to Tim's apartment." Concern filled his voice. "You be careful up there. Don't stay too long."

"I'll only be a few minutes," she said. "I'm going to change clothes and check my voicemail."

"If anything else strange happens today, you call the cops, okay?" He released the brake and the car began to ease back. "Even something small."

"Okay." She started to turn away.

"Thanks for helping me last night," he said.

Kaylen turned back. One minute he was downright rude and the next it seemed a nice guy might be hiding under that harsh exterior. "You're weird," she said. "Has anyone else ever told you that?"

Brian's scowl confirmed it.

The Camaro's engine went from a loud purr to a dull roar as he turned out of the parking space. Kaylen waved to catch his attention before he peeled out of the lot. "Tell Tim to get in touch with me," she called. "If he knows anything about what's happened…if this is because of some business deal he's gotten involved with…I'll kill him."

"You'll have to take a number," she heard before the car sped away.

Things were happening so fast, she needed a score card to keep up. She had a growing list of unanswered questions because Brian routinely avoided sharing information. There were no personal items visible on the *Destiny*. No photos, knickknacks or books. It was as though he had no past.

She grabbed the rail and climbed the stairs. How come Brian said he and Tim were only acquaintances, but he knew where Tim lived? She had never been inside Tim's apartment, and she was his girlfriend.

She had often wondered why Tim chose to live in Little Havana. He wore expensive clothes and drove a new black Lexus. He tossed money around as though he had an unlimited supply. But she had been so happy, she had put aside her questions. Besides, he was a friend of Sam's, and she trusted Sam implicitly. He would never allow her to associate with someone who could place her in jeopardy in any way, she reassured herself.

But she had to admit that Tim was as secretive as Brian, only less obvious about it. Whenever she suggested they go to his apartment, he made excuses. He'd had friends over to see a game and they'd made a big mess. His housekeeper hadn't come that week. Kaylen's condo was bigger and nicer.

Arguing with him got her nowhere. He had only laughed at her and told her she was adorable but silly. A couple of times, she had driven to his place and knocked on the door without success. The building seemed silent and deserted, although she'd had an uncomfortable feeling someone was watching her the whole time. When she had told Sam about those trips he had laughed at her, too, and asked her why it was so important for her to see inside Tim's apartment. Put that way, she agreed she was being silly.

If she hadn't been in such a hurry to get done with the dreaded visit to her condo, she would have refused to leave Brian's car until he answered the questions that plagued her all the way up the stairs. She vowed the next time she saw Brian Swift, he wasn't going to get away with being evasive. She unlocked her door and stepped inside.

She'd never realized before how dark and quiet it was in her condo. Alarm gnawed at her gut. Telling herself she was over-reacting, she laid her purse on the small table beside the front door and flipped the switch for the overhead light. Nothing happened.

All the blinds were closed. Who would have done that? The cleaning company Sam had promised to send over that morning? The alarm bells already ringing in her head intensified.

She should have asked Brian to come upstairs with her, regardless of how much he annoyed her. Coming back alone was stupid, she berated herself, anger vying with fear.

To hell with changing clothes and accessing her voicemail. She'd grab whatever clothes were in the dryer and throw them into a bag with toiletries and makeup. Five minutes, tops. Less if she really hurried. She could make herself presentable and retrieve her messages at the hotel. She no longer cared what some desk clerk thought about her disheveled appearance.

The washer and dryer were concealed in a closet on the way to the bedroom, where she had to retrieve her suitcase. Kaylen took a deep breath. First, she needed to open some blinds to avoid tripping over anything the cleaning company had moved.

Leaving the front door open, she began to feel her way slowly toward the living room, where she could dimly make out an end table topped by a lamp. The atmosphere hung heavy. No air stirred.

A hand clapped over her mouth, an arm slid across her throat, and she was pulled back against a hard, male body.

"Don't struggle." His voice sounded distorted.

Kaylen felt wool brush her cheek as he kicked the door closed.

CHAPTER FIFTEEN

Brian left all the windows down and let the wind blow the cobwebs out of his brain while he drove to Tim's apartment. His mind felt fogged from lack of sleep and pain pills.

By the time he found a space and parallel parked the car, he felt lightheaded again. The last time he'd had more than the water he had taken with his pills was the cup of coffee he'd downed at Kaylen's condo the previous morning. He'd been so busy with the charter and getting ready to meet Kaylen, he had forgotten to eat lunch. The beating had replaced dinner.

Tim would have something in his apartment, Brian reasoned, dragging himself out of the Camaro. He leaned on the doorframe while he tried to straighten his stiff and spasming body. He had to climb two flights of stairs because Tim's dump of a building had no elevator.

He pulled out his cell and hit Tim's landline again. The voicemail was still full. He tried his brother's cell while he walked into the cool, dimly-lit front hallway with worn black and white tiles and peeling beige paint. Same results. Filled voicemail. Maybe Tim was sleeping like Rip Van Winkle.

Once he got up those fucking stairs, Brian thought as he trudged up the first flight, he'd wake Tim up and lie on the couch while his brother made breakfast and explained himself. Brian vowed he wasn't going to listen to any more of his sibling's bullshit. Tim had better come up with a damned good reason for putting on a disappearing act as well as asking Brian to meet him in Kaylen's parking lot the night of her supper club opening. Although his brother had a history of being unreliable and irresponsible, Brian doubted

Tim would stoop to knocking him out and dragging him upstairs to Kaylen's bed. What possible motive could he have?

For that matter, what motive could Kaylen have for participating in that bizarre scenario? Brian felt she must be involved in Tim's latest scheme, but what role she had played was still in doubt.

As he slowly climbed the remaining stairs, he looked over the banister at a large puddle of water that had gathered in the entrance hall. There must be a leak in the skylight. Miami had been pounded by a strong storm only days before. Another was brewing out in the Atlantic. Someone needed to clean up the mess and repair the skylight before it turned into a bigger problem. He knew it wouldn't be his brother.

Brian felt exhausted by the time he reached the landing. He realized he needed something even more essential than food...rest and medication. He almost turned back, but forced himself to ignore the siren's call from his bunk on the *Destiny*. Instead, he pushed Tim's doorbell and waited. No footsteps; no movement inside the apartment. Brian let his head drop against the wall as his legs quivered. He was so damned *tired.* He pounded on the door. The neighbor opposite opened hers to the extent of the chain.

"He's not there," she said. "He hasn't been home for a couple of days. Are you his brother?"

"Yeah." Brian turned to face her and leaned back against the wall. His legs wouldn't stop quivering, and he wondered if he was going to hit the floor if he didn't sit down somewhere pretty damn quick.

"What's your name?" she asked, barely visible against the darkness of the space behind her.

"Brian Swift. I'm Tim's half-brother." He peered at her. Wisps of white hair put a halo around her head.

"What was your mother's name, and where did you live when you were growing up?" she asked.

"What's this, twenty questions?" He didn't have the time or the energy for stupid parlor games.

"He left something for you, but he told me not to give it to you unless you answered the questions correctly." The woman looked peeved and started to close the door, one faded blue eye glaring balefully through the narrowing gap.

"Okay, okay," he said quickly. "I'm sorry, but my brother sometimes likes to play stupid tricks."

The door stopped closing. "Well?" she asked.

"Maggie. Our mother's name was Maggie. She was born Maggie Webb, she married my father Andy, who died, and then she married Tim's father, Ed Madison. He took us to Baton Rouge, where we grew up on Webber Street, in a dingy little house with a view of the railroad tracks." Brian found it difficult to tell a complete stranger even that much about his private life. A sour taste coated the inside of his mouth at the thought of Webber Street. He silently called Tim a bastard.

"What happened the day you left home?" she asked.

His muscles reacted to the mention of Baton Rouge in the same way they had when he lived there…they tightened, bringing a ripple of disgust up his back and zinging into his ribs. He bit down on his lower lip while air pistoned between his teeth.

"Are you going to answer the question or am I going to close this door?" The gap between the door and the frame narrowed again.

Brian pushed aside nightmarish thoughts of Ed Madison's belt sailing repeatedly through the air to land on his exposed flesh.

"All right, all right." He pushed away from the wall. "Tim and I fought and broke a window that day. Is that what you want to hear?" If she asked any more stupid goddamned questions, he was going to kick in the fucking door and *take* the envelope.

"You get the grand prize," the woman said, mercifully dangling a small white envelope between the tips of her thumb and index finger.

Brian heard Tim's phone ringing incessantly inside the empty apartment as he took the envelope from her.

"He gave me a couple of hundred dollars to do it," she said. "Otherwise I'd have told him to go to hell. You're a pain in the ass." She shut the door in Brian's face.

"Christ, what a bitch."

Guessing she was still watching him through the peephole in the door, Brian thumbed his nose in her direction. He started walking slowly toward the stairs. *Tim always did put all his money into outward appearances, but a couple of hundred dollars tip?* Brian stopped and turned back. *His brother must have been frantic.*

He knocked on the neighbor's door.

"Go away!" She shouted from the other side. "I'm beginning to regret taking that money, even if I needed it to pay my rent."

"I want to know when he gave you the envelope."

"Are you paying?"

"My brother already gave you two hundred bucks."

"That went toward last month's rent. Now I'm working on this month."

Brian raised a clenched fist to pound on her door, thought better of it and pulled out his wallet. He'd be panhandling on the street if he had to pay for every piece of information, he thought. Fuck Tim and his screwed-up life.

"I'm out of work. I've got sixty bucks and that's it." He waved the money. "Take it or leave it."

The door opened again to the length of the chain and a wrinkled hand slid through, palm up.

"Uh, uh." Brian moved the money out of reach and fanned out the three twenties. "Information first. You're not going to grab these and slam the door in my face."

"How do I know I can trust you to give me the money after I tell you?" she countered, the washed-out blue eye glaring at him again.

"Here's a twenty on account." He placed it in her palm.

"On account of what?" she asked.

"That you don't get the rest until you tell me what I want to know."

She closed her hand over the money and drew it inside. Brian glimpsed a faded housedress in stripes of yellow, red and blue. The visible part of her leg was covered with varicose veins, her swollen ankle hung over a ragged blue slipper.

"Well?" he prodded.

"He came to my door the day before yesterday, late in the afternoon. He was all dressed up in a tux. After he gave me the envelope and the money, he left." Her hand came back through the opening. "I haven't seen him since. Now give me the rest of the money and go away."

Brian placed another twenty in her hand. "Did anyone else come to his apartment? Did they ask you where he went?" He waved the last twenty at her.

She reached out her hand again. "You don't give up, do you?"

"Never. You want this money or not?"

"Of course I do. You're not like your brother. You want more for sixty bucks than he gave me for just holding an envelope."

"I told you, I'm out of a job."

"Then you should try working for your brother's boss instead. Tim's always done up good."

Brian felt a surge of anger. *Who was she to judge?* "I'm not here to chit-chat with you," he told her, keeping his voice under control with an effort. "I'm here for information. Now give it to me or go without this." He started to put the money back into his wallet.

"Okay, okay. Two men went into his apartment that evening. They were in there for a long time. I didn't see them leave with anything, and I don't want any more to do with this. I did the job Tim paid me to do. Now give me that last twenty. You go find and talk to your brother if you want any more information."

When Brian placed the money in her hand, she snatched it away and slammed the door in his face. He stood looking at the worn wood for a moment before heading back toward the stairs. As he walked, he looked at the paper in his hand and saw Tim's spidery handwriting, giving the details of the question and answer session. He tore open the envelope and scanned the contents quickly before going back down to the lobby.

What the hell had Tim gotten into this time?

CHAPTER SIXTEEN

Fear froze Kaylen to the spot. The hand covering her face threatened to close off her nose as well as her mouth, and stars danced in front of her eyes. She knew she was going to pass out if she didn't get air in a hurry.

"All we want is the key," the man rasped in her ear. He released his hammer-lock on her throat. "If you promise not to scream, I'll take my hand off your mouth. Nod if you understand."

Kaylen would have agreed to anything at that point. She managed to nod, and he took his hand away, giving her the opportunity to gulp in air.

"Give us what we want, you'll avoid a whole lot of trouble for yourself and your new boyfriend."

Kaylen coughed, her throat tight. "I—I don't know what you're talking about," she managed. "I don't have any key." Icy tentacles clasped her insides. Cold sweat formed on her face and ran down her back.

Keep calm, she told herself. If they didn't need her, she'd be dead already. They wanted some sort of key. They thought she had it. *Why?*

"Can I sit down, at least?" she asked. Her knees felt like two quivering reeds in a high wind.

"No." He whirled her around to face him.

He wore a hideous blue and red ski mask and a pair of blue coveralls, similar to the ones worn by the maintenance men who worked around the complex. When he moved, she spotted the collar of a tailored white shirt beneath the garment.

He grabbed her right wrist and pulled her arm behind her back before bringing an impressively large knife from a pocket in one leg of the coveralls. "It'd be a real shame to mark up that pretty face of yours, but maybe you need some encouragement to remember." He placed the point of the knife against her chin.

Kaylen gasped and rose up on her toes to get away from the blade. "I swear, I don't know anything," she said, her teeth chattering.

"You know plenty, and you need to start cooperating with us. If you don't, you're gonna get yourself into a whole lotta trouble." He twisted her arm viciously.

Kaylen's cry ended abruptly when he threw her against the couch. He bent her almost double, her face sinking into the overstuffed cushions, grabbed the hem of her dress and threw it over her head.

Kaylen knew she was about to be raped and possibly murdered if she didn't do something to save herself. Her grasping fingers connected with a hard-backed book hidden between the cushions. She managed to stomp on his foot with the heel of one Jimmy Choo sandal and followed that up by swinging the book against his head. As he staggered back, she turned around and kicked him in the groin.

But things didn't go exactly as she'd planned. He was supposed to become instantly incapacitated and fall to the floor, giving her the advantage of using the book to knock him senseless. Instead, he let out an inhuman howl and pushed her so hard, she was the one who fell, sprawling face down. Her nose connected with the hardwood floor beyond the area rug and in front of her eyes, stars exploded into a Super Nova.

Blood ran into her palm as she cradled her bruised face. Despite the pain, Kaylen tried to crawl away, tears mingling with the blood. She almost made it to the front door before her assailant grabbed her.

"Bitch!" He seized her by the hair and jerked her head back. "I'm gonna make sure I take care of Swift personally. He'll end up like your last boyfriend...dead."

"What...who...who are you talking about?" Kaylen clawed at him, her fear for both Tim and Brian overwhelming any thoughts of personal safety.

"Madison. You got so many boyfriends you can't keep track?"

"Tim?" Her heart pounded sickeningly. Did he mean Tim was dead?

"Yeah, him. He's in Snapper Creek. If you don't cooperate pretty fuckin' quick, I'll throw Swift in there, too."

"No!" Kaylen's scream echoed from wall to wall.

"I told you to keep quiet!" He balled up his fist.

She shut her mouth.

"By noon tomorrow," he told her. "I'll find you." He shoved her back to the floor. "Stay put an' count to five hundred," he ordered. "An' don't call the cops, neither."

Kaylen kept her head down, but she managed to watch him from the corner of one eye. He pulled off the ski mask and kept his face averted as he left, his back visible briefly in the blinding sunlight before he ran down the stairs.

She scrambled across the room to lock the door behind him, ripped open the drapes and flooded the room with light. Despite his threats, she called the police immediately. Listening impatiently for the sirens, she grabbed one of her once-treasured table linens and held it to her bleeding nose.

CHAPTER SEVENTEEN

Kaylen's nose stopped bleeding on the way to the bathroom. Carefully, she wiped blood off her swollen face. Her eyes smarted, and she blinked away tears.

Her mind kept returning to what her attacker had said. Brian was going to be killed, *just like Tim*. Kaylen leaned over the sink and retched miserably, her empty stomach convulsing. She cupped her palm and drank from the faucet in an attempt to ease the burning in her throat before splashing her face with cold water.

Why would anyone kill lighthearted, irreverent Tim? She clutched the sink for support as she thought of him the night Bannisters opened, when he had praised her for realizing her dream, his dark eyes soft as he raised his glass in a toast.

She remembered the first time she had met him, when she visited Sam at his restaurant, and he introduced his much younger friend.

Tall, dark and handsome was a cliché but one that fit Tim Madison so perfectly, she had even come to joke with him about it. Six foot three with black hair cut fashionably long, dark brown eyes and a strong jaw-line, he turned heads everywhere he went. A superb dresser, he knew what took his looks from handsome to stunning, his designer suits molding a body honed to perfection by frequent gym workouts. He quickly got to know everyone worth knowing in her elite social circle.

Tim was the first new man she had let into her life since George's death. He had been exceptionally kind and patient with her, taking time to make her feel relaxed yet excited enough to let the relationship progress past friendship into intimacy. With the memory of their last night together in her condo, the day before the club opening, her legs gave way and she fell to her knees. *Dear God, what could she possibly have in her possession that would cause the deaths of two people?*

Kaylen knew whoever had killed Rosa would be quite capable of killing Tim. She pulled a towel from the rack above her head and covered her face, the softness of the terry cloth soothing, the clean scent filling her bruised and swollen nasal passages with a sweet aroma.

If only she could wipe the last twenty-four hours from the calendar, she would do so without sparing even a fleeting moment of regret over the loss of Bannisters. Rosa would be alive. Tim would be sending his weekly dozen red roses and suggesting they dine at another of the fancy restaurants he was so fond of visiting on Saturday nights. The comfortable routine she had established over the last few months would be intact, and all would be right in her own little corner of the world.

Kaylen threw the towel across the room. Hiding from reality wasn't going to help; neither was wallowing in misery on her bathroom floor. She got up and strode out to the kitchen, where she made herself an ice pack.

There must be something constructive she could do while waiting for the police to arrive, she told herself as she paced up and down the living room with the ice pack held against her nose.

Why hadn't she thought to ask Brian for his cell number? She had to contact him as quickly as possible. *Think,* she told herself. Brian said he was going to Tim's apartment, and she would be willing to bet that if Tim didn't answer the door, Brian would figure out some way of getting inside. He might be there now. She called Tim's landline. The phone rang and rang, but the machine made no attempt to pick up.

She called the Coconut Grove Marina's office. The man who answered promised to check whether the *Destiny* was still moored or out on a charter. He assured Kaylen he would pass her message for Brian to contact her. No, he said, he didn't have Brian's cell number. Kaylen thought he was probably lying, but forcing the issue wasn't going to get her anywhere.

Frustrated, she hung up. She needed to let the police know quickly about the threat made against Brian. She checked her watch. At least 10 minutes had passed since she talked to the dispatcher. If the cops didn't arrive in the next two minutes, she would call them while she drove to Tim's apartment. The doorbell rang while that thought was in her mind. She made sure the two men wearing suits held up their badges before she took off the security chain and let them in.

This time, Miami-Dade had sent far more than a pair of patrol officers.

"I'm Captain Hastings," the taller and younger man said, his gaze running over her. "From Vice." He indicated the graying man standing to his left. "This is Lieutenant Shaw. Homicide." He pushed a lock of dark, wavy hair off his forehead and walked past her to examine the contents of her curio cabinet. "Nice." He looked around the living room and raised dark eyebrows. "Very nice."

Kaylen watched him slide the toe of his shiny black shoe over a faint stain in the carpet that the cleaning service had been unable to remove. His appraisal annoyed her. "Did you come in response to the call I made?" she asked.

"We were in the area," Lieutenant Shaw said. "You look like someone punched you in the face."

Kaylen focused her attention on Shaw, who remained at the entrance to the living-room while Captain Hastings continued his prowling. "Someone did. When I came into my condo, there was a man waiting for me. He half-choked me and threatened me."

Hastings, who was perusing the small collection of books that had escaped destruction, turned toward her and quirked an eyebrow. "Is that right?"

Kaylen decided she didn't like Hastings or his almost-effeminate good looks. "He told me my boyfriend's dead," she told Shaw.

"Tim Madison?" Shaw stepped forward.

"How do you know his name?" Kaylen understood that as a high-profile member of Miami's social scene, her own name would be easily recognizable, but Tim's?

"The police make it their business to know a lot of things, Ma'am,"

Lieutenant Shaw said, sharp brown eyes fixed on her face.

Kaylen felt herself blush, even though she had no reason to do so, or at least none that he would be interested in. She had to force herself not to give into the impulse to look away.

"The man also made threats toward a...a...fr...uh, an acquaintance of mine." She stopped, unsure how to describe her relationship with Brian. "He dropped me off here. I'm worried he might have been followed when he left." She sat on the couch and clasped her hands together because they had begun shaking uncontrollably all over again as panic rose inside her. Shaw had bristling thick brows, a long nose and a large mouth. He felt more intimidating to Kaylen than Hastings, despite his milder manner. "Please," she said. "You've got to do something to help him."

Lieutenant Shaw looked at Hastings, standing with a framed photograph of her wedding in his hand, but he didn't move.

Kaylen's patience snapped. "People around me are getting murdered," she said, jumping up from the couch. "You've got to give us some protection!"

"Why don't you sit back down? You're not thinking rationally." Shaw pulled out his cell. "I'll call the paramedics."

Kaylen felt like hitting them both. They stood staring at her like she was a raving lunatic. She drew in a deep breath. "Some group wants a key they think I have," she said. "First there was that message on my mirror yesterday, when I found my housekeeper murdered in the bathtub, and now I was threatened by this intruder. You people don't seem to be able to do anything about it."

She knew her voice was rising, but she couldn't control it. "I don't need paramedics," she said, struggling to sound less hysterical. "You've *got* to find my friend. He went over to my boyfriend's apartment. I'm telling you, the man who assaulted me threatened to kill him."

"What's your friend's name?" Hastings had put the photograph back on its shelf. With two strides he was right in front of her.

Up close and personal, he was pretty imposing. Kaylen revised her earlier assessment of his intimidation potential as he leaned over her, his hands jammed in his pockets.

"Brian," she said.

"Brian who?"

"Brian Swift."

Again that strange look passed between the two men.

"You know him, too?" She watched them carefully. Powerful undercurrents seemed to be circling around her.

"He went over to Madison's apartment?" Hastings was so close, she felt his breath on her cheek.

"Yes. Neither of us could get him to answer his landline or his cell, and now both voicemails are full and won't accept messages." With difficulty, she broke eye contact with Hastings and appealed to Shaw. "Something's *really* wrong."

"I'll send a patrol car over there right away," Lieutenant Shaw said.

"You need the address," Kaylen said.

"I have it," he said.

Kaylen felt even more confused and frightened than she had been before Hastings and Shaw arrived on her doorstep. "Why?"

"He's a person of interest to us," Shaw said.

Hastings had moved away. He opened her curio cabinet and examined an exquisite Chinese vase George had given her for their second anniversary. "When was the last time you saw Madison?"

"Two evenings ago, when Bannisters, my new club opened." Kaylen took the vase out of his hands. It was on the tip of her tongue to say she had been tattooed and awakened in bed with a stranger, but she stopped herself. "I talked to my friend, Sam Wilson, and he told me I left with Tim after I became ill at the opening. We don't know what happened to me, or to Tim for that matter, after he took me out of the club."

Something told her not to volunteer too much information, and she knew it was Brian's voice in her head. He had warned her there would be repercussions if she said too much. Now there were two police supervisors in her condo, and they were telling her Tim was a person of interest and that they had heard of Brian, too.

What if the press got wind of all this? She cringed at the thought of the banner headlines in the tabloids: SOCIALITE KAYLEN ROBERTS

CELEBRATED THE OPENING OF HER SUPPER CLUB BY GETTING A TATTOO AND A ROLL IN THE HAY WITH A STRANGER BEFORE HER MAID WAS MURDERED IN HER BATHTUB. THE POLICE HAVE A FILE ON HER BOYFRIEND, WHO IS A PERSON OF INTEREST IN THEIR INVESTIGATION.

She suddenly felt *really* dizzy and sat down on a chair. "What interest does Tim have for you?"

"You got anything to drink around here?" Hastings sat on the chair opposite hers. "You look like you need it."

"Water," she said. "The thought of alcohol right now makes me want to vomit." She shuddered and placed one hand over her mouth. She didn't want to start retching again, but her throat was already tightening.

Lieutenant Shaw brought her a glass of water while Hastings made himself really comfortable by slouching down in the deep chair and stretching out his long legs. He crossed them at the ankles and made a steeple of his fingers, looking at her over the top of them.

Kaylen tried to ignore him. She took a big gulp of the water. It slid uncomfortably down her raw throat while, to her chagrin, her hands started shaking again. She was a pile of Jell-O, and Hastings watching her intently wasn't helping any.

"Even if Tim goes away for a week, he texts me," she said. The glass started to slip.

Shaw took it from her and placed it on the table. Another of those loaded glances passed between him and Hastings. Kaylen swore it was some sort of signal, but she couldn't figure out whether it was a warning for Hastings to keep quiet or for Shaw to do so.

"What if Tim really *is* in Snapper Creek?" she asked into the silence. Suddenly, her teeth started chattering. "It's really cold in here," she said.

"I think you're in shock, Ms. Roberts," Hastings said. "Do you need a sweater?"

She shook her head. "I don't understand why my call brought supervisors instead of patrolmen. What's going on?"

"Let's say that Vice has a vested interest in this," Hastings said. "When the call came over the radio, Lieutenant Shaw and I happened to be eating lunch together, so he came along for the ride. Since this is an open investigation, I can't tell you anything else. How did you become acquainted with Tim Madison and Brian Swift?"

"Well…" Kaylen decided short sentences would be better. Easier to keep to the facts with less chance of tripping over her own feet. "I've been dating Tim for the past three months," she said. "I met Brian recently. Quite recently."

Hastings grunted. "How recently?"

"Umm…well, the night Bannisters opened."

Another look passed between Hastings and Shaw.

"What exactly did your assailant say to you?" Shaw asked.

Kaylen repeated everything, as best she remembered. When she finished, Hastings stood. "Better check out that creek, Hal," he said to his companion.

Shaw barely inclined his head. "I was about to make that call."

He walked down the hallway and Kaylen heard him talking into his phone, although she couldn't make out the words. She wondered what Hastings had meant by saying his department had a vested interest. Wasn't this a homicide investigation because of Rosa's death?

"I talked with your friend, Sam," Hastings said, echoing her thoughts.

Kaylen remembered Sam's disapproval when she told him she was staying the night with Brian on his boat. Sam hadn't liked Brian on sight and had made no bones about it. She wouldn't put it past him to suggest Brian was involved in something illegal—something Vice could be interested in—or even Rosa's murder.

"Brian had nothing to do with any of this," she said. "He only dropped me off in the parking lot. I watched him leave before I came up here and got attacked."

"How convenient," Hastings said. "He dropped you off. From where?"

"His boat," Kaylen said. "He does charters."

"So I heard."

Hastings sounded sarcastic. Kaylen couldn't understand why.

Shaw interrupted them. "Ms. Roberts, this condo isn't safe," he said. "You should never have come back here alone."

"I know." Kaylen sighed and leaned her bruised nose on the ice-pack.

Forget the anonymous solitude of a hotel room. She needed company. "I'm going to stay with a friend," she decided aloud. "I've got to call her and make sure it's okay, but I don't think she'll mind."

"What friend?" Hastings asked sharply.

"Why should I tell you until I know for sure whether I can stay with her?" Kaylen didn't like being grilled as though she was a suspect instead of a victim.

"We need to know." His voice was hard and cold.

"After the way I've been terrorized over the last twenty-four hours, I'm not giving out the names of any of my friends unless I think it's in my best interest," Kaylen retorted. "I don't want the third degree, I want protection. Why can't you assign someone?"

"We don't have the manpower to assign an officer to you twenty-four hours a day," Hastings told her. "We've had budget cuts. You'll have to hire a bodyguard. I'm surprised you don't have one already, you being a prominent citizen."

"I'm on a tight budget, too," she snapped. "And until yesterday, I've never felt threatened by anyone. Instead of questioning me, why aren't you out trying to find out if Tim and Brian are okay?"

A furrow appeared between Hastings' eyebrows. He took a deep breath. "Those two…"

"I've dispatched a team to the creek, including divers," Shaw broke in. "If Madison fell victim to foul play and was really dumped there, I promise you we'll find him. As for Swift, I've sent patrol cars both to Madison's apartment and to the marina. In the meantime, I'd like you to come down to the station to fill out a report and talk with a couple of my detectives."

At the thought of Tim being found floating in Snapper Creek, Kaylen closed her eyes. Her head started swimming again, and she knew she was close to tears. She didn't want to start crying in front of Hastings. The man made her feel like she had gotten everything she asked for but still deserved more.

"Are you all right, Ms. Roberts?" she heard Shaw asking.

Kaylen tried to fight off the lightheadedness by opening her eyes. "I'm okay," she said, although she didn't feel anything even close to that. "My nose is going to be really sore for a couple of days, and my head's throbbing, but I'll be fine."

She wasn't going to admit the room was spinning in circles. She felt like screaming, but she wasn't going to admit that, either. Looking hysterical and stupid wasn't going to produce any sympathy from either of these two men—one because she doubted he had any to give, the other because she figured he was too well-trained to reveal his emotions.

"I have to talk to my friend about staying with her," Kaylen said. She got up and headed for the back hallway. "Is it all right if I call her?"

Hastings jumped out of the chair so fast, she couldn't believe anyone could come to standing in the blink of an eye. "You can call her after you come in for questioning," he said.

Kaylen felt like punching him on the nose to see how he liked it. "I'm not leaving here without having somewhere else to go."

"Are you sure you were attacked and that you didn't really do this to yourself?" Hastings asked. "I think this is some elaborate publicity stunt."

His opinion echoed Brian's the morning before. "My housekeeper was *murdered*," Kaylen pointed out. "I'd have to be a sadistic psychopath to want publicity that badly."

"That's enough." Shaw stepped up beside Hastings. "For Christ's sake, Bill. What's the matter with you?" He took Kaylen by the arm and steered her in the direction of the bedroom. "Make your call and pack a bag," he told her. "You're coming with me to headquarters." He gave her a little push. "Make it quick."

"Who's going to protect me after I leave there?" Kaylen asked. "Even if I did hire a bodyguard, I couldn't get one immediately."

Hastings laughed; a short, loud snort of derision. "Maybe you've already *got* police protection," he said.

Kaylen felt really confused. Forget subtle signals, Captain Shaw was glaring openly at Hastings.

"I don't know what you're talking about," she said, looking from one of them to the other. "Was Tim an undercover cop or something?"

"No damned way." Hastings made a noise like scoffing.

"Go make your call now." Shaw pointed toward the bedroom.

"Okay, okay. I'm going." Kaylen had no wish to remain in the heavily-charged atmosphere. "I'll hurry."

"Don't worry, we'll wait." Hastings leaned against the bookcase and shoved his hands into his pockets. "Wouldn't want anything *else* to happen to you."

Kaylen wished she had the courage to ask them to wait in the parking lot, but regardless of Hastings' rudeness, she didn't want to spend another minute alone in that condo. She pushed the bedroom door partially closed and called Sandy, who said without hesitation that of course, Kaylen could come and stay however long she needed.

Behind the door, she found a jacket and three cocktail dresses hanging inside thin plastic bags. Rosa must have put them there after she collected the dry cleaning. Kaylen forced aside the image of her housekeeper floating face-down in the bathtub. Instead, she tried to remember Rosa singing softly in Spanish as she cleaned. After placing the clothes on the bed along with her purse and overnight bag, she looked for her laptop and realized it was missing from its usual place. It must have been taken by the people who had ransacked her condo. She grimaced. Now they had access to her financial information, too. She'd have to notify the bank.

Tim's picture, undamaged and still in an intact frame, lay on the bedside table. Kaylen grabbed it and held it to her chest. She only wished it was Tim she held, not his image. She put the photograph in the overnight bag along with her jewelry boxes, some nightclothes, and underwear she found neatly folded in a clothes basket beside the TV stand.

She paused at the bathroom door. Despite the fact that the room looked sanitized, she had trouble forcing herself over the threshold. In her mind, she still heard water running in the shower. Mercifully, the curtain had not been replaced and the tub sat sparkling white and empty.

She hurriedly finished filling a second, smaller bag with makeup and toiletries, zipped the clothes into a garment bag and took one last look around. She really didn't believe she would ever have the courage to return to the place she had called home since George's death.

"I'm ready," she said as she walked back into the living room.

The detectives had moved away from each other to stand on opposite sides of the room.

"I can follow you to the station, so I have my car available after I've made my statement," she said, looking from one of them to the other.

"I'll ride with you," Shaw said. "Captain Hastings has to get back to his squad."

Hastings looked like he wanted to argue, but he glanced at his watch and shrugged. "Very well," he said. "I'm already late for an appointment. Keep me posted, Hal."

"Of course." Shaw motioned Kaylen out the door.

Hastings walked rapidly ahead of them down the stairs, got into his car and sped out of the parking lot without even glancing their way.

Shaw's cell phone rang. He took the call, walking away from Kaylen to talk at a discreet distance. When he returned he shook his head. "No one's at Madison's apartment. And the patrolmen couldn't find Swift at the marina, although the boat's still moored there. We'll find both of them," he assured her. "I put out all points bulletins for their cars, and we'll file a missing person report on Madison."

Kaylen wanted to go right over to the marina and sit at slip 95 until Brian came back, but she knew the lieutenant wouldn't go for that idea.

"They'll be okay, Ms. Roberts," he repeated.

"These people want something they think I have, and they're showing me that they'll stop at nothing to get it," Kaylen told him as he took the garment bag from her. "Rosa did nothing but clean my house and they murdered her. Tim's my boyfriend. If they want my cooperation, they probably think hurting him will make me talk." She sighed. "But I don't know anything, and I don't have anything they could possibly want. So I've got no way of stopping them, and they've given me twenty-four hours to produce whatever it is they want." She unlocked the trunk of her BMW and they stowed the bags inside. "I'm really worried about Brian, too," she added, slamming the trunk.

"Madison and Swift are a lot more capable of taking care of themselves than your housekeeper was," Shaw said, watching her as she walked over to the driver's side of the car. "I'm sure they're both fine."

Kaylen wanted to believe him. "Tim's probably just out of town," she said, more to reassure herself than to inform Lieutenant Shaw. "As for Brian, he probably *is* more than capable," she said, thinking of the gun and the baseball bat. "But he got pretty badly beaten yesterday, so he's not in any shape to defend himself, although I doubt he'd ever admit it."

"Swift got beaten up?" Lieutenant Shaw's bushy eyebrows rose.

"Yes, but he's okay. I went with him to the ER. He's got a couple of broken ribs and bruised kidneys. He's really sore and not moving too well today."

"I bet." Shaw got into the car.

"Tim works out at a gym several times a week, but that wouldn't help if someone shot at him," Kaylen said. She settled in behind the wheel. As if she wasn't nervous enough, she had to be transporting a police lieutenant in her car. She checked the rearview mirror, her heart thudding.

"The man who threatened you wanted to scare you into giving him information, so he told you what he thought would get results," Shaw said as Kaylen put the car into reverse. "You told me Madison takes off for days at a time, so tracking him down may be a problem. Do you know where he goes?"

"He's an entrepreneur." Kaylen backed out of the parking space with more care than she ever had before, her sweaty palms sliding on the steering wheel. "He's always involved in start-up businesses. He never tells me where he goes. Sometimes he's brought me gifts back from Mexico or South America. A couple of times he's even brought me gifts from Asia. He also does some sort of work for Sam Wilson on a part time basis, but I never asked what, and he never volunteered any information. He's not much for talking about himself."

"You'll need to give my detectives as much information as you can." Shaw settled back in his seat. "They also need a recent photo of him. Do you have one?"

"Yes," Kaylen said. She sighed with relief as she completed maneuvering the car through an area congested by two delivery trucks and a woman unloading groceries from her car right in front of the condos' main entrance. "There was a photo of him on my nightstand. It's in the trunk."

"Very good." Lieutenant Shaw pulled down the visor and put on sunglasses as she pulled her car into the street. "Now," he said, turning to look at her. "How exactly did you meet Brian Swift?"

CHAPTER EIGHTEEN

Brian parked his car on a side street in Coral Gables and walked into an old-fashioned coffee shop. He felt reasonably sure he was just another anonymous face, but chose a worn booth in a dimly lit corner to make sure he stayed as inconspicuous as possible.

A middle-aged waitress wearing a red gingham apron and matching headband brought a flask of coffee and a menu. She glanced sideways at him from under heavy bangs as she poured a rich, dark brew into his cup. "What's the other guy look like?"

"Worse," Brian said. "He wasn't wearing a seat belt."

She looked relieved. "Oh, car wreck." She jiggled the pen behind her ear. "You need a couple of minutes?"

Brian took a quick look at the laminated, hand-printed menu. "Nah."

He ordered a short stack of pancakes with bacon and scrambled eggs on the side. The waitress scribbled on her pad and grabbed the menu, which she laid in front of another customer on the way back to the grill. Brian awkwardly drank two cups of coffee in quick succession, slurping the hot liquid to avoid burning his sutured lip. His body felt like it had been hit by a truck instead of a couple of thugs, but he couldn't give in to its demand for rest. His brother was in serious trouble, and so apparently was Kaylen Roberts.

If Tim's nosy neighbor hadn't stopped him, he would have picked his brother's locks and gone into the apartment, which would have gotten him arrested for breaking and entering. Right after he left the building and climbed back into his Camaro, a squad car parked outside the building and two patrolmen ran inside.

The old woman must have decided to call the cops after all. The next time he went back, he'd better get her out of the building. She'd seen his face, she knew who he was, and she had also taken a bribe from him, which meant she'd be happy to take money from anyone else who came knocking at her door.

The waitress set the pancakes and bacon in front of him and a smaller plate of scrambled eggs at the side. "You need anything else, hon?" she asked.

Brian managed a half smile. "No, thanks."

He watched her tuck the check under the edge of his plate and walk back toward the grill. She grabbed what appeared to be the only menu in the entire place from the other customer and shoved it into the hands of a delivery man who had taken a booth near the entrance. No one looked his way. In fact, the other diners were either preoccupied with food, coffee or their phones. Time to relax, Brian told himself, but he couldn't get his muscles or his mind to cooperate.

His breakfast looked and smelled great, especially since he hadn't eaten in at least 24 hours. He salted the eggs and drizzled syrup on the pancakes. His mouth refused to open more than a couple of inches, and his jaw ached when he tried to chew the bacon. Frustrated and really hungry, he decided the eggs would go down faster. But he'd forgotten about the effects of salt on an open wound. His lip stung like he'd rolled in a hornets' nest, and he shoved a napkin over his mouth while he fought back the urge to yell his head off.

After the pain subsided, Brian cut his food into tiny pieces and forced himself to slow down. As he ate, he wondered what he could do to find Tim and help him out of whatever jam he had gotten into.

He took out the note and studied it again. His brother wanted him to take special care of Kaylen because Tim needed to leave the country for a while. Perhaps six months or even longer.

The wording was downright strange. His brother never spoke like that, much less wrote formal notes. He had been known to scribble vague messages that wound up under Brian's apartment door, or more recently jammed into the chart pocket next to the wheel on the *Destiny,* but spelling everything out…never. Brian wondered why Tim hadn't just asked him to keep an eye on Kaylen. And why did Tim think he had to get out of Miami, much less the country?

He must have really fucked up, Brian thought. Tim had to have pissed off some big shot, probably in the drug cartel. He'd been hanging around those guys or others very much like them for years. When Brian tried to tell him he was either going to end up dead or in jail, Tim had said to leave him the hell alone and let him get on with his life.

All Tim wanted to do was run around like he was a big shot, throwing money left and right, driving the most expensive car he could find and dressing like some goddamned pimp, Brian thought with a flash of anger.

No surprise that his good-looking, smooth-talking younger brother had ended up with Kaylen Roberts on his arm. The actual jaw-dropper was that Tim had kept her there for three months. Either the woman was just as crooked as the people Tim associated with, or she was so damned naïve it was laughable. How could she not know her boyfriend was a courier for a drug cartel?

Brian sipped iced water. Was there a hidden message in that note? He turned the paper over and looked for more folds, in the event the paper had to be pleated to pick out certain words. He scanned the questions on the back of the envelope and even looked inside the envelope in case Tim had written something there. But the same questions and answers stared back at him, and the same cryptic message lay across the plain white paper.

Brian tried retracing his steps, starting the night Bannisters opened. He'd gone to the parking lot, as Tim had asked, and there he'd waited, checking his watch every few minutes until he'd been leaning against his car for a good 40 minutes and Tim still hadn't shown up. He remembered it was still hot and humid, and he could smell the damp earth in the flower beds after the sprinklers had turned off at 2:00AM. And then someone must have knocked him out, because suddenly it was morning, and he was in Kaylen's bed.

Could Tim be responsible? He'd practiced sneaking up on Brian when they were both kids, and he'd carried the stupid gag on into adulthood. But if he did, then why hit his older brother over the head and tote him upstairs to throw him in bed with Kaylen?

Brian's temples throbbed. He pushed his empty plate aside and rubbed the bridge of his nose with a carefully placed finger. He couldn't even think clearly anymore, much less put meaning to Tim's stupid theatrics. Ever since the nightmare day he'd been accused of taking bribes and placed on suspension without pay, he'd been acting and feeling like he'd lost his ability to detect anything, including a way out of his own dilemma.

He still found it hard to believe that the meeting with Hal and the Internal Affairs representative had actually happened. At the end of it, he'd been ordered to hand over his gun and the detective's badge he'd worked so hard to earn after years spent in uniform. The one fact he felt sure of was that Tim was involved, just as he had always been, hanging around the fringes of his older brother's life and dicking everything up.

He figured Tim must have taken Kaylen out the side or back door of the club, probably into a small, private lot where his car was parked. Brian made a mental note to talk to the bartender and some of her patrons who had attended the opening night. Even if Kaylen couldn't remember anything, someone must know what time they'd left.

And had they been alone, he wondered? Sure, Tim was more than capable of carrying Kaylen out, but maybe someone else had helped load her into the car. It wasn't Sam Wilson, because he'd stayed behind to close the club with Kaylen's manager.

Brian downed a couple of painkillers and called the club. Rob Diaz picked up on the third ring and identified himself.

"I'm a friend of Tim Madison's," Brian said. "I can't get in touch with him. When was the last time you remember seeing him?"

"Sometime last Friday," Rob said. "At the club opening."

"About what time?" Brian watched people walking in and out of the swinging doors of the diner and waited.

"Maybe around midnight," Rob said.

The answer came too quickly. Brian wondered if Diaz had been rehearsing his answers.

"Why do you want to know?" Now Rob sounded on the offensive. "The cops already asked me the same thing this morning. What's your name?"

"The cops came to the club?" Brian asked.

"They were waiting for me in the parking lot."

By the silence following that remark, Brian knew Rob wasn't going to volunteer much more information.

"Well, thanks," Brian said. "Sorry to trouble you, but I'm worried about Tim."

"I'm sure Ms. Roberts is, too," Rob said. "Do you want to leave a message for her?"

"No." Brian hung up.

Alarm bells rang louder in his head than any complaint from his body about the lack of sleep. Where the hell was his brother? Ever since they were kids, he'd known when Tim was in bad trouble, and that feeling was with him now. He paid the check and left a generous tip for the waitress. Pushing open the heavy glass door, he stopped to scan the parking lot before walking back to his car, his senses sharpened by the caffeine and an overpowering feeling that Tim hadn't left town under his own power, regardless of what the note said.

Brian's top priority was to find out how much Kaylen actually knew about Tim's activities. So far she had managed to successfully duck his questions by throwing him off-balance with her concern for his welfare. He grimaced and then winced as pain shot through his jaw. Kaylen had been throwing him off-balance by more than concern. As soon as they got close, there was an undercurrent of sexual tension that made him lose all common sense. Instead of questioning her as he would any other suspect in a case, he found himself acting like some stupid adolescent.

He took out his cell and punched in her number, but the call went straight to voicemail. Brian asked her to call back ASAP and drove away from the restaurant. He decided to cruise past her club to check out the entrances, but the momentary spurt of energy brought on by food and caffeine quickly faded. When he almost ran through a stop light, oncoming traffic screeching to a halt and several drivers threatening to hurt him in many creative ways, he admitted he couldn't continue fighting his need for sleep and headed for the marina.

He avoided the main streets and kept a good check on vehicles following him for anything more than a few blocks. Finally sure he wasn't being followed, Brian took the back entrance into the marina, parked in a different area of the lot than usual, and took a circuitous route between cars and campers to where the *Destiny* bobbed gently, her hull rocking against the buffers strapped to the dock. He locked both the hatch and cabin doors, placed his cell on vibrate and laid it on the nightstand before crawling onto his bunk. He fell asleep within moments.

CHAPTER NINETEEN

Kaylen Roberts and Sandy Cole could have passed for sisters. Their coloring and temperaments were alike, so was their philosophy on life—live it to the fullest. They had worked together in Sam's restaurant and become firm friends over the years.

Sandy had encouraged Kaylen to start dating George, even though he was twenty-seven years older, with children almost the same age as she and an ex-wife who would have given Ivana Trump a run for her money where it came to the credo of "don't get even, get everything."

Sandy was convinced George would rebound from his wife's divorce settlement, and she was right. Despite Sylvia's efforts, George had recovered financially and ignoring the opposition of his children, had proposed marriage to Kaylen within 6 months of their first date. Kaylen, who had fallen deeply and happily in love, accepted without reservations. One of her wedding presents was the building that now housed Bannisters. At the time, it was run down and in a less-than-desirable area, but George had told her it was a diamond in the rough. His prediction was, as usual, right on the money.

Sandy had been an invaluable source of support during George's illness, and a staunch ally whenever Sylvia overstepped her bounds and tried to regulate not only her own interests in George's business, but Kaylen's as well. After George's death, Sandy became a pit bull, shielding Kaylen from the press as well as Sylvia. Kaylen blessed their friendship every day of her life.

When Sandy opened the door of her apartment in one of the art deco buildings fronting Washington at Miami Beach, Kaylen's fears ebbed at the sight of her friend's warm, welcoming smile.

"Come on in." Sandy grabbed Kaylen's bag, grunted under the weight and dumped it on a chair in the tiny apartment's living room. "Staying a while, huh?"

She lived in delicious chaos, amidst an eclectic collection of sixties memorabilia and modernistic chrome furniture. Her late father's watercolors of pastoral, Midwestern farms decorated the walls alongside Sandy's own vividly-hued oil paintings of Latin-flavored street markets. Her taste echoed the exterior of the building in which she lived. Painted pink and turquoise, with bubble glass inserts on the staircase, the apartment house radiated a sunny hospitality.

"If you think you can put up with me that long, I need to stay a few days," Kaylen said as she dropped her purse and overnight bag onto the floral print couch and draped the garment bag over the back of a burgundy leather club chair.

"Long as you need, girlfriend. You know that."

Sandy linked arms and dragged Kaylen into the galley-style kitchen, its outdated cabinets painted sparkling white and the faded blue linoleum floor buffed to a high shine.

"Have a seat." Sandy drew out a chrome stool with a black Naugahyde seat and pushed Kaylen onto it. "When you called, you didn't sound too sure of anything. You look like hell. Coffee?"

Kaylen found her mood lifting with the rapid-fire delivery and ping-pong logic of her hyperactive friend's reactions. "I'd love a cup. Thanks for stating the obvious, but do I really look that bad?"

"You want the truth or sugar coating?" Sandy poured two mugs of coffee and placed one in front of Kaylen.

"You never coat anything," Kaylen pointed out as she took a spoon from the basket of assorted tableware beside her elbow.

Sandy slid a paper napkin across the counter. "Fine, then here's the truth…you've got bags under your eyes, your hair's a rat's nest and that outfit's doing nothing for you. Obviously, you're in some sort of trouble."

Kaylen dropped the spoon she had been twisting between her fingers. It bounced off the edge of the counter and landed with a loud clatter on the tile floor. Inadvertently, she jumped.

Sandy didn't comment. She pulled another spoon from the drawer in front of her and handed it to Kaylen before planting her elbows on the counter. She clasped her hands together, one finger pointing accusingly. "Someone punched you on the nose, by the look of it. You didn't let Tim slap you around, did you?"

Kaylen felt her eyebrows lift in response, and a flash of annoyance shot through her. "No way. What do you think I am, a moron?"

Sandy blinked. "Of course not."

The annoyance left Kaylen's tired body with a gush that deflated her like a tire losing air. "Sorry," she said. She forced a smile, even though it cost her a lot of energy and didn't feel very successful, then held out her mug. "Do you have any cream?"

Sandy regarded her with a frown before pushing back from the counter. "Coming right up." She took a carton of milk out of the refrigerator and held it up. "This is all I have. Is that okay?"

"Yes. Thank you." Kaylen felt very uncomfortable. She'd landed on Sandy's doorstep at a moment's notice, asked to spend several days and then snapped at her best friend when she'd shown concern.

Sandy was rummaging in the freezer. She came out with a bag. "I'm making you a bagel," she said. "Cinnamon raisin."

"That would be great."

Kaylen took advantage of the moment to grab another napkin from the chrome holder and wipe her eyes. She carefully dabbed her nose.

"I *am* in trouble," she said to Sandy's back as she nuked the frozen bagel for a few seconds before cutting it and popping it into the toaster. "Rosa's dead, and I think Tim might be, too."

"Shit. No kidding?" Sandy took out a plate and cream cheese before turning back around. She pulled over another stool and sat opposite Kaylen. "What happened, some sort of accident?"

"I *wish* it was that simple." Kaylen sighed heavily. "No, Rosa was murdered. I found her body in my bathtub when I came home. Then today, there was an intruder in my condo. He pushed me. I fell and hit my nose. He's the one who told me Tim's body is in Snapper Creek."

Sandy's bright pink lips made an ooh. "My God, that's awful." She shook her head. "Poor Rosa, and poor you, too. What a horrible thing for you to find her like that. You must have been so scared." She shook a cigarette out of the pack lying beside a potted plant and lit it. "Why in the world would anyone want to kill your housekeeper?" She blew smoke and frowned. "And what's up with Tim? Why would anyone want to kill him? Do he and Rosa even know each other?"

Kaylen shrugged. "Only vaguely. Tim met her a couple of times when he stayed over." She pushed her hair back and wished she had something to tie it into a ponytail. It was making her neck hot, or maybe she was breaking out into a sweat just thinking about Rosa and Tim.

In fact, the whole kitchen felt hot suddenly. She fanned herself with a piece of junk mail she found sharing space in the napkin holder. "The police are investigating, but they haven't told me anything. For all I know, the man who attacked me could have lied, to frighten me even more."

Sandy flipped the switch on a small fan. A welcome breeze took the edge off the humid atmosphere and lifted Kaylen's damp hair from her face, but the napkins and mail in the crowded little area started blowing around, too. Kaylen grabbed all the fluttering papers and anchored them under the ceramic pot of a spindly, wilted Philodendron.

"Do the cops think Rosa's murder is linked to the intruder?" Sandy asked.

The toaster chose that moment to regurgitate the bagel with a resounding pop. Both women jumped.

"Oh, my God." Sandy laughed nervously, one hand on her chest. "You're making me as spooked as you are, and you've only been here a few minutes." She juggled the hot bagel onto the plate and brought it over to Kaylen with cream cheese and a knife.

Kaylen eyed her breakfast without enthusiasm.

"You've got to eat," Sandy insisted. "Do you want me to stop asking you questions?"

"No. It's okay. I should really talk about all this, anyway." Kaylen spread a light layer of cream cheese, but the sight of white, fluffy goop made her stomach churn.

"You couldn't get in touch with Tim?" Sandy asked.

"He won't answer either of his phones," Kaylen said. "Or can't. I've tried leaving messages, but no luck so far." She tried taking a bite of the food, but it tasted even worse than it looked. "I'm sorry," she said, pushing the plate aside. "I can't, right now."

Sandy inhaled deeply on her cigarette. As she blew out smoke, she watched it waft toward the ceiling. "Maybe you should get some rest first," she said. "You want to take a quick shower while I pull out the hideabed and throw sheets on it?"

Kaylen sighed again. It didn't make her feel any better, but she couldn't seem to stop doing it. Maybe because she couldn't get enough fresh air into her lungs to keep the panic at bay. "Damn it, Sandy, I'm not so sure I should be asking you to take me in. I could get you killed, too," she said.

"Don't be stupid." Sandy tossed her head, dark curls sliding back from her shoulders. "I can take care of myself."

"Tim should have been able to, but being strong and savvy doesn't seem to have protected *him* any." Desolation washed over Kaylen. "God, Sandy. I think he really might be dead." Tears clouded her vision. "I've got this horrible feeling in the pit of my stomach. I've had it since yesterday."

Sandy took one last drag of her cigarette and stubbed it out in the ashtray. "Maybe he just took off. You know how he is." She took Kaylen's bagel to the trash can. "Stop beating yourself up," she said. "Tim'll probably walk into the club next week and ask you what the hell's wrong with you, sending the police after him."

"I can only hope." Kaylen grabbed another napkin and carefully blew her sore nose. "I don't care if he's angry. I want him alive and in one piece."

"You said everyone else around you is getting hurt," Sandy said. "Who else are you talking about? Not Sam, that's for sure. It would have been in the news." She tapped one French-manicured nail on a newspaper beside the coffeemaker. "I scanned the headlines earlier."

"No, not him." Kaylen tried taking a sip of her coffee, but found it lukewarm and vaguely bitter again. "Someone I just met." She hesitated, not even sure she should confide in her best friend. "His name's Brian."

Sandy's eyes narrowed. "What are you hiding? You blinked and looked away right after you said his name."

"Well, we met under some really strange circumstances." Kaylen toyed with her knife and began poking it into the cream cheese, because she needed to keep her gaze directed on something other than Sandy's face, which she knew was probably registering the same level of disapproval as Sam's. Sometimes, she wondered if they were related, the way they both reacted to things.

"What sort of circumstances?" Sandy grabbed the knife out of Kaylen's hand. "Stop it," she said. "Who *is* this guy?"

"Look," Kaylen said. "I'll tell you what's been happening since Bannisters opened, but I don't want you to start judging me or telling me what to do. I already heard enough from Sam."

Sandy was silent for a moment, then she got up and took her empty mug and the knife over to the sink. "Okay," she said. "I won't. Shoot." She started running water and squirted dishwashing liquid into a bowl inside the sink.

For some reason, Kaylen thought how much Sandy had come to resemble her over the last few months. They were even dressing in the same color palette. Sandy wore a tailored red cotton shirt over white capris instead of the running shorts and pastel monogrammed t-shirts she had favored in the past.

"Come on," Sandy wheedled. "You've gotta tell someone, so it might as well be me. No judgments. You know that." She shut off the water and turned around, her expression non-committal.

"I know."

But a part of Kaylen's mind rebelled. She ended up giving Sandy a really abbreviated, watered-down version in which she had awakened to find Brian passed out on the floor in the living room. She kept quiet about the tattoo again. There was something so intensely *personal* about that violation. She felt as though she had been branded for some reason, and until she knew what that reason was, she wanted to keep the tattoo's existence to herself.

"So, you don't think this Brian could be connected to Tim's disappearance or the man who was hiding in your apartment?" Sandy leaned back against the sink. "Too many coincidences for me to swallow that. Did you tell all this to the cops?"

"Yes," Kaylen lied. "How about another cup of coffee? This one's cold."

Without saying another word, Sandy grabbed Kaylen's mug and tossed the cold coffee down the drain. While she emptied the glass carafe's contents into the mug, Kaylen took a few deep breaths and wiped the lie off her face.

"But you know next to nothing about this guy," Sandy said. "He could be responsible for everything." She sounded like she wanted to say a lot more than that. Her lips were tight, a dead giveaway that she was perturbed.

"He's not big enough to take out Tim," Kaylen reasoned. "And he was going on a boat charter the afternoon Rosa was murdered, so he couldn't have done that, either. He told me he was waiting for someone down in the parking lot the night he ended up on my floor. Someone hit him over the head. Maybe whoever that was mistook him for someone else, and then didn't know what to do with him."

"And so he gets dragged up a flight of stairs and left in your condo? That makes no sense."

"I know, I know." Kaylen threw up her hands in surrender. "None of what's happened over the last two days makes any sense. I've left all of it in the hands of the police. They're the ones to solve Rosa's murder and find Tim, not me. But I'm a nervous wreck." She started plucking dead leaves off the plant, because she needed to do something, anything constructive. "I can't stop going over and over everything in my mind and wondering. Is it something I did? Something I agreed to do for someone, but forgot? What about Tim? What about the club?" She dropped her head into her hands. "God."

Sandy scooped up the cream cheese container with one hand and took Kaylen's wrist with the other. "Come on," she said, tugging. "Time for you to shower." She threw the cream cheese into the refrigerator on the way to the living room, Kaylen trailing after her.

Sandy's constant need to be in motion was wearing Kaylen out, or maybe she was just plain exhausted and fresh out of tolerance for anything, she thought. Sandy was right. She needed sleep.

"You've got to stop worrying about *something*, girl, or you really will drive yourself crazy," Sandy said. "Make it the club. You've got a damn fine manager in Rob, and you can always count on Sam to check up on things over there, too." She opened a cupboard door and took out sheets. "He *loves* that shit."

"I know Rob's got a great reputation," Kaylen agreed. "But he's new to me and the club. He's got to prove himself before I feel like I can let him run it without me being there pretty constantly. As for Sam, sometimes he can be, well, overbearing. I don't want to ask him to do too much over at Bannisters or he'll think he should be running the club himself." She stretched. "You're right. I'm obsessing, and I've got to stop. I'm tired and dirty, which always makes me cranky. What time do you have to be at work?"

"Six," Sandy said. "But I've got an errand to run on the way."

Kaylen glanced at her watch. Four o'clock. More than two hours since she had promised to call Captain Shaw. She cringed. He would be really angry, and was probably digging into her entire background, right down to her miserable childhood in rural Maine. He might even have put out an APB on her. Goose bumps broke out on her arms at the thought of being hauled down to the precinct to be questioned.

She watched Sandy stack couch cushions on the floor and pull out the hideabed. After she went into her bedroom to find extra pillows, Kaylen made up the bed. She sank onto the club chair and kicked off her shoes, grateful to be somewhere that might be considered safe.

She yawned and looked longingly at the bed. She'd love to stretch out for a few hours, but she had to call Lieutenant Shaw, and she also needed to contact Brian to firm up a time for them to get together. Reluctantly, she forced herself onto her feet and dug her cell phone out of her purse, only to find it completely dead. In all the mayhem, she had forgotten to charge it.

"Mind if I use your phone?" she asked Sandy, striding back into the room with two big fluffy pillows in her arms. "I have to call the cops and tell them where I'm staying." Kaylen held up her cell. "I forgot to pack my charger."

"No problem. It's on the coffee table." Sandy dropped the pillows onto the bed and took Kaylen's phone out of her hand. "I'll see if my charger'll fit this one."

Kaylen managed to get to the coffee table without falling over the stacked cushions and had no trouble locating Sandy's phone in its bright red case, despite the clutter of old newspapers, magazines and empty soda cans surrounding it.

"I'll get you a spare key, so you can come and go as you please," Sandy called from the bedroom. "Why don't you get into the bathroom before I take it over?" She came back. "Sorry about the mess." She picked up a trash can and swept everything from the table into it. "There. Much better." She looked at Kaylen and winked. "I've got to make myself look even more drop-dead gorgeous before I leave here. You never know when Mr. Right's going to turn up."

Kaylen found herself smiling. A minor miracle after all the drama. "Sandy, you're so funny," she said. "Thank God."

"Life's too short, and we all need to laugh whenever we can," Sandy said. "Towels are in the same closet as the sheets. I'm going to iron my clothes while you're scrubbing up."

"What would I do without you?" Kaylen asked.

"You'd be in even deeper shit." Sandy took the trash can with her to the kitchen. "Don't worry about disturbing me with your comings and goings. I don't have a man in my life right now. It's you and me, babe."

"You don't know how much this means to me," Kaylen said, and her voice cracked. She swallowed quickly, afraid she was going to start crying again.

"Yeah, I do. And someday you'll pay me back. Get into that bathroom, girl."

Kaylen heard the metallic sounds of an ironing board being opened. She hurriedly showered and wrapped herself in one of Sandy's giant bath towels, a smaller one coiled around her head like a turban. Although she still felt tired, the hot water seemed to have brought her back to life.

Sandy's own shower was accompanied by a noisy but fairly pleasant rendition of Patsy Kline's "Crazy" that competed with the torrent of water. It brought another smile to Kaylen's face as she sat curled up in the club chair.

But since when had Sandy started liking country music and ballads? She had once declared that ballads were for old crooners and the old crones who worshipped them.

Kaylen decided she was getting more and more paranoid. Now she was analyzing Sandy's latest music preferences. She took out the business card Lieutenant Shaw had given her and called the precinct. Shaw was unavailable, and she was forced to talk to Captain Hastings. She hesitantly explained about her cell phone.

Surprisingly, he wasn't as rude on the phone as he had been in person. He did inform her testily that she should have been in contact with them earlier, and that she should have had the sense to make sure her phone was in working order. But as Kaylen resigned herself to a long and pithy lecture, he volunteered the information that Lieutenant Shaw had been called to Snapper Creek. As Kaylen's heart sank to a level with her feet, he informed her either he or Shaw would call with any further news, and he took down Sandy's cell number.

Kaylen felt sick to her stomach. She knew that as hard as she tried to deny it, Tim was going to be found in that creek, and she would be asked to identify his body because he had no family. At least none that he had ever told her about. He was even more alone in the world than she was, with her uncommunicative and difficult father living so far away and no other siblings.

She slid lower in the comfortable chair and leaned back, eyes closed. Tim's death would end up on her conscience, she told herself. All because she couldn't produce some key for an obsessed, callous madman who wouldn't listen to her or believe she had no idea what he wanted. She thought about all the keys she possessed, and couldn't think of one that didn't fit a door in her life. Not even one.

CHAPTER TWENTY

Kaylen jerked awake when a fully dressed Sandy bustled into the room. Cold and disoriented, she was thankful to leave a dream in which she was trying to insert an impossibly large key into the lock of Bannisters' back door.

Her rebellious body didn't want to function, but she had to get in touch with Brian. She struggled to her feet and picked up her watch. It was 4:45PM. Surely he must be back on his boat by now. She called the marina office, but the answering machine picked up. Kaylen didn't leave a message.

While Sandy stuffed keys, cigarettes, the newspaper, two bottles of water, her cell phone, and a big bag of makeup into an oversized purse, Kaylen came to the conclusion that she would have to forget about sleeping and drive over to the marina.

After Sandy finally decided she could get nothing more into the purse, which now resembled a piece of overstuffed luggage, she waved cheerfully and left, on her way to her job as manager of a slick new restaurant on Miracle Mile in Coral Gables. Kaylen searched inside her own bag and pulled out a white tank top and pink capris. After getting dressed, she shook out her towel-dried hair, ran a pick through the tangled mess and subdued it with a clip into a ponytail. Adding a flick of mascara and a touch of pale pink lipstick, she decided she wasn't out to impress Brian and headed for her car.

She drove on the MacArthur Causeway, windows down and an annoying breeze flapping the plastic that covered the cocktail dress she had hung up in the back. She decided her tired body probably wouldn't see the inside of

Sandy's apartment, or feel the comfort of that hideabed until after the club closed at 2:00AM the following morning. Hopefully, the caffeine in the cup of thankfully not bitter coffee she had purchased from a convenience store would keep her awake and alert until then.

If Brian had attempted to call her, he would have been sent to her voicemail. She'd never taken the time to set up a code to retrieve her messages remotely, and she had no one to blame for that but herself. Sandy's charger hadn't worked on her phone, but she couldn't spare the time to find a phone store and buy both a charger for her car and one to plug in at Sandy's apartment. That job would have to wait until later. Maybe she could even send one of the busboys on that errand.

Boats moored at Star, Palm and Hibiscus islands rocked gently on the currents, their hulls sparkling like blobs of white meringue floating on a blue and green tinted tropical drink. In an effort to calm herself, Kaylen shunned the heavy traffic on I-95 in favor of the more picturesque and less crowded route along South Miami Avenue.

But calm wasn't going to happen while her mind dwelled on how Lieutenant Shaw had asked probing questions about her relationship with Brian. Her face heated up at the way she had lied to him, and she turned on the air conditioning. She had told him that she met Brian in her parking lot the morning after Bannisters opened. She'd made it sound like she had awakened alone in the condo. Now she had told Sandy that she found Brian on her living room floor when she woke up.

Why in the world had she told two different stories? If she was going to stretch the truth, at least she should strive for some consistency. Kaylen found herself sighing heavily yet again. Between the lying, the sighing and the crying, not to mention the lack of sleep, she decided she was becoming thoroughly peeved with herself. She couldn't even find humor in the silly rhyme she had made up, but she did almost overshoot the marina's entrance because she wasn't concentrating.

The BMW's tires squealed as she pulled into the crowded lot, and when she drew into the first available parking space, she stepped too heavily on the brake. Her car jerked to a stop, jarring her neck.

Kaylen got out and slammed the door with a satisfying crash. If Brian's boat wasn't in its slip, she'd be really put out. Worse yet, if it was there but he wasn't on it, she'd probably start panicking. She wouldn't have a chance to tell him about the intruder or the threat against Tim, let alone warn him that she'd told a string of lies in her attempt to keep his presence in her life at a low profile.

Although she didn't see the Camaro in the parking lot, she walked briskly down the dock until she found slip 95 and thankfully, the *Destiny*. The sight of Brian, dressed casually in a white t-shirt and beige cargo shorts as he drank coffee and consulted charts at a small table on deck, made her almost dizzy with relief.

"I left you a message," he said as she climbed aboard. "I've got another charter this afternoon that I can't cancel." He pushed the charts aside and stood up. "You never called me back, but you're here now, so we can talk before I leave." A crease appeared between his eyes as she drew closer. "What's up with you?"

"I still haven't slept," Kaylen said. "And a lot happened since you dropped me off at my condo."

"More? What is it with you?" His hands cradled her elbows. "You look like someone punched you."

Kaylen wrinkled her nose and regretted it as pain shot up into her head. "No, but it sure feels like it. There was an intruder in my condo when I got there."

Brian's grip tightened. "Christ."

Talking about the attack, she could almost feel the man's arm around her throat again, his hot breath fanning her cheek as he whispered in her ear. "I thought I was going to die," she said, trembling. "He started choking me, and I didn't know what else to do, so I kicked him. He shoved me and I fell. That's when I hit my nose. I was so scared, Brian."

"Damn it, I *knew* I should have come up there with you."

"It's not your fault. I refused when you offered, remember?"

His hands tightened on her elbows. "I was tired and sore, and I took the easy way out. You could have been killed."

The warm steadiness of those work-roughened hands stilled her tremors. "They don't want me dead, or he would have done the job right then," she said.

Kaylen found herself comparing Brian's hands with the touch of Tim's smooth and impeccably-manicured ones. Without understanding why, she found herself leaning closer to Brian before she got a grip and stopped.

"I came to warn you that the intruder threatened you," she said.

His brow creased even deeper. "So maybe that's why I got jumped…the people who are terrorizing you wanted to show me they mean business."

"Maybe," she said. "You've got to be really careful. The police are interested in you, too."

His eyebrows rose. "Oh? Why?"

And then he gave her a look so piercing, Kaylen felt like squirming. She shook her head. "I don't know. Why don't you tell *me*? They already knew your name."

"Damn it, Kaylen, what did you tell them, everything? I thought we agreed to keep me out of this until we know more."

"No, I didn't tell them everything. I told them some of it, because I wanted them to get to you before the thugs did." She quickly filled him in on what she'd said, and to whom she had said it.

Brian grimaced and ran a hand through his hair, his frustration obvious. "You really screwed things up, you know."

Kaylen noticed that apart from a watch on his right wrist, he wore no other jewelry. She found herself thinking how much Tim loved gold. He wore two or three rings, a thick, heavy I.D. bracelet and a Rolex watch at all times.

"I'm not used to lying," she said. "I don't do it well and don't *like* doing it, either. Especially to the police, but my friends, too. I don't even know why I'm going along with what you asked me to do. You haven't told me anything about yourself except that you own this boat. And I'm protecting you and perjuring myself, like I'm a common criminal or something."

"There's not much to tell," he said.

"What? Oh. About yourself?" Kaylen felt anger bubbling and welcomed it. Anything was better than sweating and waiting for the roof to cave in on her. "That's not an answer," she said. "I went out on a limb for you twice today, only I wasn't very consistent about it."

"That's for sure." He had the audacity to give her a lopsided smile.

"Just what I need, you thinking this is funny," she said. "I'm in a lot of trouble. I'm keeping secrets because I'm so confused right now, I don't know who to trust. I haven't even told anyone but my doctor about the tattoo." She threw her key fob and purse on top of the charts, then sat down on a locker. "I must be losing my mind."

Brian sat beside her. "Maybe not," he said. "But you need to stick with one story or the other. What happens when the cops interview your friends, which you can be sure they will? The only thing you can do is either say you were too frightened to tell the truth, or that you didn't want your friends to know what really happened."

"Boy, you sure know how to cover your tracks fast," Kaylen said. "You didn't even have to stop to think before you came up with two plausible explanations for me tripping myself up."

"Self-preservation," he said. "A skill I learned at a very early age. I had a rough childhood."

"Where?" she asked.

"Not important, and definitely nothing to do with your situation."

"*Our* situation," she reminded him.

"Okay. Yeah. Our situation."

They sat in silence. Not an awkward silence. They shared something, not something pleasant, but definitely a connection. Probably their bruises, she decided wryly.

"How are you feeling?" she asked. "You look better."

"I ate and got a couple of hours sleep. That helped." Brian shrugged lightly. "I'll mend. I've had worse." He took her hand. "But you're not used to physical violence. Do you want to stay here? You can have the cabin, and I'll sleep on the couch in the salon. I can keep you safe, Kaylen."

"No, thanks. Being around you might be the source of my problems, not the answer." She thought about pulling her hand out of his, but didn't have the strength or the inclination. He had a way of making her feel safe, and it would be so easy for her to tell him "yes," go below and sink onto his bunk. She knew she'd be able to sleep then, and the knowledge shocked her.

"You haven't been hurt when you're with me," he pointed out, as though he was reading her thoughts. "The *Destiny's* an easier environment for me to control. Only one way on and off, one way in and out of the living areas. I've got a gun and fast reactions."

"And that's supposed to make me feel secure? What if you shoot me by mistake?"

"That'd never happen." He looked like he was about to say something else, but he didn't. He sat rubbing her hand with his thumb.

Kaylen tried to ignore the extremely pleasant sensation and keep her tired mind on track. "How can you be so sure?"

"Because it's in my better interest to keep you in one piece. You might be the key to this mess yourself, without knowing it."

She shuddered. "That's a horrible thought. Whoever these people are, they want a key. You think it's me?"

"I wasn't being literal," he said. "But you shouldn't be staying with a girlfriend when you're in danger. Whoever killed your housekeeper and threatened you will be back, you know that. If they didn't find what they were looking for by trashing your place, then they'll have to try other methods."

"Like kidnapping my boyfriend?"

"Maybe," he said slowly. "Trying to get information."

"Oh, that's too awful even to think about." Kaylen started shaking again. "You think they'd beat him or…" She couldn't voice what she was thinking.

"Yeah," Brian said. "Unless Tim's missing for some other reason, and that would be too big of a coincidence." He tilted her chin up and looked directly at her, his eyes candid and troubled. "You shouldn't be alone, Kaylen. Anywhere."

"I'm not," she said. "Not really. I'm going to hire a bodyguard. I told the police." Her teeth began to chatter. "Tim goes away all the time," she said. "Weeks, sometimes. He's bad about calling. Maybe he took me home, then left on a trip. You're jumping to conclusions."

"And you're clutching at straws," Brian told her. "You're really shaking," he added. "Are you cold?"

"Freezing. Inside and out." She shuddered. Her head felt heavy, and she laid it against his shoulder. "Too much information. I haven't slept more than a couple of hours since Friday, either."

"Sleep here," he urged. "You could lie down right now. The charter's only for a couple of hours. I can have you back at the dock by eight."

"No. I've got to go into the club early. I'm meeting my manager." Reluctantly, because his shoulder felt strong and very comfortable, she sat back up. "I can't stay here any longer."

"I'll walk you to your car," he said. "After I get done here, I'll come to the club."

"I guess you had no luck at Tim's apartment," she said.

"No. But I talked to one of his neighbors. She's nosy and lives right opposite. She hasn't seen him since early Friday evening."

"I reported him missing to the police. They're checking Snapper Creek." Kaylen swallowed, her throat feeling like it was closing up. "The intruder told me that Tim's there."

A shadow passed over Brian's face. Only a moment, and then it was gone. He stood up and pulled her gently to her feet. Something in his manner was so infinitely sad, so weary, that she placed her arms around him. "What's wrong?" she asked.

"Nothin.' Everything."

She could feel his breathing quicken.

"What are you doin'?" he asked.

"I don't know. Trying to comfort you, I think."

"Tryin' to drive me crazy is more like it."

Up close, his bruised face should have repulsed her, she thought. But for some reason, it didn't. Her hands started to slide up his back, but he stopped her.

"Don't do something you'll regret," he warned. "I don't like people playin' around with my emotions."

Kaylen felt like she had stepped over some invisible barrier he had placed between them. Unsure what to do, she tried making light of her actions. "You actually have some?" she asked. "Other than anger, I mean?"

"I feel a lot, but I keep it all hidden."

Suddenly, he moved closer. Now she felt really off-balance. "Do you?" she managed.

"If it wasn't for this lip..." he said.

He didn't finish the sentence. He didn't have to.

"If it wasn't for Tim, too," Brian added, his gaze locking with hers. "You've got no idea..." He brushed back the hair that had escaped from her clip in the breeze.

"The way Tim comes and goes, sometimes I think I'm more of a convenience to him than a girlfriend," Kaylen said, and then she felt appalled at herself. "I'm sorry," she said, wondering why she was apologizing to someone who had said Tim was only an acquaintance. "I don't believe I said that."

"You're bone-tired and scared," Brian said. "Forget it."

"I need to be held," she said. "Tight, and right now."

He pulled her against him, and Kaylen wrapped her arms around his neck. She felt the stubble where he hadn't been able to shave over the sutures. His warm lips touched her cold cheek and she closed her eyes. Her fingers took on a life of their own and ran through the soft hair at his nape as she felt his hands, firm and reassuring against her back.

"Somehow, Ms. Roberts, I thought I'd find you here," Hastings said.

CHAPTER TWENTY-ONE

Kaylen wasn't sure who jumped back faster, Brian or herself. She turned to face the captain. "Are you following me?"

The look on Hastings' face made her feel like a two-bit hooker.

"No, Ms. Roberts." He stood on the dock with one hand on the *Destiny*. "I was coming to interview Swift." He cautiously placed a shiny black loafer onto the boat.

Brian looked at the foot and stepped forward. "I didn't invite you aboard."

His tone seemed disproportionately hostile, even if he had been discovered embracing Tim Madison's girlfriend.

Hastings stayed where he was, straddling the small gap between the dock and the boat. "You want me to get a warrant just to talk to you?" he asked.

"No, but don't push it." Brian motioned him to come aboard.

Hastings stumbled onto the *Destiny*. "I hate boats," he said. "Why anyone would want to spend time on one amazes me. Damn things make me puke."

"I guess you won't be staying long, then." Brian folded his arms. "Want some Dramamine?"

"Very funny, Swift." Hastings grabbed the rail with both hands and mounted the three steps.

Kaylen realized he was having trouble keeping his balance as a barely-discernable swell rocked the boat. His complexion changed from bronze to a pale shade of green as she watched.

"Classy bucket," Hastings said, taking his hand off the rail and quickly putting it back as the *Destiny* rose and dipped in response to the wash from a passing motor yacht. He wiped his other hand across his mouth. "If you like this sort of thing." He glanced over at the table. "Looks like your charts fell on the floor, along with her purse."

His eyes shifted to Kaylen. He gave her outfit an insolent once-over before the next wave made him sit down quickly on a locker. "But I guess you had other, more important things to take care of than picking up charts," he said. He loosened his tie and looked at her again, a wry quirk at one corner of his mouth despite the sweat breaking out on his face.

Kaylen bristled. How *dare* he make judgments, especially when he was in danger of vomiting all over Brian's deck. She hadn't missed the comment about picking things up, either. She stepped forward. "Captain Hastings, I think…"

Brian's hand closed over her wrist. Somehow, he had managed to bend over sufficiently to scoop up her purse and key fob, which he handed to her.

"Kaylen." He guided her toward the steps. "You said you've got a lot of things to take care of at the club. We can talk about that charter some other time."

"Make yourself as comfortable as you can, Captain," he told Hastings. "Take deep breaths and go with the motion of the boat instead of fighting it. I'm going to walk Ms. Roberts to her car."

Hastings waved dismissively, but he did start taking deep breaths.

"Stupid bastard," Brian said under his breath as he helped Kaylen off the *Destiny*. "Don't touch anything, in case you end up taking the boat out for an unscheduled cruise," he told Hastings.

"*Very* funny." Hastings glared at them, but didn't argue. Kaylen saw him slide down the locker to get closer to the table.

"How do you know him?" she asked Brian as they headed for the parking lot.

When he ignored her and kept moving, she tried to pull her hand away. "Would you please stop?" She pried his fingers back. "I need answers."

"Ouch!" He released her. "You stuck your nails into me."

"Then listen." She rubbed her wrist. "You cut off my circulation. What's the matter with you?"

"I can't stand that man."

"Tell me how you know him," she tried again.

"I can't tell you."

"Why?"

He sighed. "Because…well…" He ran both hands through his hair. "You've got to trust me and stop asking so many questions."

"Trust you blindly, I suppose," she said. "You're making me really angry. There's so much you're not telling me. I'm not stupid, you know."

"I never said you were." He stood as still and as impenetrable as the stout wooden planks beneath their feet.

"Well?" she asked.

"I'll fill you in later, at the club. As much as I can."

"Brian…."

He held up his hand. "I know. I keep putting you off, but I've got good reason. Right now, I've gotta go back before Hastings gets bored and starts poking around."

"What have you got to hide? It's a boat. You go out on charters."

"It's my home, too, remember? I don't want him there when I'm not."

"Swift!"

Kaylen glanced past Brian's shoulder to see Captain Hastings had recovered some of his poise and stood watching them with a definite scowl. "Speed it up!" he barked.

Brian rolled his eyes.

Kaylen relented. "You're right, you'd better go back," she said. "You don't want to anger the police, especially him. I don't like him, either. He came to interview me with Lieutenant Shaw."

Brian slid his arm around her waist and urged her toward the parking lot. "It won't be the first time he's been angry with me. I'll be okay, don't worry."

Kaylen tried to ignore the sensation of Brian's arm around her, which she found very unsettling. Everything about him disturbed her. But not in the way she thought she should feel. "I *do* worry," she said. "About everything these days. Can you blame me?"

"No."

She stepped off the dock onto the blacktop. "There's my car. The blue BMW in the second row."

"With the personalized plate?"

"Yes."

"KTR TOO. Not very original."

"But easy to remember." She unlocked the car, and he opened the door for her. But instead of getting in, she turned to face him. "Do you have a criminal record?" she asked. "Is that how Hastings knows you?"

"No way." Blond eyebrows rose over those unusual, sun-streaked eyes. "That's some leap you're makin'."

"You won't tell me anything except you've made Captain Hastings angry with you in the past," Kaylen said. "So what conclusion do you expect me to come to?"

"Well, not *that*." He looked perplexed, as though unable to fathom how she could have thought he was less than an Eagle Scout. "Will it make you feel better if I swear you're not ruinin' your reputation with a felon?"

"It's a start."

He walked away. Kaylen tossed her purse onto the passenger's seat. She doubted he would even go to Bannisters that evening, much less tell her anything useful about himself.

"Kaylen."

She looked up, fob in hand.

He stood beside the hood of her car. "I'm thirty-nine," he said. "I was born in Mobile, Alabama. I left home an' came to Miami when I turned sixteen." He looked like he had just had all his teeth pulled without an anesthetic. "An' I'm left-handed, in case you hadn't noticed."

"Thank you," she said. "I don't know why that was so hard."

"I hate talkin' about myself."

"You've got a slight Southern drawl," Kaylen said. "I haven't noticed it before."

"That's because I've worked real hard to get rid of it. But when I'm totally stressed out, it comes back." He turned on his heel and walked rapidly toward the dock.

Kaylen watched until he was obscured by a group of people carrying coolers and fishing equipment. So, was she the one totally stressing him out or Captain Hastings? She wondered.

She grabbed her purse, locked the BMW back up and headed for the marina office. Surely, the manager wouldn't object to her using his office phone for a quick call, she thought.

CHAPTER TWENTY-TWO

"What the fuck's goin' on with my brother?" Brian asked as he boarded the *Destiny*. "Kaylen told me what happened at her condo. Did Hal send a team out to Snapper Creek?"

"Yeah." Hastings took a cigarette out of a silver case and lit it with a matching lighter.

"And?" Brian watched Hastings inhale deeply and exhale slowly through his nose. "Don't dick around with me," he warned. "I know you can't swim. I'll throw you overboard if you don't start talkin'."

Hastings surveyed him with a thin smile. "Try it, and I'll arrest you."

"You'd like that, wouldn't you?" Brian tried to calm down. If he allowed the guy to get under his skin, he'd only delay finding out anything useful about Tim.

"Hal sent the team out as soon as the Roberts woman reported what happened to her." Hastings took another drag of his cigarette and flicked barely-visible ash from the front of his black jacket. "He got called to the creek right before I drove here. Any news, I'm sure he'll contact you. Telling Roberts her boyfriend got dumped there was probably only a scare tactic."

Despite his personal feelings toward the captain, Brian doubted Hastings would stoop to lying about something so painful as the possible murder of a family member. He firmly told himself that Kaylen's attacker had to be lying. And until Hal Shaw called and told him otherwise, Brian decided he had to deal with his own problems, not invent new ones for his brother.

"So, what are you doing on my boat?" he asked.

"You should know that better than anyone."

Brian's thin veneer of cool developed a crack. "I'm not a fucking mind reader," he snapped.

Hastings grinned.

The crack widened. "Why don't you give it to me straight, asshole?"

"You always were a rude bastard." Hastings gave Brian a look filled with contempt. "You've never gotten rid of that dock-worker mentality. I'm damn glad I don't have to deal with your insubordination on a daily basis."

"Good thing I transferred out of Vice then, isn't it?" Brian used every relaxation technique he had learned over the years to detach himself from his flashpoint anger. He tried desperately to disengage himself and visualize Tim as just another missing person.

"Damn right." Hastings threw his half-finished cigarette overboard and took a step forward, his body language unmistakably threatening. "If you'd stayed, I would've suspended you long ago. Hal's way too soft on you. He allows you to walk all over him. Let's talk about that housekeeper's murder and your kickbacks."

Brian wanted to knock that smirk right off the man's face. "You know damn well there's no proof I took kickbacks."

He reminded himself Hastings was purposely pushing all his buttons. If he took the bait, he'd end up wasting even more valuable time sitting in jail on a charge of assault and battery. He relaxed his jaw and breathed out slowly before saying anything else. Hastings waited, his eyes reduced to slits behind his habitual Ray-Ban shades.

"And do you seriously believe I'd drown some housekeeper in a bathtub?" Brian asked. "What the hell would I have to gain?"

"That's why you're being investigated." Hastings' voice held a faint, sibilant hiss. "We want to find out."

"If you're trying to intimidate me, good luck," Brian said. "You've had it in for me ever since I caught your son dealing, but you've never been able to pin anything on me. Once this investigation's over, it'll be proved the charges against me are all lies."

Hastings made a sound somewhere between a laugh and a snort.

"And if you had anything to do with those charges, then you're the one who'll be doing all the explaining," Brian said.

"I've got better things to do than cook up charges to get you out of the department," Hastings said. "Even if you did make false accusations about Sean."

"False? *Christ.* I caught him in the act. If he wasn't your son, I would have booked him like any other dealer. My mistake. I came to you instead."

"Your word against my son's. Who do you think I'd believe?" Hastings took out another cigarette. The wind had picked up, and it took him several attempts to light it.

Brian swore he detected a slight tremor in the captain's hands, but even if he did, he had no way of knowing whether it came from anger, fear or frustration over his lack of parenting skills. And Brian didn't give a shit.

"You agreed to leave me and my brother alone if I transferred out of Vice. But now you've backed out of our deal, and I want to know why," he said.

"I'm here to ask questions, not answer them." Hastings almost lost his footing as a speedboat roared by and rocked the *Destiny.* "Pissing boat." He fell more than sat back down and glared at Brian. "Don't stand over me, like you're enjoying me making a fool of myself. Sit."

"You already made a fool out of yourself when you refused to send Sean to rehab."

"Who the hell are you to tell me what to do with my son?"

"Ignoring the problem isn't going to make it go away. I've always liked Sean. I don't want to see him turn into another Tim."

"That'll never happen."

"It's already started. Sean's young enough that you could stop him. You're his father, for Christ's sake. Tim wouldn't listen to me because I'm his brother, and he's always told me to butt out. Like you should butt out of my business right now."

Brian's anger continued to simmer, despite his best efforts. Hastings had sent IAB to ruin the life he had made for himself. They'd stuck their noses into every corner of his private life. He'd been told to make an appointment with the department psychologist after they dug up old police reports about visits to the house on Webber Street. Pure fury shot through him with the power of an acetylene torch. His fingers curled into fists, the skin over his scraped-raw knuckles stretching painfully.

He wasn't the only one losing control. Hastings leaned forward, shoulders hunched. Brian balanced his weight on the balls of his feet. He wondered if his superior was actually going to get up and start throwing punches, or whether he was going to charge from a seated position. Whichever scenario, Brian vowed Hastings would live to regret his rash behavior real fast. Despite his injuries, Brian figured he could still take the captain, and he'd get a great deal of pleasure out of smashing that pretty boy face into pulp.

He sucked in air and winced, but the sudden rush of oxygen brought the return of common sense along with the pain. If he punched Hastings, he'd never clear his name, and he could kiss his job with the department goodbye.

Luckily for both of them, Hastings must have thought better about fighting, too. His shoulders lowered and he settled back against the side of the boat. He traded intimidating looks with Brian, but it was obvious he wasn't about to test his physical skills.

"As one of your superiors, even indirectly, you *are* my business, whether you like it or not," Hastings said. "I decided to meet you here because it's a public place, and I'm well aware of your fondness for violence."

"I don't pick fights or use unnecessary force," Brian said. "Whoever's spreading that rumor's way off the mark. I boxed a long time ago, and I know how to handle myself. That's not a crime, and I don't go around beating up suspects."

"There have been complaints."

"About my temper, yeah, sure. In the past I had trouble controlling it. That's behind me." He shrugged carefully, well aware of the consequences if he moved too quickly. "I lean on people. My methods get results. You've seen my interrogations."

"I watched you when you worked under me, and I saw you begin to step over the line. Then you transferred to Homicide and became Shaw's problem. Now several people have come forward, and the public prosecutor is reviewing their statements. He expects to proceed with criminal charges."

"*What?*" Brian couldn't believe what he was hearing. "Why are they coming forward now, when I'm already on suspension?"

"People said they were intimidated by you when you were on active duty. Threatened with physical harm to themselves and their family members."

"That's a crock of shit." Brian could hear his voice rising, but he no longer cared what people on the dock heard. "And what the fuck has all this got to do with Tim's disappearance and the bribery accusations?" He pounded his fist into the *Destiny's* rail. "Someone's trying to get rid of me, and I'd be willing to bet it's coming from inside the department."

Hastings stared at a scuff on his loafer. "You're dirty," he said. "These accusations are going to stick. You can count on it."

"And you can count on the fact I'm gonna fight them. Get off my boat."

Hastings slid the Ray-Bans down his nose and looked over the top of them. "Are you going to tell me your brother's clean, too?" he asked.

"As far as taking dope, yeah."

"What about dealing?"

"No. Tim's not a dealer, either," Brian hedged.

"I'm not playing games, Swift. I want the truth."

"I think he's more than a driver now. Is that what you want to hear?"

"No. I want to hear you say he's a supplier. I want you to admit your brother's working for one of the biggest cartels in Miami."

Brian shook his head. "Tim's never admitted that to me." He watched Hastings slide the sunglasses back into place. "I'll never save myself by sacrificing Tim, whatever you try to hang on me."

"You're such a noble bastard," Hastings said. "Makes me want to puke even more than this fucking boat does."

"You made the same choice about your son that I made about my brother," Brian pointed out. "The difference between us is you're a supervisor. That makes it easier for you to hide the truth."

"I'm going to ignore that," Hastings said. "But if you try to threaten me or my son in any way, I'll make sure you spend the next few years behind bars." He leaned forward, his lips barely moving as he added, "It'll be my pleasure."

Brian grabbed the captain by his lapels and jerked him to his feet.

"You okay, Brian?" The calm voice of Jim Paxton came from behind them.

Brian let go of Hastings and glanced over at the boat moored next to the *Destiny.* His neighbor leaned against the rail, his wiry gray eyebrows drawn toward each other.

"Yeah." Brian managed to give a terse nod.

Jim backed slowly away, but instead of going below, he picked up a newspaper and sat on a chaise in the sun.

Brian forced himself to sit down at the table. He grabbed a bottle of water he had left on the seat and took a gulp. The usual hustle and bustle on the dock and surrounding boats had ceased. People had stopped to stare. The rhythmic pinging of ropes against masts and the creaking of boats suddenly sounded deafening.

"You'd better leave right now," he told Hastings.

"I'm not finished." Hastings straightened his tie and pulled his jacket back into place. Two spots of color high on his cheeks were the only signs that anything more than talking had gone on between them.

"Maybe not, but *I* am." Brian watched Hastings walk over to the other side of the table.

"I want to talk about Kaylen Roberts," Hastings said.

"I'm not answering any more questions today."

"You two looked real friendly when I arrived. What's going on between you? One brother's not enough for her?"

"Leave her *out* of this." Brian thumped the bottle against the table and the plastic split. Water showered his hands, his face and the front of his shirt. It hit Hastings' expensive suit.

"Son of a *bitch.*" Hastings unbuttoned his jacket and brushed at the water spots.

Jim glanced over, energetically shook his newspaper and disappeared back behind it. Brian wound the cap back onto the empty and shattered bottle. The motion diffused his anger, and his hand was steady as he laid the container down onto the table.

"Kaylen's got nothing to do with Tim's disappearance," he said. "Whatever Tim was up to, he didn't say anything to Kaylen about it. She told me that, and I believe her." He watched a few remaining water droplets roll down the inside of the plastic bottle.

Hastings said nothing.

"Tim called and asked me to meet him outside her condo in the middle of the night last Friday," Brian said. "He never showed, and I haven't heard anything from him since. If you're so interested in what he's doing, why aren't you out looking for him instead of trying to nail my ass to the wall?"

"Hal Shaw mobilized half his people to look for your brother."

Hastings shoved his hands into his pockets and turned his face into the wind, which had continued to build steadily. His immaculate hair stayed put. Brian wondered if Hastings used hair spray.

"They don't need me or my squad helping out," Hastings said. He glanced sideways at Brian. "I bet Madison skipped town and left you high and dry."

"He'd never do that."

Brian refused to even consider the thought that Tim had screwed up not only his own life but his brother's, too. Despite their differences, despite their frequent fights, they always presented a united front to outsiders.

Suddenly, he was in the middle of yet another unwelcome flashback. He was ten years old and reeling from a blow to the head. His drunken stepfather stood over him, with six-year-old Tim hanging off Ed Madison's arm and screaming for him to stop.

Ed had thrown Tim against the wall, and Brian had taken a couple more well-aimed kicks to the ribs before Ed lost interest. Brian heard Tim sobbing quietly. After Ed sprawled out on his bed, his snoring louder than the freight trains passing the window, the brothers had changed clothes and cleaned the blood off their faces before their mother came home.

Brian felt a deep, overwhelming sadness at the memory of Tim, his skinny legs pistoning below tattered shorts as he ran to wrap his arms around their mother at the front door that evening. It had taken a long time for either of them to tell her what happened when she was working, but she wasn't able to stop the abuse. In fact, she became a victim of it herself.

A familiar pang shot through him as he thought of how little time his mother had enjoyed freedom after Ed's death. If only things could have been different, Brian thought for the thousandth time. If only Tim hadn't been so adversely-affected by the violence in his childhood. Maybe then, he wouldn't have liked the high life so much.

Hastings' voice pulled Brian back to the present.

"...so family members frequently screw each other over." Hastings slicked back some invisible out-of-place hair from his forehead.

Brian noticed strands of gray mixed in with the black and wondered if Sean's antics weren't more to blame for those than the responsibilities of the vice squad. Maybe he should check up on the kid. See if Sean had any connection to Tim's disappearance.

"Don't confuse Tim with Sean," Brian warned. "The only thing they've got in common is disrespect for the law."

"My son's an addict. Your brother's a fucking dealer."

"No. I told you...your *son's* the dealer." Brian wanted to shake his fist, but he figured Jim was peeking around the edge of that newspaper he'd been holding up to his face for the last five minutes. "My brother hangs out with the wrong crowd," he said. "And he spends way too much money on clothes and flashy cars."

Hastings looked like he'd had a bucket of rotten fish stuck under his nose. "Your brother's running with a bunch of drug dealers who try to give themselves some class by calling themselves a cartel. And the money he spends comes from selling their drugs."

"You've never proved that."

"Yeah, maybe, but you were scared enough to back away from telling IAB about Sean."

"You *blackmailed* me to protect your son. You threatened my career and my brother's freedom. What the fuck do you *think* I was gonna do?" The longing to punch Hastings in the face was so strong, his fists crept up yet again and that time, he almost gave into the urge. "Of course I backed off." He shoved his hands into his pockets.

Hastings sat for a moment without moving, his jaw contorting. Then he took his cigarette case and lighter out again. Brian remembered when the department had given him those gifts along with a commendation after Hastings led his squad to clean up an entire section of Miami. Brian had respected his superior in those days. Even when Tim came under scrutiny, Hastings had looked the other way, and the vice squad with him, while Brian tried repeatedly to get his hot-headed and rebellious younger sibling to find a legitimate job and friends whose faces weren't in the mug books at the precinct.

But after Brian found fourteen-year-old Sean dealing drugs, he had walked on eggshells until he agreed to transfer to Homicide. Even that hadn't satisfied Hastings. He wanted Brian out of the department altogether, and he had been working diligently toward that end. The corruption charge looked like it was going to stick. Now the prosecutor might be adding more.

Hastings rubbed one hand across his face. "This discussion isn't getting us anywhere. You're going to regret holding out on me."

The swell increased under the *Destiny.* More bad weather coming, Brian thought distractedly. If he couldn't take the boat out, he couldn't earn any money. The slip fees were due in two weeks.

He firmly told himself to stop focusing on it, or any of his other problems at that moment. They were too overwhelming. "Did you seriously think we could have a civilized conversation after what's gone on between us?" he asked Hastings.

"I thought we should try," Hastings said. "Having a detective out on suspension's tarnishing the department. It would be better to resolve things as quickly as possible."

"Fuck you," Brian said. "I'm not resigning. I don't give a shit about what's best for the department. What you're really talking about is what's best for *you.*"

"You're raising your voice again," Hastings said. "Getting angry isn't going to solve your problems. Your bank account's got a balance of a hundred thousand and this boat's paid off. Explain that."

"I can't. But I'd have to be stupid to put kickbacks into my bank account. Any moron would know that's the first place IAB would look."

"So some fairy fucking godmother waved her magic wand and did it?" Hastings leaned forward, invading Brian's personal space. "You know what I believe? Either Madison arranged to put it in there or his bosses did."

Much as he hated to admit it, Hastings had a point, Brian decided. If Tim was in trouble, maybe he'd thought stashing money in his brother's account would buy him time and keep it safe.

"How long is it since you saw your brother, anyway?" Hastings asked.

Brian thought about refusing to say anything else, but knew he'd end up talking to IAB instead. "A week, maybe two."

"I wonder if I believe that," Hastings said. "You always were a great liar. That's why you did so well in Vice." He got up and started walking awkwardly toward the down-station.

"Don't even think about it," Brian said. "If you need to use the head, there's a restroom inside the marina office."

Hastings stopped and turned back to face him. "I think you've talked to Madison since he supposedly disappeared."

"What makes you think that?"

"I've got my sources."

"They're wrong," Brian said. "I've tried calling him without success. I can't even leave messages because his answering machine's full. So's the voicemail on his cell."

"Why do you think he wanted to meet you at the Roberts woman's condo?" Hastings asked.

Brian shrugged carefully, mindful that a muscle spasm could result. "No idea. He wouldn't give me details over the phone. I never saw anyone at the condos. I got sapped while I was waiting outside my car."

"Anyone who managed to get the drop on you must have been a professional," Hastings said. "You've always been a jumpy bastard."

Brian nodded. "Yeah, he was good. I never knew what hit me. I've still got the knot on my head."

"How long were you out?"

"Several hours." Brian wasn't volunteering any information about being in Kaylen's bed. "I woke up in my car."

"Hmm." Hastings' brow furrowed, and he rubbed one thumb over his chin, as he often did when thinking deeply. "There was a disturbance at Roberts' condo the next morning. What time did you wake up?"

"I dunno." Brian thought about it. "Six, maybe? I was pretty groggy. I didn't look at my watch until later." He remembered his confusion when Kaylen's scream cut through his daze and he saw her naked on the floor. The memory stirred up something he definitely didn't want to deal with at that moment. He grabbed a chart and started rolling it.

"What did you do then?" Hastings was staring, his head cocked to one side.

"I tried calling Tim's cell, but when he didn't pick up, I went home."

"Did anyone see you come back to the boat?" Hastings *knew* he didn't have the whole truth. "Can someone verify your story?"

"I doubt it. I came in the back way, and the dock was pretty deserted."

"How did you get the split lip?"

He was moving into an area Brian didn't want to discuss almost as much as being in Kaylen's bed.

"I got punched by some drunk in Kaylen's club." Brian avoided direct eye contact. Hastings' nostrils were quivering like some goddamned bloodhound on the scent.

"What's up with your reflexes?" Hastings pulled off his sunglasses and stared. "Two people got the drop on you within twenty-four hours?"

Brian's control started to disintegrate again. "Fuckin' hell, Hastings. I've been worrying about my brother," he said. "If you were in my position, I doubt your reflexes'd be any sharper than mine." He gathered up the charts. "I've got work to do, and I've answered as many of your goddamned questions as I'm going to. Tell me what else has been done to find Tim."

"His apartment's been searched and dusted, but they didn't find any evidence of a crime being committed there," the captain said. "You can check with the detective in charge of the case to get a report. I believe Hadley's handling it with his partner."

"Vickers?"

"I think that's his name."

"I'll give them a call." Brian pitched the empty bottle into a paper bag under the table and gathered up the charts. "If Tim's dead and my career's washed up, I won't have anything to lose, you know."

Hastings' lips thinned. "You shouldn't threaten me, Swift. You don't know who you're dealing with."

"I've got a pretty good idea." Spasms rippled through Brian's back and ribs. He turned away from Hastings and gritted his teeth. "You need to leave."

"I'll be back," Hastings said. "We're not done. Chances are we never will be."

"Looks that way." Mercifully, the spasms stopped. Brian wiped sweat from his brow, stowed the charts back in their pocket beside the wheel and listened while Hastings clambered off the *Destiny*.

He checked his watch: 5:30PM. He needed to search Tim's apartment himself, but he couldn't do that with a client due in thirty minutes. He started pacing the deck, feeling like a dog on the end of a very short leash.

Jim dropped all pretenses of reading his newspaper and came to the rail. "Anything I can do for you, buddy?"

Brian stopped pacing. Something in Jim's manner was so calming, he didn't even stop to think that his live-aboard neighbor might be as nosy as Tim's. "I've got a real conflict in my schedule," he said. "I don't know what to do."

"Double-booked yourself, did you?" Jim pushed his cap back and smiled. "Want some help with the charter?"

Brian felt as though someone had unlocked a door and let in a breath of fresh air. He'd been so stifled by his own problems, quickly followed by Kaylen's and Tim's, that he felt incredibly relieved by this unexpected offer.

"Could you do it for me? It's only two hours, but I've got to be somewhere else. This other thing…"

"No explanations necessary." Jim waved away the lies Brian was about to cook up. "You tell me what you want done; I'll take care of it."

"I'll give you the fee," Brian said.

"No way. We'll split it. I'm bored, and you're over-extended. We'll make a good team." Jim turned toward his cabin. "Let me put on some better shorts and I'll be right over, so you can fill me in on the details."

Brian glanced at Jim's knife-pleated navy shorts and couldn't imagine how his neighbor thought he wasn't dressed well enough for a boat charter, but he didn't argue. He needed a few minutes to change clothes himself.

By the time Jim arrived on the *Destiny,* Brian had called the clients and the caterers, found a pair of pants, a dress shirt and a tie that should get him into Bannisters, but discovered his black jacket was missing. He swore he remembered tossing it onto a seat in the up-station, but things had been happening so fast over the last couple of days, he figured he must be mistaken.

"Did you lose something?" Jim asked as Brian checked inside the lockers on deck.

"My jacket. I only own three of them, and the black one's gone."

Jim looked him up and down. "I'd lend you one of mine, but you're bigger than me."

Brian shook his head. "Thanks, but you're right. I must have left it in my car. Let me fill you in on the details of the charter."

By the time he had given Jim a quick run-down on the pleasure trip booked by an older couple, the catering truck rolled up. He left Jim making small talk with the deliveryman as the supplies were unloaded.

It was too damned hot to wear a jacket, anyway, he decided as he got into his car.

CHAPTER TWENTY-THREE

"There's another storm coming?"

Kaylen held the receiver between her ear and her shoulder while she frantically searched for more change in the bottom of her purse. She had no idea how much she'd need to finish her conversation with Lieutenant Shaw. It had been years since she'd had to use a pay phone.

"It's projected to hit the Keys in two days, unless it stalls," the lieutenant said.

"What if the search for Tim is still going on?" She found two quarters and promptly dropped them. "The creeks in that part of town are already close to overflowing. I heard it on the radio earlier today." She bent to pick up the money, only to find both coins had rolled under a nearby car.

"The search and recovery team's hoping to wind things up by tomorrow afternoon," Shaw said. "Since the last storm dumped so much water, some of the creeks are being pumped as a precaution, including Snapper. That'll help. The mud and the Mangrove roots have made searching the banks almost impossible and the creek's so dirty, the divers are having trouble seeing anything."

Kaylen closed her eyes and pictured Tim falling in cold, oozing mud before being murdered. Tears welled up behind her lids and spilled down her cheeks. She shivered and brushed her face with the back of her hand.

"Ms. Roberts…Kaylen…are you okay?" Lieutenant Shaw asked.

She stopped digging for money and pulled a tattered tissue from her purse. "No." Her voice sounded weak and barely audible even to her own ears. She wadded up the tissue and dabbed her sore nose.

"You've had a tough time." His quiet, even tones held compassion.

"Dear God, not as tough as Tim. Do you really think he's dead?" Conscious that her distress was drawing concerned stares from passersby, Kaylen turned to face the booth.

"The longer he's missing, yes." Lieutenant Shaw sighed. "There's no record of him leaving on any commercial airline, but he could have gone out on a charter."

"I think he always took commercial flights," Kaylen said. "He often complained about leaving his car in the long-term parking and coming back to find it covered with dust, but he'd never let me drive him to the airport or pick him up."

"Ms. Roberts, why were you dating a man with connections to one of the biggest drug cartels in Miami?" Shaw asked.

The abrupt change in his tone came as less of a shock than his words. Kaylen felt weak. She clutched the edge of the booth for support. "There's no way," she said. "You must have bad information. Tim couldn't...he wouldn't..."

"He did, and he has. For a long time."

Kaylen didn't know what to say. "I...I..."

She stopped trying. What was she going to say? That she was too stupid to know?

"How did you get involved with him?" Shaw prompted.

"I told you, Sam Wilson introduced us." A welcome gust of wind slid across her shoulders and lifted sticky hair off her neck. "Sam protects me. He'd *never* let me get involved with a criminal."

"Vice and Narcotics have been keeping tabs on Madison for a couple of years." Shaw said. "They suspect he makes runs from South America. But so far nothing's been proved, even though he's been brought in for questioning a couple of times."

Kaylen's legs threatened to buckle. All sorts of horrible thoughts popped into her mind. *The frequent trips. Tim's refusal to let her into more than the fringes of his personal life.*

The receiver slid out of her hands and swung on the end of its short metal cord. Behind the ringing in her ears, she heard the lieutenant speaking.

It wasn't possible, she thought, grabbing the phone. Random thoughts scurried through her mind. *She should have suspected.* Tim's secretiveness and his refusal to tell her anything about his family, his friends, or even his past should have clued her in that something was wrong.

He'd only talked about the Miami "scene." And he'd bought her so many expensive gifts, like the Dior Christal watch she wore on her wrist at that moment, and the Gucci purse. Her fingers released the strap and the purse slid onto the blacktop, its contents spilling around her feet.

She left everything where it fell, her body numb but her heart and mind racing. *He had sent her beautiful flowers every Monday. He had told her frequently how lucky he was to have her in his life. He had lulled her into some ridiculous dream. Dear God, what a fool she was…*

"Ms. Roberts? Ms. Roberts!" Lieutenant Shaw's voice sounded sharp instead of reassuring.

Kaylen ignored him, her mind whirling. Losing George had left her vulnerable and silly. Open to exploitation. Tim had bulldozed her with his likeable, easy personality, his quick wit and charm. He had overwhelmed her with his generosity and his stories of start-up ventures that sounded so exciting. She never checked any of them for substance, even though she certainly had the contacts to do so. He'd fleeced her. And evidently, he'd fleeced Sam, too.

Kaylen had difficulty swallowing. She owned a club, and a drug cartel would love to use it as a front. She thought of Sam's restaurant, empty of patrons. Yet he'd had a big house built. *Someone must have doctored his books and let him think he was making a lot of money, when in fact…* A mechanical voice told her she needed to deposit more money.

Reality snapped her out of her nightmarish trance. Kaylen saw two quarters resting on the ground next to her lipstick and pushed them into the coin slot. "I'm sorry," she told Lieutenant Shaw. "I'm so, so sorry." And again she was crying. Big hulking sobs that cut off all possibility of saying anything more.

"You need to come back to the precinct," he said. At least he wasn't shouting.

"Not today. I can't today. I just can't." She wanted to run away from everything, as far and as fast as she could.

"You must," he said. "There's a lot of relevant information you can give us, even if you don't know it yourself. You can fill in some of the gaps in the timeline."

He wasn't asking, he was commanding. Kaylen stood up straighter in response.

"You need to look at mug books. I realize you're in shock, but you've got to cooperate." He wasn't going to take no for an answer.

"I know that." Kaylen tried using her foot to push the contents of her purse back inside it, because she wasn't going to take a chance of missing anything he said. "I'm not trying to be difficult, but I can't cope with everything. It's too much." She looked in vain for another tissue and sniffed.

"One hour, Ms. Roberts. Ask for me at the desk."

"It's no good me looking at mug books," she said. "I already told you I never saw the person who attacked me."

"But you may recognize someone you've seen at your club, even hanging around where you live. We'll discuss that more when you get here."

Kaylen knew she was going in for the third degree, and all her lies would come out, including those she had told about Brian's arrival in her life.

"I'm not just asking you to point out your attacker. I want to know who else has come into your club, or who you've been introduced to either by Sam Wilson or Tim Madison," he said.

"Okay." *What else was she going to say?*

"I'll let you know if we find anything at the creek."

"Oh…okay." She started crying again.

"Don't jump to conclusions, Ms. Roberts. Until Madison turns up one way or another, he's still a missing person, and this is not a murder case," the lieutenant said. "With your help, we may be able to expedite the search."

"Anything I can do to help find Tim, of course I'll do it," she said. "But I have to keep my club going, too. My backers and my staff are depending on me. I have to make arrangements. I'm supposed to meet my manager…"

He interrupted her. "I understand that. Make some calls. One hour, Ms. Roberts."

"Yes, sir." She hung up when she heard a click and a dial tone.

She had to hire an independent accountant to go over her books, and she had to warn Sam to do the same. But she had no more change and a dead cell phone.

Kaylen decided Lieutenant Shaw might have to wait a little longer than the deadline he had set. She had to go to the club. Her meeting with Rob was in ten minutes. While there, she could call Sam to warn him about the police investigation and send out one of the staff to buy her phone chargers.

She wondered if she could get arrested for refusing to turn up on time. And if it caused a delay finding Tim, then she would never, ever forgive herself. But whatever she did, it looked like a no-win situation. Kaylen scooped everything but her keys back into the Gucci purse that now reminded her she was dating a suspected criminal and ran back toward her car.

CHAPTER TWENTY-FOUR

Regardless of the fact that Hal Shaw had sent detectives over to Tim's apartment, Brian wanted to conduct his own search.

The first thing he had to do was get rid of nosy Ella O'Grady, unless he wanted her to call the cops and add breaking and entering to the growing list of his supposed illegal activities. He drove to a grocery store a couple of miles from Little Havana, told the manager he wanted to give his needy neighbor a surprise and paid for $100 of promotional gift coupons, which he left for her in a sealed envelope at the customer service desk.

Back at the corner of N.W. 12th Avenue, where he could see the front entrance of the Cielo Azul Apartments, he used a burner phone to tell Mrs. O'Grady she had won a weekly drawing, but had to collect her prize within thirty minutes. In less than five, he saw the old woman lumbering out of the building, a straw hat on her head and a large black purse clutched under one flabby arm. Her flowered muumuu flapped in the hot breeze, giving him another unwelcome look at her swollen, discolored legs. Her blue slippers had been exchanged for white sandals that flapped off her heels, and her mouth tightened with every slow and painful step.

She managed to open the cab's door without dropping her purse, but she couldn't step off the curb to get into the back seat. Brian watched in frustration as she made several attempts, her cheeks growing scarlet from the effort. He swore under his breath. Didn't people help each other out anymore?

Just when he thought he would have to blow his cover to go help her, she started shouting, her language even more colorful than her muumuu. She knew some Spanish swear words and accompanied them with graphic arm and hand gestures. Brian was impressed by her determination. After she had delivered a tirade that ended with a one finger salute and *"Hijo de puta"* delivered at the top of her lungs, the driver scrambled out to help her. Mrs. O'Grady's ample bulk disappeared into the cab.

Brian watched the vehicle swing into traffic before he walked up the chipped concrete steps that led into the dilapidated building. Yellow paint peeled off the walls in the entry, and again he had to step around a large puddle in the middle of the floor. Judging by the size of it, he reckoned the roof was leaking as well as the skylight.

Halfway up the two flights of stairs, he decided the entire building smelled like mold. By the time he reached Tim's door, he was cradling his ribs and panting. Brian decided he had better stop thinking he was made of steel and take his pain pills on a more regular basis.

He'd also better keep an eye on the time and search fast, he reminded himself. Mrs. O'Grady would be exhausted just getting to the store, let alone cashing in the coupons for groceries. She might end up sitting while one of the associates did the shopping, in which case, she could be back in no more than a half-hour.

He ran his hand along the top of Tim's front door, found nothing, leaned over and grunted with pain as he checked under the mat. No key. He repeated the process at Mrs. O'Grady's door, except that time, mindful of the pain involved, he squatted down to check under her mat before pulling on latex gloves and picking both Tim's locks.

The apartment echoed and worn hardwood floors creaked as he walked around, checking all the less-obvious places his brother could hide something important…under drawers, beneath or at the back of furniture and behind pictures on the dark blue walls. He took the covers off the air ducts, pulled up two large area rugs and looked inside and around the toilet tank.

Defeated, frustrated and really sore after fifteen minutes, Brian stood in the middle of the living room and swore. Tim had wanted his help. He had to have left a clue to his whereabouts *somewhere*.

He ran through a mental checklist. The pad beside the phone was brand new. Despite all the creaking, he hadn't found any loose floor boards, and the only things inside the light fixtures were bulbs. Despite his meticulous efforts, nothing unusual had turned up in any of the rooms. Certainly no key or any indication of what it might fit.

Damn, damn, damn.

He returned to the spotlessly clean bedroom. Since when had Tim taken time to do anything in his spare time except buy more clothes and chase women? Brian certainly couldn't see his brother armed with a broom and a can of furniture polish. But would he allow a housekeeper to come into his private space? If so, then Brian knew he would have to find out who she was and interview her.

But something about the cleanliness and neatness of the entire apartment bothered him. The place was immaculate in a less than normal sense. It looked like it had been cleaned for an inspection by the local health department. Despite the dirty old building, no dust lay on the furniture, and his brother hadn't been seen for three days already.

Brian flipped a trio of switches on the wall beside the bedroom's doorway. A subdued glow highlighted the California king-sized bed. Tim went to so much trouble to hide where he lived, but his bedroom reeked of seduction. All show, Brian thought. The illusion was maintained even in that sterile atmosphere. Sterile. Another memory stirred in the deep recesses of his mind. Of his mother, and of Tim.

He sank onto the edge of the bed as he thought about how happy his mother had been to leave Baton Rouge behind. But she'd developed liver failure less than two years after she and Tim arrived in Miami, and Tim had stayed home to be her caregiver. Brian suddenly smelled disinfectant and an underlying odor of sickness. He closed his eyes and was transported back to the tiny studio apartment he had called home, where their mother had lain dying on the hideabed. Tim, gangly and gaunt, was 17 years old.

It was only after her death that his brother had really started getting into trouble. Brian forced his eyes back open. The past needed to stay buried. He had told himself that same thing so many times before, but guilt nagged at him. He'd been too preoccupied with his own grief to notice the lowlife friends Tim found after their mother's death. He should have tried harder to stop his brother from taking a path that led him to this apartment, and to this dangerous lifestyle.

Fluorescent lights hummed behind closet doors that occupied most of two walls. Brian looked at his watch. Twenty minutes. His body had stiffened while he sat distracted by his thoughts, and he felt incredibly tired and depressed as he stood back up. He told himself he might have no other opportunity to search Tim's place and slid back the mirrored doors. On one side, racks contained what had to be close to 50 pairs of shoes. At the other side, 10 suits hung in formation: 5 blacks, 3 grays, 2 navy blues. Brian glanced at some of the labels. Hugo Boss, Armani, Valentino. He shook his head. The price of one of those suits would probably have paid for the entire contents of his own wardrobe.

He took one highly-polished brown loafer from the rack. Size thirteen and a half. Brian figured Tim had to custom-order. He carefully placed the shoe back between its neighbors and opened drawers. Underwear and socks were neatly stacked inside, many still in unopened packets. He flipped the lid back on a large hamper standing inside the doorway of the bathroom and found it empty. *Shit.*

Only the original built-in closet remained darkened. Brian pulled a chain hanging from the ceiling. A low-powered bulb flickered on, and he stepped inside.

Tim must have been using it for storage. On a shelf above the wooden rail sat a row of baseball caps. Some emblems told of trips to the Keys, Disneyworld, the Hard Rock Café and a number of other local bars and restaurants. Others encompassed Tim's autographed collection. Brian looked in vain for the New York Yankees cap autographed by Derek Jeter, which Tim had planned to buy for over $700. Either he had recently sold it, or maybe he'd decided not to spend the money after all.

A large suitcase stood in one corner next to two duffle bags, both bearing the insignia and printed gold letters of Champions' Gym. The zippers of the bags lay open, the contents clearly visible...t-shirts, shorts, socks and tennis shoes. He pulled out the suitcase and unzipped it. Empty. *Fuck.*

He reached into his pants pocket and took out the note Tim had left with his neighbor. *Take special care of Kaylen.*

What the hell was that supposed to mean? He turned the envelope over and looked again at the questions on the back. If Tim had left a clue in any of that gibberish, he had to believe his older brother capable of more detection than Sherlock Holmes.

Ugly memories stirred. Uglier than anything Brian had remembered in a long time. The house on Webber Street. The hallway where he had been kicked and punched into near-unconsciousness so many times. The kitchen where his stepfather had thrown boiling soup onto his back as he ran, because Ed had puked after drinking, and the smell of the soup made him nauseated. Suddenly, Brian was 8 years old again, and he could feel the searing pain.

He fought to escape the clutches of his childhood. He kicked the closet door shut and marched back into the living room. *Damn Tim and his fucking quiz.*

But his stepfather's surly face appeared out of nowhere to mock him from the shadows. For a moment he felt irrational dread, but he pushed it back where it belonged, deep down inside him. Why did Tim think dredging up the past would help either of them?

Brian went into the kitchen. He had to think like a detective. Getting emotional had never helped him before, and it wasn't going to find Tim. Out-of-date O.J. sat in the fridge and a moldy loaf of bread lay on the counter alongside a half-finished jar of peanut butter.

No booze. That kind of surprised him. Tim had taken pride in the fact that unlike his father, he was no drunk, and he always kept a couple of bottles of wine or champagne on hand. He said it was to prove he had the control to either open them or leave them in the wine rack for weeks.

Brian looked under the sink. Regimental lines of cleaning supplies. Even the garbage can had been emptied. He wondered if Hal's investigators had taken the contents.

It looked as though someone had gone to a lot of trouble to erase all signs of the apartment's occupant. If Tim had emptied the garbage himself prior to going on a trip, he would have discarded the food left on the counter, and probably the orange juice, too. Brian made a mental note to check with Hal whether the detectives had taken the trash instead of his brother.

That empty suitcase was big enough to hold at least a week's worth of clothes. Brian decided Tim must have become totally freaked out to leave without any of his belongings. There were no visible gaps between the clothes in any of the closets, and even Tim wouldn't pack without making a dent in the meticulously neat rows of underwear and socks. The two guys Mrs. O'Grady had seen the day after Tim left had to have removed anything they thought useful. Brian left the apartment and quietly closed the door behind him. He should have asked her if the men had left with bags or even another suitcase.

He walked back downstairs as quickly as his ribs would allow, wondering if the dumpster had been emptied yet that week. No use him looking, he reasoned. The cops would have checked that out already. He easily picked the lock on Tim's mailbox and emptied its contents into his pockets before leaving the building as quickly as he had entered it, head down, sunglasses obscuring his eyes.

Whatever secrets Tim had been keeping, they weren't in the most obvious place. Either his brother had learned too well over the years or he hadn't even had the chance to take anything with him. Brian took out his cell and called Hal Shaw's number.

CHAPTER TWENTY-FIVE

"You shouldn't be calling me, you know that," Hal said, his voice quiet and guarded. "I'm in the middle of the precinct, you idiot."

Brian had no patience left for anyone, even his supervisor. He made no attempt to disguise the anger in his voice. "That's why I called your personal cell phone," he snapped. "Step out of the building if you're so paranoid."

A momentary silence let him know what Hal thought about insubordination. Brian silently counted to twenty while he worked on calming himself.

"I'm in my office," Hal said, his tone decidedly clipped. "I'll close the door." He put the phone down.

Brian waited, his car parked on a side street behind Tim's apartment building. He slid the seat back and wished the air conditioner still worked. The blacktop shimmered and the concrete sidewalk radiated heat.

Hal picked the phone back up. "All right. You can talk, but I can't give you any information related to your case."

Brian stretched his tired and aching body, wincing as his kinked muscles protested. "I'm not so worried about my own problems right now," he said. "Kaylen Roberts told me about Tim. I need to know what's goin' on at that creek. Hastings came to my boat and told me you got called out there."

"Damn it," Hal said. "I should've figured he'd do something like that."

Another silence. Brian didn't think he needed to comment, so he sat sweating in the Camaro and wished his supervisor wasn't so long-winded.

When Hal started talking again, he didn't sound so pissed off. "Look," he said. "So far they only found a shoe on the creek's bank. A black dress shoe.

Size thirteen and a half. It got bagged and sent to the lab. Nothing else turned up; that's why I'm back here." He paused, as though expecting Brian to interrupt him. "For all we know," he added after a moment, "that shoe could have floated downstream from miles away."

"Tim wears a thirteen and a half," Brian said. His throat tightened.

"I'll make a note of that." Hal was all business, like they were discussing some stranger. "I've got nothing else for you."

"You've gotta give me somethin' else," Brian said. "If you don't, then I'll start callin' you a lot, and not on your cell, either. IAB'll be watching." He knew his voice sounded about as prickly as his frustration level, but his professional veneer had disintegrated as soon as he realized Tim might be dead. "Why the fuck didn't you call me yourself about Tim?" he asked.

"I know you're worried…" Hal's voice was irritatingly calm and detached. "…but I can't share privileged info with you while you're on suspension, and quite frankly, knowing how short-tempered you are right now, I didn't want to tell you anything until I'd checked it out myself."

"My temper? You're worried about my *temper?*" Brian pulled his seat upright. Bad idea, the jerking motion brought spasms to his ribcage.

"That came out wrong," Hal said. "But you jumped right on it with both feet. You're touchy. Understandable with the on-going investigation. Sorry you had to hear everything from Hastings. The bastard waited for me to get tied up, so he could drop it on you and see your reaction up close and personal."

"Yeah, and he got what he wanted."

"Don't tell me you hit him."

"No, but I came close a couple of times."

"Don't you *ever* learn?" Hal's voice was definitely not detached now. "Did anyone else see what went on?"

"My neighbor, but Jim's cool."

"You'd better hope he is."

A faint rhythmic click in the background told Brian that Hal was probably tapping a pen against his desktop, which frequently happened when he became irritated.

"Hastings has been looking for a way to end your career for the last couple of years," Hal said. "Now you're under a lot of stress he's going to be pushing harder, maybe until he gets you on an assault charge."

"That's not gonna happen," Brian said with a lot more conviction than he felt. "Hal, I know you can't talk to me about my own case, but can't you keep me updated on anything new that comes in about Tim?"

"Yes, of course. Like any other family member. And I'll talk to Hastings. He's got to keep out of this business with Tim."

"Thanks." Brian wondered if Hal was expecting him to apologize for being out of line earlier in their conversation, but he wasn't about to do it. "Either something Tim's involved with has gotten me into this mess, or his girlfriend, Kaylen Roberts is responsible," he said. "I've never taken a bribe. Not even when I was asked to throw fights years ago."

"I told you I can't discuss your case," Hal said. "You want to talk about Tim, that's okay."

"Fair enough," Brian conceded. "But think about this…I got jumped by two guys in the marina parking lot last night. They did a number on me. Enough to send me to the ER, but not enough to get me admitted to the hospital."

"Why didn't you call and report this?" Hal asked. "And what did Hastings say that made you risk arrest?"

"To answer your first question, I didn't feel like it was gonna do any good. As for Hastings, he was usin' threats to try and get me to resign from the department."

"The hell you say. What sort of threats?"

"Nothin' I can't handle without your help. I told him to fuck off. I'm not gonna become some scapegoat to sweep shit under the rug for him, you, or anyone else at Miami-Dade for that matter."

"I don't expect you to," Hal said. "I expect you to fight this and give a good reason for that money to be sitting in your account."

"I don't *have* a reason, Hal. Hastings gave me one possible explanation in between insulting me and about makin' me hit him. He said maybe Tim or someone in the cartel put it there."

"Hmm," Hal said. "That's definite possibility. It would explain how the boat got paid off, too." He sighed. "But why? Were they trying to implicate you? That makes no sense. You're more use to them on active duty than you are on suspension."

"Someone needs me out of the department, even temporarily," Brian said. "You and I both know it could be Hastings. Maybe he's returnin' a favor. Maybe it's because of somethin' Tim knows." He almost said "Tim knew," but he wasn't going to start talking about his brother in the past tense. Not yet.

"Everyone knows there's bad blood between you and Hastings," Hal said. "But I still find it hard to believe he'd go that route. You're out of his department, and from what I'm hearing, he's probably not going to be around the precinct much longer. He's moving up and out. Board of Commissioners or some such position is the latest I've heard."

Brian thought about Sean's money-making venture. More than enough reason for Hastings to want an eyewitness out of the department. But surely not a reason to arrange for Tim to disappear instead of arresting him and letting the ripple effect engulf his brother.

"Hal, you *know* I'm not a crooked," he said. "But I'll admit I'm an idiot where my brother's concerned." He watched two pigeons swoop down from a chain link fence surrounding a vacant lot. They began pecking at a Burger King wrapper in the gutter.

"I can't help Tim," Brian said. "Never could, but I was too stubborn to admit it."

Further down the street, an emaciated dog knocked the lid off an aluminum garbage can sitting on the curb. The clatter awakened a bum sleeping in a doorway. A pair of filthy bare feet poked out from under a tattered blanket. Then a bald head emerged to check out the source of the disturbance. The guy threw an empty can at the dog, which veered away, its skinny tail tucked between its stick-thin legs.

"That's quite an admission," Hal said. "I've never heard you say Tim's a lost cause."

"That's because I never believed it until today," Brian said. "Hastings told me a lot of crap, but some of it made sense. He said Tim's left me hanging out to dry, and for the first time in my life, I'm beginning to believe it."

Depression flowed over him in a suffocating cloud. Was he really going to end up losing everything he had worked so hard for over the years, and all because of his goddamned selfish brother? He could end up like the bum in the doorway…homeless, jobless and hopeless.

"You sound like all the fight's been knocked out of you," Hal said. "I've never heard you talk this way." He grunted. "We've all been trying to tell you Tim's not worth your time, but you'd never listen."

"Yeah, well I just smartened up." Brian popped the top off his Vicodin and swallowed one. It threatened to stick in his throat, and he grabbed a nearly-empty bottle from the cup holder to swallow warm water. "I need you to share information with me," he told Hal. "I'm getting my balls busted here, not only by IAB, but some outside source. And I believe you're holdin' back information that could get Tim found and stop me endin' up in the morgue."

Hal took what seemed like forever to answer. Brian waited, watching the dog chase the pigeons away so it could eat the greasy wrapper.

"All right," Hal said. "I'll meet you later, but it's got to be on the QT. If anyone in the department hears about this or sees us, then I'll be out of a job, too."

"Fine," Brian said. Relief lifted some of the suffocating depression. "We can meet in the parking lot behind Finnegan's Bar. It's dark as hell back there, so no one will see us." He glanced at his watch. He still had to go to Kaylen's club afterwards. "Eleven o'clock?"

"My wife's not going to like that. She's worried enough about IAB nosing around the department without me going out to meet you late in the evening."

"You want me to call Frances and explain?"

"No thanks. That'll piss her off even more. She's already mad at me for your suspension, like it was my fault. She's your biggest defender. Pity she's not an attorney."

"Yeah. Good to know at least I've got *someone* in my corner. Tell her I'm gonna catch the bastards who set me up."

"She's already convinced of that."

"Fucking shame you're not."

"That's bullshit, and you know it. I defended you until they showed me the evidence."

Brian fought back his anger. He'd put off talking to Hal because he'd had trouble controlling himself. Hal had obviously put off talking to him for the same reason. If he didn't watch his mouth, he'd end up alienating the one person who might give him information to clear himself. "I'm innocent, Hal. I swear to you on whatever you want me to swear on…my mother's grave, a stack of bibles, whatever."

"I'll see you later." Hal broke the connection.

Brian took the expressway. He had enough time to grab something to eat before he met Hal, but after the pill and the warm water, he felt queasy. Probably because he hadn't eaten since breakfast, he told himself, glancing at his watch. The *Destiny* would be back in her slip. Maybe he could lie down for an hour.

The white Lexus in front of him stopped with a screech of brakes and the smell of burning rubber. Honking and swerving, Brian barely missed barreling into the trunk. Shaken up, he took the next exit, drove into the parking lot of a strip mall and parked in the first available space. Out of habit, he checked around to see if anyone had followed him and caught sight of his reflection in the rearview mirror. A disheveled stranger with wild eyes stared back. Brian did a double-take.

He flipped up the mirror to avoid seeing himself again. He'd never felt so out of control before. Even his hands were shaking. Something was needed to steady his nerves, and food wasn't going to do the trick.

A liquor store was listed on the shopping center's directory. He drove slowly over an annoying succession of speed bumps while he fought the urge to go find Kaylen and shake the truth out of her. He'd see her later at the club, he reminded himself. And that time, he wasn't going to dance around. She'd come clean or he'd…he'd…he gave up trying to think of a suitable method of forcing her to confess her involvement in Tim's disappearance and concentrated on avoiding a group of people pushing shopping carts across the parking lot.

At the liquor store, he glanced up at a camera mounted over the checkstand. The clerk beneath it gave him a startled glance and looked away far too quickly. Brian knew his bruised and scabbed face was enough to scare anyone. He picked up his pace and headed for the coolers.

He didn't want to arrive drunk for his meeting with Hal. He'd buy a six-pack of beer and pick up a burger from a fast-food joint. After going through Tim's mail, he'd sit and write up a report on everything. Doing something familiar, mundane and orderly might put his mind back where it belonged. He decided that ever since he'd been suspended, he'd been running around half-cocked. If nothing else, the events of the last couple of days might have finally knocked some sense back into him.

He grabbed an extra six-pack to keep on the boat. Jim liked a cold one, and Brian enjoyed his neighbor's restful company. On the way back to the counter, he passed a display of scotch and bourbon. His determination to drink only beer wavered, and he added a fifth of Jim Beam to his purchases.

All those memories of Ed Madison must be a bad influence, Brian thought as he paid. Thankfully, he knew he couldn't have inherited the alcoholism. What his own father had been like, he had little idea. His mother had rarely spoken about Andy Swift, her first husband and Brian's father, except to say he had died young. She always became so emotional at the mention of Andy's name that Brian had learned to avoid the subject.

Sweat beaded his forehead as he left the air conditioning for the heat of the parking lot. A bank of black clouds obscured the setting sun. Back in the car, Brian slid down in his seat, opened the Jim Beam and took a swallow. The liquor not only burned his throat and shot right to his brain, it brought fire to his sutured lip.

"Shit!"

Bourbon splashed over the console and Brian grabbed the bottle right before it turned upside down and emptied all over the floor mat. Now the Camaro smelled like a goddamned bar. He jammed the top back onto the bottle, pushed it under his seat and carefully wiped his mouth.

If he got pulled over now, he'd go right to the slammer. Rummaging around the glove compartment produced one stick of dried up gum, which he popped into his mouth on the way to a burger joint he spotted on the other side of the street.

Fucking heat. Brian welcomed the breeze billowing into the car from the open windows and flipped on the radio to listen to the weather report. He heard more about the approaching tropical storm and swore. Just what he didn't need, one more thing to worry about. He followed another car into the drive-through of Burger Heaven and gave his order. If he couldn't go out on charters, he'd have more time to work on his own issues as well as trying to track down Tim.

Back at the marina, he downed a beer on the way to the boat. Jim had left a note on the door to the down-station. The charter had gone well, and the caterers had already collected all the dishes and the trash. Jim was having dinner with friends. He'd left his cell number "just in case."

Brian gratefully breathed air loaded with moisture and the smell of the sea instead of the rank odors of the afternoon. Lights winked on some of the surrounding boats, and the continuous, rhythmic creak of wood and fiberglass soothed his troubled spirit. He stowed the remaining cans in the refrigerator and took his burger, fries and soda into the salon, where he consumed the less-than-appealing and mostly cold meal. After writing a check to Jim for half the charter fee, he opened Tim's mail.

Gas and electric bills. A couple of credit card statements, listing weekly flowers, restaurant meals and bar tabs, gasoline and parking fees. Unfortunately, Tim's cell and landline bills weren't there, neither was a bank statement. Most of the mail turned out to be junk—solicitations for Tim to order Mexican food, pizza or other restaurant take-out, refer a friend to the local gym or take trips to Bermuda. Brian tossed the junk mail into the fast food bag.

If Tim owned a laptop, the cops had that, too. Brian felt chagrined that he knew so little about his brother's possessions or habits, but keeping at arm's length had become a necessity if he wanted to remain a detective. Because his own laptop had been confiscated during the investigation, he was forced to open a spiral notebook. He took out a pen and wrote intently, his attention totally focused for the first time since he had been summoned to Hal's office to find IAB reps and hear the charges against him.

"How's it goin,' Brian?"

He looked up to see his neighbor standing at the top of the steps. Jim smiled, his weathered face creasing under his faded navy-blue cap. Brian thought his neighbor matched his old but well-maintained craft perfectly. Jim had retired from selling insurance to live on his boat ten years ago. Strong and wiry, he looked several years younger than his chronological sixty-nine.

Brian managed a half-smile. "Could be better, Jim. Wanna beer?"

"Sure. You want to come sit up here? Might be the last time we get to do that for a couple of days."

Brian nodded. He gathered up the papers and stowed them under the bag of junk mail before taking the drinks up on deck.

Jim had set out two chairs and was stretched out in one, facing the bay. As soon as Brian handed him the check he pocketed it without even glancing at it. He popped the top of his can and upended it as Brian carefully lowered himself into the other chair.

"Ah, that hits the spot." Jim smacked his lips and peered at Brian. "So give. What the dickens happened to you? Did you get into a fight?"

"I got punched by some drunk in a bar." Brian tried to look and sound like the incident wasn't worth talking about.

"Well, I hope you gave him as good as he gave you." Jim took another long drink.

"The bouncer broke things up pretty quickly," Brian said, taking the truth and stretching it. He quickly changed the subject. "Thanks again for taking care of that charter for me."

"My pleasure. No need to say anything more, except I hope you'll call on me again when you need help. I enjoyed taking this little gem out."

Brian managed another half-smile, even though it hurt his face. Jim's optimistic attitude made it hard to stay depressed. "Did you get any more fishing done the last couple of days?" he asked.

"Yeah, lot of good it did me." Jim crossed his thin, ropy legs, sticking out beyond neatly-creased navy shorts. A triangle of long, white and wiry hair curled from the V-neck of his matching blue and white striped t-shirt. "I went out early this morning, but those fish must have had better things to do than check my bait."

Brian always wondered how Jim managed to live on a boat and keep looking so sharp. He also cooked gourmet meals in his tiny galley, the mouth-watering aromas frequently wafting in while Brian sat in front of a peanut butter and jelly sandwich and wished for the return of a guaranteed paycheck.

"I came back around noon," Jim said. "Went below to take a nap."

The two beers coupled with the relative comfort of the chair started to affect Brian's concentration. He struggled to keep his eyes open and wished he had been able to take a nap himself.

"Next thing I knew, I heard people on your boat," Jim said. "Woke me up. Two men in suits."

Brian didn't feel sleepy anymore. "What the hell? Did they see you?"

Jim considered for a moment, eyes squinting behind his gold rimmed glasses. "Nah, don't think so. I'd stripped off to sleep, so I kept out of sight. They looked like brokers. You selling the *Destiny*?"

"No way. Did they take anything?"

Jim shook his head. "Don't think so." He wagged his finger. "You know, I'd have called you if I had your cell number. I reported the incident to the office. The manager didn't contact you?"

Brian wondered what he was paying slip fees for, if the manager couldn't even pick up the phone and tell him about trespassers. "I came home a different way and parked at the other end of the lot," he said. "I didn't go by the office at all today. No one called."

"Son of a bitch," Jim said.

"Yeah." Brian wondered if Hastings had sent detectives over to scope out the *Destiny* before coming himself. "What did they look like?" he asked, not really expecting much past a "maybe one was tall, and maybe one was short" routine from his quiet and unassuming neighbor.

"You know, I read somewhere that witnesses never remember squat when they're asked to describe a mugger or burglar, so I got a piece of paper and wrote down a few things. It's still in my pocket." Jim took out a paper and held it up. "That's not gonna work. Can't see a thing." He climbed out of the chair. "You got a flashlight in the up-station?"

"Yeah." Brian started to struggle out of the chair.

"Stay where you are. Just tell me where it's stowed."

"Beside the wheel. There's a chart pocket." Brian thankfully settled back.

"Got it." Jim returned, flashlight in hand. He held the beam over the paper. "That's more like it. One was around five seven or eight, kind of pale, reddish hair. Didn't know how to dress. Who wears brown shoes with a gray suit?" He looked at Brian for verification.

Brian made a non-committal noise. "What about the other one?" He pretty much guessed what Jim was going to say.

"Taller…five ten, maybe…Hispanic, wearing a tan jacket over beige pants, white shoes." He passed over the paper and flashlight. "How'd I do?"

"Great," Brian said. *Grover and Hernandez. Detectives from Hastings' fucking squad.* "Did you see them go below?" *He'd get them on breaking and entering.*

"Uh-uh." Jim drained his beer. "Not while I was looking. They pulled out all your charts, opened the lockers and rummaged around in the fishing tackle. If management didn't contact you, what sort of security do we have?" Jim crumpled the can, his fingers digging into the aluminum. "I'm gonna give that gold-toothed moron in the office a piece of my mind tomorrow, let me tell you."

Brian could just imagine the confrontation between Jim and the Salvadoran who spent most of his day leaning on the counter while he flashed his expensive dental work at any passing woman.

"Sometimes that place is empty when I walk by," Brian said. *He needed to move the Destiny to a more secure location, but where the hell was he going to find more money for the fees?* "I'll talk to the manager tomorrow," he said. "He needs to hire additional security if his staff can't keep out people who don't belong here."

"And I'll talk to some of the other owners. I've got a lot more time on my hands than you do." Jim took off his cap and rubbed his balding pate. "You'd think with the monthly fees the marina charges they could do better than this."

"Yeah, I know. Want another beer?"

"Nah." Jim set the crushed can on the table. "Changing the subject, how's the charter business going?"

"Good. I've got another one tomorrow morning, if the weather holds up."

"It should. Latest projections have the storm hitting the Keys in two days. That's why I got some fishing in today. Maybe those fish weren't biting because they can feel something's coming."

"I don't know if I'd give fish that much credit," Brian said. "I think you just had bad luck."

"Probably." Jim jammed his cap back on his head and stretched. "Time for me to hit the hay. If you need more help with the charters, I'd be happy to do it," he said. "Sometimes I get bored, to tell the truth. Retirement's not all it's cracked up to be."

"Thanks," Brian said. "I'll remember that, especially while my face looks like it does. Might scare off some of my clients."

Jim chuckled. "Keep a hat on and stay in the shadows."

"Let me give you my cell number." Brian got up with difficulty and headed for the salon. "Then you can call me if someone else comes nosing around."

"You bet, buddy." Jim followed him down the stairs.

Brian scribbled his number on a corner of the report paper and tore it off, handing it to Jim. "Don't put yourself into any bad situation or place yourself in danger," he said.

"Anything you want to tell me?"

"Not right now." Brian looked away from Jim's concerned stare. "I need to clear up a few things. My brother's in some sort of trouble, and it's causing me a few problems, too."

"Enough said. Family members can be a pain in the butt." Jim laid his hand on Brian's shoulder and squeezed lightly. "It'll work out."

Brian fought the urge to shrug off Jim's hand. "Yeah, I guess it will." He doubted anything would work out, but he wasn't about to unload his problems on his neighbor. "G'night."

He watched the older man leave the *Destiny* before pulling out a gym bag, into which he placed the notebook and Tim's mail. No sense in leaving anything of value on board when he was away.

He made sure his off-duty Glock 17 was loaded and stowed additional ammo in the bag, too. If anyone else tried to jump him or ransack his boat, he planned to be ready.

CHAPTER TWENTY-SIX

Kaylen pulled her sea green silk dress over her head and pushed her feet into high-heeled gold sandals. She took a vintage jet necklace from her jewelry bag and clipped it around her neck. The cold stones felt like a soothing shower of rain as they slid down her hot skin to within an inch of the dress's low scooped neckline. Rummaging around in the bag produced matching chandelier earrings. Kaylen looked at her pale face in the mirror above the vanity. She had never felt less like partying in her life.

Only three days ago, she had been eagerly anticipating the club opening. She loved the Big Band Era concept and had encouraged her patrons to dress in period clothing and role play. Now the whole concept felt jaded, tarnished by Tim's disappearance and the mayhem of the last forty-eight hours.

As she fumbled with the unfamiliar antique fastening of a jet bracelet, Kaylen scanned the menu for that evening. Crab consommé or vegetable soup, Beef Wellington or fresh salmon with new potatoes, baby carrots and peas. A vegetarian stir fry with wild rice. Garden or Caesar salads. Peach Melba or Key Lime Pie. Her stomach growled.

She opened a packet of crackers she had stowed in her desk drawer and bit into one. Dinner wasn't in her game plan. Greeting and mingling with her guests had to be a top priority that evening. Demonstrating that she was in charge, she thought, annoyed at Sam for assuming her role the night Bannisters opened.

Her cell phone sat charging on a corner of her desk, after one of the busboys had made a trip to the phone store. Kaylen found satisfaction in that small glimmer of orderliness in her otherwise chaotic life. She crammed the rest of the cracker into her mouth and took off the sandals, which already pinched her feet. Ironic that one of the few pairs of shoes to escape the destruction in her condo were uncomfortable.

She had driven back to the precinct late that afternoon, after calling Lieutenant Shaw to tell him she was running late. Perhaps he had punished her by being unavailable, because she was met by a terse, long-faced detective named Vickers and escorted to a room where she spent an hour looking at mug books without being able to identify anyone. The detective, who had an annoying habit of cracking his knuckles every few minutes, had asked her whether her list of missing items needed to be updated. Kaylen told him no.

Did she want to add anything to her statement? he asked next. He seemed to be looking right through her. Again, he cracked his knuckles, and Kaylen found herself shifting uncomfortably in the chair. No, she said. *Nothing.* She crossed her fingers under the table. She wasn't about to send detectives to Brian's boat. Finally, when she thought she would never see the outside world again, Vickers told her she was free to go.

She pulled flat black leather sandals out from under the desk. Were they too casual for her dress? She had told Brian she was a clothes horse, but tonight she couldn't even summon up the energy to look the part of an affluent club owner. No amount of concealer would hide the bags under her eyes, and bright pink lipstick had only made her complexion look even more washed out. Wearing high heels wouldn't disguise the damage, either.

Kaylen felt tired and cranky. She had spent two hours with Rob, working through receipts and order books. They had hired and fired wait staff, poured over resumes to find an additional *sous* chef and discussed wines to recommend with the evening meal. While they worked, the band arrived for an early warm-up session and evidently to practice new pieces. Tempers had frayed in tandem with jangled chords.

Kaylen suspected they had only rehearsed enough music for the first few days, deciding even before it opened that Bannisters wouldn't stay in business for more than a week. If so, Bernie Draper and his Orchestra had underestimated her and her capabilities, not to mention George's hand assisting her from the grave, she thought peevishly.

Despite the caterwauling horns, Kaylen had lingered inside the club to observe Rob's management skills. Watching his easy but commanding style, she became as impressed with him as the previous employers who had sent glowing recommendations.

When she finally glanced at her watch, it was past time for her to get showered and changed. She thanked Sam in his absence for insisting she have a full bathroom installed behind her office. He knew how little time she would have to herself some days, especially right after the club opened. Kaylen had been able to stand under steaming hot water until she felt able to face her clientele.

The phone rang as she completed her makeup. Kaylen's stomach churned. More bad news? she wondered. She hesitantly picked up the receiver. "Yes?"

Relief filled her when she heard Sam's voice saying hello. "Are you coming to the club tonight?" she asked him.

"I'm around the corner at a deli," he said. "I'm bringing pastrami sandwiches for us."

"We've got Beef Wellington on the menu tonight," she said. "I know that's one of your favorites. Don't you want that instead?"

"I thought we'd eat the sandwiches before the club opens. I know you, K.T. You'll skip dinner otherwise. Besides, it'll give us a few minutes to talk. I haven't spent enough time with you over the last few days."

He knew how she loved a pastrami sandwich on rye with a big kosher dill pickle. Kaylen's mouth watered at the thought of it. "I really don't have time to eat," she protested.

"I think you'd better *make* time," Sam said. He sounded a bit like a reprimanding father. "In case you try to leave another lasting impression with your guests."

Kaylen's first response was to snap at him, but she reminded herself Sam always had her best interests at heart. "Don't remind me," she said, careful to keep her tone neutral.

She had certainly made a fool of herself that previous Friday evening, she thought, cringing inwardly. "Okay," she said. "Bring the sandwiches."

"I'll get you an extra pickle and see you in a few," Sam said.

Kaylen hung up and headed for the kitchen.

"Ms. Roberts, are you eating alone tonight or expecting guests at your table?" Marvin, the head waiter asked when she passed his station.

Kaylen had a great deal of respect for Marvin and his professional attentiveness to her and her business. She paused. "Mr. Wilson's on his way over. He insisted on bringing deli sandwiches, but we'll have dessert and coffee later."

"Are you eating in your office?" Marvin beckoned over a busboy to remove a tray of glasses perched precariously on the edge of the serving station.

"Yes." She continued on toward the kitchen.

"I'll send in plates, napkins and drinks," he promised.

"Thanks. Diet Cokes for both of us." Kaylen pushed open the swinging doors ahead of her and stepped into the kitchen.

She scanned the staff inside the spotlessly clean inner sanctum. They all appeared cool and unruffled, despite the high humidity. Dressed in white jackets over black and white checked pants, the tall hats of the chefs bobbed as they moved between counters, stoves and ovens while directing the bustling *sous* chefs. Busboys came and went as they took more supplies from the kitchen to finish placing rolls into rows of baskets and ice-cold pats of butter onto small dishes.

The head chef, an imposing Cuban named Emrico, wielded a large knife with precision as he elbowed one of the *sous* chefs out of the way and began making julienne potatoes at lightning speed. "*This* is how you do it *correctly*," he said, shaking the knife at the terrified young man trembling beside him. "I don't want any more *mistakes!* Do you *hear* me?"

The young man nodded so hard, he looked like a puppet with a coiled spring for a neck. Emrico, chest puffed out like a pigeon, gave his cowering assistant the knife and strutted off to check the contents of a huge vat simmering on one of the stove tops.

Kaylen smothered a smile. Emrico ran his kitchen with military precision and demanded nothing less than excellence from his staff. He had taken his name and embellished it, Kaylen suspected, with an affectation that was supposed to connect him with the more famous Emeril Lagasse.

Kaylen knew Emrico's tantrums and theatrics produced meals unrivalled by any other club. Her opinion had been echoed in the stack of reviews Rob had left piled neatly on her desk. At least something in her life was going right, she thought as she inhaled mingling aromas of beef, onion and spices. The heat and steam threatened to ruin her makeup and frizz her hair, so she retreated, leaving the glaring, stark hot whiteness of the kitchen for the cool, subdued lighting of the club.

Sam brushed aside one of the ceiling-to-floor maroon velvet drapes that shielded the club from the vestibule. In one hand he held a large white paper bag, in the other, a lit cigar. He puffed energetically on the cigar, and the resulting cloud of smoke drifted upward, caught in the blades of softly-whirring walnut and brass ceiling fans and dispersed throughout the room.

"Over here," she called as she threaded her way between the tables. "Put that thing out. You know better. The whole club's going to smell like a cigar bar."

Marvin hurried past her, glass ashtray in hand. Sam grumbled, but stubbed out his cigar and watched Marvin jog toward the back exit with the offensive stogie held at arm's length.

"You've become such a killjoy," Sam complained. "My doctor's taken everything from me but those cigars. I can't eat like I used to because of high cholesterol, I can't drink because I might get cirrhosis or some other damned disease, and I've been told to watch my stress level, for Christ's sake. I ask you, Kaylen, what the hell do I have left in life to appreciate?"

"Your improved health," she said. "You've lost at least twenty pounds, and you've even started exercising a little." She bit back a comment about his drinking and that florid complexion, which looked an even darker purple in the soft glow of the dining room. No sense in starting a fight when she had the opportunity to enjoy an evening in Bannisters that she might even remember.

"Why don't we go back to my office?" she suggested, giving him a quick peck on the cheek.

"Rob, how about getting us some plates, napkins and drinks?" Sam said to Kaylen's manager as he walked over to say hello. "Diet soda for me and mineral water for Ms. Roberts."

Rob looked taken-aback, but he nodded and turned on his heel, making for the bussing area.

"That was kind of rude," Kaylen said. "Rob's not a member of the wait-staff. You might at least have asked him to get one of the busboys to do that. Anyway, I already arranged with Marvin to have those items brought to the office."

"Yeah, I suppose I could have handled that better. I'll apologize later." Sam waved the bag at her. "Let's go eat. I'm hungry."

"Me too," she said, her stomach growling again. She decided fighting with Sam in front of the staff wasn't going to make her look mature, so she followed him down the long hallway to her office.

He took the chair behind her desk. "You don't mind, do you?" he asked, plopping his ample rear into her leather seat. "My back's been hurting the last couple of days." He forcefully rocked the chair back and forth and then from side to side. "I need one of these for myself. I should have ordered it while we were in the store. This is a hell of a lot more comfortable than that old chair I've got."

Kaylen felt resentment rising inside her and tried to push it back down. For some reason, over the last couple of days Sam had annoyed her with everything he said and did. She sat in one of the red leather club chairs facing her desk while he slid what had once been a pristine large white blotter from under the deli bag, which was leaking mustard and meat juices in a widening ring.

Rob walked into the room as Sam upended the blotter and leaned it against the side of the desk. Without looking at either of them, her manager hurriedly placed a white dinner plate under the bag and gave Kaylen another plate and a pile of napkins. She quickly blotted up the mess.

"I'll get one of the busboys to bring another plate along with the drinks and a cloth to clean the table," Rob said. He sounded reproachful. He knew how long and hard Kaylen had looked before finding her beloved desk. She had made a special point to be at the club when it was delivered, and she always protected it with the blotter.

"Oops," Sam said.

Kaylen no longer felt like eating anything. "Why don't you throw that bag in the trash?" she said. "Have the Beef Wellington."

"Come on, stop fussing." Sam put one of the wrapped sandwiches on the clean plate and handed it to her. "Dig in." He rescued the other sandwich, threw the messy bag into the trash can and started eating. "Mm, that's good," he said between mouthfuls. "We don't need another plate, Rob. This is fine." He took a big bite of his pickle and munched energetically.

Rob left so quickly, Kaylen thought he might even have started running.

"What's the matter with you, K.T.?" Sam wiped his mouth with the only clean napkin left on the desk.

"You know very well what's wrong with me." She unwrapped her sandwich and stared at it. The overstuffed pastrami on rye looked less than appealing.

A knock announced a busboy with a loaded tray. He quickly buffed the desk back to a high shine, shook folded linen napkins open and draped them across Sam and Kaylen's laps. He popped the tops of the soda cans with a flourish and poured the contents into glasses filled with ice and garnished with lemon slices. The liquid fizzed energetically toward the tops of the glasses but did not spill over.

"What's your name?" Kaylen asked as he turned to leave.

"Ben, Ma'am," he said.

"Thank you, Ben. You did an excellent job," she told him. "We'll have to talk about training you to be a waiter."

"Thank you, Ma'am." He beamed widely, revealing uneven teeth under his wispy moustache.

Kaylen thought he looked all of seventeen, with slicked-back hair and ill-fitting pants held up only by the white apron knotted tightly around his waist. Even his white shirt was at least a couple of sizes too big. His thin neck stuck out of the collar like a giraffe's. She made a mental note to get him trained as soon as possible. He looked like he desperately needed to be working for more than minimum wage, and he certainly had the potential to do more than set up tables or clear away the remains of peoples' meals.

"Eat," Sam told her, interrupting her train of thought.

"I've got no appetite." She took a sip of the soda. Delicious. She drained the glass.

"More?" Sam raised his can. "I asked Rob to get mineral water for you. Lucky for him you're enjoying what was sent instead."

"I had already asked Marvin for Diet Cokes, so no mistakes were made, especially by Rob." Kaylen didn't attempt to hide her irritation that time. "I'll put the pastrami in the fridge. Maybe I'll feel like eating it later." She pushed her sandwich to the edge of the desk and placed her empty glass beside it.

"Any news about Tim?" Sam asked after a few moments of strained silence.

"Nothing." She leaned her elbows on the desk and massaged her temples. "A missing person report's been filed, and I gave them a photo."

Sam poured the remains of his soda into her glass and pushed it toward her. "Drink up. You want a shot of scotch or something in it?"

"No." She had already told him she didn't want any more to drink, but he'd ignored her. Kaylen's irritation grew.

"What about Rosa's murder?" Sam leaned back in the chair and studied her, his hands laced across the black vest beneath his dove-gray tux. "Any leads?"

"Nothing." Bringing up Rosa's murder put a knot the size of a grapefruit into her stomach.

"K.T.," Sam said. "You're holding something back. You can tell me anything, you know." He took her glass and sipped from it.

"I didn't want to worry you." She had trouble looking at him. She knew he would be upset. "There was an intruder in my apartment when I went back up there to get some clothes."

"What?" He stopped lounging and reached across the desk to take her hand. "Are you okay?"

His hand felt hot and slightly moist. Kaylen wanted to pull away, but she didn't want him to think she was rebuffing him. "I must have done a really good job applying my makeup," she said. "You didn't notice my nose?"

Sam looked embarrassed. "Well, kind of, but I thought you had a big zit or something."

"A *zit?*" She jerked her hand away.

"Sorry," Sam said.

"If I had a zit this big, I'd be at a dermatologist's office getting it taken care of, not sitting here with you." She got up and took her sandwich over to the little fridge next to the filing cabinet.

"I suppose so." Sam stood up, too. "Are you telling me you got attacked and didn't call me?" He walked around the desk and stepped into her path.

Kaylen almost ran into him. She stopped no more than two inches from his vest. "I got pushed, not attacked," she said. "I tried to fight him off, which was probably pretty stupid of me, and I fell." When Sam's large hands enfolded her bare upper arms, she realized how fragile she really was as tears rushed into her eyes. "The last couple of days have been absolutely horrible," she said. She allowed him to cradle her against him, the rapid beating of his heart a little alarming.

"You should be staying at my house." His voice rumbled in her ear as her head rested awkwardly on his shoulder.

"I'm already staying with a friend. I'll be okay."

Sam began stroking her hair, which felt really strange and more than a little unsettling. She had never been physically demonstrative with him, but she decided he was trying to comfort her, so she tried to relax.

"You're not okay," he said. "You need me to take care of you. George would want that." His hand went from her hair to her back and began stroking the bare skin above her dress.

"George would have wanted me behind a twelve-foot fence with armed guards around the perimeter." She pulled away from Sam's touch. "George isn't with us any longer, so I have to make my own decisions. I'm not a young girl any longer, Sam. I'm able to take care of myself."

"Okay." He threw up his hands. "Be stubborn. But you're not doing a good job of handling everything right now. What are you going to do about that condo? You can't stay away from home indefinitely."

"Sell it," Kaylen said without hesitation. "That's if I can find a buyer who doesn't mind that someone was murdered in the bathtub."

"K.T., people don't care about that sort of thing these days. You're living in a highly-desirable area."

"I'm not living there now," she reminded him.

"So, where *are* you staying?" He looked perturbed, his eyebrows drawn toward each other and the corners of his mouth turned down.

"The police told me not to tell anyone, even friends," she said. "You can still reach me on my cell, so it doesn't matter if you don't know where I am every hour of the day."

"I'm your closest friend, honey. I can give you anything you need, from emotional support to a chauffeur. I can certainly give you security and peace of mind." He seized her hand again and held it within both of his. "I want to give you *everything* you need," he said. "Let me take care of you. I can't replace George, but I can be a good substitute."

Kaylen didn't like the emphasis he'd placed on *everything*. It sounded uncomfortably like an offer of sex. She had to struggle that time to escape his grasp.

"Why are you acting like this suddenly?" she asked, completely confused and slightly revolted by his unwanted attention and innuendos. "You and I are friends…good friends…but never anything more than that. Tim's missing, and I told you I've had a horrible couple of days, but I'm not looking to you for the comfort I think you're trying to offer."

Sam's face registered a fleeting expression Kaylen could only interpret as rage, quickly followed by his usual, affable smile.

"You're misinterpreting things," he said, his tone reminding her again of a parent reprimanding a child. "I was referring to me taking over the club until you get your life straightened out." He leaned against her desk. "I'm thinking of selling my restaurant. In spite of everything I've done over the last few months, that new place down the block has beaten my butt. Frankly, I'm tired of the joint. But this…," he gestured in a wide, all-encompassing arc. "This would make a great new challenge."

Kaylen stood speechless. Sam had morphed into a stranger. She wondered if her mouth was hanging open with shock.

"You could sit back and enjoy the results without all the stress," he said, apparently oblivious to her reaction. "You could shop, sunbathe and completely relax." He smiled, all benevolence. "If you felt like it, you could even drop by now and then. Play owner. Order specialty items for the menu, try out some new wines."

Kaylen found her voice. "Whatever gave you the idea I don't want to be involved with the club?" she asked. "I really appreciate all the great advice you've given me over the past few months, Sam, but I'm not giving up the reins for anyone, even you. Besides, I thought things were going better at your restaurant since you redecorated and changed the menu?"

Sam shook his head. Kaylen noticed he no longer had a comb-over. In fact, his hair looked thicker, suspiciously so. He must have bought a hairpiece.

"The restaurant's been running in the red for the last six months," he said. "The tables fill up pretty well at lunch because I've got the die-hard regulars who always come in. But I'm not getting any new customers, and it's half-empty in the evenings, even though there's a line down the street at Conchita's Cantina. You've been in my place lately. You had to notice."

"I did," she said. "But you can't give up after all the years you've had The Hideaway. You could try different advertising, new dinner specials."

Sam waved his hand dismissively. "Been there, done that." He pushed away from the desk and invaded her personal space again. "What I need is a new challenge, K.T. Bannisters is just the ticket. If you don't want me here permanently, at least let me help until your private life gets straightened out."

She stepped back. Only a pace, but his eyes narrowed. "Bannisters is probably the only thing that's keeping me from losing my mind right now," she said. "I put all my problems on a back burner this afternoon, and they're staying there until this evening's over. Then I'll *have* to confront reality. But not now." She checked her watch. "Show time," she said. "The doors are open."

She kicked off her flat shoes and slid her feet into the three-inch heeled sandals that made her at least a half-foot taller than him. It felt good to be looking down at Sam. Empowering. Kaylen felt she needed the advantage.

She strode over to the door and looked at him over her shoulder as she turned the knob. "Coming?"

He shoved his hands into his pants pockets and followed her out into the hallway. Kaylen promised herself she would enjoy that evening if it killed her. But the cliché unsettled her even as she thought it. A shiver that had nothing to do with air conditioning crossed her bare shoulders, and for some indefinable reason, she wished Brian was with her instead of Sam.

CHAPTER TWENTY-SEVEN

At 10:50PM, Brian backed the Camaro into a space at the end of a deserted lot behind Finnegan's bar and waited impatiently for Hal Shaw. He had a lot of questions, and Hal had better answer them.

Brian trusted no one else in the department, including his last new partner, Paul Sanchez. None of the detectives in the squad had contacted him after his suspension, which didn't come as much of a surprise. Brian figured they were relieved they wouldn't have to walk on eggshells where Tim was concerned. He also wondered if they were really putting a lot of effort into searching for his brother.

Shaw's charcoal grey Accord drew in next to the Camaro. Brian had parked under the cover of two spindly trees growing between the chain link fence on the easement and the tall brick walls of a deserted paint factory on the other side of the fence. In the dim light, the two vehicles blended with their surroundings.

Hal didn't waste time on preliminaries. The moment his butt hit the passenger's seat he asked, "What the fuck's been going on since I saw you last Monday?"

"Plenty," Brian said.

Hal peered at him. "Christ, you look like shit."

"Yeah, I know." Brian grimaced. "Beaten up. No sleep." He caught himself nervously drumming his fingers on the steering wheel and stopped. "Worried about Tim as well as my job."

Hal rubbed his hands on his knees. "Having a family member missing must be pure hell."

"Worse," Brian said. "I'm worried about Kaylen Roberts, too. Some intruder attacked her in her condo. She needs protection, Hal. She's talking about hiring a bodyguard."

Shaw leaned back, putting his face into shadow. "She made a report about the attack. We're investigating, but no leads so far. No one saw the guy enter or leave her place, and since he wore a ski mask, there's no physical description to go on. We can't use department manpower to protect her twenty-four seven. I told her that."

Brian had to ask what he didn't want to know: "Any more news from the creek?"

"Nothing." Hal kept looking straight ahead, like he couldn't deal with Brian's appearance. "No news may be good news. We still haven't found Tim's car, either."

"I've got a really bad feeling in my gut," Brian said.

"Me, too," Hal said. "It's like Tim walked out of his life. No trace of him anywhere. His apartment's clean. Too clean, Vickers said. Like it wasn't lived in."

"Yeah," Brian said. "I was in there today. No dust on any of the furniture, nothing out of place, and all the trash taken out. But there was a loaf of bread and an open jar of peanut butter on the kitchen counter. Who cleans an apartment but leaves a mess in plain sight? It looked like he didn't even bother to pack. He left a big empty suitcase behind. All the closets and drawers were crammed full. It makes no sense."

Hal stared at him. "What the *fuck* were you doing in there?"

"It's not a crime scene," Brian said.

"Do you have a key?"

"No. I picked the locks."

"Breaking and entering," Hal said.

"Tim would never press charges," Brian reasoned. "And I had to know for myself what was or wasn't in there."

Hal's fist pounded against the dashboard. "Damn it, Brian, you're never satisfied unless you're double-checking after everyone. What made you think you'd find something in Tim's apartment that we didn't?"

"I bet you'd do the same thing if you were in my shoes." Brian didn't like being interrogated, much less disciplined like some rookie. "Did your guys take anything out of there?"

"No." Hal had a grip on the door handle, like he was about to get out of the car.

Brian knew better than to say anything else at that moment. He sat looking through the windshield at the tree branches waving inches in front of his face on the other side of the glass.

After a minute or so, Hal let go of the handle. "They didn't even get a chance to take the trash, because there wasn't any. Damn, it's hot in here."

He shifted in his seat and rolled the window down a crack. Tepid air slid through the opening, providing a brief stir in the stale atmosphere.

"Vickers and Hadley dusted for prints and came up with nothing, not even Tim's," Hal said. "You saw it…he left valuables out in the open, rings, necklaces, watches. Five hundred bucks in tens and twenties on his night stand, rolled up and held in place with a diamond-studded money clip. If someone other than your brother went through that place, robbery wasn't the goal."

Brian glanced at his supervisor and saw a grim set to Hal's mouth.

"No paperwork of any kind," Hal said. "No bank statements, utility bills, nothing. He didn't use online banking. We checked. He used cash or checks to pay his bills, which are up to date through the end of this month except a couple of the utilities. He's got a reasonable amount in his checking and savings accounts. Nothing too big, nothing close to being overdrawn. Tim was very careful not to draw attention to himself." Hal finally turned around to face Brian. "We wondered if he stored everything at another location. You know anything about that?"

Brian shook his head. "No. And he definitely didn't leave stuff with me, if that's what you're asking. I don't know anything about Tim's finances. He stopped confiding in me long ago. I always got too angry and lectured him. He didn't want to hear it. Kaylen said Tim never gave her anything to hold for him, either, but the intruder told her she has twenty-four hours to produce some key."

He wondered if Tim had placed a momentary stop on his mail, because the box had been stuffed full the day Brian went to the apartment. He said nothing to Hal about clearing it out, or he would have gotten a sermon about that, too. Sometimes, Brian thought wryly, his relationship with Hal mirrored the one he had with his brother.

"It must be a key to a safe deposit," Hal said. "Unless it's to another apartment, even a house. Maybe the address we have is a decoy, designed to keep everyone away from his real home. That building's a dump."

"Could be," Brian said. "With Tim, who knows?"

"Maybe he said or did something to piss off his friends in the cartel," Hal said. "The word on the street is that he stole something from them."

"Okay, so if they want whatever it is back, I can see them terrorizing Kaylen, but why beat *me* up?" Brian asked. "The last thing the cartel wants is to get the attention of the cops."

"Pounding on you isn't going to stir up a lot of sympathy at the precinct right now," Hal pointed out.

"Pounding on me at any time wouldn't do that," Brian said. "I know I'd never win any popularity contests, even without having Tim for a brother."

"That's true," Hal said.

He didn't elaborate. He didn't have to. Brian was well aware of his own flaws in the personality department. He tended to rub people the wrong way and didn't care enough to change.

"Maybe it was a simple case of him deciding it was better for you and Kaylen to take the heat instead of him," Hal said. "Tim's into self-preservation."

"I dunno, Hal. Even if he left me to fend for myself against thugs, I can't see him leaving Kaylen in danger," Brian pointed out. "Anyway, what would the cartel gain from it? I don't know shit, and I'm willing to bet Kaylen doesn't, either. They never even asked me if I did before they started beating me."

"You think they were warning you away from Kaylen?" Hal asked.

"Maybe. I seem to remember someone telling me to keep out of things, but it was hard for me to think straight after being kicked in the head."

"You didn't take their advice by the sound of it."

"No. If anything, it made me want to stick to Kaylen like glue. If she's got something they want, they're not going to give up, and that may lead me back to Tim, one way or another. Especially if you don't find anything else at the creek."

"When was the last time you talked to him, anyway?" Hal asked.

Brian hesitated. He'd already told Hastings it had been a week or two.

"The truth, Brian. Not what you told Hastings."

Brian shifted uncomfortably and brought his feet back. The bottle of Jim Beam bumped against his heel. He dragged the seat forward before Hal noticed the bourbon.

Hal noticed everything, Brian thought, pulling himself up straight. He should have taken the time to brush his teeth and use mouthwash before leaving the *Destiny*. His breath probably smelled of liquor.

"Friday," he said. "Six o'clock in the evening, give or take a few minutes. He called my cell."

"What did he tell you?" Hal leaned against the door and waited.

Brian went over the details of their conversation: The urgency in Tim's voice, the insistence that Brian drive over to Kaylen's condo and wait downstairs. "I woke up in bed with her the next morning," he finished.

Hal stared at him. "You had sex with Kaylen Roberts?"

"Hell no. I was knocked unconscious and put in her bed sometime after two-thirty in the morning. I must've had a concussion, because next thing I knew, she woke up and found me. She started screaming and fell out of bed. Or maybe she fell out of bed and started screaming. All I know is, she was on the floor and naked. Believe me, if I'd gotten her that way, I would have remembered. Good God, I would have."

"So now *she's* lying, too." Hal wiped one hand across his face. "She never said a thing about you being in her bed. Did you tell her to do that?"

"No." Sweat ran uncomfortably down the back of Brian's neck. Hal was right, it was incredibly hot in the car. He cracked his own window open. "She tried to protect me. She doesn't know why she did that, and neither do I."

A slow smile broke onto Hal's tired face. "She must like you a lot, Swift."

"She's Tim's girlfriend, for Christ's sake. She's almost as worried about him as I am. There's nothing going on between us."

"I'll let that drop for now," Hal said. "I'm more interested in knowing what happened after Kaylen started screaming."

"She tried to run, and I tackled her." Brian couldn't look at Hal. "I know. It was a stupid thing to do, but I was groggy and confused."

He hated admitting how unprofessionally he'd acted over the last couple of weeks, but he needed Hal's help, so he stumbled along with his report. The more he talked, the worse things sounded, especially when he recapped Hastings' visit to the *Destiny*. Hal had stopped avoiding eye contact and instead was staring as though he couldn't believe what he was hearing. Mercifully, his cell rang while Brian was trying to decide whether it was worth attempting to justify his behavior.

Hal's end of the conversation consisted mainly of non-committal grunts. After the call ended, he took a moment to put his phone on the dashboard before facing Brian. "Tim's car was found in long-term parking at the airport," he said. "It's been taken to the lab. So far, it looks like it was wiped clean."

Brian let his breath out slowly. "If Tim skipped the country, he wouldn't have bothered to get his prints off anything," he said.

"I know," Hal said.

Brian waited. Hal always paused before jumping to a different subject, and when he spoke again, it was usually with a question that would startle the listener. His interrogation techniques were legendary in the department. He lulled suspects into a false sense of security, then when they least expected it, he'd catch them off guard and nail them in a lie.

"Can you tell me if the blood found at the base of Kaylen Roberts' couch is yours?" Hal asked.

Brian felt a trickle of sweat run down his temple. "I don't know."

He wiped the sweat away with one finger and caught Hal watching out of the corner of his eye.

"Maybe I was on the floor in the living room before I got tossed into her bed," he said. "I had a knot on the back of my head when I woke up."

"The lab'll be testing DNA. They'll expedite the results. Hopefully they can get hair samples from Tim's grooming kit."

"He left his hairbrush and razor behind?" A prickle of unease ran through Brian. "Tim was so damned vain, he never went anywhere without a grooming kit."

"They found it in the trunk of the car. Maybe it fell out of his luggage and he didn't notice."

"Maybe." Brian couldn't grasp that straw of hope.

"They also got copies of Tim's phone records," Hal said. "No unusual activity there, either. He'd bundled his services at the apartment, so they were easy to trace, but he may have other accounts, even other cell phones. The laptop we found in his apartment told us nothing. Brand new, the tech said. He didn't even have an email account set up. Maybe that was a decoy, too, and he took his personal one with him. Do you know anything else you haven't told me?"

Brian figured honesty was the only route to go at that point. "I talked to his neighbor across the hallway on Saturday. She told me two guys went into his apartment Friday evening and spent a couple of hours. They'd have had plenty of time while they were there to check the place out, take his trash and swap his laptop for a new one."

"We talked to her, too. She wanted to be paid for her trouble and was damned uncooperative."

Brian had to smile.

"What's so funny?" Hal asked sharply.

"I gave her sixty bucks just to find out what I told you. She's ready to shake anyone down, even cops."

"Hadley had to threaten to take her downtown before she let him inside her apartment," Hal said. "He stood the whole time he was in there. The only chair that wasn't covered in cat hair or other crap was the one she sat on."

"Did she tell him she saw me?"

"No. She only said Tim was a nice neighbor who left boxes of food outside her door every week. She said she's going to miss that if he's not coming back. Apparently he gave her money toward her rent several times. He also gave her phone cards. She used them to talk with her son in Montana." Hal made a noise somewhere between a snort and a chuckle. "Funny. I never saw Tim in the role of benefactor."

Brian tried to visualize Tim hauling boxes of groceries up to Ella O'Grady, but the image wouldn't present itself. "That's one fucking weird story," he said.

"Tell me about it." Hal sighed. "Damned heat." He rolled the window all the way down. "Unless you start shouting, I don't think anyone's going to see or hear us."

Brian refused to react to Hal's gibe. "That's why I told you to meet me here. I used this place when I worked in Vice. No one ever comes back here at night. Not even the bar's customers. I heard some guy got capped back here when a drug deal went sour."

"That's real comforting." Hal stopped slouching. He looked out the side window and then at Brian. "So you're *sure* Tim never mentioned having a safe deposit box?"

"Positive. My brother never kept anything in a bank that he didn't have to. Tim was always the idiot with the roll of cash." Brian stopped himself. "*Is* the idiot with the roll of cash," he corrected.

A sinking feeling hit him harder than any punch would have done. He now knew how victims' families felt when he interviewed them. Tim was his only brother. His only family. He knew Hal was speaking, but all he heard was mumbling.

"Brian?" Hal's hand was on his arm.

Brian pulled away before he could stop himself. Since childhood, he'd had an aversion to personal contact.

"Are you okay?" Hal's voice sounded harsh with emotion.

"Yes...no...I don't know...." Brian couldn't breathe. It didn't matter if the window was open or not. He got out of the car. Oppressive heat bore down on him, and he wished he had a bottle of water under his seat instead of bourbon. He loosened his tie and opened the top button of his shirt.

Hal got out, too, and walked around to where Brian leaned against the car's trunk, hidden under a canopy of leaves. The branches overhead rustled angrily, stirred by the strengthening wind.

"I'm sorry," Hal said. "I know how much Tim means to you."

"Yeah," Brian said. "This waiting's gonna drive me crazy, and I can't be there to see what's bein' done to find him, which makes it worse."

"We're doing everything we can," Hal said.

"I'm tryin' to believe that, but I know I'm the only one in the department who's gonna lose any sleep over Tim." Brian heard the dry scraping of leaves on concrete. His cheek stung as a gust of wind lifted dirt from the surface of the parking lot to shower them with grit. "The rest of the squad's probably real glad to see the back of both of us."

"You're still a cop, Brian." Hands jammed in his pants pockets, Hal rocked slowly back and forth. "The guys are going to put their own personal prejudices aside and do their best to find Tim."

"They'd better do it in a hurry," Brian said. "That storm's comin' in fast. When it rains again, any evidence at the creek'll be wiped out. If Tim's there, he'll get washed out to sea or buried under mud. Didn't they find anything except that shoe?"

"Lots of vehicle tracks and footprints. Looks like people go out to the creek on a regular basis for one reason or another. Impressions were taken, but most of the tracks were too messed up to be useful. Nothing else showed up until they found Tim's car at the airport." Hal sighed, long and heavy. "They've checked outgoing flights, but Tim wasn't listed. Canvassing employees at all the airlines is a big task. The only thing we have to go on is the time the car arrived in the lot. The surveillance camera shows the visor down over the driver's seat and a man with sunglasses and a baseball cap behind the wheel. The quality's poor. You're welcome to come in and try to ID the man. He's got the same coloring and build as Tim, but I'd stake my career it's not him."

"I doubt it is, either." The words Brian had refused to utter came out in a rush. "I think my brother's dead."

Unwilling to let Hal see his emotional meltdown, Brian turned away. He fought for control and found none. For one horrifying moment, he thought he was going to break down completely. He gulped in air and tried to put some distance between himself and Hal. Big mistake. Disoriented in the darkness, he tripped where tree roots had split and lifted the blacktop.

Hal grabbed him. Brian reacted instinctively, jerking away and falling against the chain link fence. The metal bit into his flesh, but he used the support to regain his balance. Slowly and reluctantly, he turned to face his supervisor.

Hal stood on the other side of the Camaro. Brian rubbed his smarting elbow. "I didn't mean to do that."

"I know," Shaw said.

One night, after a particularly difficult case had been solved and the squad had gone to blow off steam at McGinty's Tavern, Brian had told Hal about being beaten by his stepfather, who resented having a child around who wasn't his own. His supervisor sat quietly listening while they sipped draft beers and had never brought the subject back up.

The lieutenant stared across the lot at the American Flag snapping energetically on the side of the copy shop across the alleyway from Finnegan's. "Don't believe Tim's dead until there's concrete proof," he said. "You know better than anyone he's been too slick to catch."

"No one's indestructible, Hal." Brian looked up to see clouds scudding across a hazy moon. "They just think they are."

He'd made the mistake of thinking he was invincible himself. But in less than two weeks, his world had fallen apart.

He decided he didn't care if he lost his job or ended up in jail, as long as Tim was alive and well. If his brother was sunbathing and drinking tequila in Mexico, that would be fine with him.

"I've gotta go," Hal said. "I'll keep you posted, whatever happens. Screw IAB."

"Thanks, I appreciate it." Brian watched Hal walk toward the Accord. "I'll be investigating, too," he said. "If I come up with anything, I'll let you know."

Hal turned on his heel. "You'd better," he warned, his tone all business and authority again.

"Yeah, yeah." Brian waved.

"Fuck you," Hal said.

CHAPTER TWENTY-EIGHT

Brian pulled onto the expressway. He hated reminiscing, but his brother's disappearance kept dredging up memories he thought he had buried for good. The emotions he had kept in check for so many years were all bubbling toward the surface, and he knew he couldn't go to Bannisters until he dealt with them.

As he kept pace with the traffic flow, he reluctantly allowed his mind to drift back to that last day in Baton Rouge. He'd left home for good the day the window broke, before his step-father arrived home from work to discover the damage. Brian had told his mother to place the blame on him and tell her husband she had no idea what started the fight. He was sixteen, and he was afraid he was going to kill his step-father the next time the man lifted his fists to any of them.

He still remembered the tears on his mother's face. She had wanted Brian to finish high school, get a job and take them to a safe place away from the violence. For years, he had told himself he was long past feeling regrets, but tonight, he couldn't shake the emptiness and a wish that his mother had been more courageous and independent.

Her one act of true defiance had been to run out the door behind him, press $40 into his hand and tell him to buy a bus ticket to Miami, where his cousin, Harry, lived. Brian knew she had given him the grocery money for the week, but Tim said he could cover the loss. Brian didn't need to ask how. Tim had been shoplifting for years to supplement the family's meals because Ed Madison drank away most of his paycheck.

Brian felt his muscles tighten. The beating he had taken two days before was only slightly worse than the ones he had endured at the hands of his step-father. He had willingly borne the brunt of Ed's assaults, but after he left, as his brother put it. "Ed made up for lost time with me and mom, and then some."

Brian eased his grip on the steering wheel as his fingers cramped. Whenever he felt frustrated or angry with Tim, he reminded himself how those years on Webber Street had adversely affected his brother and his mother as much as they had him. He reasoned that although he'd left that day, they had endured another three years of beatings while he got on his feet and paid their bus fares to Miami.

Bringing his focus back to the present, he found he had automatically returned to the marina. He parked, turned off the ignition and pulled back the seat.

He stared up at the roof of the Camaro. If only he could have sent for Tim and their mother earlier, maybe things would have turned out differently, but he had barely managed to keep off the streets himself until he got a job unloading cargo at the docks and joined the union.

Brian wondered what would have happened if he hadn't become friends with a couple of beat cops. They convinced him to get his GED, which ultimately led him to the academy and a better life. But right after he graduated and began walking the beat himself, his mother became seriously ill. *They never got a break.*

He took a long drink from the bottle of Jim Beam. The tension eased from his body as fire wound its way to his belly. The only selfless thing his brother had ever done was to quit his job at the local supermarket so he could take care of their mother. She died two years after arriving in Miami. Tim took her death the hardest.

Brian looked at the Jim Beam, twisted the top back on and shoved it under the seat. He had too many bitter memories of bailing Tim out and paying his fines after fights had landed him in court for public intoxication. They didn't need another member of the family under arrest, that time for a DUI.

Tim had gone to AA meetings and sobered up after a while. But after scraping through high school, a short stint in community college ended when Tim got bored. He became a drain on Brian's limited funds as well as a discipline problem. He stayed out all night and slept all day. Brian kicked his brother out.

A couple of months later, Brian spotted him getting into a new Jaguar. He discovered Tim was driving a reputed member of the Cuban mafia around town. The liaison didn't last long, but from then on, Tim could always be found on the fringes of Miami's criminal circle. He dressed well and drove expensive cars, although he continued to live in the same dingy building Brian had visited only the day before.

Brian made good on the promise he had made to his mother as he moved up the ranks. Tim kept getting into trouble. Brian kept getting his brother out of it.

A couple walked past the car, their voices starting Brian out of his reverie. He looked at his watch. 12:30AM. Kaylen's club didn't close until 2:00AM. He turned the ignition back on.

CHAPTER TWENTY-NINE

Kaylen stood beside a table filled with patrons from one of George's favorite charities. She beckoned Marvin over. "Champagne for my friends, please. On the house." He nodded and walked quickly away.

"Thank you, Kaylen. Wonderful club. We'll be back often." Beyond the warm glow of the small lamp in the center of the table, a man with buzz-cut hair and dark eyes that sadly reminded her of Tim's, raised his half-empty wine glass to her, and the seven people seated with him followed suit.

"I'll hold you to that." Kaylen smiled at Tony Jimenez. "All of you," she added, glancing around the table. "I can't promise free champagne every time you come, but you'll always get the royal treatment for special occasions." She left them and walked toward the next table.

Sam weaved his way toward her through the throng. "See," he said loudly, when they were only a table apart. "I told you there was no need to worry. I've got this place running on smooth wheels."

A ripple of annoyance passed through Kaylen. Now all the diners within range of his booming voice thought he was in charge of Bannisters.

"Thanks again for stepping in while I was ill," she told him, trying hard to keep her voice from rising. "But now I'm perfectly capable of taking care of the club myself. You'll be able to relax for a change, Sam. You work far too hard at your own restaurant to come here in the evenings and try to help me out."

When he started to protest, she cut him off quickly, but with a smile. "Why don't you take a break? Have a brandy and a cigar while I visit with my

181

customers." She sat in the only empty chair at the table beside her and beamed at the twenty-somethings occupying the other seats, the men wearing black dinner jackets, their dates dressed in black and white sleeveless dresses. They looked like they had stopped by the club on the way to some job that required uniforms. "So, how are you enjoying yourselves?" she asked. "I'm Kaylen Roberts, the owner of Bannisters. Welcome to my club."

Their enthusiastic responses came in a chorus. Kaylen watched Sam as he stalked over to the bar and spoke briefly to Julio, the bartender, before giving her a reproachful look. She avoided his gaze and tried to appear interested in the compliments paid to her club, her hair and her dress, but she continued to watch him from the corner of her eye. Brandy in hand, he took a brief cell phone call and headed for the lobby, an unlit cigar in his mouth.

Kaylen knew there would be an argument as soon as the club closed that night. Sam wanted Bannisters badly, and she had better try to curb her temper. If she alienated him, he might badmouth her to her backers. As soon as that thought arrived, she reproached herself. How could she think Sam was trying to do her harm? His biggest problem was a control issue. Hers was having a mentor for whom she had once worked. The more secure she became, the more he wanted to put her into a position of dependence. She could never repay his kindness, generosity, guidance and emotional support. But, she wasn't about to let him run her life, business *or* personal. She wondered how she was going to handle the dilemma diplomatically, when all she wanted to do was tell him to go manage his own failing business instead of trying to meddle in hers.

"Ms. Roberts?"

She blinked at the young man sitting next to her. "Sorry. What did you say?"

"I asked if you'd like to join us in a glass of wine."

Another man on the opposite side, his tie askew and a lock of sandy hair falling over one eye, raised a bottle of Merlot.

Kaylen's feet ached and Sam needed to cool off. "Sure." She watched as the glass in front of her was filled to the brim.

Wine cascaded over her fingers as she raised her glass. Purple droplets stained the white table cloth. "Cheers," she said.

"To you, Ms. Roberts," they chorused. "And to the continued success of Bannisters," added a girl with copper curls and a low-cut, strapless white dress.

Bernie Draper's Orchestra swung into a rousing rendition of "Ragtime." Kaylen glanced surreptitiously at her watch and slid her aching feet out of her sandals. 1:00AM. She wished she had worn the flat shoes after all.

CHAPTER THIRTY

Finding a "FULL" sign blocking the entrance to Bannisters' parking lot, Brian had to cruise around the block twice before he found space on the street. He gently eased the Camaro between an old convertible with a disintegrating rag top and a Ford Focus sporting a large dent on the left side.

He reached into the back seat for his black jacket. His groping hand found nothing but upholstery. He got out of the car and looked on the floor, under the front seats and even in the trunk before he really believed it was missing.

It wasn't worth much, so why would anyone steal it? He thought about the short period of time he had left William Hastings on the *Destiny*. Maybe the captain had taken perverse pleasure in throwing it overboard. Brian wondered if he would be allowed inside Bannisters while wearing a white dress shirt with a plain black tie and beige pants. Maybe they kept a couple of jackets around for people like him. *Or maybe not.*

As he walked along a deserted sidewalk lined with darkened storefront windows, he tried to fathom why Tim had wanted to meet outside Kaylen's condo. If Tim's apartment was clean, his car empty and his girlfriend wasn't holding a key to some magical lockbox, then he had to alter his way of thinking.

Tim never acted in a linear manner. Since childhood, he had loved to drive Brian crazy with his convoluted schemes. Why would this time be any different? Images of a naked Kaylen came to him. Visions of her trying to cover herself with a tattered black dress. That rose tattoo on her flawless thigh.

Annoyed honking told him he had strayed off the sidewalk and was about to cross the crowded thoroughfare without any regard for his safety. He waved at the irate driver and made his way to the crosswalk. Tim was a total prick.

Brian waited impatiently for the light to change. Tim may have placed them in bed together for more than his perverse pleasure. If so, then Kaylen's tattoo might not have been left only as a lasting souvenir of her relationship with him. Brian decided he had better get a closer look at it.

But how he was going to convince Kaylen to cooperate was another matter. She would never lift the hem of one of those figure-hugging cocktail dresses to voluntarily show him her thigh, except in his dreams. An obvious thought occurred to him, but he wasn't going to take advantage of her vulnerability to get her back into bed just so he could see that damned tattoo.

And that had to be the only reason for getting her into bed again, he told himself firmly. Kaylen Roberts was so far out of his league, it was laughable to even consider she might be interested in him unless she was too scared out of her wits to care whose arms she had around her.

He strode up to the club entrance behind four men dressed in tuxes, their female companions clicking alongside in high heels and black dresses. A stout figure stepped out the front door and stopped in front of the two men guarding the entrance as Brian walked up to the ropes. *Sam Wilson,* Brian thought, seeing cigar smoke curling into the air. At least Wilson knew him, even if he didn't seem to like him very much.

"Hi," Brian said, looking from the muscle-bound men blocking the door to Sam. "I've lost my jacket. Can I borrow one? I need to go inside and talk to Ms. Roberts."

Each over six feet tall, the two men formed a formidable barrier. They looked at Sam for orders and continued barring the doorway, arms crossed, legs planted wide.

"No jacket, no entry," Sam said. "We don't provide patrons with jackets. Guests of Bannisters know the dress code and come in tuxes."

"I got in the other night," Brian said. "I wasn't wearing a tux then."

"We tightened the rules after that. You got into a brawl at the bar."

"I didn't start it." Brian forced himself to relax. No sense in antagonizing any of these guys, or he wouldn't get to see Kaylen at all

"Ms. Roberts doesn't want to see you anymore." Sam drew deeply on his cigar and blew a suffocating cloud of smoke right at Brian. "She's staying with me, and I'm providing her with security. Your services, if you could call them that, aren't required."

Brian managed to avoid breathing in the smoke and swore under his breath. Wilson knew about his fractured ribs, the son of a bitch, and how much pain coughing would cause. "I'm not a security guard," he snarled, "I'm a ...," he stopped himself, "...a charter boat captain," he finished.

"Well, then, you're absolutely useless." Sam dropped the cigar and ground it out beneath his heel.

To Brian, the implication was unmistakable. Sam wanted to crush him like the cigar. Despite his resolve not to let the guy push his buttons, Brian's fists clenched. The guards moved forward.

No more fighting, Brian thought. His body couldn't take it. Normally, being outnumbered and unarmed wouldn't have made him think twice, but the events of the last couple of days had made him more cautious.

What would getting into a brawl accomplish? Kaylen coming out to save his ass again, if she heard the commotion? He'd never get any closer to Wilson than he was at that moment, and in his already-weakened state, he probably wouldn't even land one good punch on either of those guards. He had her cell phone number. He'd call her later, after the club closed.

"You can't stop me seeing her," he told Sam. "She came to the boat today. We're friends."

"Kaylen doesn't need friends like you. She's upset and confused." Sam's gravelly voice lowered even further. "Stay away from her."

Brian turned to leave as a group of chattering people got out of a limo. The bouncers stood aside and allowed them to enter while Brian walked back to his car. He had to bump both vehicles to get out of the parking space, then hit the gas pedal hard. The car peeled off down the street.

He fought his anger. He'd been treated like dirt. He drove onto the closest freeway. Maybe if he cruised around for a while, he'd calm down. If he'd still had his badge, they wouldn't have kept him out, jacket or no jacket.

Frustration joined his anger, simmering so close to the surface that it took everything he had not to push the needle past 80 miles an hour. Luckily, traffic stayed light and he didn't run into any cruisers.

He drove out to Pembroke Pines, saw the gauge had dropped to "E" and pulled off the highway into a gas station with a little convenience store, where he filled the tank and bought a cup of strong coffee. He pulled out his wallet and realized he barely had enough money to cover his purchases. After donating to the Ella O'Grady rent fund twice in as many days, his cash reserves were dwindling fast. He looked at his watch. 2:45AM. He'd been driving around for over an hour, and he had a charter early in the morning. His anger at a more manageable level than when he left Kaylen's club, he turned back toward Coconut Grove and sipped the acrid brew he had purchased under the label of Regular Grind.

His cell phone rang as he approached the exit for the Grove.

"Brian, it's Hal."

Brian swerved onto the shoulder. "What's up?"

"You'd better come to the department."

"You've got news about Tim?"

Hal's voice sounded low and guarded. "There have been some developments. You want me to send a squad car to pick you up?"

"No." Brian heard traffic whizzing past, then the blast of an eighteen wheeler's horn. He realized he had stepped on the gas and was back on the freeway. "I'm on my way."

He quickly checked his rearview mirror before gunning the motor, the speedometer rising rapidly as he headed for the interchange and the trip back into Miami.

CHAPTER THIRTY-ONE

Kaylen pushed open the door of the all-night cafe and glanced around. Sandy waved from a booth in the back as a waiter armed with a large menu stepped forward.

"I'm joining a friend," Kaylen told him. "I can seat myself." She took the menu from his hands. "I'd love a Diet Coke."

The young man smiled, his shoulders visibly relaxing. "Coming right up."

Kaylen smiled back. "Long night, huh?"

He rolled his eyes. "And a biology test at eight in the morning." He walked off toward the bussing area.

"Hi, kid." Sandy folded the newspaper she had spread across the table and laid it beside her on the bench. "You look more tired than my feet feel, if that's possible." One bare foot emerged from the booth and her toes wiggled, the frosted pale pink nail polish glittering. "These puppies have been in use from two o'clock this afternoon. They passed barking and went into howling after the dinner rush."

"I know what you mean." Kaylen slid her own feet out of her tight shoes. "I don't know what possessed me to wear three-inch heels tonight."

Sandy raised her eyebrows. "Are you nuts? You never wear heels that high unless you're trying to impress the hell out of someone. Are you?" She grinned. "What about that guy you met?"

"Brian?" Kaylen shook her head. "I don't think there's much that would impress him. No, and he stood me up. He was supposed to come to the club tonight."

The waiter brought her drink.

She glanced at his badge. "How's the BLT here, Eli?"

"Okay." He looked pleased that she had actually taken the time to read his name. "But the club sandwich is better," he said, pen poised over notepad. "There's also a really good corn chowder, with biscuits made from scratch."

"Sandy?" Kaylen looked at her friend, whose forehead had crinkled into a frown of concentration usually reserved for life-changing decisions.

"What about splitting a club sandwich and each of us having a cup of that chowder?" Sandy suggested. "We should probably skip the biscuits, though. Too fattening."

"Sounds like a plan." Kaylen handed Eli her menu.

Eli scribbled on his notepad, stuck the pen back behind his ear and walked off at a rapid pace.

"If his suggestions are good and he keeps up the service, I may have to take him away from all this," Kaylen said. "We had to fire three wait staff tonight. I caught one eating in the middle of the dinner rush while another left two tables of patrons without any attention for close to twenty minutes. The third dropped a tray of food onto the kitchen floor and blamed one of the *sous* chefs." She sucked greedily on her straw and half-emptied the glass.

Sandy made conciliatory noises.

"I guess dropping the tray wasn't enough for him, either," Kaylen said. "He also tipped a woman's Peach Melba right into her lap."

"What a nightmare." Sandy finished her coffee and toyed with the handle of the mug. "Did she make a big scene?"

"No, thank goodness. I apologized profusely and promised to pick up the cleaning cost. Her dress may be ruined. If so, then I'll pay for a replacement."

"With your luck, it's probably a designer piece," Sandy said.

"Don't even go there." Kaylen shook her head. "I also picked up the bar tabs on the two tables with the long wait." She sighed and leaned against the back of the booth. "It was an expensive evening, and a stressful one, too."

"That's club ownership for you." Sandy said. "All the decisions, all the headaches, all the bills."

Kaylen shrugged. "Even after those incidents, I still love it. I needed a challenge, and now I've got it. I just wish Sam wouldn't be such a thorn in my side. He's become so pushy and…," she searched for the right word, "…overbearing."

"He sounds like your father," Sandy offered.

"There's a lot of that going around these days." Kaylen poked her straw into the ice cubes and finished the rest of her drink.

"How so?" Sandy pushed her empty mug aside as Eli served steaming cups of chowder and exchanged Kaylen's empty glass for a full one.

"I seem to have spent the entire day with domineering men." Kaylen sampled the chowder. "Mmm. Eli's right, it's really good. I may have to steal the cook, too."

"Would you stop workin' and start dishin'?" Sandy laughed at Kaylen's expression. "You're a diner here, not an employment scout."

"That's true. I have to unwind, and you're the person to do it with."

Kaylen felt the tension slide from her shoulders as they ate and chatted about Sandy's new job, sharing her wardrobe until Kaylen's clothes were replaced, and going on a shopping expedition together. But talking about shopping brought up visions of Rosa, Tim's disappearance, and her homeless situation. She felt toast from the club sandwich sticking in her throat. She started choking and grabbed her soda.

Sandy toyed with a French fry, twirling it around in the ketchup at the edge of her plate. "I shouldn't have mentioned the clothes," she said when Kaylen set down her empty glass. "I'll help you, girlfriend. We'll put your life back together. Sam will help, too. He cares so much about you."

"He cares too much, sometimes, Sandy. He treats me like I'm still new to the business and working for him at his restaurant." Kaylen thought about him caressing her in the office. "Other times, he tries to step over the line from friend and mentor to acting like he's my boyfriend or something." She shuddered. "It started right before the club opened. And since Tim's been missing, it's gotten worse. He hugged me tonight and put his hands all over my back. That's not like Sam."

"I'm sure he only meant to comfort you," Sandy said, her expression troubled, her voice a little sharper than necessary.

Kaylen sat back. She hadn't expected what sounded like a rebuke. "You weren't there," she pointed out. "His touch wasn't that of a friend. I *do* know the difference."

"Do you?" Sandy folded her arms, her eyes glittering in sharp contrast to their usual friendly sparkle. "You never seem to do anything, but you've got scores of guys chasing you all over the place."

"That's not…," Kaylen began, but Sandy wasn't finished.

"You had Tim," she said. She raised one arm and snapped her fingers, like she was a magician. "Now suddenly he's missing, and you're telling me about this new guy, Brian, wanting you."

Kaylen felt very defensive. *What was the matter with Sandy?* "You make it sound like I had something to do with Tim's disappearance."

Sandy made a dismissive noise; like Kaylen shouldn't be surprised anyone would think that.

"As if *that* wasn't enough…," Sandy rapped her knuckles on the table for emphasis, "…now you're imagining Sam's got ulterior motives, for God's sake." She leaned forward. "Get real, girl—not every man in town is after your bod. Especially not Sam Wilson."

"What's gotten into you?" Kaylen felt as though she had been slapped in the face. *Sandy of all people scolding her? Defending Sam as though she…she…* "You're in love with him," Kaylen said, incredulous.

"With who?" It was Sandy's turn to sound defensive, her eyes opening wide. "Sam?" She laughed, quick and brittle. "Are you nuts?"

"No, I'm not. That's one thing you could never accuse me of being. Stupid, maybe. Gullible, absolutely. But nuts? No."

"Sam Wilson doesn't want the likes of me," Sandy said. Now she sounded downright angry. "He wants class and money. I don't have either. So why would I waste my time falling in love with someone who won't love me back?"

A thought so incredibly egotistical came to Kaylen that she tried to dismiss it, but it refused to leave her head. If Sam couldn't have her, would he take a substitute who looked marginally like her? Nonsense, she assured herself. Absolute garbage. But an ice-cold tremor ran up her back when she looked across the table at her friend and really *saw* how much Sandy had changed her appearance over the last few months.

Sandy shook her head, the brown curls bouncing. "I'm not interested in Sam. Never was, never will be."

Then why did you change the color and style of your hair to look more like mine? Kaylen thought.

"Didn't we just have that conversation about me liking your new manager, Rob?" Sandy laughed again, the sound forced, mirthless. "What's the matter with you?"

"I'm learning to be paranoid," Kaylen said. She thought about the changed color palette of Sandy's clothes. The change of jobs to move into a managerial position at the new restaurant much further away from home, and with longer shifts and less benefits. Maybe *not* so paranoid.

She couldn't spend another minute in her friend's company. The questions popping into her head sounded accusatory and ridiculous. But if she asked Sandy why she had changed everything about her appearance and even changed her job, Kaylen knew that Sandy's lies would finish that friendship for good. So instead, she grabbed her purse and jammed her protesting feet back into the high-heeled shoes.

"Look, Sandy, I'm really sorry if I'm offending you, but I can't think straight tonight." She pulled $50 out of her purse and laid it on the table beside the check. "I really appreciate you meeting me for dinner, because it's the first real food I've eaten since the night Bannisters opened, but I'm leaving." She slid out of the booth and stood up. "I've got a lot of thinking to do."

"You're not coming home?" Sandy looked worried, suddenly. She grabbed Kaylen's wrist. "Look, I'm sorry if I said anything to upset you, K.T. I know you're tired and overwhelmed. Let's go back to the apartment and sleep. You'll feel better in the morning, I promise."

Kaylen had to pry Sandy's fingers off her. They left a blanched spot that quickly turned red. "No, thanks." She rubbed her smarting flesh. "I'll be okay. I just need to be alone for a while."

"Where the hell are you planning to go at this hour of the morning?" Sandy glanced at the check. "You've left too much money. At least let me get the tip and give you some change."

"It's on me tonight," Kaylen said, conscious that her voice held a slight tremor.

Sandy had called her K. T. Sandy had never, ever called Kaylen by George's nickname. Only Sam had insisted on perpetuating that. A distinct feeling of unease swept over her. Eli had seen her get up and came over when she beckoned.

"Take this," she told him, handing him the money and the check. "And this." She took out her business card, managed to scribble Rob's name on the back without her hand shaking too noticeably and thrust the card at him. "Call tomorrow afternoon at three and ask for him."

Eli turned the card back over and studied the raised lettering on the front. "Bannisters?" He looked surprised. "You're Kaylen Roberts?" His cheeks turned pink, and he almost dropped the card. "Ms. Roberts, your new club is…"

"Yes, I know. It's really popular. The pay and the tips will be better than here. Rob's the manager. Call him." She gave Eli a quick but wobbly smile, more to convince Sandy she was at ease than anything else. "It'll be worth your time." She turned toward the door.

"Kaylen, we're not finished." Sandy slid out of the booth.

"I'm sure we're not, but I can't do this right now."

Without giving her friend a chance to say anything else, Kaylen walked swiftly out of the café, her thoughts so disturbing that she dropped her keys right beside her car.

"Damn it to *hell.*" Mindful of her tight dress, she carefully stooped to retrieve them. When she straightened up, she watched Sandy get into a red Mercedes convertible and back out of the parking space without giving her another glance.

Now where in holy hell had Sandy gotten the money to buy that?

Kaylen's cell phone rang.

CHAPTER THIRTY-TWO

Escorted by a uniformed officer, Brian walked into Hal Shaw's office at 4:00AM.

"Thanks, Rodriguez." Hal stood. "Shut the door on your way out, would you?"

The officer nodded and closed the door, leaving Brian and Hal alone.

"Have a seat." Hal pointed to the chair in front of his desk.

"I'll stand." Brian didn't like the tight-jawed look on Hal's tired face. "What's the news?"

"The creek got pumped because of the storm coming in…"

"Cut the crap, Hal."

"Fair enough." Shaw's shoulders sagged. "We found Tim. His body had gotten wedged under the roots of a Mangrove tree. That's why the divers missed it before."

Brian had thought he was prepared for Tim to be found dead, but as soon as Hal spoke, he realized he wasn't. His legs went out from under him, and he fell into the chair he had refused only moments before.

"I'm so sorry, Brian," he heard faintly against the rushing in his ears. He tried employing the same techniques he had so flippantly told Hastings to use when he became seasick on the *Destiny*.

Take a deep breath.

His brother was gone. No more arguments, no more laughs, no more getting Tim out of yet another scrape.

Breathe out.

No more of Tim's annoying, disrupting but always stimulating presence.

Brian felt hollow, sickened, dizzy. Hot and cold, all at once. His heart seemed to have dropped to his feet and taken his chest along with it.

Breathe in.

Hal was still speaking. "This isn't what either of us hoped for," he said. "But with his apartment and car dusted clean, we also knew the outcome probably wasn't going to be good."

Brian abandoned the deep breathing techniques.

Hal brought him a bottle of water. "Wish I had something stronger," he said. "Christ, you're as white as a fucking sheet." He pushed the intercom. "Gabe, where the hell are you?"

A muffled voice answered, "Right here."

"Bring in two cups of black coffee," Hal said. "And try to dig up some booze. Check Verne's bottom drawer."

"Lieutenant, you know how Detective Vernon...," Gabe began.

"Yeah, I know, but screw his privacy. If the drawer's locked, I'll give you the master key."

Brian took a mouthful of water. "Tim's body. Is it still at the creek?"

"For another hour at least," Hal said. "Then it'll be brought in for autopsy. Preliminary findings weren't easy, because of the..." He stopped.

"You don't need to sugar-coat things for me." Brian looked down at his shoes. "I know what goes on." He started to peel the label off the water bottle. *Anything to keep his hands busy.*

"We're not talking about a stranger, Brian. You won't be able to detach yourself."

A knock on the door announced the arrival of Gabe Weston, the clerk. He delivered two steaming mugs of coffee with a sideways glance at Brian. His boyish face looked uncharacteristically haggard, blond brows drawn together under a mop of sun-bleached hair.

"I heard about your brother, Sergeant," he said. "I'm really sorry." He put the mugs on the desk and slid a flask out of his pocket. "Lieutenant, reporters are already gathering downstairs as well as at the recovery site. I'm keeping out anyone who doesn't belong in the squad room."

Hal took the flask and opened his bottom drawer. "Keep it that way until I tell you otherwise," he told Gabe. "Anyone's brought in for questioning, the detectives are to take them in through the side door. If the press gets wind of Tim's identity before we're ready to release a statement, I'll find out who leaked the info, and they're suspended without pay. Pass the word."

Gabe nodded vigorously. "Yes, sir."

Hal rummaged around and produced a Styrofoam cup. "Thanks, Gabe." He shut the drawer with a decisive click.

The clerk took the hint and left the room.

"Hold my calls unless there's an update from the creek," Hal said before the door quietly closed.

He poured liquor into the cup and handed it to Brian. "Here. This'll take the edge off."

Brian took a sip and fought a desire to gag. "I want to go out to the creek."

"You can't. You know that. You're…"

"On administrative leave. You don't have to keep beatin' me over the head with that." Brian slid the cup onto Hal's desk. "I can't drink this. I'll puke."

Hal pitched the container into the trash. "I wasn't going to say anything about your suspension. I was going to remind you that as a family member, you're not allowed at a crime scene."

Brian ran a hand over his face. It felt numb, like it didn't belong to him. "Yeah, I suppose so."

"You should go home," Hal said. "Is there anyone I can call for you?"

Brian shook his head. "You know better than that." He shifted around on the chair. "I'll need to make arrangements. How long do you think the coroner's gonna keep him?"

"Several hours. I'll have a better idea when the crime unit finishes and the bod…he's brought in. Do you want me to find somewhere you can wait instead of driving back to the Grove?"

"No. I'll wait on the boat." Brian stared into his coffee, like it was going to tell him who had killed Tim. "I want whoever did this found fast."

"I've put Mills and Browning on the case," Hal said. "With you out of commission, they're the best I've got."

Brian tried sipping the coffee, but it tasted almost as bad as the scotch. "Any preliminaries?" he asked. "Was he shot?"

Hal took a sip of his own coffee, grimaced and pushed it aside. "Looks like he was in the water the last four days, so there was decomp. Cause of death wasn't easy to determine. If the creek hadn't been so swollen, we probably would have found him sooner. The pumping sent the level down, and a patrolman on the bank spotted him."

"You'll call me as soon as the coroner finishes?"

"The minute it happens."

Brian stood up and made for the door. He had to get out of the building before the pressure cooker inside him blew.

"Let me get you a ride at least." Hal picked up the phone.

"No. I'm okay."

"You're sure?"

"Damn it, Hal. How many times do I have to tell you?"

"All right." Hal put the phone back down. "Call Franklin's Funeral Home after you get back to the boat. They're good. Discreet. Tell them you'll let them know when your brother's body's released."

Brian nodded. He opened the office door. Ignoring the pitying glances of three detectives working at their desks, he walked quickly across the squad-room.

"Goodbye, Sergeant," Gabe said as Brian passed. The phone rang and he picked it up, but Brian felt Gabe's wide brown eyes watching him all the way out the door.

As soon as he left the squad room behind, Brian sped up. He pushed the door to the stairwell so hard, the resulting crash rang down the hallway. By the time he hit the bottom of the stairs, he was running despite the discomfort to his ribs. He left the stale atmosphere of the precinct for the clammy night air of the parking lot. Bile rose up his throat, sending him on an all-out dash for the bushes behind his car. He vomited until nothing else remained in his stomach, after which he endured miserable dry heaves for a while.

When those quit, he leaned against the Camaro until his head stopped spinning and he could lower himself into the car. The enormity of Tim's loss weighed him down. He allowed all the guilt and recriminations to flow over him.

Several times over the last few months, Hastings and Shaw had both warned him that the only way he could keep Tim out of escalating trouble was to get his brother to leave Miami. But Tim had refused, telling Brian to butt out of his life. Brian knew he should have tried harder, but he had become so involved with fighting for reinstatement and trying to figure out how to pay his bills, he had slammed out of Tim's apartment and stayed out.

What a stupid, stubborn idiot, Brian thought, but he wasn't sure if he meant Tim or himself. He was as bad at asking for help as his brother. Maybe that's why he had ended up on administrative leave, as Internal Affairs liked to phrase it. Maybe stubborn and stupid behavior had not only caused his own problems, but also Tim's death.

Brian stared into the darkness. Tim had always done what he wanted with his life. No compromises, no regrets, and certainly no thoughts about consequences. He never listened to any advice that involved putting a dent in his lifestyle, even after he knew that he had fallen out of grace with the cartel.

Mindful of the vans setting up shop outside the main doors of the precinct, Brian drove slowly away. No sense in drawing attention to himself. He had no intention of becoming fodder for any of the local TV news broadcasts.

His mind filled with memories of Tim as he drove back to the marina. He pulled in at what should have been daybreak, but ominously dark clouds obscured the rising sun. An unsettling glow illuminated the *Destiny's* windows. Brian shook off a feeling of impending doom. A tropical storm was bearing down, not an apocalypse because his brother had been murdered.

He hurried below deck, stripped off his clothes and took a shower, punishing his body with frigidly cold water. Finally, the grief left and rage took its place, boiling freely and making him immune to the icy needles.

He toweled off quickly, brushed his teeth and gargled with mouthwash to get the sour taste out of his mouth before getting dressed. He hesitated over whether to take more Vicodin, but decided slowed reactions were better than painful ribs.

He concealed his gun under a windbreaker and pocketed clips. On the way out, he grabbed the baseball bat. It felt good in his hand and might even keep him from shooting the truth out of people. He headed for the dock.

Jim glanced up from his preparations for the coming storm. He held a length of rope in his hands and a pile of gear lay at his feet, ready to stow below deck. He dropped the rope and came over to the rail closest to the *Destiny*. "Where are you going in such a hurry?" he asked.

"No place you need to worry about." Brian was in no mood to chit-chat with his neighbor. He had heads to break.

"Well, okay. None of my beeswax. But unless you plan to be back soon, you're cutting it fine to get your boat ready for the storm."

"I've got something more important to take care of than the *Destiny*."

Brian had never thought he'd find anything more pressing than attending to his boat, but at that moment, all he could think about was tracking down the people responsible for Tim's death. He gripped the bat harder.

"In that case, you want me to batten down the *Destiny* for you when I'm finished over here?" Jim asked.

Brian hadn't expected an offer of help. He noticed Jim wore a pair of shabby jeans and a faded t-shirt. If his trim and neat neighbor had abandoned his ironing, the storm must be coming faster and harder than he thought. "Thanks," he said. "I'd appreciate it. I've got something to do that can't wait."

"You be careful," Jim said. "I'd sure miss you if you weren't around."

When was the last time anyone had told him he'd be missed if something happened to him? Brian asked himself. He couldn't remember. People might respect his skills, but they sure didn't care for his abrupt manner, and frequently he thought they were relieved when he left. He brought Jim his spare set of keys.

"Thanks," he said, tossing them over.

Jim easily caught them. "I mean it." He leaned on the rail. "Can I do anything else to help you out?"

"No. This is personal."

"You need to calm down a tad before you leave," Jim said. "What's got you so riled up?"

"Somebody killed my brother."

Jim shook his head slowly, side to side. "I'm real sorry to hear that, Brian.

My condolences." He maintained eye contact, his gaze steady. "That's a tough rap. But do you seriously think you can get answers by swinging a bat at someone's head?"

"Maybe. If I swing at the right person."

"You'll end up in jail. I don't think your brother would want that."

"He'd want his killer brought to justice."

Jim stared at him across the narrow divide between the boats as they rocked on the swell. "You're way too hot right now. Come over and have a cup of coffee. We can talk things out until you're calmer."

"I don't *want* to calm down. Staying angry will keep me focused."

"It'll screw up your objectivity," Jim said. "You'll only hear what you want to hear, not the truth."

"I don't need or want a fuckin' lecture, Jim." Brian turned away.

"You know, I saw your brother here about a week ago," Jim said.

Brian swung back to face him. "Doing what?"

"He was walking around on deck." Jim's brow furrowed. "His name was Tim, right?"

Brian nodded. "Yeah, Tim Madison. We're…," he stopped and corrected himself. "We were half-brothers. Why didn't you tell me you saw him?"

"He said he'd made a mistake and forgotten where he was supposed to meet you. Asked me not to tell you, because he didn't want you to think he was stupid."

Tim was on the Destiny a week ago? Brian realized it was only a few days after he had stormed out of his brother's apartment

"Nice young feller," Jim said. "Good sense of humor. Able to laugh at himself."

"Sometimes." Brian remembered Tim's big laugh. He shoved the image away before the grief bubbled back up.

"Why don't you let the police handle this?" Jim asked. "They'd be a lot more effective."

"The fuck they would."

Jim tut-tutted. "That's your anger and grief talking. For God's sake, Brian, come over here, and you can vent all you want."

"I'm not just some jackass blowin' off steam," Brian said. "I'm a fuckin' detective with Miami-Dade. I'm not waitin' around while some bastard gets away with Tim's murder." He left Jim staring after him and strode onto the dock, where people gave him a lot of space.

Brian shoved the Camaro into gear and headed for Little Havana. He knew where most of the lowlifes in his brother's circle hung out. Screw Jim and his pissing coffee. Screw Hal Shaw and his directive to keep out of things. The cops had done nothing more in the last week than find Tim's rotting corpse.

Brian pushed his foot down hard on the accelerator as the first raindrops of Tropical Storm Norman spattered the Camaro's windshield.

CHAPTER THIRTY-THREE

Kaylen drove distractedly toward Coral Gables and Coconut Grove, her mind mulling over the dinner conversation and putting innuendos into everything Sandy had said.

She reprimanded herself for becoming totally paranoid. Suddenly, she was looking at her friends with suspicion, like they were all members of some conspiracy. She told herself to stop it immediately. But the memory of Sandy getting into that red Mercedes was too vivid.

Kaylen's cell phone rang.

"Hi, honey," Sam said.

"Hi, Sam." Kaylen wondered if he was calling to tell her off again. She knew she didn't sound excited to hear him, but she was too tired to care, and she still didn't know where she was going to spend the rest of the night.

"Where are you?" he asked.

"I'm about to do some cruising. I had a really late supper with Sandy."

"Why aren't you headed back for her apartment?"

Alarm bells went off in her head. "Why would I be?"

"Well…," the phone stayed silent long enough for her to wonder if the signal had faded. "…I'm thinking that's where you're staying, that's all," Sam said.

"I told you I wasn't giving out that piece of information to anyone."

So much for hiding out at Sandy's place, Kaylen thought. Even if she wasn't part of a conspiracy, Sandy was definitely a blabbermouth.

At least Kaylen knew where she was *not* going to spend that night, or any other, either. When she was sure Sandy had left for work the following afternoon, she'd pick up her belongings and live out of her car. She could always shower at work and store her clothes and makeup there, too.

"I'm not just anyone," Sam grumbled. "Although you're treating me more and more like some damned stranger who's in your life only to annoy you."

"I'm not going to fight with you again about this." She coasted to a stop at a red light. "Both of us said more than enough after the club closed."

"Agreed, and that's not the reason I'm calling, anyway."

"So, what's up?"

"My restaurant had a fire tonight."

"What?" She was glad for hands-free technology or she would have dropped the phone. "Where did it start? The kitchen?"

"No, outside," he said. "In a dumpster that had been pushed up against the building. The whole back wall of the kitchen is damaged, so the restaurant'll be closed a while. I'm here with the arson investigators."

"I'll be right there," Kaylen said without hesitation. Their fight earlier didn't matter. Sam needed support, and she was already driving in the right direction.

"You don't need to do that," Sam said, but his protest sounded hollow.

"I can be there in about twenty minutes. I'm not tired, and you need me." She heard voices in the background.

"I've got to go, K.T. They want to ask me more questions."

"Fine. I'll see you in a few."

She drove quickly, her mind racing. He'd said the dumpster had been placed up against the side of the building and the fire had started inside it. Was it an accident or arson? And if it wasn't an accident, who would try to destroy Sam's livelihood?

As she came up the block, she saw all the flashing lights. Emergency vehicles lined the street and blocked the alleyway. Kaylen took the first available parking space and walked the rest of the way, stepping over hoses and getting her feet wet. The chill wind off the ocean brought goose bumps up on her arms. The oppressive heat had blown inland. She wished she had thought to bring a sweater and shivered. The restaurant's windows were fogged up and the door stood wide open, a thick hose snaking inside. Yellow tape blocked her way, as did a patrolman.

"I'm a friend of Mr. Wilson's," she said. "He called and asked me to come."

"Sorry, no one goes back there," the patrolman told her. "The investigators are still on-scene."

"Sam?" she shouted. "Sam!"

"Ma'am, don't do that. You'll have to leave."

"I am *not* leaving." She pulled out her cell phone. Sam answered on the first ring. "I'm stuck out front, behind the tape," she told him.

He came around the corner of the alley moments later, accompanied by a tall, thin man who introduced himself as Miles Barnes, the lead investigator. They held up the tape so she could duck underneath.

"You're freezing." Sam took off his jacket and draped it around her shoulders.

"Thanks." Kaylen put her arms into the sleeves and fastened the double-breasted jacket, grateful for Sam's lingering warmth. She took his arm. "That's better, but now *you're* getting cold."

"We're going inside," he said. "The smoke damage is pretty bad at the back, but the office is okay, and they gave me the go-ahead to get my personal stuff out of there."

They followed Barnes through the dining room, where they had to pick their way around upended chairs and tables.

"The firemen had to knock a couple of holes in the ceiling, so the water damage is pretty bad," Sam said.

Kaylen looked around. "This place looks more like it was hit by a hurricane than a fire."

Barnes, his long face sharpened by a deeply-cleft chin and an equally-deep frown line between dark brown eyes, handed Sam a large flashlight. "Don't wander around outside this room," he warned.

Kaylen noticed he wore heavy boots and wished again that she hadn't chosen to wear the high-heeled shoes, which couldn't have been less practical in the middle of the ruined restaurant. Her cocktail dress wasn't an asset, either, she decided as the hem caught on the leg of an upended chair and ripped.

Barnes helped her pull the dress free. "I'll be back in a couple of minutes," he told Sam. He trudged off through the standing water toward the kitchen.

Sam pushed a couple of chairs aside to get to his desk. "When they're all done, I'll call in an emergency board-up service," he told Kaylen. "With that storm on the way, I doubt there'll be any damned plywood left in Miami by now, and I'm not even sure it's worth the effort, but I can't leave the goddamned place wide open."

Flashing red lights outside the restaurant windows cast a pulsating glow throughout the dining room. Smoke damage had almost obliterated the Everglades mural. The flamingo stalked toward darkness instead of a tropical paradise.

"I still say you shouldn't be here." Sam used a long pole to open a small window high on one wall.

"I had to come." Kaylen turned her back on the devastation. "This was your baby."

Sam grunted and pulled papers from a desk drawer. "I'm going to have to find another baby. This one's a complete write-off." He stuffed the papers into a plastic bag on his chair. "I don't think I've got the patience to sit around while the insurance settles, then start all over again." He opened another drawer and took out a receipt book.

"Can't you take the settlement and buy another restaurant someplace else?" Kaylen suggested. "You said your business had fallen off here, anyway."

"No," Sam said. He continued to go through drawers in his desk, the bag filling rapidly.

Kaylen felt awkward suddenly, as though she was intruding. Instead of standing around while he tried to salvage his possessions, she told herself, she should be helping. She found an undamaged box sitting on top of a filing cabinet and began to gather photographs from the credenza. Sam with his arm around George's shoulders as they stood outside The Hideaway, a large banner hanging over their heads that said "UNDER NEW OWNERSHIP." Another showing the original staff, frozen into stiff poses against the Everglades fresco.

From one corner of Sam's desk she picked up a small gilt frame and found it contained a photo of herself, dressed in a uniform of black capris and a fuchsia-pink t-shirt, a white apron tightly girded around her waist. She looked young, gangly and awkward, with a tray balanced precariously on one forearm and a pair of shiny black dress shoes on her feet. In another frame beside it, Sam stood shaking hands with the mayor while his late wife, Pearl, looked on with a radiant smile.

Kaylen loaded the photos into the box. "The bank could give you a loan until the insurance pays off," she said. "Then you can do whatever you want."

She almost suggested Sam come over to help her more with Bannisters, but she knew he'd resume his bossy behavior. It was in his nature.

"Nah," Sam said. "Too much work. Early retirement sounds a whole lot more tempting." He opened his cigar box, took one out and cut the end off it. "Do you think they'll give me a ticket for smoking inside the restaurant?" he asked with a short laugh.

"Doubtful, under the circumstances." She managed a smile, even though she didn't feel like it. "Don't make any rash decisions, Sam. What do you think happened here? Someone pitched a cigarette into the dumpster?"

Sam shrugged. "I'll leave the who and the why to the guys out back."

His cigar smoke joined the already-overpowering odors of burned wood, plastic and food. Kaylen wished she hadn't eaten that late supper. She needed an antacid.

"I don't understand you," she said. "If Bannisters went up in flames, I'd want to know why. Instead, you're talking about closing down."

"I can't see the point of trying to out-guess the investigators," Sam grumbled. "They get paid to find the answers."

"Maybe they do," Kaylen said. "But I don't understand how the fire got started, or how it got so big before anyone noticed. That dumpster would have been pretty noisy to move, not to mention heavy, even with the wheels. How come nobody in the kitchen heard anything?"

"Have you forgotten how loud it gets in a restaurant kitchen?" Sam asked.

"Of course not." Kaylen added a plaque from the local Chamber of Commerce to the box and closed the top. "It's pandemonium at Bannisters.

But your kitchen's smaller, and you don't have Emrico screaming at the *sous* chefs."

Sam chuckled. "That's true. But my chef likes to play Salsa music and sing at the top of his lungs while he's cooking." He took a bottle of Courvoisier from a cabinet and handed her a snifter. "Let's stop speculating and make a toast to The Hideaway."

The last thing Kaylen wanted was to put liquor in her stomach.

"What's the matter, is the glass dirty?" Sam asked.

Kaylen looked into the snifter. "No. It's clean enough. I don't much feel like drinking, that's all."

"Nonsense," Sam said. "Brandy'll make you feel a lot better. Warmer, too."

"Oh, all right." She didn't have the strength left to argue. It was way too late, and she definitely did need some sort of comfort. She held out the glass. "Only a splash for me."

Sam poured a whole lot more than a splash for both of them. He raised his snifter. "Cheers."

Kaylen clinked her glass with his and sipped. She had to admit he might be right; the brandy felt good as it slid over her tongue and down her throat.

Sam swallowed half his own generous serving in one gulp. "Ah, that hits the spot." He brushed off his chair with a bar towel, sat down and leaned back. "If one of the busboys hadn't taken an unscheduled cigarette break, the whole restaurant would probably have caught fire. Maybe that would've been better under the circumstances. Less mess to clean up later."

"That's ironic," Kaylen said. "He goes out to smoke and finds a fire. Are the investigators sure he didn't start it?"

"Yeah. My chef saw him slipping out the door, got mad and went after him. The kid ran right into him, coming back the other way." Sam swallowed the remainder of his drink. "The employees were going to fight the fire with extinguishers, but it had gotten into the kitchen by then. Marvin convinced them all to get out while the fire department was on its way. Good thing he was here to take charge."

Sam offered her the Courvoisier again. Kaylen shook her head. She finished her drink and set the glass on the desk as Sam poured himself another one.

"You'll miss working, you know." Kaylen watched him rock back and forth on the chair, his hands folded across his stomach. "You'll get bored."

"Nah." Sam stubbed out his cigar. "I've got several other things going for me, including a stake in a couple of those start-ups Tim was telling you about before he left town."

"I don't think Tim went anywhere," Kaylen said. The warming effects of the brandy evaporated. "According to Lieutenant Shaw, he wasn't an entrepreneur, either." She suddenly felt afraid for Sam. "You didn't give Tim a lot of money, did you?"

Sam made a non-committal noise and took a sip of his drink. Kaylen heard footsteps behind her as Barnes came back into the room. She wondered what Sam would have said if they hadn't been interrupted. Maybe The Hideaway wasn't losing revenue after all. Maybe Sam had taken his capital and invested it in some shaky business of Tim's.

"Did you find anything new?" Sam asked the investigator.

Barnes nodded. "A can of accelerant and a black jacket behind another dumpster. We found some ID in the jacket's pocket, so we'll be able to wrap this case up fast."

"That would be a blessing." Sam stood up. "I know you're on duty, so I won't offer you a brandy." He pointed toward the snifter in front of him. "But maybe you can come over to Kaylen's club, Bannisters, in the next couple of days. I'll buy you a drink there."

"Thanks for the offer." Barnes shook the hand Sam offered him. "I may take you up on it." He headed for the door. "We're done here, if you want to make arrangements to get the place boarded up."

Kaylen decided she should head for the door herself. No point in hanging around any longer. Sam had calls to make, and her fatigue was getting the best of her. She stifled a yawn. She needed to check into a hotel and get some rest.

Sam evidently saw the yawn. "You look exhausted," he said. "Why don't you come home with me? I've got a half-dozen guest rooms. You can get a good night's sleep, then we'll have brunch tomorrow."

Kaylen shook her head. "No, but thanks."

Sam grunted. "George would turn over in his grave if he heard you refusing my help."

Kaylen took off Sam's jacket and handed it back. "George would be only too happy to see me standing on my own two feet."

"I don't think he'd be sending up a cheer about you being homeless." Sam shrugged back into the jacket and buttoned it.

"That's only a temporary situation." She caught herself sighing and hoped he hadn't noticed. "I'm going to call a real estate agency tomorrow and put my condo on the market."

Sam rocked back and forth on his heels. "I suppose you'll be angry with me again, but I figured what the hell. I contacted a real estate agent this morning."

"Sam…," Kaylen interrupted.

"Let me finish, K.T." He stuck his hands in his pockets. "The agent said she could sell your condo real fast, even with its history and the water damage. She can show you a couple of really nice places right down the street from here. One of them's even got a lease option on it, so you won't have to risk jumping into a sales contract."

Kaylen felt more disappointment than anger. He'd done it again—acted in a territorial and dictatorial manner. But with the best intentions, she reminded herself.

"You should have asked me before you did that." She tried to keep the edge out of her voice. "But I've got to thank you for saving me a lot of leg work."

Sam looked pretty smug. "The lease option even has furniture. You could use that until you have time to find something you like better. Maybe some of your old furniture's even salvageable."

"I don't think I want anything else out of that condo." She shuddered. "I'd keep seeing Rosa every time I looked at it."

"Your decision." He took a card out of his pocket and handed it to her. "The agent can meet you at the Seahaven Condos as early as ten tomorrow morning."

Kaylen doubted Lieutenant Shaw would be finished grilling her by that time. "I can't make it then, I've got another appointment. I *will* call her, though." She looked at the name on the card. "Suki Adamson. Her name even *sounds* like a realtor."

"She seemed like a nice gal. After I spoke to her on the phone, she stopped by and gave me the card. You could be in your own place within twenty-four hours, if you like the lease option."

"You're right." Kaylen pocketed the card. "I told you, I'll call her. She can show me some listings, and then I'll make a decision."

"Okay." He sighed. "You're a stubborn woman, Kaylen."

"And you're a damned pushy man, Sam." She smiled to belie her sharp words.

"Why won't you let me take care of you?" He walked around the desk to stand closer to her. "What's the big deal? George took care of everything when he was alive."

"George was my husband." She backed up a step. *And Brian already told me he would take care of me,* she thought.

Sam moved forward to close the gap. "I could…"

"Don't go there, Sam." She backed away again, her buttocks colliding with the door frame. She sidestepped quickly. "Once that thought's in the open, you can't take it back, and it will be between us all the time."

She put a hand on his arm, more to stop his advance than to reassure him. Sam placed his own big, warm hand over hers and it took all she had not to jerk away as his thumb massaged her wrist.

"K.T," he said. "You know I love you a lot."

"Do you tell Sandy you love her, too?" she blurted.

"What?"

Kaylen knew him too well, and she saw the quick shift before he stared at her with wide-eyed innocence.

"You're sleeping with Sandy." She pulled her hand away.

"Are you sure you didn't get hit over the head when that guy attacked you?" His voice sounded a full octave lower.

"Sandy's driving a Mercedes and calling me K.T. She's never done that. I'm always 'girlfriend' to her, or Kaylen."

"Maybe she thinks you need reassuring right now. She knows K.T. was George's pet name for you."

"Sandy calling me by George's pet name isn't normal. It's not at all reassuring. And she can't afford that car, regardless how much she's getting paid to manage that new restaurant."

Sam sighed. "I can explain the car, if that's what's worrying you so much. Sandy called me. She wanted new wheels, and she wanted something flashy. She asked if I knew of a good dealership. I told her I could do better than that. One of my friends was moving to Mexico and didn't want to take his car, so she got it at a great price."

"It looks new."

"It's not, K.T., er, Kaylen. It's a couple of years old. The owner got it detailed right before Sandy picked it up."

Kaylen looked at him. His jaw was set. She wouldn't get another thing out of him.

"I'm not swallowing that explanation," she told him. "Something stinks, and if you're lying, then you and I are really going to start fighting, whether you're one of my best friends or not."

"I'm not boffing Sandy, for Christ's sake. You've lost your mind."

"Maybe I have, but I can't afford not to be suspicious of everything and everyone right now."

"Even me?"

"Maybe especially you." She couldn't look at him. She knew his blood pressure would be out of the ball park and his face beet red.

"You're the one I want," Sam said so softly, his words almost got lost behind the sound of the fire hose being pulled out of the restaurant.

Depression washed over Kaylen. Her life as she knew it had now completely ended. The one person she had always counted on to give her support without strings attached was trying to lasso her with a steel cable.

"Just because I married one older man doesn't mean I want to get romantically involved with another," she said. "Do I really need to remind you how quickly I lost George?"

Sam grabbed both her elbows and shook her, not unkindly. "Look at me,

K.T.," he urged, when she avoided his gaze. "I'm a healthy sixty-year-old. My cholesterol's down, I've lost weight, and I've even got a personal trainer because I'll be damned if I'm going to join an f-ing gym."

Kaylen sighed. *Why did he have to do this now? Why couldn't they just remain good friends? Why the hell did sex always have to enter into every relationship she had with a man?*

"I'll even quit cigars, if that'll make you change your mind." He tilted her chin with one hand until she couldn't avoid his gaze. "Anything you want."

She tried to step back, but his grip on her tightened. "Those are wonderful things that you needed to do for yourself," she told him carefully. "You shouldn't be doing them for me."

"Oh, honey." He released her, his expression sad as Kaylen had never seen it.

"Why won't you give me a chance?" he asked. "I love you so much. Always have. I was waiting for you to give me some sort of signal that you were ready to be with me. But George didn't wait. Neither did Tim, damn him."

She felt so dispirited and confused. Her life was already too complicated, and she refused to feel sorry for Sam and give him any kind of false hope. "I've *got* a boyfriend," she said. "You introduced me to Tim. Why would you do that if you didn't want us to be together?"

"I never thought you'd get so involved with him that you'd date him for three months," Sam said. "And I figured because he was such a player, he'd dump you and move on. Then you'd come running to me for comfort."

"You used Tim?" She couldn't believe what she was hearing. "And you set me up to get my heart broken? I don't even know you anymore."

"Don't get mad," Sam said. "I was stupid, and it backfired. Tim fell in love with you."

"No, he didn't," she said. "We were just having fun. He was great to go out with, nothing more. I wasn't looking for another husband. I'm still not."

"Damn it, Kaylen. You need a man, not a boy." Sam pulled her against him, the contact abrupt, unwelcome. "I can change your mind about what you think you want."

She felt his heart beating madly. Hot breath fanned the bare skin above her low-cut gown.

Anger and revulsion swept through her as his lips pressed against her neck, then inched lower. She struggled to free herself. "You don't have any right to tell me what I need!"

"I do when you're acting like some adolescent in heat with that guy, Brian."

"Let me go!" Kaylen tore herself from his grasp. She picked up her keys and purse. "You'll regret this tomorrow," she said. "But I won't forget what you just did, what you said."

"I hope you don't." The buttons on Sam's vest strained as his chest heaved. "I want you to come to a more sensible conclusion. We're two of a kind. We make a great team, and despite my appearance, I can perform very well in bed, too. You'll learn to love me. You already know me as a close friend."

She gritted her teeth. The thought of being intimate with Sam was too repulsive even to contemplate. "You and I will never, ever end up in the same bed," she said. "Make no mistake about that."

"Never say never." Sam no longer looked sad. In fact, he looked exceedingly angry.

She wasn't going to continue arguing with him. She wanted out of that building as fast as she could get there. "Let's try to pretend the last few minutes never happened," she said. "Before you make me say something very ugly to you."

"By all means." His voice was sheer ice. "I wouldn't want to push myself on you when you find me so disgusting." He stalked back to his desk, where he jerked open a drawer and slammed a well-worn copy of the Yellow Pages onto the oak surface.

Kaylen left him thumbing through the pages, the edges ripping audibly as he turned one after another. She drove down the street until she found the condos he had mentioned. They looked secure and inviting, with bright lights over heavy iron security gates and a guard visible inside a small booth. He looked at her car as she pulled over to the curb. A couple of signs announced FOR SALE, and one said LEASE WITH OPTION TO BUY.

She would definitely call Suki Adamson in the morning, right after her interview at the precinct. But not to view one of those condos. She'd ask to be shown something else. Something Sam hadn't seen and didn't know about. Or maybe she'd even skip calling Suki and find her own realtor. No more depending on friends, she thought. They were all becoming unreliable, secretive, or in Tim's case, just plain missing.

Swinging around, she passed the restaurant and drove toward the marina. If Brian wouldn't come to her, then she'd go to him. But she found the gate locked, and she needed to punch a code into a keypad before she could enter. All her concerns about security, and she hadn't even thought about the marina being locked up for the night.

She backed up and parked while she looked for Brian's phone number in her purse. Her cell rang.

"I need you to come to my office right now, Ms. Roberts," Lieutenant Shaw said.

CHAPTER THIRTY-FOUR

"Come in." Shaw stood up as Kaylen was ushered into his office at 6:00AM. "I apologize for bringing you in here so early."

Kaylen shrugged. "I wasn't asleep. I'd just left Sam Wilson's restaurant. He had a fire."

Shaw nodded. "I got a report."

"Is that why you called me?" Kaylen asked. "I don't know anything about that. I was having a late supper with my friend, Sandy, while it was happening."

"No." He motioned her to take a seat. "It's about Tim Madison."

"Oh." She sat. He looked grim. Her heart pounded uncomfortably. "You found him," she said.

"Yes." Lieutenant Shaw sighed heavily. "His body turned up in Snapper Creek. Preliminary findings put it there at least four days."

"Oh, how awful." Kaylen closed her eyes.

"Are you okay?" the lieutenant asked.

He sounded concerned, like he wasn't sure if she was going to pass out.

"No," she said. "I haven't been okay since the night my club opened."

Tim hadn't abandoned her and his life in Miami. He hadn't left town without telling her. Oh, God! She had told Sam there was nothing between her and Tim except a good time.

Kaylen felt so ashamed, so horrified at herself and her flip attitude. She tried the word dead on for size, but it wouldn't fit Tim. He had been so full of life, it was impossible to imagine him any other way.

"I can't believe it," she said. Tears welled up in her eyes. "Are you absolutely sure it's him?"

"Yes." Lieutenant Shaw took a seat behind his desk and slid a box of tissues and a bottle of water toward her.

Kaylen's throat had tightened up. She unscrewed the cap from the water and took a sip.

"Brian took it very hard," Shaw said. "Tim was his only brother, after all."

She choked and dropped the bottle.

Shaw jumped back up. "Are you all right?"

She waved at him, her head reeling. His *brother?* She couldn't breathe, coughed again, grabbed a tissue.

"I don't…don't understand." Kaylen carefully blotted her still-sore nose, wiped her eyes and tried to compose herself while Shaw stared at her, the furrows on his face deepened with concern. "They don't look alike," she reasoned. "They don't even have the same last name."

"They're half-brothers," Shaw said. "Same mother, different father. Tim never told you?"

"No," she said. "Tim told me he didn't have *any* family. But my God, why didn't Brian say something? He knows I've been so worried about Tim. He must have been even more worried than me. He told me Tim was an acquaintance. He said something like 'when it was convenient for Tim.'"

"Brian couldn't tell you, Ms. Roberts. He may be on administrative leave, but he's still a detective, and this is an open investigation. He couldn't take a chance he'd jeopardize the case."

"He's a *what?*" The tissue box fell to the floor, too.

"A homicide detective."

"He told me he's a charter boat captain." She was having trouble breathing again. "I must be dreaming. This can't be true. He…he…" She couldn't continue.

She covered her face with her hands. She felt so lightheaded. *She had almost kissed Tim's brother. He'd held her in his arms while Tim lay dead in some creek.*

The lieutenant broke into her anguish. "Ms. Roberts, I'm sure you're really shocked and confused right now, maybe even angry, but let me assure you, I have full confidence in Brian Swift. He's an honorable man with a deep love for his brother. He's completely shattered by Tim's death."

Kaylen tried to push her own feelings aside. If she was so upset about Tim, how bad did Brian feel? Her mind rebelled at the notion of feeling sorry for him. He had covered up his relationship to Tim. His mask had never slipped, not even that horrible morning when they had awakened in the same bed. Not even when she'd helped him the night he'd been beaten, and she'd mistakenly thought him so vulnerable.

She had almost placed her trust and safety in his hands. "The bastard," she said.

"Tim?" Lieutenant Shaw looked at her with pity. "Yes, he was. And I don't understand how you couldn't see that before."

"I'm talking about Brian." She wiped the tears off her face. "Doesn't he have any conscience at all?"

"He's always felt responsible for Tim. Brian blames himself for not being able to keep his brother out of trouble."

"How much trouble was Tim in?" Kaylen asked. *No wonder she had thugs lying in wait for her and threatening her. Now she began to understand.*

"Probably even more than any of us knew." Lieutenant Shaw sat back down and grabbed a pen, which he started rhythmically tapping against his desk. "Because of the way you've been threatened, we're thinking he must have taken something vital to the cartel he worked for, and we think he hid it somewhere in your possessions. It couldn't have been in your condo, or they would have found it when they searched it. You've got to have it with you, sewn into an article of clothing or inside the lining of something, maybe a purse. Even hidden in a piece of jewelry. He didn't give you a locket or a charm bracelet, did he?"

"Tim worked for a cartel? My God, my club will have to close. After the media gets this story, none of my customers will feel safe in there."

Kaylen knew her life would never, ever be the same again. All her best laid plans were collapsing like a house of cards.

She pulled off her watch and pushed her purse across the desk. "Here. Look for yourself. These are the only two things I have left that Tim gave me."

Shaw checked out the watch and upended the purse, picking through the contents with the end of his pen before splitting the lining and feeling around inside. "You've got nothing else? You're absolutely sure?"

"Absolutely," Kaylen said. "Everything else stayed behind in the condo."

"Why did you lie to me before, Ms. Roberts?" Shaw asked.

"I didn't," she said, confused.

"What about waking up in bed with Brian?" he asked.

Kaylen colored up. "Oh," she said, unable to think of an appropriate response. She gathered up her belongings and dumped them back into the purse.

"He told me," Shaw said.

"Oh," Kaylen said again. She stared down at her knees. If Brian had told Shaw that much, then he probably had also told his supervisor about them being naked, too.

"Brian said you don't know why you lied," Shaw said. "Is that true?"

"Yes," she said. "I was embarrassed, and Brian thought it was a publicity stunt a rival club owner had cooked up. He thought news crews could be waiting outside the condo, but they weren't."

"If we can figure out what Tim had that was worth killing him for, then maybe we'll have the missing piece of the puzzle." The lieutenant laid down his pen. "Without that, you're still in danger and so is Brian."

"But why?" Kaylen asked.

She looked up and saw nothing in Shaw's face that looked like speculation or anger. In fact, she realized the Lieutenant's expression hadn't changed throughout the time she had been in his office, except when he talked about Brian.

"Apart from being Tim's brother, the only thing he's done is hang around me," she said.

"And someone doesn't like that," Shaw said. "They want you to be alone, unprotected. With Brian close by, they don't believe they can scare you into giving them what they want."

"But I don't *know* what they want. If I did, and I had it, I'd give it to them." Kaylen nervously ran the straps of her purse between her fingers. "I don't want to live like this. I spent most of last night in my car, driving around because I was too scared to stay with my friend or go to a hotel."

"I want you to trust Brian," Shaw said. He had picked the pen back up and was tapping it again. "There are people out to ruin his career, and I believe he's become a target because of his connection to Tim."

"You really believe in Brian's innocence," Kaylen said. "Good for you. I can't be so sure. You said he couldn't tell me who he really is, but I think even if he could have, he wouldn't. How can I trust someone who won't tell me anything?"

"You'll have to take a leap of faith," Shaw said. "I'm telling you Brian's been framed, and it's about to happen again with that restaurant fire. The preliminary findings are pointing to him, but the time-line's off. I already told the arson investigators Brian was in my office when the fire started. Whoever tried to set him up didn't count on Tim's body being found tonight."

Kaylen tried to envision Brian in the role of a victim, but she couldn't. "You're asking a lot from me," she said.

Into her mind came a memory of Tim on the last night she had seen him, talking to Sam, laughing with the bartender and other patrons. So at home with all her friends. He was the one she should really be mad at, she thought. He had deceived her all the time she had known him. Even more than Brian, who had been withholding information because he was a detective. And she thought she had been depressed and confused *before* she came to Lieutenant Shaw's office.

"So where *is* Brian?" she asked. "Back at his boat?"

"Probably. At least that's where he told me he was going after he left here. He's not answering his cell. I was hoping you'd had some contact with him."

"I'm Tim's girlfriend, not Brian's."

"Not anymore," he pointed out, a little too matter-of-factly for her.

Kaylen thought of Tim lying face-down in murky water, and her throat tightened.

"You seem to be at the center of everything, Ms. Roberts," Shaw said. "You're the last one to see Tim alive. Your housekeeper was murdered in your home. You've been attacked by an intruder in the same condo. You're friends with Sam Wilson, whose restaurant got burned tonight. You've got a lot of explaining to do."

And she might have the key to the whole mess on her thigh, she thought, suddenly.

She remembered Brian telling her she must have been drugged. He was right. Drugged and then tattooed. And if she wasn't careful, she would no longer be more useful alive than dead. If the people who had done all those other terrible things knew that what they were searching for was on her thigh, they'd have no further reason to keep trying to get information out of her. They would kill her and get it from her leg.

Instinct took over. She had to get out of the precinct and find Brian. He might be devious, but he'd never hurt her, and he'd never threatened to do so, even when he was really angry. She stood abruptly, the chair scraping behind her. "I've got to use the restroom."

Lieutenant Shaw shook his head. "That won't do, Ms. Roberts."

"I really, really do have to go," she pleaded, trying to look sufficiently distressed. She thought of Tim again and tears trickled down her cheeks without any effort on her part. "I drank three cups of coffee at supper…," she managed, her voice quivering. She put the tissue she still held in her hand up to her mouth. "….and with all that coughing…"

"Oh, very well."

They walked across the squad room to the reception desk.

"Gabe," Lieutenant Shaw said to the tow-headed young man behind the desk.

"Yes, sir." Gabe stopped tapping on a keyboard.

"I want you to escort Ms. Roberts to the restroom and then send Detective Kemp to supervise Ms. Roberts and bring her back to my office."

Gabe got up quickly. "Please follow me," he said to Kaylen.

He led her down a long hallway to the restroom and pushed open the door.

"I know where Detective Kemp is," Gabe said. "It'll only take me a minute to get her."

"Thank you." Kaylen gave him a weak smile and stepped inside.

Gabe closed the door.

She made a loud production of going into a bathroom stall and slamming the door. Conquering her revulsion at the idea of lying on a restroom floor, Kaylen shimmied under the locked door. She chanced a look into the corridor, found it deserted, and ran on tiptoe for the exit sign.

She opened the heavy door just enough to slide between it and the wall, abandoned all caution and ran headlong down the steps. Outside, rain spattered onto the blacktop and bounced off the vehicles in the parking lot. She walked quickly to her car, expecting to hear shouting behind her the whole way.

She set out for Coconut Grove and the marina. If she had to scale a fence in her damned designer dress, she'd do it. The hem had already ripped once that evening, anyway. If Brian wasn't on the *Destiny*, then she'd sit on the boat and wait until he came back.

She almost ran off the road exiting the freeway, her speed too fast for the narrow ramp. Kaylen saw a street sign lining up with the hood and veered away, pumping the brakes and listening to the resulting screech of tires. The BMW reacted well to her frenzied efforts, coming to rest in the parking lot of an auto supply store.

She cursed herself for being the idiot she was, retrieved her purse and phone from the floor, found Brian's cell number and punched it in. The phone rang and rang until his voicemail finally picked up. She left a terse message, asking him to call her immediately, then continued on at a more sedate pace.

The last thing she needed was a cruiser to pull her over for speeding. She'd probably end up back at the precinct, and then she'd have to not only face Lieutenant Shaw, but call Sam and eat crow while she begged for bail money.

CHAPTER THIRTY-FIVE

Brian spent three fruitless hours threatening people more than punching them as he searched for answers to Tim's murder. His anger fizzled as rain drenched everything including him, squalls dumped from low gray clouds moving over Miami. Finally he found Sean Hastings in Little Havana, seated on a stoop sheltered by a tattered canvas awning that sent rainwater in a steady stream onto the cracked blacktop in front of his wet and dirty tennis shoes.

Brian had discarded his rain gear, which didn't allow him to move around as easily as he wanted, and he barely managed to avoid getting soaked as he ducked under the sagging cover to take shelter beside Sean. The teen's only response was to shift his feet slightly. He sat hunched up, forearms on his knees, barely blinking as he stared straight ahead.

"I want information," Brian said. "Who killed my brother?"

Sean wiped his nose on his sleeve and yawned.

Brian slammed the bat against the doorframe at a level with Sean's ear. "Don't ignore me."

Sean didn't even flinch. He muttered something under his breath and pulled out a crumpled pack of cigarettes.

"Did you just tell me to fuck off?" Brian made a grab for Sean's shirt, but the teen jumped to his feet, surprisingly agile when he had appeared to be flying high only moments before.

"Yeah, asshole. That's what I said." Sean bounced into the middle of the alley. He pulled a silver lighter from his pocket and lit a cigarette.

Brian recognized that lighter. He had seen it in William Hastings' hand only days before.

"Been home lately?" he asked.

Sean put the lighter back into his pocket. "What's it to you?"

Brian shrugged. "Nothing. But I bet you know what happened to Tim."

"Nope." Sean took a long drag on the cigarette and blew smoke out his nostrils. "I stay the hell away from cartel business."

"I don't believe you," Brian said. "Tim's body was found only a couple of hours ago. But you weren't surprised when I told you he was dead."

Sean shrugged. "Word's been out on the street for days."

"Then you've got to know who's takin' credit."

Sean shrugged. "Why ask me? You've got snitches. Every cop does." He looked at Brian from under overgrown, greasy bangs. "Oh, that's right. You're not a cop anymore, are you? So no one has to talk to you, including me." He grinned, the gesture snide and mocking.

"You owe me," Brian said.

"For what?" Sean stopped slouching and became at least two inches taller. "You ratted me out to my dad, shithead."

"To get you into rehab," Brian said. "That's old business. You know what happened."

"Yeah, I ended up on the fuckin' street." Fingers shaking, Sean tried to take another drag of his cigarette, but it had become sodden with rainwater. He pitched it into the gutter.

Brian didn't want to waste time talking about Sean's issues, but he'd be damned if he would let an old wound screw up his opportunity to get information.

"It wasn't supposed to go down like that," he said. "If I'd known your father would react the way he did, I'd have found some other way."

"Liar," Sean said. "You used me to get that transfer to Homicide. You didn't like the way my dad ran Vice. You were taking bribes. You still are."

"I was forced into taking a transfer after I caught you dealing and he refused to do anything about it."

Sean's eyes narrowed. "No way." He sounded unsure.

Brian pushed his advantage. "I'd have cuffed you and taken you to holding if I'd wanted you to end up in jail."

Sean chewed on his lower lip. He tried to zip up his sweatshirt, but the zipper wouldn't cooperate.

Brian stepped out from under the cover of the awning. Rain hit him, the drops heavy, stinging his face and soaking through his shirt. Sean's bloodshot brown eyes peered at him, dull, lifeless but definitely wary.

He leaned forward, invading the teen's space. "Was your father involved in Tim's death?"

Sean snorted and spat a revolting mixture of blood and mucous right beside Brian's shoe.

"Shove off, dickhead," he said. He started to edge away. "I'm not giving you crap. You fucked up my life."

Brian watched the teen, thin shoulders hunched under the hooded sweatshirt, open and flapping in the wind. Sean shuffled off, his feet almost completely covered by tattered and filthy jeans that dragged in the puddles. Brian sadly remembered the kid as a freshman in high school, open and friendly, clean and well-dressed.

"I can help you get straight," Brian said as the distance between them lengthened. Frustration surged through him when Sean didn't even falter. "It's not too late," he added, although he had his doubts.

Sean shuffled toward a dilapidated apartment building with half the windows broken out.

Brian followed warily, his hand on his gun. "Sean…"

"I said 'fuck you' already, Swift." Sean saluted with his middle finger for emphasis. "Go find someone else to bully. That's all you're good for, anyway, beating people into saying things they regret later."

"Who the hell gave you that idea?" Brian sped up as Sean broke into an uneven jog.

"I heard stories from my dad."

"You would. He didn't like you hanging around me."

"Turns out he was right." Sean took shelter in the doorway of the apartment building as rain hurtled down. "Now he's getting promoted, and you've been booted out."

Brian had to raise his voice over the thunder of rain on cement. "Once the investigation's over, I'll be reinstated." He ducked into the same doorway and grabbed Sean's arm. "I'm not here to argue with you about my business. I want information to find Tim's killer."

"I told you, I don't know anything." Sean tried to pull himself free. "You're hurting me. Let go."

"A name," Brian persisted. His grip tightened and he watched Sean wince.

"Asshole!"

Sean's other hand came out of his pocket. Brian saw the blade right before it sunk into his chest. He veered to one side. A chop sent the knife skittering away. He twisted Sean's arm up behind him, the teen's heels rising off the ground until he was dancing around on tiptoes.

"Lemme-go!" He squealed like a young girl. "You're fuckin' killin' me, man."

"Stop talking like a piece of street trash." Brian eased up his pressure, but kept Sean immobilized. "Cooperate and you can go shoot up."

"Go piss up a rope."

Brian tightened his grip again. Sean squealed even louder than the first time. A window slid open high above them.

"Hey, man, what you doin'?" a voice demanded. "I'm gonna call the cops."

"Shut the fuck up and go back to watching the *novelas.*" Brian glared up at the guy leaning over the sill, yellowed lace curtains blowing around his grease-stained t-shirt.

"Cabron," the guy said, but the window slammed shut.

"Now." Brian pulled Sean up against him and put him into a headlock. "Talk."

Sean dug his fingernails into Brian's hand.

Brian squeezed tighter.

Sean tried to slam his heels onto Brian's toes. When that failed, he kicked wildly, but Brian managed to hold on. Running out of air, Sean also ran out of energy. The flailing stopped and he sagged.

Brian loosened his choke-hold enough for the teen to breathe. "A name," he repeated. "That's all I want." He thought about the lighter. Sean must have gone to his parents' home and lifted it. "I asked if your father was involved," he said.

"Yeah," Sean said. "He is."

Brian released him. Sean staggered across the alley and leaned against the wall.

He wiped his nose on the sleeve of his shirt. "Is *that* what you wanted to hear?" He gave Brian a look filled with contempt. "My father set your brother up. He got two guys to beat the crap out of him. I heard him talking on the phone the night that new club opened. He said Tim had something he was gonna get back."

"I thought you'd been kicked out of the house," Brian said.

"My mom sneaks me in for a meal and a bath sometimes. I went to take a leak and heard my dad on the phone. After he got done, he came into the kitchen and caught me eating. He chucked my sandwich across the room and threw me out the door. I was afraid he was gonna get his gun, so I ran." Sean shivered and pulled the ends of his sweatshirt together. "I felt sorry for my mom. I'm sure he smacked her around after I left."

"Did he do that often?" Brian asked.

Sean shrugged. "Not until he gave me drugs to sell."

"You're telling me your father was your supplier?" Brian now knew why Hastings had made it so difficult for him to stay in Vice.

"Yeah. I don't know where he got the shit from. I didn't ask. I made a lot of money, so what did I care?"

"Did your mom try to stop you? Is that why your dad started slapping her around?"

"Yeah." Sean's teeth were chattering. "I've gotta go," he said. "Your beef's with my dad, not me."

"Do you have any idea who your father was talking to on the phone?" Brian stepped closer again.

"No." Sean looked nervous as well as shaky. He rubbed the arm Brian had pulled up against his back. "He never said."

He tried to inch along the wall, but he came into contact with a group of overstuffed garbage cans and stopped. Water poured down from a gutter high above their heads, splashing water all over his jeans. Sean tried to move away.

Brian pinned him beneath the stream. "Are you telling me the truth?"

Sean covered his head with his arms. "I swear," he said. "I fuckin' swear. Lemme outta here. I'm freezin'."

"If you're lying to me, I'll find you and beat the crap out of you," Brian promised.

"You already did that. I've got bruises all over my throat, an' I think you dislocated my arm."

"There's a free clinic two blocks away. Do yourself a favor and go there."

Brian started to walk away, then changed his mind and went back. "You want to get clean, call me or come to the boat."

As he stepped out of the alleyway, he looked down at himself. His shirt was about as torn and filthy as Sean's and spattered with blood. His knuckles were raw, his arms covered with scratches and the indentations made by Sean's broken and filthy nails.

No wonder Sean thought he got information by beating it out of people. And after he'd half-choked the kid, he wondered if he'd gotten anything really useful. Sean would have said anything to get away, and maybe he thought Brian would shoot his father, thereby getting rid of two people he didn't want in his future.

Brian needed to get cleaned up in a hurry. He didn't want to go back to the *Destiny* looking like he'd been in another fight, and even though Sean had verified what he had already suspected…that Hastings was involved in Tim's death…he had no proof other than the teen's statement. A judge would never consider Sean to be a reliable witness, even if the kid was willing to make a deposition.

Brian looked around when he reached the street and realized he was only three blocks from Tim's apartment. He walked there, his ribs aching in protest now the adrenaline had left his system.

He emptied the mailbox on the way in, collecting more pizza delivery coupons, utility bills, an invoice for Champion's Gym, and a "Thanks for the referral" from another gym right around the corner from the apartment building. Brian couldn't imagine Tim frequenting a place without connections that might benefit him financially, but maybe his brother liked to sweat closer to home and impress people at Champion's.

He picked the lock and entered Tim's apartment. The place smelled musty. He opened a couple of windows that didn't lead to the fire escape and stripped off his clothes.

The gas and electricity had been turned off. He opened the bills and saw they were final notices. As he took a cold shower, he wondered why Tim had disconnected his utilities. Was it because he had already planned to leave?

Brian toweled off and walked into the bedroom. He opened packets of new underwear and slid back one closet door. His brother the clothes-horse, he thought, surveying the contents. Kaylen had coined that phrase in regard to herself. She and Tim were alike in their fondness for shopping. Brian rejected new clothing in favor of a pair of beige chinos and a blue Henley shirt that seemed to have been worn at least a couple of times. Seeing his reflection in the mirrored closet doors, he rolled up the pants that hung over his feet. He looked like he had shopped at Goodwill.

Ironic, he thought. The outfit had probably cost a couple of hundred dollars new. He sat on the end of the bed while he tried to slide into Tim's skin as well as his clothing. What had motivated his brother to pick up the phone and call after they had argued so bitterly that they had agreed never to see each other again?

His resting place gave him a view of the small closet where Tim stored his baseball hat collection. In the dim glow from the bedside lamps, the two red bags were barely visible. Why would his brother have two identical gym bags? Were they merely another sign of Tim's excesses, or something else entirely?

Brian retrieved the bags and swung them to the bed. They both bore the logo of Champion's Gym. One felt slightly heavier than the other. He looked inside. Although they were both filled with similar items, only one looked like it was used on a regular basis.

Why would Tim have filled another bag with new clothing? Brian dumped the contents of the second bag onto the bed and ran his hand around the lining. He found another zipper.

The handles of the other bag were folded back. With difficulty, he pulled out a slightly smaller gym bag, navy blue and emblazoned with the logo of Smithy's Gym—the same place that had sent the coupons and the thank you note. He checked inside the first bag. Nothing except half-empty toiletries and Tim's clean but definitely used workout clothes.

His cell phone rang, and he dropped the contents of Tim's grooming kit all over the floor. He sat for a moment, looking at the mess. *If he didn't get a grip, he'd never figure out the fucking clues Tim had left.* He picked up his phone from the bathroom vanity. The call back number was unfamiliar. He thought about ignoring it, but as he bagged his dirty clothes, a beep announced an incoming message.

He decided whoever had called could wait until he was on his way to the *Destiny*. He threw his dirty clothes down the trash chute on the way out and left with Tim's mail and both Champion's Gym bags, the Smithy's bag safely stowed inside one of them.

CHAPTER THIRTY-SIX

"No, I haven't seen or heard from Kaylen," Brian told Hal as he drove toward the marina. "I can't believe you managed to lose her."

While he listened to Hal's frustrated explanation regarding Kaylen's escape from the precinct, another call interrupted.

"Hold that thought," he told Hal and took the other call.

"Brian." Kaylen's voice sounded tight and angry. "I have to see you. Now."

"Do you realize Lieutenant Shaw's got an APB out on you?"

"I don't care. You've got a lot of explaining to do."

"Where are you?"

"Close to the marina."

"I'll meet you there in ten minutes."

"You'd better." She hung up on him.

"What's going on?" Hal asked. "You put me on hold, you bastard?"

"That was Kaylen."

"Are you meeting her?"

Brian needed to talk to her before anyone else did. "In an hour," he said.

"Where?"

"Bannisters."

Hal would never forgive him.

"Why are you waiting an hour?" Hal sounded suspicious.

"Her request."

"You'd better be telling me the truth."

Hal definitely smelled a rat. Brian put his foot down. The marina was 5 minutes away. "I'll talk to you later." He turned off his phone.

CHAPTER THIRTY-SEVEN

Kaylen saw the plume of smoke even before she arrived at the marina. Fire trucks, police vehicles and onlookers jammed the parking lot and spilled onto the dock. She cursed her outfit, the glittering rhinestones on her bodice picking up the numerous flashing lights and blinking wildly in response. She'd look completely conspicuous and totally out of place wearing a beaded cocktail dress, and she doubted she would be able to find Brian in the chaos. She called his cell, but was told the user was unavailable.

She parked across the street and watched people fighting the wind for control of their umbrellas while she wondered what to do next. A young couple passed by, wearing hooded rain gear.

Kaylen lowered her window. "I'll give you fifty dollars for one of your jackets," she called.

They stared at her, their faces tanned and curious, then started to sidle away.

She opened her purse and pulled out money. "A hundred." She waved $20 bills.

"Geez, lady." The boy looked at his companion. "Whadda ya think, Mo?"

"She looks bigger than me, Carl. Give her yours." The girl huddled down inside her slicker.

Carl grimaced, but took off his yellow jacket and passed it through the open window. He and his friend dashed off down the street, dodging under the awnings of restaurants and stores.

Kaylen glanced in the direction of Sam's restaurant. A truck stood outside, men unloading plywood. She pulled on the slicker before leaving the BMW. Rain and wind swirled around her as she waited for a break in the traffic.

A gut feeling told her the *Destiny* was the cause of all the smoke. She jogged across the road, through the open gates and into the back of the marina's parking lot. Augmenting the fire boats, three fire trucks and six police vehicles jammed the blacktop, uniformed officers and firemen shouting to each other as they moved rapidly between their vehicles and the dock. The police had already marshaled onlookers away from the scene, and yellow tape cordoned off part of the marina. Kaylen saw an ambulance. Her stomach churned.

Perhaps Brian hadn't turned off his phone. She broke into a run. *Oh, God. Maybe he'd been on the Destiny.*

She tried to convince herself someone's breakfast had gone up in flames and she was being ridiculous. But when she got closer, she saw she wasn't wrong. Brian's boat was now only a charred shell. Two paramedics pushed a gurney toward an ambulance, the head of the victim showing above a blanket, an oxygen mask covering the lower half of the face.

Brian!

Kaylen didn't care if she was wanted by the police. Brian had been injured, and she hadn't even been able to tell him she shared his grief over Tim's death, or how much she realized she needed him. She broke through the crowd only to collide with someone else, who promptly shoved her aside.

"Hey!" She stumbled and braced herself for a fall, but strong hands pulled her back to her feet.

"Look where you're going, damn it," said a familiar voice.

"Brian!" She threw her arms around his neck. "Oh, thank God. You're safe."

"Kaylen?" He peered under her hood. "What the hell are you doing here? Come on." He grabbed her hand, and they ducked under the yellow crime scene tape.

Two officers stepped out in front of them. "That's my boat," Brian said. "Who's in charge?" He tried to evade the patrolmen, but one threw out his arm.

Kaylen watched Brian's fist curl. "Don't," she said. "Please."

"What's going on?" A man in a wrinkled black raincoat left a group standing at the edge of the dock.

"Mills." Brian started forward again. "That's my damned boat. Let me pass!"

"It's okay." The middle-aged detective, his black, curly hair liberally dusted with white and beaded with water, motioned for the officers to let Brian through.

Kaylen held on tight to Brian's hand as they headed for the *Destiny's* slip at a rapid pace.

"What the hell happened?" Brian asked Mills.

"We got calls, telling us a boat suddenly exploded into flames." Mills pulled up his coat collar as rain pummeled his face. "She went up so fast, there wasn't much the fire department could do, even though they were here inside of five minutes. They managed to save the boats on either side of yours, although the older one at the slip to the left took a lot of damage. Arson's on the way. You didn't leave anything on her that could have triggered this, did you?"

"No way." Brian frowned. "My neighbor, Jim, was going to help me out with storm preparations. Is he okay?"

"That's him." Mills pointed to the gurney being loaded into the ambulance. "He took one on the head. A couple of people found him laid out on the dock. The paramedics said he's going to be okay. Randall's going with him to the hospital, so we'll get a statement as soon as he's able to talk. Right now he's pretty groggy."

Brian ran a hand through his hair. "Christ, what a fuck-up of a day."

"I heard about your brother. I'm really sorry, Swift." Mills shifted from one foot to the other. "You'll have to come to the station and make a statement about your boat."

"Fine. Whatever." Brian nodded in the direction of the *Destiny's* burned hull. "Am I a suspect for this, too?"

"No. Several people came forward to tell us they saw you leave around six o'clock. The fire didn't start until maybe three hours later." Mills tried to peek under Kaylen's hood, but she kept her face averted. "Who's your friend?"

Brian slid his arm around her. "No one you need to know about," he told Mills. He winked. "I picked up some company."

Mills flushed. "You'll have to get rid of her. Give her cab fare. She's not getting a ride from the department."

Kaylen couldn't even begin to imagine what Brian was thinking, telling Mills a horrible story like that.

"Look here…" she started.

Brian gave her a less than gentle squeeze.

"She's got her own car," he said. "I'll take her back to it." He pushed Kaylen in the direction of the parking lot.

"Yeah, okay. But don't take too long." Mills turned his attention to the fire chief tramping toward him.

Kaylen had trouble keeping up with Brian in her high heels. The hood of her slicker kept sliding off her head, her purse kept falling off her shoulder, and she turned both her ankles several times. By the time they arrived at the back of the marina, she was panting, wet and totally out of sorts. Brian watched with a quirked eyebrow while she straightened the slicker and dabbed her face with a tissue she found in her purse.

"This isn't a fashion show, princess," he said. "Where's your car?"

So much for comforting him, she thought. He had definitely ruined his chances of having her apologize for anything. "Across the street." She started to point.

He grabbed her arm. "Head for it. Look like you're arguing with me."

"That'll be easy." She struggled out of his grip. "You're so rude and… and…" she searched for the right word, "deceitful," she said.

He had the audacity to laugh at her. "Is that the best you can do?"

"No, and I'm not finished, either." She shook her finger at him. "I don't know why I even bother with you. Why did you lie to me about being Tim's brother?"

"You're doing good," Brian said. "Keep walking, but speed it up. I figure we've got two or three minutes before they realize we're both gone. Give me your fob."

He had sidestepped her question about Tim yet again. Kaylen cradled her purse against her chest. "No way. No one drives my car except me. It's brand new."

"Give me the goddamned key fob, Kaylen." He snatched the purse right out of her arms.

"Give that back," she said.

He ignored her and rummaged around until he produced the fob.

Kaylen was done with being manipulated, lied to and treated like she was stupid. "Fuck you, Swift," she said. She slapped him so hard, her hand stung.

"Fuck you, too," he said. He unlocked the doors. "Get in," he told her.

Kaylen hesitated. He looked so angry, she wondered what he might do to her once they left the crowds behind. The imprint of her hand showed on his cheek, and his ear was the color of an over-ripe tomato.

"Do I really have to tell you again?" He jerked open the driver's door.

"No." She climbed into the passenger's seat and buckled her seatbelt.

He maneuvered the BMW through the maze of backed-up traffic as though he was taking a Sunday drive on a deserted country road. Kaylen held her breath a couple of times while they squeezed through spaces she knew could result in a new paint job, but somehow Brian missed everyone and everything to pull off onto a side street and leave the marina behind.

"What were you thinking, running away from the precinct?" he asked, his voice calm, as though nothing had happened between them.

Kaylen decided she wouldn't remind him, especially since he was driving her car. "I had to find you," she said. "I realized my life won't be worth anything if whoever wants the key realizes it may be on my leg."

"That tattoo," he said, as though he already knew.

"Yes. Although I don't think it's anything but an inked rose."

Brian turned right and headed north. "Did you use a magnifying glass when you looked at it?"

"Well, no, but there's nothing wrong with my eyesight."

As they drove through Coconut Grove's central district, Kaylen watched merchants hurriedly taking display racks inside their stores and retracting awnings before the strong wind gusts ripped them.

"Where are we going?" she asked. "The rain's coming down harder. We've got to take shelter."

"Little Havana," Brian said. "I think it'll be safer to go there than anywhere else. People will be too busy preparing for the storm to take much notice of us, and nobody there will recognize you, either. I'm sorry I couldn't tell you about my relationship with Tim, but it's complicated."

"That's what Lieutenant Shaw said."

Kaylen reorganized the contents of her purse, found her brush and worked on her tangled hair. She felt less anxious keeping her hands busy, but she wondered if Brian would make another snide remark about her paying attention to her appearance.

But his silence made her even more anxious, and Kaylen felt a need to clarify her feelings. Brian's lack of emotion made it difficult for her to interpret his mood. "The rational part of me understands that because you're a detective, you couldn't tell me everything," she said. "But the rest of me is really upset with you." She laid the brush back in her purse. "I've been terrified." Her voice quivered and she cleared her throat. "You could have eased my mind. It wouldn't have taken much. I just would have liked to know you were on the right side."

Brian's hand covered hers, and tears sprang into her eyes at his touch.

"From here on out, I'll do my best to make you feel less scared and confused," he said. "Scout's honor."

"You'd never make it as a scout," she said, sniffing. "Not with *your* mouth."

"That's probably true," he said.

"I bet you're a big discipline problem for Lieutenant Shaw, too," she said. "You're not much on following orders, are you?"

"No, and neither are you." Brian joined a throng of traffic moving slowly toward the expressway.

"I've had to start using my own judgment a lot more lately than in the past," Kaylen said. "Lieutenant Shaw told me to trust you earlier today, but I've still got reservations about that."

Brian laced his fingers through hers. "You won't regret it if you *do* trust me."

Kaylen looked at their hands and sighed. "I don't really have much choice at this point. I've pretty much run out of other options."

She hesitated, unsure whether she should allow herself to appear as vulnerable as she felt. "People are keeping things from me," she said. "I'm even worried about my best friend, Sandy. She's acting really weird. I think she's been sleeping with Sam and they've kept it a secret. And Sam's been coming on to me, which is doubly creepy if he *is* sleeping with Sandy."

"You've known Sam for a long time, haven't you?"

"Almost as long as I've lived in Miami…over ten years. Sandy not much less time than that."

"So what has she done to make you think she's acting weird?" Brian asked.

While they drove the expressway, Kaylen told him about Sandy being so insistent they go back to her apartment, about the new car Sandy could never afford, and about Sam telling her he loved her.

"And to top off the weirdness," Kaylen said as they arrived on the outskirts of Little Havana, "Sam didn't even seem to be upset he'd lost his restaurant to a fire. It sounded like he had invested in some of Tim's start-up businesses and planned to use the income from those instead of his restaurant, but he was evasive about even that."

"Tim wasn't involved in any start-ups," Brian said. "If Sam gave him money, then he probably either spent it somewhere or was planning to leave town with it."

Kaylen sighed. "I thought that, too. I'm really worried about Sam," she said. "He might be too proud to admit he had the wool pulled over his eyes. He spent so much on his new home, I was surprised when he told me his business was losing money."

"Maybe he torched the restaurant himself," Brian said.

"He'd never do that." Kaylen shook her head. "He practically lived there. He was always trying to improve his service, bring in new foods, new coffees…" she trailed off, thinking of the bitter blend she had been served on her last visit to The Hideaway and the horrible brew Sandy had poured for her.

"What's wrong?" Brian asked.

"He gave her the new coffee," Kaylen said.

"I don't understand."

"Sam had a new coffee at his restaurant. He made sure I tried it. Ugh, it was awful…bitter…full of chicory. When I arrived at Sandy's apartment, she gave me the same coffee. It's a specialty roast, so she couldn't have gone out and bought it."

"Sounds like your suspicions may be right, then."

"More deception," Kaylen said. "I don't understand it. Both of them must know I want them to be happy. Why would they try to keep their relationship a secret?"

"You'd better ask them the next time you see them," Brian said. "I'll never get the chance to ask Tim any more questions."

"Did he lie to you all the time, too?" Kaylen asked. "He didn't only lie to me about what he did for a living. At first, he said he lived in Coral Gables, but he always made excuses when I wanted to go to his apartment. He finally told me he was managing a friend's building in Little Havana, but it was a crappy place and he wasn't taking me there." She shook her head. "I was so stupidly naïve. It was like I wanted to believe him because he was so charming and fun to be with." She refused to tell Brian about going over to Tim's more than once and knocking on his door without finding him home. She felt too humiliated already.

"Tim lied to everyone," Brian said quietly. "Even me."

The wind picked up and tossed a large cardboard carton into the path of the BMW. Brian barely reduced speed as he maneuvered around it. Kaylen held onto the door frame and wondered where they were going to end up that afternoon. Not some fleabag hotel in Little Havana, she vowed.

"Tim left clues for me that I haven't even figured out yet," Brian said. "If he hadn't tried to be such a smart ass, I may have saved all of us a lot of pain."

Kaylen saw his knuckles whiten. She looked at his rigid profile. "You don't have to hold everything in, you know."

"I've been trained not to show emotion," Brian said. "But I'm hurtin.' Tim was my only family. He meant everything to me, but I'm not even sure he was gonna ask me for help when his life was in danger. I keep wondering whether he was the one who made it look like I was taking bribes. Maybe he was even the one who knocked me out and took me up to your bed."

"But why would he do that? Did he want the cartel to think you were taking their money, or did he want the police to arrest you?" Kaylen looked at the debris floating down the gutters and into the storm drains. She felt like the empty Styrofoam container she saw bobbing its way into the sewer...at the mercy of outside forces over which she had no control.

"I don't have all the answers yet," Brian said. "But I'm working on them. You're right in saying people are keeping secrets. No one associated with this case is telling the truth. It's like you're all wearing masks."

"I'm not," Kaylen said. "This is the real me." She pulled down the sun visor and stared at her reflection in the mirror on the back of it. "A little too much of the real me right now."

"I like the real you." Brian glanced at her and smiled. "The windblown look suits you, princess."

"Thank you," she said, grateful for the compliment.

"I wasn't sure if I could trust you, either, when I first met you," Brian said. "For all I knew, you could have been working with or even against Tim."

"Did you *really* believe I'd scare the hell out of myself, murder my housekeeper and trash my own home, not to mention risk the business I had sunk all my money into?"

"People have done a lot stranger things than that, believe me."

"Yeah, I know, because you've seen everything as a detective. Why didn't you at least tell me that? I'd have felt a little reassured about your motives."

"I'm on suspension, accused of taking bribes. How would telling you that reassure you about anything?"

"I suppose it wouldn't, if you put it like that." She found a hair clip in her purse and used it to anchor her curls away from her face. "Somehow, you always manage to talk your way out of everything. It makes me kind of mad."

"Force of habit," Brian said. "I learned over the years to cover my bases."

"It must be very lonely," Kaylen said. "You never let your guard down, do you?"

"I did once, with you. When you spent the night on the boat."

"Yes," she said, remembering. "I guess you did. A little."

Brian pulled the car over to the curb. "We're here."

Kaylen looked around. "This is the entrance to some filthy alleyway in a slum. What are you talking about? At least let's go to a hotel somewhere."

"We can't, unless you've got cash and you're willing to go somewhere they won't ask for ID," Brian said. "I'm pretty much tapped out. I've got about thirty bucks." He turned off the ignition. "We've got to ditch this car. Hal will have issued an all-points bulletin with the make and license plate by now."

"We're not going to walk around here," she said. "I'm not getting out, and you can't make me. It's dangerous. And I'm not leaving my car here to be stripped, either."

"Better your car than you," he said.

He opened his door and got out. Without giving her another look, he started walking away.

"Hey," Kaylen said. She grabbed her purse and opened her door. "Hey!"

"Stop shouting. I'm not deaf, and you're going to attract more attention than we need." He stood looking at her, rain running down his face, his clothes drenched. "Come on. You won't melt."

"I'm not worried about the rain." She reluctantly got out of her car and closed the door. "I'm worried about getting mugged."

"You'll be fine."

He opened his jacket briefly. Kaylen saw the holster and the gun.

"That makes me feel *so* much better," she said. "I hate guns."

"Would you like to announce the fact that I've got one to the entire population of Little Havana, or are you going to shut up and get a move on?"

"You're so sarcastic," Kaylen said. "I think I might hate you more than your gun."

"You don't hate me." He grinned briefly. "I'm growing on you. Admit it."

"I'm not admitting anything," she said. But she returned the smile. "Why are you wearing clothes that are too big for you? Your pants are rolled up."

"I had to borrow them." He took her hand. "Come on, I've got to double back and pick up some stuff I stowed in my car."

"Where is it?"

He was speeding up again, and Kaylen clung tightly to his arm as she tried to dodge the worst of the puddles.

"Parked about a quarter mile away from the marina. I got stuck in traffic, so I left it and took off on foot. People rubber-necking the fire. I forgot to get my rain gear out of the trunk."

"We should have gone there first," Kaylen said. "Before we drove over here."

"I wasn't going to take a chance on us getting caught," he said. "Mills isn't an idiot. If the fire chief hadn't distracted him, I doubt he'd have let us leave the dock so easily."

Kaylen realized her teeth were chattering. "I'm so cold," she said. She opened the slicker and pointed to her dress and shoes. "I'm not wearing the right clothes for hiking. How far do you think we'll have to walk before we can find a cab in this weather?"

"Don't you ever wear anything but strapless dresses and stupid shoes?" he asked.

"I never went to bed last night," she said. "So I didn't get a chance to put on something less formal. Next time I run from the police, I'll make sure I've got a change of clothes in my purse."

"Now who's being sarcastic?" Brian shook his head. "I'm cold, too. Come on, Calle Ocho's a half-block from here."

"What's on Calle Ocho?"

"Everything, including a cab stand." He put one arm around her waist and propelled her toward the street, barely visible through the sheeting rain.

Kaylen took a quick glance back at her BMW and decided she would probably never see it again.

CHAPTER THIRTY-EIGHT

"You're leaving me here?" Kaylen fought panic as they stood on Calle Ocho.

"You'll be fine." Brian hunched down as rain and wind swirled around them. "Go buy a magnifying glass at that variety store. They should sell soap and toothbrushes there, too. I'll meet you in the sandwich shop across the street in less than an hour. Do you have money in that suitcase of a purse or just makeup?"

"I've got debit and credit cards as well as cash."

"Stick with the cash," he said. "At least for now. Nothing that can be traced."

"Why can't I go with you?" Kaylen asked. "I came to you because I don't want to be left alone for five minutes. Now you want to leave me here for an hour."

"They'll be looking for the two of us. Besides, I can move faster if you're not with me. Keep your slicker closed and try to blend in. If you weren't so damned tall, you could pass for a Cuban."

"Very funny." She shivered again as the wind buffeted them.

"You should get some other shoes," he said. "No one wears high heels in a storm. There's a shoe store on the corner, next to the sandwich shop. "

"You're giving me a laundry list to take care of while you're getting what out of your car?" she asked.

"My rain gear and a couple of bags."

"I can buy you another slicker," she said. "Bags, too. What do you need empty bags for?"

"They're not empty." Brian shoved his hands into his pockets. "Don't argue with me. God, I'm freezing my butt off."

"You're not the only one."

"True," he said. "As soon as I get back, we'll find somewhere to stay."

"I can't believe I've come to this," Kaylen said. "I'm homeless and on the run. It's not supposed to be like this. I'm a socialite, not a felon." She felt like crying again, but she was sick of acting like a baby. No doubt Brian would tell her she was a *big* baby, too, she thought.

"You'll be okay," he said.

He drew her close, and she wrapped her arms around him. He was incredibly cold and wet, but he still brought comfort to her.

"I'll be back as fast as I can." His lips were against her ear. "Between your tattoo and the other clues Tim left for me, we'll figure things out. Then you'll be able to get your life back to normal, and I'll get reinstated. All this will go away, or at least everything but Tim's death."

"I don't know what 'normal' is any more," she said. "But I'll hold onto that thought while you're gone." She tried to smile, but the result was very wobbly. She took a couple of $50 bills out of her purse and pressed them into his hand. "Take these. Thirty dollars won't be nearly enough for the cab fares, and I'm not staying here alone for more than an hour while you're running all over town."

Brian looked relieved. "Thanks, princess. I owe you."

"The next time you see me, I'll be wearing pants and flat shoes, if I can find anything that fits me in these stores.".

"That's my girl." He ran off.

Kaylen felt incredibly alone, standing in the torrential rain falling onto Little Havana. She glanced at her watch. Sixty minutes would go fast, she told herself as she walked into the variety store.

CHAPTER THIRTY-NINE

Kaylen bought pink tennis shoes and gladly trashed her designer heels, which horrified the young girl at the shoe shop. As she left the store, Kaylen saw her shoes come out of the garbage can and hoped they wouldn't pinch their new owner's feet as they had hers. She found cropped jeans, a navy-blue t-shirt and a fuchsia sweatshirt in a tiny dress shop two doors down from the variety store.

She didn't know what to do for Brian. She doubted guessing his size would result in anything that fitted. And while he was ordering her around like a short order cook, he hadn't asked her to buy him anything, either. She decided he must have an outfit in one of those bags he had gone to pick up.

The biggest immediate problem they still had, after dry clothing and food, was somewhere to stay. Kaylen took Suki Adamson's card out of her purse. Brian had told her not to use credit or debit cards. Signing a lease would definitely leave a big trail of breadcrumbs. She called Sam.

"I want you to lease that furnished condo for me," she told him. "You'll have to sign the paperwork. I want a six-month lease, but if that won't fly, go ahead and sign for a year. I'll write you a check. Don't tell Suki it's for me."

"Why not?" Sam sounded bewildered. "Are you in more trouble, K.T.? I told you to come stay with me."

"That could send the cops to your door, if not a drug cartel."

"What?"

Kaylen imagined Sam's face was probably pinker than her new sweatshirt.

"I sort of ran away from an interview with a homicide lieutenant."

"You need to come to my house right now. You're running from the police and a drug cartel? Have you lost your mind?" Sam wasn't bewildered anymore. He was all business. "I'll get my attorney over here to meet with us."

"No attorney is going to be willing to drive to your house in this weather," Kaylen said. "I need somewhere close-in not only to ride out the storm, but to live in. You told me yourself that I need a roof over my head."

She heard him sighing heavily and waited.

"All right," he said.

He sounded resigned, and her spirits lifted a little.

"I've got Suki's card in my hand," Kaylen said. "I can give you her numbers right now."

"No need. I've got her card on top of my desk," Sam said. "I was going to call her to get the number of a guy in their commercial division, so I could see how much it was going to cost me to buy another restaurant. I'll call you back in a few, as soon as I've talked to her."

"Thanks, Sam. I really appreciate it." Kaylen took cover under an awning right before a deluge sent shoppers scattering from the sidewalks.

She waited for a break in the rain, the smell of fresh bread wafting out through the open doorway behind her. She thought about staving off her hunger with a roll, but told herself she was going to eat a meal as soon as Brian got back.

Sam called moments later. "That condo's been leased already," he said.

Kaylen's hopes plummeted.

"But she has another condo without a view of the bay," Sam said. "It's only a short walk from the marina, and it's a furnished one-bedroom overlooking the pool."

Hope returned. "Is it available today?"

"It's vacant. She can negotiate."

"Please. I can't face the hotel scene in this weather."

"Okay, honey. Don't get upset. She said the place has been empty for a while, so the owners are pretty motivated."

"Remember, don't use my name," Kaylen said.

"Yeah, I know. I'll get her to fax or email the lease over right now and I'll sign it. I just watched a weather update. This storm's going to shut everything down within the next couple of hours. It's a doozy."

"Thanks, Sam. Tell Suki there's a big bonus if she gets everything finalized within the next hour. That'll get her moving."

Sam chuckled. "You sound like George."

"I'll take that as a compliment."

"It is," he said. "I'll call when I've got the key. Stay dry, honey." He hung up.

Kaylen called her manager, Rob. "Close the club for tonight," she told him. "And I may need to keep it closed through the end of the week. Does it need boarding?"

"I already called a service," Rob said. "They're ready to start as soon as I get the word from you."

"You've got it," Kaylen said. "But how did you manage to get that agreement in place? Did you offer them a bonus without checking with me first?"

"No. They're my cousins on my mom's side," Rob said. "They owe me a favor, and they've got access to plywood."

"Oh." Kaylen wondered what sort of favor could elicit a promise to work in the face of a tropical storm.

"You'll lose a lot of money and maybe some staff if we stay closed," Rob said.

"I know," Kaylen said. "But I've got some personal issues. I can't manage the club until I take care of them."

"Whatever you have to do shouldn't interfere with the club running smoothly." Rob's voice held a gentle but firm rebuke. "You hired me on as the manager."

"That's true," Kaylen said. "But I'm still the owner, remember?"

"Sorry," Rob said. "I overstepped my bounds."

"That's okay." Kaylen smiled. He sounded contrite, but still offended. "My issues may end up causing problems for the patrons and staff. I'm not going to discuss them with you, but I want you to know I'm not coming to this decision lightly."

"Then I'll call the staff today and notify them," Rob said. "Is there anything I can do personally to help you out?"

"No…well, maybe. Can you get me a car on the QT?"

"My uncle's always willing to lend me his LeSabre," Rob said. "I'll call and tell him my car broke down."

"Thanks, Rob. I'll take good care of it." She hoped she could say the same thing about Brian, who drove like he was in the Indy 500.

The rain slowed enough for her to walk down the street to the sandwich shop while she made arrangements for Rob to bring the car over. After she ordered, she took two cans of soda and sat at the back of the shop, where she couldn't be seen through the big window. Brian arrived a couple of minutes later, wearing a rain slicker and carrying two red gym bags. He joined her at one of the chipped and scarred yellow Formica-topped tables.

"I ordered chicken noodle soup and meatball sandwiches. That'll warm us up," Kaylen said.

"Sounds great." He dumped the bags on the floor. "The cabbie said the storm is almost at hurricane strength. We've got to find a hotel and wait this out."

"I've done better than that. We should have a furnished condo in less than an hour. Sam's signing the lease for me and calling me back as soon as he's got the keys."

Brian leaned across the table. "No one should know where you are," he whispered. "Or who you're with. Did you tell him about me?"

"No way," Kaylen whispered back. "He hates you on a good day. I told Sam I was sick of being homeless and I didn't want to ride the storm out at a hotel. But I did tell him I couldn't stay with him because of well, *you know…*" She smiled as the young girl from behind the counter brought their soup and sandwiches.

"Would you like anything else?" The girl gave Brian a really long look.

"Coffee?" he asked.

"Yes, I will make a pot." She smiled and sashayed back toward the counter, her hips swaying under her tight and very short black skirt. "It will only take a couple of minutes," she called.

Brian watched her, his eyebrows drawn toward each other. "I hope she doesn't have a TV back there," he said. "She gave me a strange look."

Kaylen wanted to laugh, but since they were supposed to be keeping a low-profile, she controlled herself. "She was flirting with you," she said. "You don't do much outside of work, do you?"

"No." He dug his spoon into the soup.

"Ouch," Kaylen said. "I won't bring up that subject again."

"Good. Eat your meal. Who knows when we'll get another."

Kaylen's phone rang as she was finishing her sandwich.

"Look at the caller ID before you answer," Brian cautioned.

"It's Sam," Kaylen said.

The girl brought Brian's coffee while Sam was telling Kaylen he had access to the condo keys already.

"Do you want me to meet you over there?" Sam asked.

"No. Better I meet you at the restaurant. Oh…" she stopped. "I'm so sorry, Sam. I forgot about the fire."

"That's okay, honey. I'll get one of my men to drop off the keys at the condo management office."

Kaylen didn't want the manager to see her or Brian, but she didn't know what else to suggest. "Sounds good," she said. She listened as Sam gave her the condo address and wrote it down on the back of Suki's card.

The girl was lingering. "Would you like coffee, too?" she asked Kaylen.

"No, thanks." Kaylen pulled a $5 bill out of her purse. "Do you want anything else?" she asked Brian.

He shook his head, his attention on the street outside. Kaylen paid for the coffee and told the girl to keep the change.

"My father said to tell you we are closing in ten minutes," the girl said. "He thinks we will not get any more customers." She looked at Brian again. "He was upset with me that I made a whole pot of coffee."

"Fine," Kaylen said. "Give me a big cup of it to go and bring my husband one, too." She took out another $5. "This should cover the cost."

"Thank you, Madam. Thank you very much," the girl said as she took the money. With a disappointed glance at Brian, she went back behind the counter and Kaylen heard her speaking to someone in the kitchen as water ran and pots clanged.

"Husband?" Brian shook his head. "Now she's *really* going to remember us."

"No she won't. She's checked you off her list and completely forgotten you exist by now." Kaylen popped the last bite of her sandwich into her mouth and wondered how a small place in Little Havana could come up with such a tasty meatball.

"I'm not happy about this condo," Brian said.

Kaylen bristled. He wasn't going to order her around like she was his property. "I refuse to go to some filthy pay-by-the-hour hotel," she said. "Either with you or by myself. I need a home, where I can lock the door and know I'm the only one with a key."

"I'll be with you at all times," Brian said.

"I don't care. I'm not staying somewhere with bed bugs." She folded her arms across her chest. "You can't make me. Forget it."

"Christ, you're hard-headed." He glanced toward the empty counter. The discussion in the kitchen continued at a fairly loud volume. "What if you can't trust Sam?"

"That's nonsense." Kaylen picked up her purse. "I'm going, and you can't stop me. Either come with me or leave me to fend for myself. If I die, it'll be on your head, whether it's the storm that kills me or the cartel."

"Okay, okay." He threw up his hands. "I'm not going to keep arguing with you over this, but I think it's a big risk."

"Thank you." She put her purse back down on the empty seat beside her. "I really would have gone without you, you know."

"I realize that. I'll make the best of a bad situation."

"It would've been worse in a flea-bag hotel with a flimsy door," she said. "I guarantee you that. And you'd have been worried about me the whole time. Admit it."

"Yeah, I do, unfortunately." He rubbed his hand across his face. "I'm even getting too punchy to argue with you."

Kaylen wondered if she looked as drawn and tired as Brian did, and whether he was right about the waitress remembering her last customers of the day, bedraggled and out of place in the little café.

"How far away is this place?" he asked, breaking into her swirling thoughts. "Do we have to take a cab or can we walk?"

"Neither," Kaylen said. She felt a lot more secure about the second request she'd made while Brian was gone. "I got us a car. It should be here in a few minutes. My club manager's bringing it."

"Damn." Brian's eyebrows rose. "You're not just a pretty face, princess."

"That's right. I'm resourceful, too." Her inner churning slowed.

He'd given her a backhanded compliment, even if he had tacked on that horrible nickname again. Kaylen wasn't sure if she should be flattered or resentful.

Brian smiled suddenly, a little lopsided because of the healing scar on his mouth, and Kaylen somehow forgot about the resentment part. There was something reassuring about him, even with his rough exterior.

"When do you get those sutures out?" she asked, changing the subject.

"A couple more days."

"Does your mouth still hurt?"

"A little, but it's a whole lot better. I actually got to enjoy this food. Maybe because I haven't eaten since breakfast yesterday."

"This is the first meal I've managed to finish since last Saturday." Kaylen pushed the remains of her pickle around her plate before deciding she was too full to eat it. "Must be the company."

"If I make you feel safe enough to eat, then I'm happy," Brian said. "I know it can't be anything else."

"Don't sell yourself so short." Kaylen leaned forward. "That little girl behind the counter developed a big crush on you immediately. And when you're not insulting me, you're fairly pleasant to be around."

"Not as pleasant as Tim, I bet." Brian crumpled up his napkin and laid it on his plate. "He worked hard on his conversation skills and likeability. I bust heads for a living. I don't need to be charming."

"And you don't try to be, either." Kaylen placed her hand over his. "But I know that under that abrasive exterior, you've got a heart. Otherwise you wouldn't be here with me."

251

"I need you, princess. You said it yourself…you may have the answer to both our problems."

"Don't call me princess," Kaylen said. "I've told you that before."

"Then don't play around with my emotions. I told you *that* before. You're trying to make that girl jealous."

Kaylen withdrew her hand. He was right.

"What's in the gym bags?" she asked, eager to change the subject again.

"I'll show you as soon as we get to the condo." Brian stood up. "I think our ride's here. There's some guy double-parked outside in a Buick LeSabre, and he's waving."

CHAPTER FORTY

Kaylen felt much safer after she closed and locked the door of her new home.

Suki Adamson hadn't lied when she told Sam the place was a good deal. The condo was elegant without being cold and impersonal, the decor soothing in tones of blue and beige. Brian threw the gym bags into a corner of the bedroom and flipped the light switch. Lamps on the bedside tables illuminated a king-sized bed covered with a pale blue satin comforter.

"Well, something's gone right today, apart from us getting a decent meal and transportation," Brian said. "Comfortable, clean and the utilities are on. I've got to shower and warm up." He took toiletries and clothes out of one of the bags. "Do you want to go first?"

Kaylen shook her head. "No. You're the one in the wet outfit. You look exhausted, too. After you shower, I'll keep watch while you take a nap."

He shook his head. "You've seen too many movies. What are you planning to do if someone breaks down the door? Scream and come get me? Bolt the front door and put a chair under the knob if you're afraid until I get out of the bathroom. I'll nap on the couch. Then if anyone tries to get in, I'll hear them."

"Fine," Kaylen said. "Whatever you say. You're in charge." She took off her slicker and draped it over the back of a chair.

"Christ," Brian said. "Being with you reminds me why I don't have a girlfriend." He went into the bathroom.

Kaylen heard the shower running. Her cell rang.

"I'm sending one of my men over with groceries," Sam said. "He was the one who dropped off the keys, so he was in the area already. Let him in."

"Okay." She wondered how Brian would like that, but they had to eat again if the storm was going to interrupt everything for the next few hours at least.

"Do you want me to come over and keep you company?" Sam asked.

"No," Kaylen said. "I need to get some rest." That was true. No sense in telling him Brian was with her. "I'll call you when I wake up," she promised. "I'm not going to open the club tonight."

"Nobody'll be out partying in this," Sam said. "Not if they have a lick of sense left, anyway."

Kaylen glanced out the living room window at the steady downpour. "That's for sure."

"I'll call Rob and tell him to make sure none of the staff tries to turn up," Sam said.

Kaylen felt herself bristling again. "I already did that," she said, trying hard not to sound defensive. "He's making calls." She watched the wind toss the trees around, their branches bending into impossible positions that threatened to snap them. "What's the latest on the storm? I heard it's almost at hurricane strength." She bit her lip. She had almost said: "Brian told me."

"It's lost a little strength over the last hour," Sam said. "But it hit the Keys pretty hard."

"I like my new place," Kaylen said.

"Good."

"Sam, are you okay?" she asked. His conversation sounded stilted.

"You haven't been watching the news."

"No. I haven't seen a TV or newspaper in days," she said.

"Then you don't know."

"Know what?"

"About Tim," Sam said. "Honey, the cops found his body. He's dead."

"I *do* know about that," Kaylen said quietly. "Lieutenant Shaw told me this morning."

"Tim was murdered," Sam said. "I should be with you."

"No," she said. She made a decision. Worrying about what Sam thought of her wasn't important anymore. "I'm okay, and I'm not alone. Brian's here. He's taking care of me."

There was silence.

"Sam, are you still there?" she asked.

"Yes." One word, but it conveyed his displeasure.

"I know you don't like him," Kaylen said. "Although I don't know why. He's never done anything to you."

"He's a crooked cop," Sam said.

"How do you know that?"

"It's all over the news. And he's Tim's half-brother, Kaylen. Did you know *that?*"

"Yes," she said. "I know everything." That was a lie, she thought. She knew so little, and yet she was hiding in a condo with this man and placing her life in his hands, all on the word of his supervisor and her gut feelings.

"I'm coming over there to pick you up," Sam said. "Right now."

"No, you're not. And if you try, I won't open the door."

"K.T..."

"Non-negotiable," she said. "Back off. I've been confused enough over the last few days. I'm not confused about Brian. I *know* he's innocent." And suddenly, she believed that was true.

"You're not thinking straight," Sam said. "You need my protection."

"I'm fine." She meant it, and peace came to her at last. "I think I can take care of myself, but if I can't, Brian will. He won't let anything happen to me. And Lieutenant Shaw knows we're together."

"If you were here at my compound, you would be surrounded by state-of-the-art security. That would be a lot better than being with one man, even if he *is* a cop."

"Maybe," she said. "But right now, there's a storm blowing through and I'm safe behind a locked door with a detective. I'll take that over you trying to send a car for me or putting yourself at risk to come pick me up yourself. Be sensible, Sam."

"I'll call every hour," he said.

"Don't you *dare*. I didn't sleep at all last night. I'm going to bed. I'll call you later, I promise."

"I'll hold you to that," Sam said. "I'm not happy about this, K.T."

"I know, but you're going to have to trust my judgment sometime, and it may as well be now." She waited for him to answer, but he said nothing. "I'll call later," she said again. "I'm hanging up now," she added.

"I love you," he said.

"I'll be okay," she said.

He hung up the phone.

The doorbell rang. Kaylen looked through the peephole and saw a man standing outside, his arms filled with a large box.

"Groceries from Mr. Wilson," he said.

She slid the chain into place and opened the door a crack. "Thanks for bringing them," she said. "I'm not dressed. Please put the box down outside the door. I'll pull it inside after you leave."

He set down his burden and disappeared from view. Kaylen counted to 20 before cautiously opening the door. She dragged the heavy, damp box over the threshold, locked the door and propped a chair under the knob before pulling Sam's gift into the kitchen and stowing everything. By the time she finished, the shower had stopped running and the condo was completely silent except for the drone of the refrigerator.

When she walked into the bedroom, she saw Brian asleep on one side of the bed. He was dressed in a t-shirt and shorts with one leg almost hanging off the bed, as though he had decided to lie down for a moment and that moment had been all it took. Kaylen shivered. The bedroom felt really cold.

She pulled the covers over Brian and stood watching him. The tightness in his face had relaxed, leaving him peaceful. She tried to see any resemblance to Tim, but decided there wasn't any. It was something of a relief to her…she was beginning to have real feelings for this man. The fact that he was her deceased boyfriend's brother made that an unsettling revelation.

She sighed. Comparing Brian to Tim was like comparing apples to pears. Or maybe more like rough-grained sandpaper to a polishing cloth. But she knew she would rather have that sandpaper on her side. Brian might not have

Tim's finesse, and he might not be as tall, handsome or buff as his brother, but if her life was threatened, she knew who she would want to have standing in front of her.

The thought soothed her, and she made sure both Brian's feet were covered by the comforter before she helped herself to a t-shirt and shorts from the open gym bag. She needed to rinse out her underwear, shower and get some sleep herself.

When she returned from the bathroom, he hadn't moved an inch. She slid under the covers and lay shivering between the cold sheets. His warmth was too inviting, and she moved over beside him. He turned to face her and flung one arm across her. She burrowed against him, closed her eyes and slept dreamlessly for the first time since that fateful morning she had awakened beside him.

Until she awoke with a jolt.

CHAPTER FORTY-ONE

Kaylen thought someone had kicked the door in. She wondered if she had dreamed it, but Brian was on his feet, gun in hand, heading for the living room.

The wind had intensified, howling with a low monotony, and the windows rattled in their casements. She glanced at the clock. It was two in the afternoon, but the sickly light filtering in through net curtains made it feel a lot later. Rain cascaded from the overloaded gutters and gurgled in the downspouts.

Brian came back into the room. "It's okay," he said. "There's a big plant rolling around outside your front door. It must have blown over from one of your neighbors."

"Oh, thank God." Tears welled up in her eyes, and she began to cry, softly but forcefully.

"It's just a plant," Brian said. He sat down beside her and placed his gun on the nightstand. "It's nothing. Go back to sleep. I'm gonna watch TV. The power's still on, at least for now."

But she couldn't stop crying. The numbness that had kept her functioning was gone, as though the dreamless sleep had released it. Kaylen needed comfort, and she sought it from the one person she felt could understand her feelings. She wrapped her arms around Brian and buried her face against his neck. He smelled faintly of the soap she had found in the shower stall, his skin warm, his pulse leaping strongly against her cheek.

Reluctantly, it seemed, he put his arms around her. Kaylen felt confused.

He hadn't hesitated before. Why would he now, when she knew so much more about him and Tim no longer stood between them, except as a ghost?

"Do you have any idea what you do to me?" Brian's voice sounded uncharacteristically shaky.

She raised her head and looked at him through her tears.

"I want you," he said. "All the time I'm near you. I've been trying to ignore it since the day I woke up in your bed."

Kaylen pulled his head down. She craved close, intimate contact, and she knew Brian needed it just as desperately. His lips met hers, awkwardly at first because of the sutures, but the kiss deepened as he laid her against the bed, his body aligning with hers. Her hands slid up his back, under his shirt, to encounter ridges where there should have been none.

Startled, she stopped kissing him. "Brian, what happened to you?"

He pulled away from her. "We shouldn't be doing this," he said. "It's wrong."

"Because of Tim? I'm sorry he's dead, really sorry," she said, because she didn't know what else to say to make Brian feel less guilty. "But this isn't wrong."

She tried to regain the mood by throwing off her t-shirt and kissing him again.

His muscles felt like coiled steel, but slowly he relaxed as she rimmed his ear with her tongue and rubbed against him. Kaylen couldn't wait any longer. She grabbed the bottom of his shirt and dragged it upward.

He pulled away again. "Don't," he said.

"Why?" She frowned. "We're not going to make love with our clothes on."

"I'm not taking my shirt off," he said.

"That's too weird. I want to look at you, to touch you," she said.

He closed his eyes. "I want that too."

"Then what's the problem?" She pulled him back down onto her and kissed him again. He responded, but he was still holding back. "Tell me," she said.

"No more questions," he said. "Sometimes, you talk way too much."

His hands and lips claimed her breasts hungrily. Kaylen arched her back, incredible sensations flowing over and through her. The heat of his mouth contrasted erotically with the cold air in the room. Her nipples hardened to the point of exquisite pain. Barely able to breathe, she closed her eyes as he moved down her body in a relentless path, arousing her quickly, his movements forceful behind the teasing fingers, the probing tongue, and the nipping teeth. He pulled her shorts low over her stomach. His tongue rimmed her belly button; his hand slid down to her thighs. He caressed her through the shorts before his fingers slid beneath them. Her muscles quivered, expectant, but suddenly he stopped. She raised her head to find him looking at her.

"Are you sure you want this?" he asked. His fingers slipped an inch closer to their goal.

"Yes." Her voice was guttural, low. Almost unrecognizable to her.

She wanted him more than she could ever have imagined. She spread her legs wide apart. Brazenly. She felt completely uninhibited. Wanton like she had never been. She took his hand and slid it completely inside the shorts.

"Now," she said. She rubbed herself against his fingers, her head thrown back. She felt his lips against the pulse throbbing strongly at the base of her throat as he took the gift she had offered him, giving her pleasure in ever-widening circles.

Her shorts were torn from her and thrown across the room. His followed immediately after. She rose to meet his powerful thrust, clasping his hips with her knees, pulling him further into her, her eyes locking with his.

Lost somewhere between the present and infinity, she welcomed the swirling emotions, the heat and the ever-building urgency, the feeling of being completely alive. She basked in the rush of fulfillment and lay content beneath him when he slumped against her, his body trembling. Her hands slid up his back again, and that time he didn't try to stop her. Roughened skin felt knotted beneath her fingertips.

"What happened?" she asked.

"I was beaten and burned as a kid." He rolled away from her, his emotional withdrawal more painful than the physical distance. "My step-father," he said. "Most of the scars faded over the years, but a couple of times, he was too drunk to care what he did with the belt buckle, and another time he threw boiling soup on me."

"Brian, I'm so sorry."

"You don't need to be. It was a long time ago. I don't like talkin' about it. Subject closed."

She felt awkward. Very naked, and completely uncomfortable with her unblemished, unflawed body. She wanted to put her arms around him and snuggle up next to him, but she was afraid he'd reject her.

"Do…do you still think Tim may have been the one who stripped you and put you in bed with me?" she asked.

Chilled, she wanted to pull the comforter over herself, but would he think she was trying to separate herself from him? Involuntarily, she shivered.

For once, Brian seemed unaware of her discomfort. He stared at the rain coursing down the windows. "Yeah, even though I thought he had more respect for me. He knew how difficult it is for me to…" his voice trailed off.

Tears sprang into her eyes. She wanted to take away the years of pain. "It doesn't matter to me," she said. Abandoning her qualms, she put her arms around him.

"Sooner or later, it matters to everyone," he said. "So don't lie."

Kaylen wasn't sure whether telling him she wasn't a liar would help or completely destroy the intimacy they had just shared. She kept holding him, placed her cheek against his shoulder and waited to see if he would withdraw from her again.

But when he turned to look at her, the harshness had left his face. "You know, Tim gave his neighbor a note to hold for me. It told me to take special care of you. I think he was afraid to write what he really wanted to say, in case someone else got to read it, but I believe he wanted us to be together. For me to do more than make sure you're kept safe."

"Oh, Brian. If I could believe that, it would give me some peace."

"Kaylen…" he faltered. His hand was gentle on her face. "I don't know where this thing's goin'…"

"Shh." She held him close, tight. "Now *you're* the one who's talking too much."

"I…" He choked up.

Kaylen felt pretty choked herself.

They kept their arms around each other as the sounds outside intensified to the volume of a runaway locomotive hurtling down a track. Reluctantly, she broke away first. "I bought a magnifying glass," she said. "Do you want to look at the tattoo now?"

"Yeah." He managed a smile. "Thanks. You know, for everything."

She had never seen him look so unguarded and vulnerable. She kissed him lightly. "Any time. With or without your shirt."

"About Tim…"

"Not now. Not while all this is going on," she said.

They kissed again, and the kiss quickly deepened, but when he reached for her, she put her finger against his lips. "I want you as much as you want me, but we've got to get moving," she said.

"I know." He rolled onto his back and stared at the ceiling. "I don't want to get out of this bed."

"As long as you don't blame me for that." She kissed his shoulder and forced herself to sit on the side of the bed. "I'll make coffee and get the magnifying glass," she said. "Are there sweats in one of those bags? I'm really cold."

Brian swung one of the bags onto the bed for her to look through while he pulled on his shorts. Kaylen found sweats and welcomed the warmth, although she had to roll up the pants. The shirt reached almost to her knees. "Are these Tim's?" she asked.

"Yeah. I found the bags in his closet."

"Why would he have two identical bags full of gym clothes?" she asked as she walked out the door.

"That's what I wondered the last time I went over to his apartment."

Brian followed her. He found the thermostat in the hallway and adjusted it before walking into the living room to flip on the TV. The furnace kicked on and welcome warmth blasted from a duct beside the breakfast bar.

"I found another bag inside one of them." Brian's voice mingled with the sounds of a news broadcast. "It's from a different gym that's close to Tim's place." He turned up the volume. "Listen."

Kaylen had the bag of coffee in her hand when she heard her name.

"Nightclub owner and socialite, Kaylen Roberts is wanted for questioning in connection with the murder of her boyfriend, Tim Madison, and her friend, Sandy Cole. Madison's body was found in a creek yesterday evening. Cole's remains were discovered early today in a burned-out motor yacht at the Coconut Grove Marina."

CHAPTER FORTY-TWO

Brian dropped the remote when he saw Kaylen's face turn white. He managed to get to her before she collapsed. He carried her into the living room and laid her on the couch.

"I swear I had no idea there was going to be an announcement about your friend. Are you okay?" He brushed the hair from her eyes. Her forehead felt cold and clammy.

"No." She was crying again.

"I'm so sorry." He cradled her against his chest. "What the hell would Sandy be doing on my boat? I've never even met her."

"I don't know." Kaylen's voice sounded muffled. She sniffed. "Maybe looking for me? I told her about you."

"Is there anyone you *didn't* tell about me?" Brian asked. "Telling you to keep quiet about your involvement with me doesn't seem to have worked at all."

"Sam and Sandy are my best friends." She stopped. "God, I can't believe anyone would kill her. For what reason?"

"Maybe because she looked like you and they made a mistake?"

"She didn't used to," Kaylen said. "She suddenly started dressing like me and changed her hair color fairly recently. She used to be blonde."

"Do you know why she did it?" Brian asked. "Did you ask her?"

"No, not until last night." Kaylen sat up. "I felt kind of flattered in the beginning, but then her efforts creeped me out. I think she did it to please Sam, because he has a thing for me. But I don't know why she wouldn't want to be

264

herself any more. When I finally did confront her, she got so defensive and angry. She told me I was mistaken, thinking they were having a relationship."

"Do you think you made a mistake?"

"No." Kaylen took a travel pack of tissues out of the bag containing the magnifying glass and opened it. She blew her nose hard.

Brian decided she wasn't such a dignified socialite after all, and he liked the out-of-character slip.

"Well, I will say that destroying the boat makes more sense to me now, even if I don't know why she was murdered," he said. "I bet she was either killed there or was already dead when she was brought on board. The fire was set to cover the homicide."

Tears ran down Kaylen's face again. Brian cursed his insensitivity. He was talking about this woman's best friend, he reminded himself. This woman who was no longer a stranger, but had become a lover. *His brother's girlfriend.*

He instinctively started to edge away. He'd done the one thing he vowed he wouldn't, lowered his defenses and had sex with her. He'd got to re-establish the distance between them.

"Maybe you should go stay with a friend," he said. "To keep you safe while I try to figure things out."

"I'm not going anywhere," she said, and she slid right back up against his side. "I know what you're trying to do, but it's not going to work. You let me in, and now you're stuck with me."

"Christ," he said. He needed a distraction. Things were getting way too personal. "Let's have that coffee." He left her on the couch, ran water, and filled the coffeemaker.

"Brian, I can't sit around crying while you're making coffee," she said. "I need support, and you're going to have to give it to me, whether it's uncomfortable for you or not."

He dumped grounds into the basket and pressed the button to start the brewing cycle. "Look, I realize you've got every right to be upset…"

"And so do you. God knows, you've lost even more than I have."

"Who's countin'?" He couldn't go there. His own loss was too raw, too painful. The coffee bag fell to the floor, its contents spilling over his bare feet.

"Shit," he said. "Why can't you just let it go?" He opened cabinets and slammed them closed, catching his fingers in the last one. "Where's a fuckin' *broom?"*

Kaylen was in front of him suddenly, and her arms went around his waist. "I understand how you feel. I really do. More than you know." Her face was disconcertingly close, unable to be ignored.

She kissed him softly, the warmth of her lips penetrating his defenses and chipping at the ice surrounding his soul.

"When I lost George, I couldn't talk about it for weeks," she said. "I was so angry. I felt so abandoned. You're trying to do the same thing."

Looking at her, Brian knew his life was never going to be the same again. *Damn Tim, or bless him. The jury was still out.*

"Enough lecturing from me." She gave him the ghost of a smile. "Let's see if my tattoo has anything written into it. Then we can give the information to the police, so they can find out who killed Tim and probably Sandy and Rosa, too."

Brian thought about Hastings' possible involvement. If Kaylen's tattoo held a key piece of the puzzle, walking into the precinct was the last thing they needed to do. He watched her as she picked up the bag containing the magnifying glass.

"I've got to keep you away from everyone until we figure things out ourselves," he said.

"I don't think that's wise," she said. "You're all alone. What if the cartel finds us here and kidnaps me? You're in no shape to stop them."

"I'm healing fast," Brian said. "You saw that for yourself in the other room, didn't you?"

"Putting it so crassly, which is what you do best…yes. But what if you're outnumbered?"

"I'll deal with it."

Kaylen shook her head. "It's not only us in danger anymore. Even your neighbor got hurt."

"Yeah. I feel real bad about Jim. I didn't want to involve him, but he wouldn't keep out of the way. I hope he's okay."

The coffee had finished brewing and a welcome aroma filled the kitchen. After slamming around in the cabinets, Brian knew exactly where the cups were stored. He filled two mugs.

"I've got to admit that's the best idea you've had since we got up," Kaylen said. "Can I have some cream? It's in the refrigerator."

Brian opened the door. "How is it we've got at least a week's worth of groceries in here?"

"Sam," Kaylen said. "He sent one of his men over with a box of food. He always does things like that, looking after me."

"Does he know I'm here?" Brian tipped a small amount of cream into her coffee. "Light or dark?"

"Medium," she said. "Yes, I told him. He's not happy. He wanted to come over and pick me up."

"I bet. And if he knew what happened between us this afternoon, he'd probably arrange to have me shot."

"Probably." She laughed a little too forcefully. "I told him I was safer with you than anyone else."

"Thanks for the vote of confidence." Brian placed both mugs on the coffee table.

Kaylen took a sip. "You make good coffee," she said. "That makes two things you do well apart from busting heads."

"I've got my uses." He tried the coffee himself. "Yeah, it's good. Did this come from Sam?"

"Yes," she said. "I'm glad it's not that bitter stuff he and Sandy gave me before." She put the mug down quickly and her coffee slopped onto the table. "What am I thinking? I'm sitting here talking about Sam and he could be in danger, too. I've got to call him, warn him. If they killed Sandy, he could be next." She got up. "Where did I leave my purse? My cell's in it."

"On the dining table." He got up, too, and headed for the bedroom. "I'll call Hal, ask him to give Sam protection."

Kaylen grabbed her bag. "I'll tell Sam you're sending the police. He's so defensive about asking for help, even though he's always telling me *I* should."

CHAPTER FORTY-THREE

"You may think your place is like a bunker, Sam…"

Brian divided his attention between Hal yelling in his ear about being irresponsible and going off half-cocked and Kaylen, in the living room.

He watched her as she sat cross-legged on the couch, her cell phone up to one ear. Her chestnut hair cascaded in thick curls over her shoulders. The neckline of Tim's too-large sweatshirt hung off one bronzed shoulder. Even without makeup she was stunning, and Brian wondered what the fuck she saw in him.

He thought back to the morning he awakened in her bed. He'd never have placed a bet that he'd get any closer to her than that, much less that she would have been the one to initiate sex with him. He wondered if she understood how deeply she had affected him, and he worried that in the long run, their encounter might mean a lot less to her than it did to him.

Hal finally paused for breath.

"Do you seriously think I'd sit by after someone off'd my brother?" Brian asked. "Are you gonna tell me you'd have done anything different?"

"Damn it, Brian, I'm the one who should be asking all the questions, and you're the one who had better be answering them. Meet me in an hour, and bring Kaylen with you. Otherwise, I'll put out a warrant on you, too."

Brian looked through the blinds at sheets of rain blowing sideways, a classic sign of a tropical storm. "If we can get that far, we'll meet you in the parking lot of Finnegan's. But make it two hours."

"Why the hell do you want more time? I'm going to need a goddamned pontoon to get anywhere by then. Do you know how bad the weather is out there right now?"

"Yeah. I can see the rain from where I'm standing. Look, Hal, all I'm gonna tell you is that what I have to take care of is more important than giving you an easier drive. I don't care if I get my badge back or not."

"*...and what makes you so sure you can trust everyone around you?*"

Brian heard Kaylen's voice rise. He glanced at her again, and she pointedly stared back. He looked away.

He finished up with Hal and went back into the living room. She was still arguing with Sam, knees bent and feet on the couch. When Brian sat down, she shifted back until only her toes rested against his thigh. A distance was re-establishing itself between them, and he found he wasn't sure he liked that after all.

Kaylen ran her free hand through her hair while she listened. Finally, she sighed. "No, I *still* don't want you to send anyone to pick me up." She looked at Brian. "No, I don't care if you don't like him, Sam. I already told you that. I called to warn you that you might be in danger, not to argue with you about Brian again." She rolled her eyes and pushed her hair off her face. "I've got to go. I'll call you again later." She hung up. "He's too pig-headed," she said. "He told me the police can go fuck themselves."

Brian slid the magnifying glass out of the bag. "Hal's past mad. He's gonna give himself a stroke if he keeps yelling like he just did. He told me to bring you in. I told him I need a couple of hours. He threatened to have us both arrested, but he'll simmer down."

"You hope." She sighed. "I'd say sorry, but I think you were already in a lot of trouble before you even met me."

"Yeah, and I have Tim to thank for most of it. We've got to find out what he took and where it's hidden. Take off those sweatpants so I can get a closer look at that tattoo."

"I'm not wearing any panties," she protested. "Give me a minute."

"Kaylen, we just had sex. Why are you worrying about underwear?"

"I...I...oh, why am I trying to explain myself to you? You don't even want to take off your shirt. You're the one with all the issues, not me." She retreated to the bedroom.

Brian rolled the magnifying glass between his fingers while he watched images of storm damage flickering across the television screen, the sound still muted after Kaylen almost passed out. Reporters held microphones while behind them, debris blew across streets ominously empty for the middle of the day. A lone figure battled the elements for possession of a red umbrella, turned inside out by the wind. Kaylen walked back into the room as a weather report flashed onto the screen, the Doppler showing a bright green circulating mass moving onto land in an irregular, stop-start pattern.

"Okay," she said. She was wearing a pair of Tim's shorts, the waistband grasped firmly in one hand to stop them falling off.

She draped one long, shapely leg across Brian's lap, the tattoo standing out in brilliant colors on her tanned thigh. Brian tried hard not to think about the very recent pleasure of having her legs wrapped around his hips.

"Can you bring that lamp closer?" he asked.

She obliged, and he forced his attention back to the matter at hand, instead of letting his mind drift to thoughts of investigating more of Kaylen's body than her leg.

He traced the outline of the pink rose with his fingers, and then followed the green stem. A blue ribbon threaded its way past a branching set of leaves, to coil amongst two petals lying beneath. A series of dots meandered along the ribbon, discolored the stem and even the fallen petals. He turned his head to one side, then the other, until his eyes interpreted the message his brother had left behind.

The dots weren't random at all. They formed a pattern. Tim had left a cryptogram on his girlfriend and taken the chance his brother would find it.

"Do you see something?" Kaylen asked.

"Yeah. It's not easy to read. But he didn't want anyone else looking at it to understand there was a message. It's got numbers drawn into it. One-zero-five-six-three-eight."

She took a pen out of her purse and wrote on the paper bag that had held the magnifying glass. "Is that a phone number?" She looked at the numbers. "No, there'd have to be seven numbers, not six."

"I think it's a combination, but for what?" Brian gently lifted her leg off his lap and stood up. He had to get away from her if he was going to think straight. Feeling agitated and slightly aroused, he paced up and down between the couch and the breakfast bar. "Hal and the cartel are looking for the key to a safe deposit box. I think they're on the wrong track."

Kaylen took the magnifying glass and tried to position it so she could see the message herself. "Hopeless," she said, giving up. "Obviously he didn't expect me to find it. I can't believe Tim would do this to me."

"He must have been desperate. Maybe his original plan was to tell me what he'd done, but something went wrong. The cartel must have sent people to get him. Maybe they tried to beat the information out of him, but he was so stubborn they ended up killing him. Since I was already at your apartment, they could have decided to place the blame for Tim's death on me by putting me in your bed. Like we were lovers, and I'd gotten jealous."

Kaylen watched him pacing, her brow furrowed. "The walls of the condo are pretty well soundproof," she said. "That was a big attraction for me when I moved there. It could have happened that way. They could have called the cops the next morning to report a disturbance. To make sure we were found together."

"Yeah," he said. "But you woke up too early, before the call went in to the dispatcher. Which screwed up their plan." Brian stopped pacing and leaned against the breakfast bar. "If they'd known what he'd done, they would have taken you, or..."

"...or killed me and taken photos of my leg." She shuddered. "But why would you think Tim's responsible for this?" She pointed toward the tattoo.

"Because he started tattooing when he was fifteen years old. He practiced on me." Brian sat back beside her and pulled up the right sleeve of his t-shirt. "Look at this thing."

Kaylen's eyes widened. "That's one misshapen bird," she said, touching his upper arm.

"It's supposed to be an eagle," Brian said. "I told him to go practice on other people and not to come back to me until he knew what he was doing." He showed her his other arm. "Five years later, he did this."

271

"Now *that's* an eagle," Kaylen said. "Flying. Gorgeous. You can see all the feathers."

"And he got better and better," Brian said. "He used to work in local parlors when he was in his early twenties. He had a lot of regular customers, especially women, of course. That's when he started doing roses. They were his specialty." Memories flooded into his mind, bringing Tim so close, Brian could almost reach out and touch the essence of his brother.

A sudden gust of wind slammed the potted plant against the front door again. Brian pushed the memories back deep inside himself.

"So, what sort of lock would these numbers open?" Kaylen asked. "I think you're right about the safe deposit box. That would need a key, not a combination of numbers. The cartel's on the wrong track as well as the police."

"I think it's gotta be a locker combination," Brian said. "That extra gym bag Tim had hidden inside the bigger one. It's from a little neighborhood joint no one would expect Tim to frequent. They've been sending Refer-a-Friend coupons to him, and I recently picked up a Thanks-for-Your-Referral letter from his mailbox."

He hauled Kaylen off the couch and pushed her toward the bedroom. "Get dressed. We're going there."

She dug in her heels. "Are you out of your mind? The gym's going to be closed."

"Then I'll break in." He pushed her again, harder. "Hurry up. You're gonna wait with the car while I get whatever Tim left for me."

CHAPTER FORTY-FOUR

Brian walked through the door of Smithy's Gym and up to the small reception desk, manned by an elderly black man wearing a navy-blue t-shirt with the Smithy's logo emblazoned across his concave chest. A younger, slender white woman emerged from the back office. Her bright red hair clashed with purple lipstick and an orange t-shirt.

She smiled at Brian with a big gap showing between her upper front teeth. "We're only going to be open another hour," she said. "The storm's forcing us to close early."

Brian wasn't sure if Tim was well known in the place or not. "I'm here because of Tim Madison," he said.

"Oh, yes. Mr. Madison used one of our Refer-A-Friend coupons. We wondered when you'd be coming by." She opened a file drawer. "What's your name, again?"

Brian took his best guess, based on Tim's repeated, unwelcome references to their childhood and an old alias Tim had used. "Webber Street," he said.

"Welcome to Smithy's," the woman said. "I'm Cecilia. This is Gerald. His brother, Floyd's in the gym somewhere. There are still a couple of sparring partners back there. You could get in a short workout before we close." She thumbed through the folders. "Ah, here it is." She pulled out a file. "Your locker number's thirty-nine. He already put a lock on it for you. He said you'd know the combination."

Brian nodded and pushed open frosted glass doors beside the reception desk to reveal an old-fashioned boxing gym.

Damn Tim. Of all the gyms he could choose to stash his secrets, he had to pick somewhere that didn't have toothpick-thin women taking spinning classes and young execs running on treadmills. The place smelled of disinfectant, with an underlying odor of sweat and puke. The handful of patrons in Smithy's wore old sweats and headbands. Two muscle-bound black guys worked hard at the punching bags while inside one of three rings, a couple of Hispanics danced around, making air jabs.

Brian nodded at a middle-aged man leaning on the ropes. *Must be Floyd,* he thought. The guy had seriously over-developed pecs and a bald pate shining like a glass dome under the midday sun. Brian picked up his pace. He planned to retrieve whatever was in his locker and get the hell out of there ASAP.

He found locker 39 in a secluded corner and used the numbers from Kaylen's tattoo to open the combination lock. He popped it off and swung back the metal door to find another gym bag stuffed inside. He pulled on the handles. It was heavy and firmly wedged into the narrow opening.

A hand clapped onto his shoulder.

"You about ready to spar?" asked a deep voice.

CHAPTER FORTY-FIVE

"What were you *doing* in there?" Kaylen asked as Brian climbed back into the passenger's seat of the LeSabre. "I got really worried. You were gone almost thirty minutes."

He turned to face her. "I had to get in the ring with some guy."

Her mouth dropped open. "Brian, your cheek's swelling."

"Yeah, he managed to get in a couple before I knocked him out."

Kaylen shook her head. "I can't believe you took the time to fight. So like a man."

"Cut the comments and get us out of here," he said.

Kaylen reversed out of the parking space. "Did you find anything?"

"This bag."

He glanced at the side mirror as they pulled away from the curb. Through sheets of rain, he saw a black sedan move into position two cars behind them.

"Take a hard left," he told her.

Kaylen glanced at him as though he had two heads. "What are you talking about?"

"Take a left now!" He made a grab for the wheel.

She reacted by jamming her foot on the accelerator and turning the wheel at the same time. The tires squealed in protest, the rear of the car going into a fishtail spin that threatened to take them into a 360.

Brian grabbed the dash as they shot across the road onto a side street, the rear of the car mounting the curb and missing a drugstore by inches.

"Is that what you wanted?" Kaylen asked, her voice shaky around the edges.

"Yeah, but without the theatrics." He released the dashboard. "Make a right in the next block, but cut out the skidding. My ribs can't take much more today."

"I'd like to punch you myself," she said.

"Is it your driving, or can't this car move any faster?" he asked.

Kaylen gave him a look that would have turned Medusa to stone. They picked up speed, water and debris flying in all directions. They hydroplaned over a big puddle before she turned the wheel and took the next corner too fast again. They barely avoided a warehouse on the opposite side of the narrow street.

"Shit, woman," Brian said. "How did you get your license?"

"I've driven a truck through a blizzard," Kaylen said. "But I couldn't do it with *you* in the passenger seat. God, you're unbelievable. Why are we even doing this?"

"We picked up a tail. Black sedan."

She glanced in the rearview mirror. "I don't see anything behind us."

"Maybe we managed to lose them. Or maybe you scared the crap out of them and they backed off."

"Yeah, right." She shook her head. "What next?"

"We find out what's inside the bag."

"What if it's booby-trapped?"

"Tim would never chance blowing me up, Kaylen. Get a grip."

"Get a grip? *Get a grip?*"

She stomped on the brake. The seatbelt locked and body-checked him. "What the fuck are you trying to do now?" he asked. "Cripple me?"

In response, Kaylen stopped the car in the middle of the street. "I'm sick of you swearing at me and ordering me around," she said, and then she was out of the car and stomping around the back of it. She jerked open his door. "Get out," she said. "You're driving. I'll look in the goddamned bag."

"Now who's swearing?" he asked.

Kaylen threw up her hands. "You'd drive a saint to it. You're an absolute pig, Brian Swift."

"And you're a prissy socialite, princess."

They both got into the car and slammed the doors, practically in unison.

"Here." He gave her the bag.

She tossed it into the back seat, pushed dripping wet hair back from her face and folded her arms across her chest.

Brian couldn't resist baiting her. "I thought you were afraid there was a bomb in there?" he asked as he joined the dwindling traffic heading south on SW 27th.

"If I really thought there was, I would throw the bag at you right this minute."

He smothered a smile and kept quiet. Better to let her simmer down instead of annoying her further, he decided, even though it appealed to him. He liked her ruffled instead of cool and aloof.

At least she seemed to have lost their tail. To make sure, he took the South Dixie Highway instead of going straight back to the condo. To the right, the elevated Metrorail ran out to Dadeland. Climbing figs gripped the concrete uprights with green tentacles, while strip shopping malls flashed by, murky in the incessant rain.

The wipers slapped ineffectively with a rhythmical squeak as visibility diminished and the storm swept onshore. He glanced frequently in the rearview mirror but saw nothing suspicious. Visibility dimmed further and the LeSabre hydroplaned over deep puddles covering half the road.

The long stoplights aggravated Brian, and he pulled off at Le Jeune Road.

"What are you doing?" Kaylen asked. "We keep going further out of town."

"I'm going to double back to the highway. On this empty road I can see anyone following us."

Rain blew in gusts that rocked the car. Thick vegetation overshadowed the road with a tropical canopy of green. Barely visible neat hedges or stone walls bordered the narrow road. Flashing lights and a barrier blocked Sunset. A cop waved them down, flashlight in hand.

"Flooded out," he told them, shouting above the boom of rain hitting the street. "Take Davis."

Brian drove on. He felt Kaylen's hand on his thigh.

"I'm really frightened," she said. "I'm sorry I called you a pig."

"It's okay, princess. We'll be fine," he assured her, but he wondered if he had done something really stupid. Even turning the wipers on high couldn't clear the windshield.

A sign read Fairchild Tropical Garden, almost obscured by torrential rain that pounded the roof and echoed inside the LeSabre. Water meandered down the inside of the windshield.

"Find out what's inside the bag," Brian said. He realized he had given her another order. "Please," he added.

Kaylen watched the weather closing in on them. "Can't we turn around?" she asked. "The water's rising. Who knows if Davis isn't flooded out, too?"

"If Sunset's flooded, then Coral Gables Waterway is probably spilling over. It's better we head inland."

She looked doubtful, but took off her seatbelt and retrieved the gym bag. Unzipping it, she threw rumpled clothes into the back seat before taking out an attaché case.

"Put your seatbelt back on," he said. "I don't want you going through the windshield while I'm driving."

"I bet you don't," Kaylen said. "Do you have the combination for this case?"

"No, but it's probably unlocked. Tim wouldn't try to stop anyone getting this far."

She snapped the locks but nothing happened. "Yes, he would. Got any other ideas?"

"I could shoot the fuckers off."

"Brian, I know you're aggravated, but do you always have to cuss?"

"Force of habit."

She glared at him.

"Okay, I'll try to cut some of it out."

"I'd appreciate it," she said.

"Look," Brian said. "Tim's got me on some hell-bent trip down memory lane. Try twelve fifty-six."

"What's that?"

"Our house number on Webber Street in Baton Rouge. Where we lived after my mother remarried."

Kaylen stared at him. "What happened to your father?"

"Try opening the case," he said.

She sighed. "Another unanswered question." She lined up the numbers and the locks sprang. She opened the lid. "Oh, my God."

Brian tried to keep the car on the road while he glanced over. Kaylen was looking at neat stacks of money.

"They're all hundreds," she said.

"He robbed the cartel, the idiot."

They almost ran off the side of the road right in front of a bridge. The car came to rest inches from a sign that read *Slippery When Wet.*

"Sorry," he said. "Are you okay?"

"Good thing I didn't have to pee," she said.

"Nice attempt at a joke." He took her hand, cold and shaking. "Are you still mad at me?"

"No," she said. "I don't have the time or the energy to stay angry. Something scary happens in your world about every five minutes."

He put the LeSabre into reverse and backed up carefully. "If those bills are all hundreds, there's twenty-five hundred to every inch."

"You know that right off the top of your head?"

"Practice, princess. Count the stacks."

He eased the car back onto the road.

"Twelve stacks across and six down, about eight inches to a stack," she said.

"Do the math."

"I need a calculator. Let's see—six times twelve is seventy-two, then eight times twenty-five hundred…" She rubbed her forehead. "I can't do it."

"You don't have to go any further," Brian said. "It's well over a mil. Tim'd never try to leave the country with less than that to live on. See if there's anything in the pockets."

She dug around and pulled out a leather-bound book. She started flipping pages. "There's a journal filled with dates and names." She scanned. "He has initials in some places…WH, LG, PV, SW. Some are meetings. Some have amounts jotted in the column next to the entry. Large amounts. All dated. Looks like Tim's scrawl."

"Give it to me." He snatched the journal out of her hand. "He must have kept tabs on everyone. No wonder they wanted this. Somehow they must have found out. It's not the money they want, it's this."

He caught sight of the black sedan right as it drew level with the LeSabre. Through the rain, he saw an open window and a gun. He floored the accelerator, the journal flying from his grip.

CHAPTER FORTY-SIX

Brian's window shattered, sending a shower of glass into the car. His right hand flew up to his face as the LeSabre careened across the wet road like it was on a skating rink.

Kaylen made a grab for the wheel, but the car was already mounting the ridge marking the end of the narrow shoulder. Back wheels kicking dirt, it took off and became airborne, engine screaming, heading for a small roadside park. When the vehicle came down with a spine-jarring crash and sank into the mud, the hood flew up and a hubcap took off like a Frisbee at the beach.

Kaylen took one look at Brian and fought to release her seatbelt.

He moaned, blood running between his fingers.

"I'm getting out," she said.

"No." His voice sounded faint and filled with pain. "They'll kill you."

She looked around. "There's no one out there, Brian. They left."

"No way." He seized her arm. "I'll get us out of here. Give me something to wipe the blood out of my eyes."

She grabbed one of Tim's shirts from the back seat. "Here, I'll help you."

"No." He snatched the shirt from her and mopped his face.

"I can get us out of this," she insisted. "I grew up in Maine. Mud can't be more difficult than rocking a car out of a snowdrift. You'll have to get into the passenger's seat."

"Can't. I'm shot."

"Shot?" She felt dizzy. "Where?"

"My left shoulder."

"And you think you can drive?"

"Have to."

"You can't even see. At least let me put the hood down."

"No time."

He put the car into reverse, but as soon as the engine revved and the wheels spun, his foot was back off the accelerator.

"Passin' ou…"

Horrified, Kaylen caught his head before it hit the steering wheel. She turned off the ignition.

They were trapped. An unconscious Brian was too heavy for her to lift. Any moment now, their attacker might come back. She grabbed her phone and dialed 911. No service.

Brian had a gun and a cell phone. She searched his pockets, ran her hand around his waistband, but found nothing. Panic set in. They were going to be killed for that journal and the money. She had nothing to fight assassins with but her fingernails. She wrenched the door open. What the hell was she going to do? She couldn't get her breath.

Stop it! She told herself. She could hear her father's voice in her head, clear as day: "This is the reason I wanted sons. What use is a girl on a farm? All you do is run around like a chicken with your head cut off whenever something goes wrong."

She forced away the image of her father, his thumb almost severed after an accident with farm machinery. She was twelve years old, and her father terrified her even when he wasn't hurt.

She pulled up the hood of her sweatshirt and scrambled out of the car. Brian was left-handed. The phone and the gun were on the other side of the vehicle.

Her feet sank into the mushy grass as rain and wind buffeted her face and body. Her hood blew off, and she had to wrestle the elements to get it back on her head. Kaylen shivered as water soaked through her clothing and trickled down her skin. She searched warily for signs of either a vehicle or people before fighting her way to the front of the car.

Slamming the hood, she noticed a plume of smoke between the trees across the road and breathed an acrid stench of burned rubber carried by the wind. Twin beams of white light illuminated the undergrowth with an eerie glow, while the red tail lights of the sedan were almost obliterated by the torrential downpour. Brian wasn't the only driver who had lost control on that wet road.

It might not be much of a break, but she'd take anything at that point. Mindful that the occupants of the other car could recover any minute and climb out to finish what they had started, she slid around the car, opened Brian's door and bit back a gasp. Beneath the torn slicker, his shirt was soaked with blood. His freely-bleeding face made her light-headed. She swallowed the bile rising in her throat and grabbed his cell.

"All circuits are busy," she heard. *Dear God. Now what?*

She remembered he had hidden his Glock under the seat before going into the gym. She felt around until she found it, made sure she wasn't going to blow off her foot with a live round in the chamber and then carefully stowed it in the pocket of her slicker. If they were close to Fairchild Tropical Garden, then they were also not that far from Sam's new home. She had only visited once before, and it had been evening then, all landmarks invisible in the darkness. She tried 911 again, and that time the phone rang. Kaylen listened impatiently until the operator came on the line.

"Which service?" The operator's voice drifted in and out. The line crackled. "Fire or paramedics?"

"Both," Kaylen said. "There's been a bad car accident." Reception faded.

"...currently unavail...," the operator said.

"I need help!" Kaylen felt hysteria trying to regain a foothold.

"...hour...," she heard before the signal faded completely.

"Shit!" She put the phone in her other pocket.

She was going to have to do something herself or Brian would bleed to death before help arrived. She tried to get his slicker off. He moaned.

"Oh, thank God. You're conscious. Can you hear me?" She shook him. "You've got to help me. I can't get to your arm."

"Leave it." His eyes opened briefly, then closed.

"Don't pass out again. Come on, Brian. Help me get the slicker off."

He bent forward over the dash while she pulled and tugged until finally she got his arm out of his sleeve. She forced herself to ignore his groans, wadded up a pair of Tim's sweatpants and made a pressure bandage by securing them with Brian's belt. She wrapped a t-shirt around his head to stop the blood running into his eyes. A sheen of sweat covered his face, contorted with pain. His eyes stayed closed.

"You're really bleeding," she said. "I've got to drive. I can lift your legs onto the passenger's side, but then you've got to help me get the rest of you over there. I can't move you by myself."

He didn't protest, and she wondered whether it was because he had lost consciousness again. No matter. Not having him ordering her around made it easier for her to think.

She slipped more than walked back around the car, falling to her knees twice in the soupy mud, her pants soaked through and her cheap tennis shoes refusing to give her any traction. The rain pelted her mercilessly, icy darts striking her face with the power of rice thrown at a wedding.

Cold and shaking, she grabbed Brian's legs and dragged them over to the passenger's side. She heard him swearing under his breath. *Fine. Let him swear all he wanted, for once.* At least he was still conscious. If he passed out again, she knew she wouldn't get into either of the front seats, because he'd be blocking both of them.

"Brian, are you listening to me?"

He barely acknowledged her, his face covered with blood, but one of his reddened hands grasped hers. Kaylen pulled and he moved, but the effort cost him dearly. He fell backwards, his head striking the door, and there he lay. She grabbed the waistband of his pants and managed to drag his buttocks halfway between the seats. Her back spasmed in protest, and she wiped her hand across her forehead.

Sam. She'd phone Sam. But Brian's cell was already ringing in her pocket.

"Sergeant Swift?" The voice was male.

Kaylen grunted in what she hoped was a tone Brian might have used.

"Sergeant, this is Gabe from the precinct. Lieutenant Shaw was in an accident. He's been taken to the hospital. He managed to call in and told me to contact you because he was on the way to meet you."

CHAPTER FORTY-SEVEN

"Who is this?" Kaylen asked.

"Who are *you*, and what are you doing with Sergeant Swift's phone?" The caller's voice definitely sounded unfriendly.

"You've got to help me," Kaylen said. "He's been shot. We're stuck in the mud in some roadside park near the Fairchild Tropical Garden."

"Did you call nine-one-one?"

"Yes, of course I did. They were no help at all. The storm's caused too many accidents. The operator told me it would be hours. At least I think she did, because I couldn't hear half of what she said. He's bleeding."

"Where?"

Ass. Was she the only one left with any brains? Kaylen's frustration vied with the underlying panic. "I *told* you, we're in a roadside park..."

"Not your location." The man's voice softened. "What's your name?"

"Kaylen Roberts."

"Ms. Roberts, this is Gabe Weston, the homicide clerk who escorted you to the bathroom before you ran off. I'm asking you what part of the Sergeant was shot. His leg?"

"Oh...no." Kaylen flushed, embarrassed. "His shoulder. His left shoulder. Somebody shot him through the driver's side window. He's bleeding badly, and his face got cut by flying glass. We need help right now. I don't care how bad the weather is. You've got to get someone out here...please."

"I'll call it in immediately. Are you past the Tropical Garden or before?"

"About three miles before."

"I'll call you right back." The connection severed.

She saw movement in the car. Brian was trying to scoot over to the passenger's side. She brushed glass off the driver's seat so she could kneel on it without cutting herself as she pushed him. With her help, he got over far enough for her to slide behind the wheel.

"I called for help," she said.

"'s comin'?" His breathing was labored, his face the color of paste.

"Gabe Weston called."

"Clerk…" His voice trailed off.

"Yes."

Brian moaned, and his chin dropped onto his chest.

"Don't you dare die on me," she said. "I need you."

"Not dyin'," he murmured. "Hurtin'."

"I'm going to get us out of here."

When she got no answer, she dragged the floor mats from the car. On her hands and knees, she shoved them as far under the wheels as she could get them. Anything to give traction. She wiped mud and blood from her hands onto her pants and shuddered with a revulsion she hadn't felt since cleaning up after chickens were slaughtered at her father's farm. Brian wasn't the only one taking a reluctant trip down memory lane.

She started the car and began shifting between reverse and drive, trying to work into a rhythm that made the motions more effective without sending the wheels deeper into the quagmire. She'd been a teenager the last time she'd ended up in a snowdrift, and on that occasion, she'd had to give up and walk two miles back to the farm and confess to her father that she'd run off the road because she wasn't paying attention after drinking a beer with her friends at the local bar.

Kaylen gritted her teeth and shifted into neutral to let the transmission cool along with her emotions. She knew getting panicked would only result in them needing a tow truck to get out of the park.

Damn Brian. This was all his fault. If he hadn't refused to turn around, they could have been back in the condo now, warm and dry. She looked over at him, slumped against the doorframe, and recanted quickly.

She tried rocking the car again, slowly gaining inches. If anyone was still conscious in that other vehicle, they certainly would be able to hear the LeSabre's progress, but there was little choice. The longer they stayed in the mud, the harder it was going to be to get out of it. Rain fell in a relentless torrent, limiting visibility to a few feet beyond the hood. Kaylen shifted back into neutral and reluctantly got out to see if she could move the floor mats, but they had disappeared under water that had now risen to within an inch of the car's chassis.

One more time, Kaylen told herself. Either she'd wreck the transmission or she'd get them out of there. *Don't spin the wheels*, she reminded herself. That would only drive the car deeper into the mud. She started rocking again…drive to reverse and back again. With a shudder, the LeSabre grudgingly started moving. Kaylen kept the wheels as straight as possible while she edged out of the park and onto the highway. When she heard the crunch of gravel beneath the tires, she let out the breath she'd been holding.

Gabe still hadn't called. She decided she had better head for Sam's house. The smoke from the other wreck had died down, and she worried that anyone who had escaped the blaze might have recovered enough to come over and finish what they had started. Her heart hammering painfully, she drove the ailing car down the road toward Sam's compound.

The LeSabre had sustained significant damage. Grinding noises and difficulty steering alerted Kaylen to the fact that they weren't going much further. Keeping her foot lightly on the gas, she coaxed the car up to imposing wrought iron gates set into a high brick wall, pushed the button on the call box and waited impatiently while the engine knocked and missed like it was about to go belly up. The wipers slapped ineffectively at the deluge delivered by the heavens. Kaylen hit the button a second time before taking out Brian's cell and punching in Sam's number.

"The power's out," Sam told her. "The gates are unlocked, but you'll have to get out and push them open. I can send down a couple of my men to help you."

"It's okay. I can do it myself. I don't want to wait."

One more time, she thought. One more trip out into the rising water and they'd be safe. She pulled on the emergency brake and waited a moment, worried the car would roll off and she'd get Brian killed, before getting out and pushing back the filigreed iron gates.

Brian hadn't stirred since they left the park. Kaylen placed her fingers on the side of his neck and found a weak pulse. She eased the car down a winding path between tall trees and thick undergrowth filled with aerial roots from Mangrove trees, wet, dark and unwelcoming in the fading light.

"Where are we?"

Brian's voice startled her, and she jammed on the brake. "Sam's," she said. "Gabe never called me back. I've got to get help for you."

"Sam's?" With a great deal of effort, he turned to look at her. "How long…I've been out?"

"Not long. He lives near the Tropical Garden."

"*Fairchild?*" He struggled to sit up, his breathing short and fast. "Near Snapper Creek?"

"I suppose, if that's near the Garden." A knot formed in the pit of her stomach. "Why?"

"Tim found…Snapper Creek."

Kaylen stared through the windshield. It couldn't be. No. She refused to consider what she knew Brian was thinking. But even if her stubborn side wouldn't accept it, self-preservation screamed at her. She grabbed the wet journal and shoved it into the attaché case.

"Turn," Brian said.

"We'll get stuck. I'm not going through that again. I've got to get rid of this case. We'll play dumb and hope."

"Give me…phone." He took it from her, leaned against the door and started pushing numbers with his right hand, his motions clumsy.

Kaylen tried to ignore the blood dripping from the fingers of his left hand into an ever-widening stain on the beige carpet. She got out of the car and dashed into the undergrowth. Near the wall, a large tree with a split trunk looked like a recognizable landmark. Half-hidden from the driveway, it might be the best chance she got for a hiding place.

She jammed the case into the split and ran back to the car. If she was mistaken about Sam, she'd beg his pardon for the rest of her life. If she wasn't, then the only way they would stay alive was if the contents of that case stayed hidden.

CHAPTER FORTY-EIGHT

Kaylen drove the chugging LeSabre into the wide forecourt outside Sam's front entrance. Sam stood on the top step, one of his employees holding an umbrella over his head despite strong gusts of wind threatening to turn it inside out. Four other men flanked them, and she spotted two more at the perimeter of the parking area, hoods up, rain pouring down their black slickers.

She wished she had listened to Brian and tried to turn around in the driveway. Sam looked angrier than she had ever seen him, and the men on the edge of the parking lot were armed with shotguns.

She reluctantly rolled down the window. "Thanks," she told Sam as he walked down the steps. "I didn't know where else to go. We were in an accident and Brian got shot."

"Is that right?" Sam said.

"He needs help, and the paramedics can't come quickly enough."

Kaylen knew she was nervously prattling, but as she watched Sam's face for any sign of concern, for even a glimmer of compassion, she saw none.

"You shouldn't have brought him here, K.T." Sam's florid face looked purple in the waning light. "Come on, let's get you inside." He opened her door and took her arm. "Christ, you're covered in blood. Are you hurt?"

"No. It's from Brian."

She gripped the steering wheel tightly. Sam didn't even look surprised, shocked or remotely interested in where all that blood had come from, once he knew it wasn't hers. The engine sputtered and coughed, the car shaking even more than Kaylen herself. Coming to Sam had been a complete mistake, she thought. Another betrayal, and at a time when she so desperately needed help.

Sam pulled, not at all gently. "Out," he said. "I've got to get you inside the house."

"No. You're hurting me. Let go." She tried to shake him off, but he only tugged harder.

"Out, Kaylen. …gonna…kill me."

Brian's voice sounded so weak, she swore she had imagined it, but when she turned he was looking at her, face ghastly white, eyes glassy. His shallow panting terrified her. She slid her right hand into the pocket of her slicker. She'd hated all those hunting trips with her father, but for once, she thanked her stars she knew how to handle guns, no matter how much she loathed them.

"I won't leave you," she told Brian. She slid the gun out of her pocket. "They'll have to kill me, too."

"Stop it, K.T. You're being silly and making things harder for yourself." Sam tugged at her again. "You're in danger. You have no idea."

"Is that right?"

"Let go of the damned wheel!" Spittle flew from Sam's mouth. "You've got to come with me. I'm telling you, they'll kill you, too, if you don't."

"How could you even *think* I'd willingly come with you?" She saw beyond the benevolence, the charm, and the fake concern. *How could she have been so dumb? So totally trusting?*

"Idiot!" Sam sounded like he was talking to an errant child. "Remember what happened to Tim, Rosa and Sandy." He pointed at Brian, his short, stubby finger trembling. "Look what's happened to *him*. You've got what they want, and they're going to get it from you. It'll go easier if you're with me."

Kaylen pushed his hand away. "And who *are* they, Sam? Business partners of yours? Friends?"

"It doesn't matter. You've got to get out of this car *right now*." He grabbed her forearm again and jerked it painfully. "Now!"

She bit him.

With a howl, he released her and grabbed his hand. "Bitch!"

Kaylen pointed the Glock at him. It felt cold, unwieldy, and very heavy, and she had to concentrate to keep it level.

Sam backed up. "Have you gone crazy? What the hell are you thinking, girl?"

"I'm thinking this is the first time I've really seen you for what you are, and I don't like you at all."

"You're actually going to try to use that thing?" He gazed at the gun, his little eyes round and prominent, like Goobers.

"You bet. Remember how I grew up on a farm? I went hunting with my father every weekend, and he always kept a handgun in the house."

Sam backed up quicker that time, tripping over his own feet even as his men closed in. He staggered and fell onto his rear end, water flying up all around him. His flunkies rushed to his aid. Kaylen took advantage of the commotion to hit the gas. Spinning tires threw gravel like artillery fire and the group scattered, two of them dragging Sam out of the way, his mouth wide open as he clutched them for support.

"Fuckin' A," Brian murmured.

The LeSabre responded sluggishly, but Kaylen managed to turn the vehicle in the direction of the gate. Her door swung within reach. She grabbed it and slammed it shut.

"Oh, my God." She clung to the wheel. "I forgot to put on your seatbelt." She glanced over at Brian, his chin almost on his chest. "That must have hurt like hell."

"Don't…tell…'bout…the money an'…an' the journal." He raised his head. The effort sent his eyes rolling.

"For God's sake, Brian…"

"Promise." His voice was barely audible.

"I promise," she said.

His head dropped.

She saw a kaleidoscope of lights in the distance, making their way slowly along the road. Kaylen headed the car toward them like a floundering ship to a homing beacon.

CHAPTER FORTY-NINE

Brian heard his name, far off, like someone shouting down a well. He tried blocking it out, but it persisted, growing louder.

"Brian."

Kaylen's voice, very close. A hand on his arm, gentle but firm. He opened his eyes and she swam into view, haloed by a blinding light. He snapped his eyelids shut.

"Jim, can you tilt the blind?" she asked.

Brian heard rattling.

"That's better." She kissed his cheek, her lips soft against his skin. "Come on, Brian. Time to wake up."

He squinted, found the room shady, and tried to focus. Kaylen's face came into view, a little hazy around the edges. Despite her smile, her eyes looked sad, her face thin and pinched.

"Not dead, then," he croaked through parched lips.

"No, thank God." She brought a plastic cup from the tray table, scooped something into a spoon and raised it to his lips.

"Ice chips," she said. "The nurse said it's okay, but take it slow."

He opened his mouth, and she slid in a couple of chips. The cold on his dry tongue woke him up.

"Hmm." He rolled the ice around and swallowed. "More."

"I said 'slow.' You didn't even chew." She frowned, but she gave him another spoonful.

"How ya doin', buddy?" Jim's face appeared over Kaylen's shoulder.

"Groggy." Brian chewed, frigid liquid sliding down his throat. "How long?" he asked.

"Three days in and out. You don't remember anything, do you?" Kaylen sat carefully on the edge of the bed.

"Nurse isn't going to like that," Jim said. He took a seat on the bedside chair.

"She'll just have to deal with it." Kaylen pushed more ice chips between Brian's lips.

He chewed and swallowed a lot quicker. The fuzziness had cleared, but his limbs felt heavy. When he tried to take the cup from her, his left arm wouldn't move at all.

"You had surgery," she said. "You're feeling the effects of the drugs. They've had you on some strong stuff since they operated. The nurse told me to wake you up so they can get fluids into you and take out the IV."

Brian tried to raise his right hand to his left shoulder. Totally uncoordinated, his arm refused to cooperate and fell on his chest.

"No more drugs." He wanted to wipe his face, but he was afraid he'd poke an eye out. "Tell 'em. I've gotta get out of here." He struggled against the bedclothes. "You've got to get off. I'm all tangled up."

"You're not tangled up. You're weak. You need to stay in bed."

"She's right." Hal came into the room, or at least Brian saw his foot and leg first, propped on an extended wheelchair legrest. The remainder of Hal came through the door right after, the wheelchair pushed by his wife, Frances.

"That's some cast," Jim said from his seat in the corner.

"Damn thing." Hal raised his hand. "I know, I know, Frances. It could have been a lot worse."

Brian gave up his futile struggle against the sheet and blanket. Exhausted, he lay back.

"So," Hal asked. "How are you feeling?"

"Like crap."

Kaylen started to get off the bed but Brian stopped her, sliding his hand into hers. She smiled and sat back down.

Frances wheeled Hal around to the foot of the bed.

"Here." Jim got up and motioned Frances to take his seat by the window.

The door opened. "How many people are in this room?" A nurse, stethoscope around her neck, squeezed past the wheelchair. "No more than two at a time."

"What about me buying you a cup of coffee, Kaylen?" Jim asked.

"Okay." She squeezed Brian's hand and got up. "I'll be back in a few minutes."

She kissed his lips lightly, her hair brushing his cheek. Brian thought maybe he had died after all and ended up somewhere he hadn't expected to go.

"Is it safe?" he asked Hal. Although he couldn't do anything to defend Kaylen, the idea of letting her out of his sight made him dizzier than the drugs.

"There's a guard at the door twenty-four seven," Hal said. "If Kaylen's going anywhere, she has to be escorted by more than a friend." He looked at Jim. "No offense."

Jim shrugged. "None taken."

"Giddings!" Hal shouted over his shoulder.

A uniformed officer popped his head around the door as a man in a white coat walked in behind him.

"Dr. West." The nurse pursed her lips. "I told them…"

Dr. West's arm shot out, his index finger pointing toward the door. "Out. All of you."

"I just got here," Hal protested. "I'm his supervisor."

"And you can come back in five minutes, along with one other person." The doctor seized the wheelchair and turned it around.

Frances sprang up. "I'll do that."

"Go to the lounge," Dr. West said. "I'll make sure one of the staff gets coffee for all of you, and then I'll come out and talk to you."

"To tell us off individually, or as a group?" Jim grinned and offered Kaylen his arm. "We were just talking about going for coffee. This way, we won't have to go so far, or pay for it."

"I want another uniform outside the lounge," Hal told Giddings, still hovering at the door. "And make it yesterday." He glowered and Giddings disappeared. Hal squared his shoulders. "I'll be back," he assured Brian as Frances wheeled him away.

The nurse wrapped a blood pressure cuff around Brian's arm and started pumping as Jim and Kaylen trooped out behind Frances. "One thirty-five over seven-four," she said. She placed cool fingers on Brian's wrist and looked at the clock. "Eighty," she said.

"I'm surprised it's not higher after all that." Dr. West pointed to Brian's left hand. "Make a fist."

"It takes more than a roomful of people to get me riled up." Brian's fingers reluctantly curled and tongues of fire shot up his arm. He winced.

"Still in a lot of pain?" Dr. West frowned.

"I feel lousy. Drugged up. Sleepy. And moving hurts like…" He looked at the nurse and bit back what he was going to say. "What the hell did you do to me?" he finished instead.

"Extensive work. The bullet did a lot of damage. I put pins and a plate in your humerus, and you've got a brachial plexus injury, which unfortunately means nerve damage. But your girlfriend saved your life with that pressure bandage. You almost bled out."

"She's great," Brian said. "But she's not my girlfriend." He didn't know how to describe his relationship with Kaylen. It was too complicated, and he felt too tired. His eyes started to close, and he forced them back open. "You've got to get me off whatever you're giving me. I can't go on feeling like this. I can't stay awake."

"You'll be in a lot more pain," Dr. West warned.

"I'll deal with it."

"I imagine you will. You look like it's no stranger."

Brian didn't want to discuss the origin of his other scars. "I want real food. None of that Jell-O and broth shit. I hate that stuff."

"If I give you a regular diet, you'll puke." Dr. West sighed. "I'll try you on a soft diet, but that's as far as I'll go."

"And no IV's or shots, either."

"Fair enough, but you'll have to take something."

"Darvocet or Vicodin. I do fine on them." He was slipping away again. If only that dull ache in his shoulder would stop building in intensity, he thought. He wondered if despite his resolve to stop taking the drugs, he'd soon be begging for a return to the twilight zone he'd lived in for the last three days.

"You'll need Physical Therapy after I clear you to resume some of your activities. I'll see you in my office to remove the staples." Dr. West was already heading for the door, his lab coat rustling with every step. "You'll get appointment instructions at discharge. If you tolerate the diet changes and your pain's adequately controlled, I see no reason why we can't send you home by the end of this week. I'll have nursing teach your friends how to do the dressing changes and help you monitor for infection."

"Good," Brian managed to mutter. Getting a discharge date sounded positive.

"You'll need someone to assist you at home for at least the first week or two," Dr. West said. The door swished open. "No showering until those staples come out."

Brian forced himself out of Never-Never Land. "How long am I looking at being off work?"

The door closed and Dr. West came back to stand beside the bed. "Three to six months. Maybe longer. I'm not sure how far that shoulder's going to come."

His voice was no longer clipped and professionally distant. Brian saw a furrowed brow and concern in the surgeon's eyes.

"You're almost forty, Sergeant Swift," Dr. West said. "Judging by your history, you're tougher than most, but toughness will only go so far with this type of damage. Brachial Plexus injuries are hard to predict. You could get back everything, or very little. You might consider finding another line of work. This is your dominant side we're talking about."

CHAPTER FIFTY

Brian lay staring at the blinds after the doctor and nurse left. What if he couldn't go back to work, even if he was reinstated? He no longer had a home, a boat and now, probably even a job. What was he going to do…live in his car after he scraped up the money to get it out of the impound lot? Assuming the insurance company agreed to replace the *Destiny*, how could he run a boat with one arm, and his right one, at that?

When he heard the door swish open again, he closed his eyes and feigned the sleep that had come so easily such a short time before. He heard whispers as Kaylen tried to convince Lieutenant Shaw he needed to hold his questions for another day.

"Not happening," Hal said. "I've got to talk to him now. Wheel me up beside the bed."

Brian pulled the covers over his head.

"That's not going to work," Hal said. "I talked to the doc. He said you're depressed and in a fair amount of pain, but you got plenty of sleep over the last three days. So stop hiding."

"Christ." Brian threw back the blanket. "I can't even get away from you in the hospital."

"Kaylen, why don't you go to the cafeteria with Frances and Jim?" Hal said, the question more like an order. "You look like you could do with a break."

"I'm fine," Kaylen said. "But I can take a hint."

"Don't go far," Brian said. "You shouldn't be wandering around the hallways alone."

"Jim's right outside the door." She bent down and kissed his cheek. "I'll be back in a few minutes," she whispered.

He watched the graceful sway of her hips as she left. He knew he'd never stop looking at her, whether she was coming into a room or going out of it.

Hal placed Brian's badge on the bed. "I asked West how long you'd be off work. At first, he refused to tell me squat. After we had a short and very informative discussion about police procedures, he told me your prognosis for getting the use of your arm back is what he calls guarded. I refuse to believe that."

Brian picked up the badge. It felt good to hold it after the weeks of speculation and accusations. "Thanks for the vote of confidence," he said. "I hope you're right."

"Your job's waiting for you, as soon as you've healed," Hal said. "In the meantime, you're out on full disability for as long as it takes. I had to move quickly to get everything done before Hastings made Chief."

"I thought he was holding out for a political appointment?" Brian placed his badge on the nightstand.

"Didn't get it," Hal said. "So now he's got a lot of power in the department while harboring a big grudge, which already looks like it's going to center on you as his least-favorite staff member. He's already asking questions around the precinct. He wants exact times on what went down from the moment your boat blew up to when Kaylen brought that car out of Wilson's compound. For instance, he wants to know what you guys were doing in that condo for four hours."

"Sleeping," Brian said. "And then not sleeping, if you know what I mean."

"Too much information for me," Hal said. "But Kaylen may be the best thing that's happened to you in a long time."

"She is," Brian said. "But I'm not sure I'm ready for it, or comfortable with it, either. I keep reminding myself she was Tim's girlfriend."

"Maybe you need to stop analyzing everything so much," Hal said. "Especially right now."

Brian needed to change the subject. He wasn't about to open up to Hal or anyone else about his inner misgivings and feelings of guilt over his involvement with Kaylen. "What about IAB?" he asked.

"I thought I could get the investigation stopped, but they're getting involved again because of the business over at Sam Wilson's. It should be pretty routine. Nothing you need to worry about…they may not even need to interview you." Hal shrugged. "Because you almost bled out, they can't accuse you of instigating anything. You had to have been unconscious most of the time after you got shot." He cleared his throat. "West said it's amazing you didn't die. It took several units of blood and four hours of surgery to piece you back together."

"Yeah, I know. He said Kaylen saved my life." Brian waited for Hal to continue, but he didn't. "I misjudged her, Hal," he said. "I didn't think she could hold up in a crisis, but she did real good."

"She's facing charges brought by Wilson."

"For what?"

"Using your gun to make threats. What in hell were you thinking, giving it to her?"

"I didn't. She took it while I was unconscious. I heard her tell Wilson she knows how to use it, too. I think she said something about hunting, but I kept passing out, so I missed some of that." He shifted uncomfortably on the pillows.

"Do you need your pain shot?" Hal asked. "You're sweating."

"No. I'm not taking any more of that crap." Brian moved again and gritted his teeth. "I've got to get out of here, and that's not going to happen if they keep me drugged up."

"There's no hurry." Hal repositioned his wheelchair so he was facing the bed. "The medical examiner's final report on Tim's death confirmed it was a homicide. Mills is leading that investigation. Your brother took one hell of a beating…multiple rib fractures, collarbone, smashed nose. They must have tried like hell to get information out of him. Then they went too far and ended up lacerating his liver. That's what killed him." Hal stopped. "I'm sorry," he said. "Damn sorry." He shook his head. "If only Tim had come to us for help, maybe he would still be alive."

"I think he was in too deep," Brian said. "And too stubborn to admit he couldn't handle it."

"Do you know why they came after you and Kaylen?" Hal asked. "I know I've asked you this before, but I'm asking it again…did Tim give either of you anything?"

"No." Brian felt sweat trickling down his face. Technically, he thought, the tattoo couldn't be considered a gift.

"Is that the truth?" Hal asked. He looked suspicious.

"Yes." Brian used his foot to kick off the blanket. "It's hot in here."

"No, it's not," Hal said.

"I found Sean Hastings and got some information from him on his father." Brian filled Hal in on what Sean had said.

"Even if he agreed to testify, I doubt his statement would hold up in court," Hal said. "We'd need something a whole lot more concrete than that to bring charges against Bill Hastings."

"I think his wife knows what's going on."

"She's not required to testify against him. You know that."

"Yeah, but Sean told me there's spousal abuse. That may motivate her. Getting away from him would end that. Maybe even get Sean to check into treatment. We've got to find a way to get to her."

A knock at the door announced the nurse. "You look very uncomfortable, Sergeant Swift," she said. "You need something for pain."

"I told Dr. West I'm not taking any more shots," Brian said.

"I've brought you the Vicodin you agreed to take." She placed a small cup containing a pill onto the tray table and picked up the empty plastic pitcher. "You need to push fluids now you're awake and the IV's out. I'll get you some iced water." She looked at Hal. "You'll have to leave if you upset him," she said before she walked out.

Kaylen came through the door before it had swung completely shut. "Sorry," she said. "Jim and Frances found out they both attended the same college in the Midwest. I felt like a third wheel. I tried staying in the lounge area, but it made me too nervous, so here I am."

"I'm not done." Hal sounded pissed.

"I don't mind Kaylen hearing this," Brian said. "Although she doesn't believe it, I don't have many more secrets left."

"Fair enough." Hal shifted around in his wheelchair.

"Why don't I put a pillow under your cast?" Kaylen suggested. "And maybe one in your back?" Without waiting for him to respond, she did it.

"Thanks." Hal sounded surprised. "That *does* feel better."

"And you," Kaylen said to Brian. "You look awful." She went into the bathroom, and he heard water running. She came back with a cold cloth, which she used to dab his face before laying it across his forehead.

"Thanks," he said. The coolness slowed the nausea. "You always know what to do."

"Yes, with things like this, I do," she said. "I had a lot of practice taking care of George."

Brian didn't want to remind her of her terminally ill husband. He tried to sit up straighter, but he couldn't find the strength. Kaylen sat on the bedside chair and took his right hand, her touch incredibly soothing.

"So how did you wind up getting shot?" Hal asked him.

"I wasn't paying enough attention," Brian admitted. "The weather was so bad, I didn't even see the car, much less the gun, until right before the bastard shot me through the window."

"Kaylen said you were tailed from her new condo to a gym close to Tim's apartment. What were you doing at the gym?"

"Following a hunch," Brian said. "Trying to get some information on the place. I thought maybe Tim had been there, and I was right."

"We interviewed the staff and a handful of clients. They said you used the name Webber Street."

"It was some stupid alias Tim had used before. The name of the street we lived on in Baton Rouge, when we were kids. He set me up with a locker, too."

"Anything in it?" Hal asked.

The nurse came back into the room. She looked at the cloth on Brian's forehead and then at Hal. "It's time for you to leave," she said.

"I'm in the middle of an investigation," Hal protested. "I only need a few more minutes."

"Are you nauseated, Sergeant?" The nurse, whose badge said her name was Peggy, filled a cup with iced water.

"Yes," Brian said. He put the pill into his mouth and swallowed it with the water she handed him.

"I'll bring you something for that, too, then." She placed an emesis basin on the bed. "I want you gone when I get back," she told Hal. "Otherwise I'll call security and have you removed."

"I'm a police lieutenant," Hal said. "I'd like to see them try."

"I don't care who you are," Peggy said. "You're making my patient ill, and I want you out of his room."

"It's okay," Brian said. "If you can take care of the nausea, I can handle the lieutenant's visit. Otherwise he'll be back here tomorrow."

"Well…" Peggy gave Hal a stern look.

"You can time me if you like," he said.

"I'll do that. No more than five minutes." Peggy left, the door closing behind her with a loud click.

"All right," Hal said. He glanced up at the clock on the wall. "Let's get this over with."

"The only thing in the locker was a gym bag," Brian said.

"Which is what we found with the search warrant. Filled with new clothes, but in a size that would fit Tim, not you."

"That was my brother, always looking out for himself. He probably figured he would use that locker for storing his stuff, too," Brian said. "What were you saying about Wilson bringing charges against Kaylen?"

"He's doing *what?*" Kaylen stood up, the chair crashing against the nightstand behind it.

"As soon as he made bail, his high-powered lawyer started making noises in that direction," Hal said, with a glare at Brian for bringing that up. "Wilson denied threatening either you or Brian. He said you were overwrought and imagined things that didn't happen. Says he tried to help you out of the car but you scratched and bit him, then told him you were going to shoot him. He's thinking about charging you with assault. The deposition said he sustained a sprained ankle and a severely bruised tailbone. Now he's added a herniated disc from falling after you pushed him."

"I *pushed* him? Ooh, the *bastard*." She sat back down. "He tried to drag me out of the car, Lieutenant. He made it very clear that Brian was going to be murdered. I wasn't going to let that happen."

"I know…I know." Hal waved his hand. "I read your statement. I find it hard to believe Wilson's got the balls to do that, too." He cleared his throat. "Sorry about the language."

"Believe me, hanging around Brian, I've heard a lot worse." She took Brian's hand again and squeezed it gently. "I've kind of gotten used to it."

She stroked his wrist with her thumb. Brian wished Hal would hurry up and leave, and that the nurse would bring the anti-nausea medication. He wanted some alone-time with Kaylen, now he wasn't feeling spaced-out from the drugs. There was so much he wanted to tell her. He hadn't even had the opportunity to thank her properly for saving his life.

"Do I need an attorney?" she asked Hal.

"Yes. Do you want a recommendation?"

"Maybe," she said. "I've dealt with a lot of corporate lawyers, but this is different."

"Let me know. You can call me anytime." He pulled a card out of his pocket and scribbled on it. "I've put my home and cell phone numbers on there." He placed the card on the tray table. "Anything happens to this guy," he jerked his head toward Brian, "you call me, too."

"I will. Thank you." Kaylen picked up the card and took it over to her purse. "Sam said I was the target, not Brian," she said. "That he got shot by mistake."

Hal shook his head. "Wilson denied saying anything close to that before he lawyered-up."

Kaylen folded her arms and gazed out the window at the palm trees swaying gently in the breeze. "I can't believe I was so naïve. That I didn't see Sam or Sandy for who they really were." She turned on her heel and looked at Hal. "You're not going to tell me George was mixed up in any of this, are you? I don't think I can take any more horrible surprises."

"No," Hal said. "Whatever Wilson's into happened behind your husband's back. We believe your husband was shoring up Sam's restaurant for some time, probably as a favor for an old friend, but when he became ill, the assistance stopped for some reason, and Wilson had to look elsewhere."

"George handed most of his financial affairs over to Sylvia, his ex-wife, and his accountant six months before he died. Between the cancer and the chemo, he'd become too sick to function as a CEO anymore." Kaylen bit her lip. "Every day was either spent at some doctor's appointment, the lab or the hospital. The days he didn't have to leave the house were spent feeling really ill." She stopped and stared out the window again.

Brian saw the rigid lines of her shoulders. "Sylvia probably didn't feel any compulsion to keep pouring money into the restaurant," he said.

"She placed part of the blame for the breakup of her marriage on Sam," Kaylen said. "She told George that. It didn't matter that they were already divorced before I met George at the restaurant. So no, I doubt she would have given Sam as much as the time of day. Definitely no money to bail out his business."

"What about Sandy's death?" Brian asked. He covered his entire face with the cloth. It helped not to be staring up at the light above his bed. He didn't have to watch Kaylen's distress any longer, either, without being able to get up and comfort her.

"No suspects, except maybe Wilson, although we can't find a motive for him to either kill her himself or have someone do it for him," Hal said. "Mills talked to the people she worked with, starting with the manager and working his way down to the kitchen staff and busboys. They thought she was engaged to Wilson, who may have used her to try to get information that he could only get from Kaylen's best friend. He frequently visited her and the restaurant she worked at. It's an expensive place, and he dropped a lot of money on meals and bar bills. He also left big tips, sometimes as much as a hundred dollars."

Brian took the cloth off his face.

"How devious could he be?" Kaylen shuddered. "He pulled the wool not only over my eyes, but Sandy's, too. And she was willing to breach my confidence for what? A relationship with a man she must have at least suspected wasn't who he seemed to be?" She grimaced. "I feel so betrayed, so angry." She tossed back her hair and folded her arms across her chest.

"Anyway, enough harping about things we already know…how could Sam throw money around like that? I thought he was going broke?"

Brian pushed the bed control to raise his head. "Sam's relationship with Tim should tell you that. Tim was involved with a drug cartel…"

"I know that," she said. "But what could Sam possibly be doing for them?"

"What about that coffee you said was so bitter you couldn't stand it?" Brian regretted touching the bed control. His shoulder started throbbing like an invisible knife was being pushed around in the joint. "Maybe it was used to pack around drug shipments and he had to get rid of it somehow, without drawing attention by dumping it in the trash."

"He had regular shipments of specialty roasts," she said. "Even after The Hideaway started losing money, he was always trying something new. They were really expensive, too, he said. And frequently, the quality of them was substandard."

"I'll have Vickers check into that," Hal said.

"What did you find out about the guys in the black sedan? The one that ambushed us?" Brian asked. He eased the bed back down and put the cloth back over his face.

"Small time wannabe mobsters," Hal said. "They died on impact. Nobody came to claim their bodies at the morgue, so we made plans to ship them out with county funds once the coroner was done with them. The burials got delayed because of the storm." He stopped speaking.

Brian slid the cloth off his face in time to see a look passing between Hal and Kaylen. "Tim's still at the morgue, too," he said into the silence. "It's okay to talk about it. Jim's been a big help with the arrangements."

"Yeah, he has," Hal said. "He's a good man. You're lucky to have him as a friend." He watched Kaylen wipe sweat off Brian's face. "Where the hell is that nurse?" he asked. "Press the call button, Kaylen."

"Please come back and finish up tomorrow," she said. "I'll make sure Brian takes his medication before you get here."

"Yeah," Brian said. "I'll cooperate. I can't take any more questions today. I'm about to vomit. You don't want to stick around for that."

Hal pulled his cell phone out of his pocket. "I've got enough for today. I'd better get Frances back up here." He looked at Kaylen. "Are you going to stay at the hotel tonight?" he asked. "You look about as pale as Brian."

"No." She pressed the call-light. "I'm not going anywhere."

CHAPTER FIFTY-ONE

Brian felt considerably better the next afternoon, until he saw the IAB representative, Gil Morrison, walk into the hospital room behind Hal Shaw's wheelchair.

"I thought you said I wouldn't have to talk to IAB," he said as Hal wheeled himself closer to the bed.

"That's not the lieutenant's decision," Morrison said. He looked at the low bedside chair and pulled over a metal straight chair from its position near the window. He sat down and pulled a laptop from a black case. "Is this the only table?" He pointed to Brian's tray table.

"This is a hospital room, not a hotel." Brian looked at Hal. "You could have warned me."

"Lieutenant Shaw was instructed not to do that," Morrison said.

Brian felt hot and irritable. "If you're not going to let the lieutenant speak for himself, what's he doing here?"

He wished he hadn't tried so hard to convince Kaylen to shower and change clothes at the hotel. Even Jim was out of the room, eating lunch in the cafeteria after Dr. West had given strict orders for Brian to take it easy. He had spiked a low-grade fever after Hal's last visit.

"I'm here to tie up loose ends and clarify your statement," Morrison said. "Lieutenant Shaw insisted on coming with me." He pulled out a voice recorder, placed it on the tray table beside the laptop and punched a button.

"I want it to go on record that I object to this meeting," Hal said. "Sergeant Swift shouldn't be subjected to an interview until he's medically stable."

Morrison made a derisive noise that sounded like a snort of annoyance. "I already checked with hospital administration and was told the sergeant is indeed stable." The gaze he directed at Hal was filled with contempt. "Your protest is duly noted, however, Lieutenant Shaw." The tone of his voice held nothing of the condescension that Brian detected in his manner as Morrison leaned closer to the recorder. He went on to state the date, time and location of the interview..

"Now, Sergeant, I want you to state your name for the record," Morrison said.

Brian thought about refusing to state any such damn thing, but he knew that would only result in spending more time with Internal Affairs. He swallowed his anger and complied.

"Now," Morrison said. "I want to bring you up to speed on what the investigation has revealed. No evidence was discovered that you accepted bribes from any parties. The funds deposited into your account were all cash deposits. They were made at a couple of small branches on the outskirts of Miami by a man whose build resembles your brother's, although it would be hard to definitively identify him from the video recovered. He wore a number of different baseball caps, all pulled down low over his forehead, and kept his head down. A cashier's check was used to pay off the balance owing on your boat. It was sent directly to the finance company."

"Tim did all that?" Brian used the trapeze over his head to pull himself upright. "I can't believe it."

"There's more, Sergeant." Morrison crossed one leg over the other and jiggled his foot. "Your brother made you the beneficiary of his half-million dollar life insurance policy, plus you're the sole beneficiary of his will. He has considerable holdings in Little Havana. He owns three buildings on the same street, including the one where his apartment is located. He has interests in two restaurants...a fifty-three percent share in Samuel Wilson's Hideaway and twenty-five percent of Conchita's Cantina right down the block from Wilson's establishment. Stocks and bonds in his portfolio have a current value of approximately a million dollars. We also believe there was a Swiss bank account, but up to now have been unable to identify its exact location or possible contents."

If Brian thought he was feeling lightheaded before Morrison walked into the room, he knew he was mistaken. He thought about the attaché case filled with money and wondered if he'd been hasty in deciding Tim had robbed the cartel. Maybe instead, his brother had emptied that Swiss bank account to finance his escape from his life in Miami. The journal may have been only a form of insurance against interference from his former acquaintances and business associates.

"However," Morrison said. "The investigation into the legitimacy of your brother's affairs has not yet been completed. Given that his murder appears to be related to the drug trade, you will not be able to access his funds until their origins have been determined."

"Are you okay?" Hal's voice sounded far off and fuzzy around the edges.

The next thing Brian knew, Peggy's face was peering down at him, her fingers on his wrist, and the head of his bed was going down fast.

"No more visitors," she said, her voice low but firm. "Out. Both of you. Right now. And don't come back until Doctor West gives you written permission."

CHAPTER FIFTY-TWO

"Talk to me," Kaylen urged the following afternoon. "What's wrong? You've barely said anything since Lieutenant Shaw's last visit with that awful internal affairs man. Peggy told me he tried to have her arrested for obstructing his investigation. Jim took her to dinner last night to make up for it." Kaylen smiled. "Personally, I think he's got a major crush on her."

"How can you even think about stuff like that?" Brian kicked off the blanket. "Jim's friggin' love life. Christ!"

"I'm sorry if I upset you," Kaylen said. "But I can't be dark and gloomy like you all the time. It makes me too depressed."

"I should be out helping solve Tim's murder. Instead, I'm stuck in this bed. Everything's a mess, and I can't seem to stop running a fever so I can get out of here." Brian threw his pillow at the bedside chair. It missed and landed on the floor.

Kaylen picked it up. "That's not going to help. Getting angry and frustrated is only going to make your temperature climb. You've got to calm down."

"Fuck calm," he said. "It looks like my brother wasn't a total loss after all, and if there's a way to clear his name, I mean to do it."

"You're not the only detective in the squad," Kaylen said. "You can't expect to get right back to work after surgery, regardless of whether you want to investigate Tim's death yourself or not. Lieutenant Shaw won't allow it, anyway. He put you on disability."

"I am *not* disabled." Brian pushed the tray table out of his way.

Kaylen grabbed the water pitcher right before it fell over.

"I wouldn't be in this sorry-ass shape at all if you'd gotten help out there quicker," he said. "Next time I get shot, remember to tell them 'officer down.'"

"Next time?" Kaylen frowned. "There's not going to be any next time. I can't go through this again."

"I'm not asking you to. If you want to bail on me, you're free to leave. This is my life. I'm a cop. Sometimes, I get shot." He managed to get his legs out of the bed and struggled to sit up. He couldn't do it with his shoulder trussed up like he was a Thanksgiving turkey. He grabbed the bed control and rolled his head up higher. The pain in his arm nearly took his breath away.

"You probably risk getting shot way more than anyone else, with your attitude." Kaylen pulled the tray table further away. "Do you want me to help you myself or call the nurse? You can't make it out of bed alone."

"Who said?" He pushed himself toward the edge and eyed the chair. It looked like it was two miles away.

Kaylen pushed it closer without asking him. He thought about telling her to leave things alone, but he was afraid she'd move the chair back again and let him fall on his ass. He tested his legs. They trembled. *Damn!*

"I need help," he muttered.

"What was that you said?" Kaylen turned her head and put her hand behind her ear.

"I said, damn you, I need help."

"Finally." She looked up at the ceiling, arms held wide. "The man asks for help."

"Don't gloat. I'm already pissed off." He grabbed her arm.

"I think we need a nurse." She looked worried. "Peggy's off today and you've scared everyone else half to death. I'm pushing the call-light, but I can't guarantee anyone will come in a hurry."

"I don't need...any more...help." He managed to push himself up and swayed, afraid to move his feet and risk falling.

"Sergeant Swift!" A middle-aged nurse in a highly starched uniform came so quickly, Brian swore she must have sprouted wings on her heels, like Mercury.

Together, they got him half-on, half-off the chair. The effort left him panting like a horse coming into the winner's circle at the end of a race.

"You're going to need more assistance than we can give you getting back into bed," the nurse warned as she helped him push back further onto the chair. "You'll be tired. Don't you dare try it without pulling the call-light. It'll take a couple of male orderlies to transfer you safely."

Kaylen nodded. "I won't let him move," she promised.

"Make sure you don't." The nurse put her hands on her hips. "I was warned about you, Sergeant. I'm the nursing supervisor. Peggy told me how difficult and non-compliant you are. We'll all be very relieved when you get well enough to go home." With a swish of the door, she left.

"Wow," Brian said. "She should have gone into the prison system. She'd make a great warden." He looked at Kaylen's pinched, white face. "Sorry I snapped at you. Why don't you take a break? Jim's around here somewhere. He can stand guard over me to make sure I don't do anything that would get me into trouble with Nurse Ratched or the doc."

"Jim's not here. And I'm not leaving again until I'm sure you're able to take care of yourself. Your judgment's still affected by the drugs. If I hadn't been here, you'd have landed on the floor."

"Yeah, well, maybe," he muttered. "Where's Jim? Taking Peggy out on another date?"

Kaylen folded a sheet and tucked it around his bare legs. "He went to the funeral home to complete the arrangements."

"Oh." Brian knew Tim's body had been released by the coroner. "When's the funeral scheduled?"

"Four days from now." Kaylen sat on the edge of the bed. "I know you want to go, but I think you'll still be too weak, even if we take you in a wheelchair."

"I'll make it," he said.

"How could we get you in and out of a car when you need at least two people to get you to a chair?"

"Give me a break," he said. "This was my first time out of bed."

She took his hand. "I wasn't trying to make you feel bad. I'm simply telling you what I see. And a car ride is going to be very painful for you because you won't take your pain medication on a regular basis. That's why you're so cranky."

"I am *not* cranky." He jerked his hand away and slammed his fist onto the arm of the chair.

"I'm not going to argue with you again." She frowned, and her lips went into a pout of disapproval.

Brian avoided her gaze and made a big production out of readjusting the sheet covering his legs.

"There's something you're not telling me," Kaylen persisted. "You've been really down in the dumps ever since the surgeon came to see you. I think you're using that visit from internal affairs like a smoke screen, to cover the real reason you're so angry and depressed."

Brian looked at his lap. *Too weak to go to his brother's funeral. Too damaged to go back to work. Too feeble to defend himself.* "My life's over," he said.

"That's nonsense. You'll be feeling much better in a couple of weeks."

He shook his head. "I'm all washed up." He explained to her what Dr. West had told him. What a long road he had ahead of him. How he didn't know what he was going to do with the rest of his life.

"You could try not feeling so sorry for yourself," Jim said from the doorway.

Brian and Kaylen both jumped.

"Sorry," Jim said. "I couldn't help overhearing. I came to tell you everything's set for the funeral."

"With what?" Brian couldn't keep the lid on his feelings any longer. "Hal said I'm getting back pay, but Christ knows when that's coming. And until IAB's finished pokin' around, I won't see any of the money Tim left me. I got a call this morning from some rep who told me Tim's illegal activities may cancel out his life insurance policy." He laughed bitterly. "I used the last of my charter money to put gas in my car. I don't even have enough left to get it out of the impound lot."

Jim placed his neatly-folded newspaper on Brian's tray table. "The department's gonna issue you a check for back-pay during the next couple of days, and it should be a fat one," he said. "You were so out of it when Hal told you that, I don't think you heard him. Your insurance company'll reimburse on the *Destiny*. That claim's in the works, and they're gonna issue a check in the next few days, too." He sat beside Kaylen on the bed. "Hal already got your car out of hock…it's back at the marina parking lot. Kaylen got hers back, too, didn't you, honey?"

Kaylen nodded. "My Beemer stood out like a sore thumb in that alleyway. It got picked up and sent to the impound lot before yours did."

"Your coworkers even set up a fund to pay for Tim's funeral," Jim said. "You're going to be okay, buddy. Stop worrying."

Brian digested everything for a few moments. "I can't believe the guys at the precinct would do anything for Tim, even indirectly," he said, bewildered.

"Whatever beefs they had with your brother, they don't have with you," Jim said. "They've told me there's enough to pay for all his expenses, and the money's going to the funeral home tomorrow morning."

"I don't know what to say …"

"Just say thanks," Jim said quietly. "That's more than they expect. They know they let you down. Hal gave Mills my number and he called today. I think he was afraid to call *you,* because he figured you'd slam the phone down on him."

"They all hung me out to dry," Brian said. "They didn't even attempt to back me up."

"And they're trying to make up for it. Give them a chance, Brian. You've got to learn to be more forgiving. You did it for Tim. Why not your coworkers?"

"I'll think about it."

"That's a start."

They didn't understand, Brian thought. Saying sorry wasn't enough. He'd heard that too many times, after his mother got home from work and found him covered with cuts and bruises yet again and Ed Madison laid out snoring on the couch. Sorry was only a word. It didn't stop abuse, it didn't take away pain, and it didn't fix things. It just made the person saying it feel better.

"Things'll work out," Jim said. "You can stay with me until you get a new boat." He looked at Kaylen. "What about you, honey? You're not going to keep hanging out at the hotel after Brian gets discharged from here, are you?"

Kaylen sighed. "No, but I'm not going to stay at that condo again. Lieutenant Shaw believes we got followed from there." She took the rubber band off Jim's newspaper and used it to pull her hair back into a ponytail. "I try not to think too far ahead, these days."

Jim rapped his knuckles on the footboard of the bed. "Maybe you're out on disability, Brian, but it doesn't mean you can't keep working this case. I'd like nothing better than to help you in any way I can. I did a stint in Naval Intelligence during the Vietnam era. I'm a bit rusty, but being on the fringe of this investigation is getting my juices flowing again." He rubbed his hands together. "Sam Wilson's limping around on crutches and thumbing his nose at the cops. You've got to stop being a victim and start thinking like a detective again."

"Damn right." Kaylen folded her arms across her chest. "All you are right now is a nightmare patient, overbearing and grouchy."

"I am *not* overbearing." Brian felt anger boiling to the surface, and he couldn't stop it, didn't want to stop it. He turned toward Kaylen. "You started all this. You got Sam Wilson mad at me, and the fuckin' cartel sent a hit man."

She shook her head and held her ground, far from intimidated. "You're not blaming all this on me. You wouldn't have gotten shot if you hadn't refused to turn around and head back into Miami instead of taking us out joyriding onto a deserted stretch of road in the middle of a tropical storm." She shook her finger when he tried to interrupt her. "And if you hadn't passed out, we wouldn't be sitting here right now. You finally stopped barking out orders long enough for me to start thinking for myself. I've been surrounded by dominant men my whole life…my father, Sam, George, and now you. If I'd realized the only way to shut you up was to shoot you, maybe I'd have done it myself, only sooner."

"Oh? And when would that be? Before or after I saved your life?" He glared at her and she glared right back. And then he saw the corner of her mouth twitch.

"Beast," she said, and then she sat on the armrest of his chair and wrapped her arms around him.

As suddenly as his anger had appeared, it left, and took the desolation with it. He held her back, hard, with his good arm.

"I'm going to the funeral," he said.

CHAPTER FIFTY-THREE

And go to the funeral Brian did, a pale ghost wearing one of Tim's too-big suits, the sleeves hurriedly shortened and the pants cuffed by a tailor who agreed to measure Brian in the hospital and make the alterations on short notice.

Against her better judgment, Kaylen pushed him in a wheelchair to the graveside service at the Woodlawn Park Cemetery in Little Havana, after he got Dr. West to release him from the hospital a day ahead of schedule.

"I'm okay," he assured her, the lines deep around his eyes and at the corners of his mouth. He got up shakily and moved to one of the chairs placed in front of the simple oak coffin, decorated only with a spray of white lilies.

Jim took the wheelchair from her. "Go sit with Brian," he whispered in her ear. "Even if he tells you to go away at some time today, don't do it."

"I won't." She squeezed Jim's arm before walking over to sit beside Brian. She took a bottle of water out of her black shoulder bag. "Want some?"

He shook his head. "The only thing that would do me any good right now would be a stiff drink, and I can't have that while I'm taking all these pills."

Kaylen slipped her hand into his. "Anything else you want," she said. "I'll get it for you."

"I know."

He managed a weak smile that tugged at her wounded heart. Maybe he'd be the one to hold *her* together instead of the other way around. All the events of the last three weeks threatened to tumble from the clear blue sky and suffocate her like a cloud left over from the tropical storm. Tim's presence seemed almost palpable.

"Nice day," Jim remarked as he took a seat on the other side of Brian. "It'll be a short service. I told the minister you'd been in the hospital, so no dragging things out."

"I appreciate everything you've done." Brian stopped speaking and looked straight ahead. His jaw clenched.

Kaylen thought about asking him if he was in pain, but she was afraid he was suffering more than physical distress and kept her mouth closed. Hal and Frances arrived, along with four stern-faced men in dark suits.

His left arm supported by a sling, Brian turned slowly as they moved into the second row of chairs. "Thanks for coming." He sounded surprised.

He introduced Kaylen again to Detective Mills, and then to the other three...Detectives Hadley and Gomez, new to her, and Vickers, whom she had already met over mug books at the precinct.

"We had our issues with your brother, but he didn't deserve to die this way. No one would." Mills extended his hand and Brian shook it. "The rest of the guys are on duty, but they wanted us to extend their condolences, too."

"Thanks for paying Tim's funeral costs. I was..."

Mills shook his head. "Least we could do." He cleared his throat. "You had it real rough, and we should have stood behind you a lot earlier than we did."

"Yeah, well..." Brian glanced at Kaylen. "I don't make it easy for people. I know that." He looked at his feet, encased in thick socks and Tim's shoes, laced up tight to keep them on.

Kaylen wondered if she should have ignored Brian's wishes and sent Jim out with her credit card to buy him a new outfit instead of having him use items from Tim's wardrobe.

"Here's the minister," Jim said.

Kaylen heard the words of the service. She even remembered some of the details, like the ashes to ashes and dust to dust section, the feeling of Brian's hand lying still and cold within hers, and the stir of wind that ruffled the white curlicue of ribbon wrapped around the lilies' stems. But she couldn't shake the feelings of numbness and detachment until the service was over and the small group got up to leave.

She turned away to speak with Frances for a few moments. When she turned back, the rest of the mourners were trooping toward the cars, Jim walking slowly beside Lieutenant Shaw, now limping along on crutches. Brian had left his chair to stand in front of the coffin, his head bowed. Kaylen didn't know whether to give him privacy or go to him. She remembered her own desolation as she stood in front of George's coffin before it had gone to the crematorium, and how isolated she had felt. She heard Jim's whispered words again about not leaving Brian alone. Hesitantly, she walked over, hooked her arm through his and stood beside him.

"I failed him, you know." Brian's voice was low and filled with emotion. "I should've tried harder to get him to straighten up. He was so hard-headed, like his father. He'd blow me off. Tell me he had everythin' under control."

"You can't take the blame for this." Kaylen made no attempt to wipe away the tears coursing down her cheeks. "He loved the lifestyle...fast cars, expensive clothes, women like me." She shuddered. "I was so shallow. I didn't look past the handsome face and the sweet talk."

"He conned everyone, Kaylen. Not just you. He even lied to me. I'd always give him the benefit of the doubt and believe he would change. It caused a lot of friction with the squad, especially Hal, who said Tim stood in the way of both my career and my personal life. If I'd had to depend on the merit system instead of a test to make sergeant, I'd still be waiting."

"And if I'd been looking for commitment, then I'd be waiting, too." She took a tissue out of her pocket and dabbed at the tears. "What a waste of a life. He had so much going for him, and he threw it all away."

"I still can't believe I'll never see him again." Brian bit his bottom lip.

"Me, neither." Kaylen slipped her arm around him. He felt as rigid as the coffin in which his brother rested.

"I thought I was the one in danger of losing my life, because of my job," Brian said.

"Tim must have known how much his lifestyle placed him at risk." Kaylen looked at the casket and felt a powerful, unsettling sense of infinity. "He must have said *something* to you."

But Brian shook his head. "The only time we ever talked about death was after our mother passed away. Tim said he never wanted to be cremated. He wanted a real grave with a headstone, so people would remember him...like we'd ever forget." Brian smiled thinly. "I think it'll always feel like he's just waitin' around the next corner, instead of lyin' here."

"And that's what will keep his memory alive. Not the grave and the headstone." Kaylen tried in vain to see behind Brian's sunglasses and took them off. His eyes were murky, muted by pain. She stroked her fingers gently over the new scars on his cheek. "You'll remember. We both will. Tim left an indelible mark on us. I'll never think of him here, like this." She nodded toward the coffin. "I'll always think of him the last time I saw him alive, at the club, dressed up in a brand-new tux and looking so fine all the women in the place wished they were me."

"That was Tim," Brian agreed.

"I'll also remember the way he took care of me when I was sick," Kaylen said. "He was so gentle and caring." She smiled ruefully. "Of course, Tim being Tim, he was probably the one who made me sick in the first place, but I've got to forgive him, because he sent me you."

Brian lowered his head again. She gathered him in her arms and held him, looser than she would have liked because she was afraid of hurting him. Their cheeks touched. She felt moistness on her face and didn't know if it came from her own eyes or from his. She wanted to tell him everything was going to be all right, but she doubted it, and she couldn't lie. She wanted to kiss him and comfort him, but doing so in front of his dead brother's casket wasn't right, either.

So instead, she held him and closed her eyes against the harsh brightness of the summer day while he grieved at long last for the brother he would never see again.

CHAPTER FIFTY-FOUR

Kaylen quietly closed the bedroom door at Vickers' apartment and joined Jim in the kitchen. She spotted a mound of multicolored cut vegetables in a bowl on the counter.

"You're cooking?" she asked. "Aren't you too wiped out after that funeral?"

"We've got to eat," he said. "Especially Brian, but us, too."

He took the lid off a large pot bubbling on the stove, and an aroma of garlic and onion wafted over. Kaylen inhaled appreciatively. "Yum, that smells good."

Jim carefully tipped all the vegetables into the pot and took the empty bowl to the sink. "It's chicken stew," he said. "Nothing fancy." He smiled. "Glass of wine?"

"That would be great." Kaylen kicked off her shoes and perched on a stool at the opposite side of the breakfast bar. "I need something to relax. God, this has been an awful day." Tears welled up, and she grabbed a napkin.

Jim poured her a Chablis. "How's Brian doing?"

"Resting, finally. Thank God there's an elevator in this building. We'd never have gotten him up a flight of stairs. I had to help him get undressed and onto the bed." She took a sip of her wine. "Oh, that's good."

"Think I'll have a beer." Jim took one from the refrigerator. "Want a snack? Cheese and crackers?"

"No thanks." Kaylen placed her hands at the small of her back and stretched. "I could do with an Advil. Brian's heavy. My back's feeling it."

Jim frowned. "You should have asked me to help you get him into bed, honey."

Kaylen lowered her voice. "I've had enough trouble getting Brian to admit he needs help from *me*. He'd be mortified if I came out and got you."

"Because I'm an old man?" Jim looked offended.

"No, silly. Because you're a man, period. The worst day at the hospital was the first time he got out of bed. The nursing supervisor sent two orderlies to help him get back, and they picked him up like a baby. He was so ashamed and angry. Any sign of weakness is totally unacceptable to him."

"I still think he would rather you didn't hurt yourself," Jim said.

"I'll keep that in mind." Kaylen slid her fingers up and down the stem of her wineglass. Jim was old school…the man had to be the one who provided the help. He and Brian had a lot in common, she thought, not only their love of boats.

"This is a nice place," Jim said. "Generous of Detective Vickers to move in with his sister and her family for a few days." He adjusted the flame under the pot.

Kaylen suddenly felt flushed and slightly dizzy. She couldn't believe she was getting a buzz off one glass of Chablis until she realized she hadn't even made coffee that morning, much less eaten breakfast or lunch.

"I don't know how we'd have managed without all the help we've gotten over the last few days." She propped her elbows on the counter. Her head felt incredibly heavy, and she laid her chin onto her clasped hands. Time to give credit where it had been earned a hundredfold. "Especially yours, Jim."

"My pleasure," he said. "But even if you two had to do it alone, you would've made it. You guys are great together, you'd have figured things out." He pulled the other stool into the kitchen and sat opposite her. "You were meant to be together."

Kaylen's spirits plummeted lower even than at the graveside. "I was Tim's girlfriend. How in the world can I have feelings for his brother, and in so short a time?" Unwilling to see Jim's expression, she covered her face with her hands. "At best I feel fickle and at worse, well, I feel like a slut, if you want to know the truth."

"Oh, honey, you're neither," Jim said. "You've got to stop beating yourself up."

"I can't," Kaylen said. "I'll never get a chance to explain myself to Tim, neither will Brian." She felt tears welling up again and swallowed hard. "I don't even know where I'd start to do that, anyway." She took the napkin Jim slid across the bar and wiped her eyes. "How would you tell your boyfriend that you think you're falling for his brother? And how do I even know I'm not confusing gratitude with something a lot deeper?"

Jim patted her hand. "You're taking on way too much right now, trying to make life-changing decisions right after Tim's funeral."

"I suppose I am." Kaylen blew her nose and mentally cursed the wine for loosening her tongue to a virtual stranger, however kind and decent Jim seemed to be.

"You and Brian have to give yourselves time to come to terms with Tim's death," Jim said. "Having lost your husband, you should know that already. When my wife died, I thought I couldn't go on, but I did." He took a long pull on his beer, his tanned, wrinkled throat muscles convulsing rhythmically as he swallowed.

Kaylen watched as he carefully placed the bottle onto a coaster and used the sleeve of his shirt to wipe away the ring of condensation it had created on the granite counter top.

"I couldn't go on with my life in our house, though, or in front of all our friends," he said, his expression distant and troubled at the memory. "I had to sell the place we'd lived in for almost thirty-five years, shut down my business and move halfway across the country."

She remembered her own feelings of being rootless and without goals or direction. "All the time George was dying, I thought I was adjusting to the inevitability of losing him, but I wasn't," she said.

"Sometimes I think it's harder on those of us who are left." Jim smiled faintly at her before walking across the kitchen to take bowls out of a cabinet. He carried them into the dining area.

Kaylen took utensils from a steel basket and added napkins and glasses to set three places at the table. "I don't know if I should wake Brian or not when dinner's ready," she said. "It's hard to decide what he needs most, sleep or food."

"He needs *you* more than anything else," Jim said.

"I doubt he feels that way." Kaylen leaned back against the wall. The solidity of it comforted her while her emotions churned so painfully. "Brian feels guilty, like it's his fault Tim's dead, even though he said Tim wouldn't listen to his advice. Despite me telling him I was never, ever serious about Tim, he still thinks it's wrong for him to feel anything more than protective toward me. I don't know if he'll ever be able to get past that."

"Brian's an honorable man. He's also the elder brother. Guilt comes with the position." Jim took his empty bottle to the trash. "Like it does with being a parent."

"I wouldn't know about that." Kaylen felt the need to finish her wine. "I'm an only child, and my dad and I aren't close." She picked up the glass and drained it.

"Hmm," Jim said. "Sounds like there's a story behind that, but I doubt you're gonna share it with me right now."

"Good guess." Kaylen managed a smile to lessen the sharpness of her words. "I don't know you well enough yet for that."

"Fair enough." Jim smiled back. "Let's talk about Tim instead. Seems right today. What attracted you to him?"

"He swept me off my feet." Kaylen said. "He was so charming, so personable, so generous. He sent me red roses every Monday and took me out to dinner every Saturday night, unless he had to go out of town. Then he would call or text to tell me how much he missed our standing date."

"Quite the romantic," Jim said.

"Yes. Suave, sophisticated, worldly. He dressed immaculately, always in designer clothes. He drove a black car that never showed any dust, even at the height of summer with the wind blowing sand off the beaches onto everything. He was perfect. Too perfect. That's maybe why I was attracted to him in the first place, but why I never fell in love with him."

"A total opposite of Brian," Jim said. "In every way."

"Totally," Kaylen said. "And that's not a bad thing."

"No, it's not. With Brian you get no frills, but you sure know where you stand."

"That's the truth." Kaylen rubbed her temples. "Brian's rude and dictatorial. But he's got such a good heart, and he's absolutely fearless. He took a bullet while protecting me. Tim would never have done that. He'd have run the other way at the first sign of trouble, in case he messed up his suit." She grimaced. "That was mean and in poor taste. I'm sorry." She yawned before she could stop herself. "Must be lack of sleep."

"No one's perfect." Jim took a last swallow of his beer and put the bottle in the trash. "Not even Tim. Not even you."

"I know that. We all go through life searching for someone who's close to that, though, don't we?"

"And that may be the mamma of all mistakes." Jim stirred the contents of the pot with a wooden spoon. "Dinner'll be ready in about thirty minutes."

Kaylen yawned again. "I should never have had that drink."

"You're worn out. It's got nothing to do with a glass of wine. Why don't you take a nap? Dinner'll keep. Like Brian, you may need rest more than food right now."

"Maybe you're right."

But when she tiptoed into the bedroom and closed the door, Brian opened his eyes.

He tapped the bed. "Lie down."

She slid fully dressed under the covers and snuggled up against him. "Somehow, I always end up in bed with you," she said.

"No complaints from me." He put his arm around her. "Get some rest. You'll need to be fresh when we go back out later to get the attaché case."

"Today! Are you crazy?" She pulled away from him. "You just got out of the hospital, and Sam's men are all over the compound. How are you planning to get us in there?"

"Over the wall. I'll do something to knock out the cameras. They'll think it's another power outage. By the time they know it's not, we'll be gone."

"I thought you stopped taking all those drugs? You're hallucinating if you think you're going over a wall in your condition."

"We'll see about that." He rolled over to face her. "I feel much stronger already."

"Yeah, right. And that's why you came up here in a wheelchair."

"Last ride I take in that thing," he said. "But it looked good if anyone followed us."

"You faked everything? You made me hold you up getting in and out of that car four times?" Kaylen sat up. "Why, you...you..."

"Go on," he said. "Say it..."

"Fraud," she said. "You should have been an actor, not a cop."

"Sometimes, working undercover required acting. I had plenty of practice."

"I'm sure." Kaylen didn't feel sleepy any more.

"Is Jim still here?"

"He's in the kitchen, cooking our dinner."

"You've got to convince him to go back to the hotel," Brian said. "I don't want him to go with us. He was lucky the last time. I don't know what he was thinking, tackling one of those guys on the dock. He's sixty-nine, for Christ's sake."

Kaylen looked at Brian's pallid face. He'd had no rest since he left the hospital that morning. "Jim's not the only one around here who doesn't know his limits," she said. "If there's a confrontation, how do you think you're going to defend us with your arm in a sling?"

"You'd be surprised what I can do when I put my mind to it. But you've got to get rid of Jim. He thinks he's going to use those old skills he picked up during the Vietnam War, but they'll get him killed. Things have changed, and I doubt he's able to do as much as he thinks he can. And he won't take orders from me. You, I don't have to worry about."

Kaylen felt like telling Brian she wasn't taking any more of his orders, either, but she couldn't take the chance that he'd leave her behind, too. He needed her, she told herself, and not just to drive him around, whether he was willing to admit it or not.

"We've gotta stop by a store to pick up rope an' a couple of other things before we go out there," Brian said. "Hal brought my service piece to the funeral today, but we need more ammo. I'll show you how to load a clip."

"I already know how to load a clip," Kaylen said. "I think you and Hal are *both* crazy," she added as she got back out of bed. "Hal brought a gun to a funeral?"

"Well, he couldn't bring it to the hospital, for Christ's sake. IAB confiscated the gun you used to get us out of Sam's compound. Morrison said it's part of the investigation. Hal told me he wasn't going to leave us defenseless under any circumstances, and since I already had my badge returned, why shouldn't I get my Glock back, too?"

"Guns." Kaylen shook her head. "I already hated them *before* you got shot. Now I hate them even more."

"So if you don't like being around them, how do you know how to use one? Is that something George taught you?"

"No. My father, the gun-toting farmer. He insisted on educating me, like I was ever going to pick one up and fire it at anyone or anything. I'm a pacifist." She put her hands on her hips. "Are you going to tell me you can load that Glock one-handed, and you're going to be able to hit more than the side of a barn using your right hand?"

"I can," he said. "We're taught how to reload with one hand, in case we get injured in the field and have to do it. I may not be able to hit someone with the same accuracy using my right hand as my left, but I guarantee I'll bring him down."

"You've got an answer for everything," Kaylen said. "You make me so angry." She shoved her feet back into her shoes. "Oh, what's the use of arguing with you? You're going to do this anyway, so I might as well go along to make sure you don't get killed."

"You're really mad at me, aren't you?" Brian sounded surprised.

"Of course I'm mad. I put myself at risk to save you when we went to Sam's. Now you want to go back there and endanger yourself just to get that damned bag of money."

His brow furrowed. "It's not the money I want, it's the journal. I can use it to bargain our way out of this. Otherwise, do you seriously think either of us will ever be able to stop worrying about another hit man doing a better job?"

Kaylen wanted to shake him, but that wasn't a choice. He looked almost as white as the sheet he was lying on. "It doesn't matter whether you give them the journal or they take it," she said. "Whichever way, we lose."

"I thought about that a lot while I was supposed to be resting in that hospital bed. I've got to set up a meeting with Hastings."

"What good is that going to do? He's slimy...I don't like him."

"I think he's the one giving all the orders, and not just at the precinct."

Kaylen felt a ripple of fear ice her back. "Oh, God. Now he's in charge at Miami-Dade, he hears everything."

"Which is why I'm keeping quiet until we've got the attaché case again. Then I'll contact the FBI and let them use the information from that journal to start rounding people up."

"You really believe that'll stop the cartel?"

"From threatening us anymore, yes. I figure all they wanted was to stop Tim sharing information about their activities. I'm not even sure they know anything about the money. I think he had cash stowed in a Swiss bank account and emptied that to finance his trip out of Miami. Whether he skimmed money belonging to the cartel or profited from his business dealings, I'm still not sure."

"If that's true, and the cartel doesn't know about the money, then why was he running? He could have given them the journal himself."

"I don't have all the answers yet, princess. Tim never did what would seem logical to anyone else. But I doubt a drug cartel would believe that was the only copy of his journal, or that Tim would leave town without telling me where it was hidden."

"Okay." She nodded. "That makes sense. What doesn't is Sam. Why would he be involved in all this?"

"The financial benefits," Brian said. "He told you his business was in trouble, and he'd had that big house built. I bet he was in a panic. Anyone would be with debts mounting up. The cartel may have contacted him through Tim, offering Sam a way out."

"Or maybe he was already involved, which gave him the funds to have the house built in the first place," she said.

"Good guess," Brian said. "You're turning into a partner instead of a sidekick."

"Coming from you, that's actually a compliment, not a put-down." She smiled, and for the first time that day, it didn't feel like so much of an effort. "But then why would he try to burn down his own restaurant? He needed it. He wouldn't be able to live in that big house without any visible means of support. Someone would question that. He's too big a part of the Miami community for people not to notice. He said he wasn't going to have The Hideaway rebuilt. Instead, he was going to take early retirement, which sounded ridiculous. Sam loved to work. He was never happier than when he was at the restaurant."

"People's priorities change. Maybe he was happy with his life until he was offered more than he ever dreamed of."

"And the financial rewards would have meant he was been able to meet me on common ground, too, which he was never been able to do since I married George." Kaylen sighed. "Men are so stupid. They think all women want is for them to have money."

"Not all of us do," Brian said quietly. "Some of us know it takes a whole lot more than that."

Kaylen didn't have an answer for that comment. "If we're going back to Sam's, we've got to eat," she said. "I'll bring you a bowl of Jim's chicken stew." She paused at the door. "I'll tell him we want to be alone. He'll understand and leave."

"Does he really think I'm capable of *that*?" Brian grinned at her.

"Men also think they're invincible," she pointed out. "Look at you…you think you're capable of climbing a wall. So why wouldn't Jim believe you could give me an hour or more of ecstasy?"

She felt a great deal of satisfaction when Brian pulled the sheet over his head. Putting on her best game face, she made for the kitchen.

CHAPTER FIFTY-FIVE

It was close to six o'clock when they approached Sam's compound. They found the gates closed and the cameras back in service, moving to record the progress of Kaylen's BMW as it passed by.

"Keep driving," Brian told her from the passenger's seat. He hunkered down, a baseball cap hiding his blond hair and one of Tim's black jackets zippered over his left arm, immobilized against his chest in a sling. "We need to find a way in at the side of the compound."

Kaylen wondered if any of Sam's men would recognize her car. Without street lamps, the dark blue vehicle might not attract as much attention as she thought. But still, she worried.

"There's a turn-off ahead," Brian said. "Take it slow."

Kaylen checked all her mirrors for other cars before driving down a narrow track that threaded between the wall and the thick vegetation bordering the swampland. Her heart thundered in her ears as she eased the car over potholes and tried to stay away from reeds marking the edge of dry land.

"Stop," Brian said.

Kaylen gently tapped the brakes and the car glided to a standstill.

"Lucky for us, Sam's a cheap son-of-a-bitch," he said. "Turn off the engine, but leave the fob on the seat, in case we have to leave in a hurry. We're getting out."

Kaylen followed his instructions without arguing, despite her misgivings. "What do you mean, Sam's cheap?" she asked.

"The cameras are ten feet apart beside the road, but about thirty feet apart back here."

She quietly closed her door and looked at Brian over the roof of the car. "Maybe he's got some other type of security on the other side of this wall, like attack dogs. Did you consider that?"

"I thought you'd know. You never visited here?"

"He only moved in a couple of months ago, and I've been too busy with the club to socialize much. He sent a limo for me once, and it took me right to the house. I wasn't looking at his security system. Why would I? I don't think like you…suspicious of everything and everyone."

"Obviously." Brian grimaced. "Then I guess there's only one way to find out what's back there." With difficulty, he hoisted himself onto the hood and peered at the top of the wall. "Give me the rope," he whispered.

"There's got to be a better way of doing this," she said.

"You want to continue looking over your shoulder for the rest of your life, or you want this to be over?"

Sarcasm again. She decided to throw it right back at him. "Do I really need to remind you that you almost got killed the last time we were here?"

"I'm not planning on dying, Kaylen." His voice was calm, reassuring. "But we need that case, and unless you think asking Sam nicely will make him hand it over, we're gonna have to take it."

He was trying not to frighten her, and it was actually working. "You don't even know where I put it," she pointed out. "You were nearly unconscious."

She joined him on the hood. It protested with a sharp metallic noise that sounded deafening. They both stood silently waiting for a response from the other side of the wall. Kaylen realized she was holding her breath and let it out slowly when nothing stirred except a warm breeze rustling its way through the reeds.

"Get down," he hissed.

"No," she said. "I'll go."

"You wouldn't know what to look out for. And what if there really are attack dogs in there?"

Kaylen tossed her head. "If there *are* dogs behind that wall, then they've got to be deaf. We're making so much noise arguing about everything."

"Okay. I'll give you that," he said, actually conceding a millimeter. "But you've also got to watch out for cameras and motion detectors. I'm the one with all the experience."

Kaylen decided reasoning with him wasn't getting her anywhere. "So what's your plan again?"

"Climb that tree, secure the rope around a branch and drop it over the wall."

"At least let me climb up and tie the rope, then," she said. "You can't do that with one hand."

He looked doubtful. "Well...all right, but that's it. Then you come right back down."

More orders. Kaylen pushed her exasperation aside, reminding herself Brian was compensating for his weakness by a show of force. She draped the rope around her neck and took a deep breath. She couldn't even remember the last time she had climbed a tree.

"Here, I'll give you a boost." Brian made a cradle with his hand and braced it against his knee.

Kaylen put her heel into his palm and held onto the tree trunk. When he pushed, she managed to grab a branch and hoist herself up. She scrabbled around for a toe hold. Her nails sank into the wood, still wet from the tropical storm, but she swallowed her revulsion and held on tight.

Brian grunted as he pushed her foot again, propelling her upward. Kaylen knew he didn't have much strength in reserve. With renewed determination, she got a better hold on the branch and pulled herself into the tree. Panting, she promised herself that once that attaché case was in the right hands, she would use her gym membership on a regular basis and not just skip meals to keep her weight down.

"Tie one end around the trunk and drop the other end over the wall," Brian said. "Then come back down."

Kaylen did as she was told, right up to the point where he had instructed her to come back down. Instead, she flung one leg over the wall.

"What are you *doing?*"

She heard his panic even as she teetered on the edge of the abyss before taking the rope in both hands and lowering herself over the other side. She swung for a moment while she tried to get her bearings, the rope biting painfully into the palms of her hands. Kaylen decided she didn't care if she fell, but she wasn't going to stay in that exposed position. She remembered she had to wrap the rope around one leg, but she did it so sloppily, she couldn't control her descent.

The ground came up with a rush, and she dropped onto it with a jarring thump that shot all the way from her tailbone to the top of her head. Winded, she sat where she had landed. Now she knew how Sam must have felt when he tripped over his own feet and ended up with a herniated disc.

"Kaylen!" she heard.

"I'm okay. Stop talking or someone's going to hear you."

She got up and pulled twigs out of her hair while she tried to get her bearings. Old-fashioned carriage lamps cast a subdued glow over the driveway as it meandered between thick plantings of bamboo, ferns and oleanders. Kaylen trod carefully, mindful that snakes and other disgusting creatures might be lurking in the undergrowth. Branches snapped underfoot and leaves rustled as she passed. She heard Brian's sarcastic voice in her head, telling her she was making more noise than a scout troop at a jamboree.

Afraid to take the easier route and be seen by the cameras, she continued on her way, trying to remember how many twists and turns the driveway made before it came to the tree with the fork in its trunk. They should have come in daylight, she thought, but she realized the chances of being discovered would have been magnified. The twilight provided some anonymity, but also made it more difficult for her to see where she was going.

She wished she had Brian's gun in her pocket, but then he would be unarmed as well as disabled. To quieten some of her fears, he had shown her he could still reload his own weapon. He had dropped the magazine and inserted a new one, jamming it home against his thigh, all one-handed. He also told her he could pull the slide back by catching the rear sight on his jeans pocket or scraping the top of the gun along the open window of the car. After that, she had stopped telling him he couldn't defend himself.

Kaylen recognized a rock formation beside the driveway and picked up speed. *To hell with the noise.* If she didn't get a move on it would be completely dark, and then she'd never find her way back to the damned rope. Brian, believing he was the one who would be scaling the wall, still had the penlight in his pocket. She pushed aside the thick, spiky leaves of a small palm and stepped into a chuck hole. As she fell, she heard a car approaching.

She forced herself to lie still and listened as the engine's purr grew louder. Gravel crunched. Cautiously, she got onto her hands and knees and peered through the palm fronds. A black limo passed by with tinted windows rolled up tight. It kept going at a leisurely pace, disappearing around the next curve in the direction of the street. She gulped in air heavy with the scent of damp earth and composting leaves before pushing her way through a stand of bamboo to see the tree's distinctive shape outlined against the darkening sky.

The case still nestled in its fork. Kaylen grabbed it and squatted back down. No small army appeared. She watched the cameras perched on the wall, but they didn't rotate. Maybe Sam couldn't afford to keep his security measures going, or they were only there for show. Whatever the reason, she was truly thankful. She stayed within the cover of the vegetation on the way back, mindful that another misstep into a chuck hole could result in a sprained ankle.

"I got it," she told Brian.

"Good, then get back over here."

He sounded irritated. Kaylen bit back a tart comment. If she was in his shoes, she'd be drained and short-tempered, too. She had also disobeyed one of his orders, and he wouldn't take that lightly.

As well as a handle, the attaché case sported a long leather strap, which she swung over one shoulder. She grabbed the rope and tried to climb, but couldn't remember what to do. She tried putting her feet on the wall and going hand over hand, but her tennis shoes slid on the wet bricks. She tried putting the rope between her feet. That only resulted in her swinging around like a monkey at the zoo. The case weighed her down and the strap bit into her neck.

Totally exhausted, she let go of the rope and leaned against the wall while she caught her breath.

"What the fuck are you doing?" Brian's voice floated over.

"Filing my nails. What the hell do you think? I can't climb that damned rope. It's hopeless."

"Well, you can't *stay* in there. You've *got* to climb."

"I failed gym in junior high because I couldn't."

"Then why did you go over the wall in the first place?"

"Because you couldn't, but you wouldn't admit it. I'll take the case to the gate and push it between the bars. I think it'll fit. If not, then I'll empty the contents into your hands…well…hand."

"And then you'll still be on the wrong side of the wall."

"I'll throw myself on Sam's mercy."

"I reckon he's a bit short of that right now. Besides, I think he left in that limo a few minutes ago."

Kaylen sank to the ground. "What am I thinking, anyway?" she asked, more to a nearby Banyan tree than to Brian. "You can't drive the car away from here, even if I do get the case to you somehow."

"Go stand about twenty feet from the gates," Brian said. "And no arguments."

Kaylen thought about telling him she wasn't going anywhere, but she knew that really wasn't an option. Neither was going up to Sam's door, unless she wanted an untimely and probably painful death. She heard her car backing up. Brian was unbelievable, she thought, shaking her head and running for the entrance. *But why twenty feet?*

Her brand-new Beemer sent Sam's filigreed wrought iron gates flying back as though they were made of aluminum. The car came to a stop, grill crumpled but engine still running. Kaylen sprinted for the passenger's side and wrenched the door open. "You're insane," she said.

"Get in." He put the car in reverse as she sat. "We've got company."

Kaylen barely had time to close the door before they tore backwards out of the compound.

"Put it into drive when I tell you," he said as they swerved into a turn that almost sent them into the swamp.

She grabbed the gear shift.

Brian stomped on the brake. "Now!"

Kaylen did as she was told. The BMW shot off down the street with another car in close pursuit. She heard gunfire. "Oh, God. We're going to die."

"Not after all this, we're not." Brian accelerated, the scenery flashing by.

Kaylen looked at the speedometer. The boasts of the manufacturer were evidently grounded in truth, because the needle was already passing 70 as they flew down the narrow street. She turned her attention to the side mirror. Lights kept pace, the vehicle behind them a black hulk in the waning light. "We've got to get off this side road," she said. "Take Kendall to Ponce de Leon."

"I'm on it, already." He swerved to avoid a tree, downed by the storm and partially blocking the road.

Kaylen closed her eyes and held her breath. She heard screeching tires and only hoped that if they were about to die, it would be quick. A ridiculous thought crossed her mind of their bodies being thrown in on top of Tim's coffin to save the cost of additional burials. The screeching stopped.

"Missed Kendall," Brian said.

"No shit." Kaylen stared through the windshield at the center white line disappearing rapidly beneath the front of the car as they straddled the middle of the road. Steam slid out from both sides of the hood.

They passed a small side street and flashing blue lights illuminated the windows. A patrol car swung in behind the chase vehicle.

"Just great. The one time I don't want the cops, here they come." Brian took a sharp left onto Douglas, and the wheel whipped through his fingers. "Help me. I can't hold it!"

Kaylen grabbed the wheel and they both hung on as the Beemer skidded from one lane to the other and back again.

When she was able to glance back, she saw the chase car had missed the turn, careened into some parked cars and come to rest. The patrol car had fared only slightly better, mounting the curb and taking out a small tree on the easement. Brian accelerated again and the flashing blue lights dimmed into the distance.

Neither of them spoke until he pulled onto a side street and stopped. He dimmed the lights.

"I almost killed us," he said. "You'd better drive." He opened the door. "I've gotta call Hal. The radiator's cracked and we're gonna have to ditch this car. While I'm doin' that, I want you to call Jim. I didn't want to involve him, but there's no choice. Ask him to bring my Camaro and meet us."

"Where?"

"There's a strip mall to the right after he exits the highway and takes Douglas. He can call when he's close, an' I'll give him better directions."

Kaylen watched Brian haul himself out of the car as she pulled out her cell. Jim answered on the first ring, like he had been expecting a call. He sounded peeved when she told him they had been in a wreck and needed the Camaro.

"I offered to help Brian," he said. "But he sent me to the hotel like I was just getting in the way. Now he asks you to call me instead of doing it himself."

"He's talking to his supervisor," Kaylen said. "Please don't be mad, Jim. Brian was afraid you'd get hurt. He wanted to do everything himself, but I wouldn't let him. Then he had to rescue me. It's all my fault."

"I doubt that," Jim said, but then, totally unexpectedly, he chuckled. "I don't think I'm ever going to complain about being bored again. This is a case of 'be careful what you ask for.'"

"Does that mean you're coming?" Kaylen asked.

"Wouldn't want to miss any more of the excitement," Jim said. "Guess I'll have to prove myself to Mr. Do It Himself. I'm on my way. Hope I remember how to drive stick without wrecking Brian's transmission."

"Well?" Brian was leaning against the doorframe.

Kaylen climbed out of the car. "To put it mildly, Jim was a bit upset," she said. "But he's coming. He said he's going to prove himself to you. I think you should be apologizing to him, instead. What about Lieutenant Shaw?"

"More pissed at me than Jim, probably, but he'll get over it." Brian sat heavily on the passenger's seat as she slid behind the wheel. "Give me the case, would you?"

Kaylen handed it over and eased the Beemer back onto the main road. A dull hiss made her fully aware they had to speed up if they wanted to get anywhere before the car stalled out.

Brian rummaged around in the case. "I called Hastings while you were wandering through Sam's compound. We're meeting at the marina in an hour. Jim's boat, since it's still waiting to go into dry dock for repairs." He put the rain-damaged journal to one side and took out an envelope wedged at the bottom of a pocket. "Jim'll be less than thrilled about that location, but I couldn't come up with a better one. I know the layout of the place, and I can sit down." He took the penlight from his pocket and clamped it between his teeth.

Kaylen felt defensive. He hadn't congratulated her on getting the attaché case. He obviously still retained an opinion that her abilities extended to little more than standing around looking fashionable in a cocktail dress. "I wasn't 'wandering through' Sam's property," she said. "I was being careful not to get caught."

"Making the amount of noise you did? I could hear you crashing around in there from the other side of the wall."

"As you have so carefully pointed out on multiple occasions, I was never trained for this job as your sidekick." She hit the accelerator and the Beemer bucked in response, the engine coughing.

Brian took the penlight out of his mouth. "Sidekicks do what they're told, without arguing about everything. Robin doesn't argue with Batman. Tonto never talked back to The Lone Ranger."

"The women in those shows were relegated to screaming and fainting whenever things got rough," Kaylen said. "If I did that every time you got into trouble, then you wouldn't be sitting here with your brother's stuff."

"You're right. I'm sorry. I was trying to joke with you, to make you less worried."

"It's working. You're making me mad."

He had the audacity to grin at her.

"I'm starting to hate you again," she said.

"Good." He tore open the envelope with his teeth and unfolded a couple of sheets of notepaper.

"What's on those?"

"Dunno." He scanned the papers with the aid of the penlight, until it suddenly dropped into the attaché case and started rolling around, its beam catching Kaylen in the eyes.

"Hey, you're blinding me! What's wrong?"

"Tim left me a letter."

Kaylen grabbed the penlight and aimed it at the papers. "Read."

"Later." He stuffed the letter into his jacket pocket.

"Anything else in there?" she asked.

He took the penlight back from her. "An airline ticket to Rio, first class." He peered at the ticket. "The red eye, on the night Tim disappeared." He looked through the pockets again. "His passport." Brian turned his attention back to the journal, rapidly scanning page after page. "I never knew Tim was so organized. He'd been keeping tabs on these guys for a while."

"Why do you have to be the one to meet Hastings?" Kaylen asked. "Why don't you let Hal do it, or the FBI or something?"

"I've got to go. They want me to wear a wire so they get everything they need to lock the bastard up for good. I can't prove he was responsible for Tim's death unless I get him to confess."

Kaylen's attention wandered very far from her driving. The car weaved. Horns sounded and cars swerved.

"Watch it!" Brian shouted. "Stop light!"

Kaylen hit the brakes hard and the car ground to a halt.

After all they'd been through, she thought, he was going to sacrifice himself to send Hastings and the cartel to jail. "You can't," she said. "You mustn't."

"I have to." His voice was amazingly calm. "No one else can do it. I'm not letting these sons-of-bitches get away with Tim's murder."

"Then I'm begging you. Please don't do this." Fear gripped her insides with icy fingers. "Hastings has been looking for any excuse to kill you, and he'll think this is his best chance to do it. I'll go. I've got the tattoo. He won't harm me. He thinks I'm a stupid socialite."

"It's non-negotiable, Kaylen. He won't tell you anything, but he'll talk to me. He hates me so much, he'll want me to know what happened to Tim before he tries to kill me."

She struggled with her seatbelt, got it off and threw her arms around Brian's neck. "I can't lose you."

"It'll be okay, princess."

His voice was soft and reassuring. Kaylen sobbed against his neck.

"I won't take any unnecessary chances." He shook her gently. "Look at me."

She raised her head. His scarred face had become infinitely dear to her. The thought of never seeing him again was too much to bear.

"I already told you I'm not planning on dying tonight, Kaylen." His hand cradled the back of her head. His lips brushed hers. "I've finally found a reason to be careful," he said against her mouth.

CHAPTER FIFTY-SIX

"If you're going to send me away again," Jim said from the back seat of the Camaro as they waited for a cab to arrive in the marina parking lot, "then at least let me take Kaylen out of danger, too."

Brian felt her grip tighten on his leg. "She won't go," he said. "I've already tried to convince her."

"I won't," Kaylen said. "But you have to, Jim. You've got to take this out of here for us." She handed him the attaché case.

"Must be mighty important stuff in there," Jim said.

"There is." Brian saw cab lights approaching. "I don't want it anywhere near Hastings."

"It'll be safe with me," Jim promised. "You're not going to get my boat blown up are you, right before she gets spiffed up in dry dock?"

"I'll do my best not to let anyone put another scratch on her." Brian watched Jim get out of the car. "Thanks again. We'll see you in a couple of hours."

"Make sure you do, buddy," Jim said. "You, too, missy." He smiled at Kaylen.

"If I don't call you within two hours, take the case to the FBI," Brian said. "The contact person is Britton."

"Okay." Jim nodded and flagged down the cab.

"And don't open the case yourself," Brian added.

Jim waved and left without a backward glance.

The cab's rear lights died to a glow as it exited the marina.

Kaylen shook her head. "If he knew what was in there, he'd have a heart attack."

"Which is why I didn't want him peeking. Jim's a man of his word. He won't look."

Brian wiped sweat off his face. He needed his pain pills. The constant ache in his shoulder had turned knife-like again, shooting up his neck and radiating down his left arm all the way to the tips of his fingers. He threw open the door and lifted his right leg out of the car. It felt like someone had filled it with lead while he wasn't paying attention.

"What are you doing?" Kaylen asked. "Put your leg back in the car and rest. We're meeting Hastings in fifteen minutes."

"You're *not* going to this meeting," Brian told her. "Since you insist on staying here, you'll have to sit in the car with the doors locked until Mills comes to pick you up." He tried to control the tone of his voice, but he sounded weak and irritable even to his own ears. "I need my jacket. Jim hung it over the back seat, and the Vicodin's in one of the pockets. I can't take this fuckin' pain any longer, even though I wanted to face Hastings without being drugged out."

"Sit tight. I'll get it." Kaylen opened her door. "There's water in my bag on the floor by your feet," she said as she got out.

Brian gratefully slumped back and closed his eyes. He wondered if he'd even be able to walk onto Jim's boat under his own power, much less deal with Hastings. Sometimes, he admitted, he had delusions about being Superman or something.

His eyes flew back open when he heard a scuffle and Kaylen's muted scream.

"Get out of the car, Swift," Hastings said.

Brian saw the barrel of a gun pointing through the open door. Past it, he saw Hastings with a hammer lock around Kaylen's throat.

"Out, bastard." Hastings motioned with the gun.

"How did you find us?" Brian sat upright.

"You think I'd wait until the last minute to come to a meeting you'd set up?" Hastings laughed. "I saw your car turning into the lot."

"*Shit!*" Brian knew he should have forced Kaylen and Jim to drop him off a block away, but he also knew he would never have been able to walk that far.

"Come on, Swift. Stop stalling," Hastings said. "Hands where I can see them."

"My left arm's useless. I can't do anything with it."

"So I heard, but maybe I'll put a bullet into it to see if that's a lie."

"Help yourself. I'm in so much pain, it won't make any difference." Brian got slowly out of the car and stood, right hand in the air.

"Toss your gun."

Brian slid the Glock out of its holster and lobbed it into the bushes surrounding a nearby palm tree. He forced himself to concentrate despite his pain, his mind flipping through various scenarios to resolve the situation, rejecting them all. Kaylen looked terrified, eyes wide and breathing ragged.

"Now, where's that list, fucker?" Hastings tightened his grip on Kaylen's throat and she gasped.

Brian steeled himself not to react. "You think I'd be stupid enough to bring it with me?" He kept his voice neutral and put his hand in plain sight on the Camaro's roof. "I came to make a deal with you."

"You think you can bargain your way out of this? What are you, stupid?" Hastings' pretty-boy face contorted into an ugly caricature.

Brian tried to shrug and regretted it. Pain slammed into his neck. "Not as stupid as you," he said before he could stop himself. He instantly regretted it when Kaylen rose up on her toes. "Ease up," he told Hastings. "Your beef's with me, not her."

"If I'd had my way, you'd be wearing cement shoes and hanging out at the bottom of the bay." Hastings' gun pointed steadily at Brian's head.

"Obviously, you're not in charge of this operation, or it would've happened by now." Brian watched Hastings' lip curl. "You know as well as I do the cartel's gonna have to deal with me. If they try messing with Kaylen or me, that journal goes to the media and the FBI."

He warily watched the barrel of the gun and wondered how fast he could duck to retrieve the Ruger he kept in his glove compartment. Not fast enough, he decided. Hastings could break Kaylen's neck and still manage to shoot him through the open car doors.

"Do you seriously think I'm going to stand by while you hold this over my head for the rest of my life?" Hastings suddenly pressed the gun barrel to Kaylen's head. "No goddamned way."

Brian's fragile control snapped. The bastard was going to shoot Kaylen and there was nothing he could do to stop it. "Well, I'm not gonna stand by while you get away with Tim's murder, you son-of-a-bitch," he said. "You're goin' down."

Anger bolstered his failing strength, and he prepared to lunge for the Glock. It was a huge risk, but he'd be damned if he was going to wait for Hastings to take out both of them.

But as he prepared to commit potential suicide, the sound of a gunshot made him dive for cover instead. His left elbow hit the ground and for a moment, he became completely incapacitated, fighting off nausea and blackness. Swearing under his breath, he used the floorboard of the car to lever himself up, popped open the glove compartment and grabbed the Ruger.

He chanced a look before slamming the door to shield himself. Hastings was down on his knees, hands clutching his throat. He looked bewildered as he brought up a bloody hand and stared at it. Kaylen, on all fours, was crawling frantically toward the Camaro.

"Get down!" Brian ordered. "For Christ's sake, Kaylen, get down!"

She dropped to her belly and cradled her head in her arms. He heard her whimpering and wished he could get to her, but that would be a stupid mistake, and he'd made far too many already.

He crawled to the front of the Camaro and looked around for the shooter. A spotlight illuminating the marina's sign outlined a figure walking out from behind a clump of bushes near the gate. Brian saw a gun dangling between the man's fingers and heard what he realized was sobbing.

"Miami-Dade Police! Drop the gun!" Brian showed himself briefly before ducking back behind the car. "Now! Drop it or I'll shoot."

As the man lurched across the parking lot, the overhead lights revealed Sean Hastings closing in on his father, coughing up blood and gasping for breath as he crumpled onto the blacktop.

"I couldn't let you kill anyone else, Dad," Sean shouted. He wiped his face on his sleeve. "You lied to me. You told me Brian was responsible, but I know you had Tim murdered. Mom heard you. She heard everything. And you beat the crap out of her." The teen started keening like a grieving widow at a funeral.

Brian looked for Hastings' gun and saw it laying a couple of feet away from the dying man. He half-ran, half-stumbled over to a car closer to Sean and leaned against it. He wanted to sit down, but knew he wouldn't have the strength to get back up.

Sean kept moving toward his father, face down and gurgling. Brian had to disarm the teen, but wasn't sure how he would fare with only one hand. If the kid put up a fight, all bets were off as to who would win.

When Sean passed him, Brian ran full-tilt at the boy, barreling into him and sending him sprawling, the gun flying from his hand. More by luck than judgment, Brian landed on top of Sean and managed to straddle him. He held his gun to the back of the teen's head. "Don't even think about moving," he said.

"Carefully kick that weapon away from Hastings," he told Kaylen, on her feet and hovering as though she couldn't decide whether to jump on Sean, too, or run for help.

Hastings coughed one final time and lay still. Kaylen slid the gun away then pushed him with her foot before hesitantly leaning over to place her fingers on his neck.

"There's no pulse," she told Brian. "What do you want me to do?" She looked with revulsion at Hastings. "Do I *have* to give him CPR?"

Brian heard sirens in the distance. Lights had come on in several nearby boats. "Leave him alone, hon," he told her. "There's nothing you can do."

Sean wailed even louder.

"Get my cell out of the car," Brian told her. "Hal's on speed dial. Tell him there's an officer down, but I've got the shooter in custody. Make sure he understands that and tells everyone else. The police and the FBI will get here fast from the other side of the dock. I'm not going to risk getting shot again because some asshole makes a mistake and thinks I'm the suspect. Understand?"

"Yes." She ran for the car.

"And bring my handcuffs from the glove compartment," he added. Beneath him, Sean's body shook convulsively. Brian was afraid to ease off and risk losing his prisoner. "It's going to be all right, Sean," he said. "Everything's going to be okay."

Sean only sobbed harder. Brian took a deep breath. "Sean Hastings, you have the right to remain silent…" he began.

CHAPTER FIFTY-SEVEN

Brian pushed open the door marked 'Chief of Detectives' and walked into Hal's new office.

"Have a seat," Hal said from behind an elegant mahogany desk. "You sure managed to cover your ass very successfully with your brother's case, while making the rest of the department look like a bunch of morons."

"That wasn't my intention," Brian said. "I…"

"No interruptions," Hal said. "And no excuses. You always have those, and this time I'm not listening."

Brian sat.

"You're getting a commendation," Hal said. "I'm in two minds as to whether you deserve it, but you took a bullet and saved Kaylen Roberts' life, which makes you a hero with the local community, so it's also good PR for the department."

"A commendation?" Brian didn't believe he'd heard correctly. How could he have gone from department pariah to decorated officer in less than a month?

"I told you, no interruptions," Hal said. "Not until I ask you a question, which hasn't happened, yet."

He leaned back in his chair and drummed his fingers on an armrest. "I've never seen anyone bounce back the way you do. That's what makes you such a valuable member of this department. But let me give you a warning…if you ever go maverick on me again, I'll take your badge myself, and I guarantee you'll never get it back. Do you hear me?"

"Yes, sir," Brian said.

"Good. I'm glad we understand one another." Hal leaned forward and grabbed his pen. "You're the finest officer I've ever had, and you almost got yourself killed. Why the hell didn't you ask me to help you with Hastings?"

"It wasn't because I don't trust you, if that's what you're thinking," Brian said. "Otherwise, I wouldn't have called you or met with you, would I? But I didn't trust anyone else, and they weren't going to help me out, anyway." He avoided looking at Hal. "I know that's partly my fault, and I'm not going to rehash my mistakes. I've got to go forward and try to mend my relationships with the rest of the squad."

"They're receptive," Hal said. "You saw that at Tim's funeral."

Brian nodded. "I'd like to get back to work as soon as possible, in whatever capacity. Behind a desk, if necessary, although I think I'll probably hate it."

"You're nowhere near ready to come back in any capacity," Hal said. "You'll need a medical release before you can do that, and from the information I've been given, you have appointments set up that extend through the next couple of months."

"Yeah," Brian said. "I do."

"You'll also have to complete all the scheduled visits with the department's psychologist." Hal looked like he was expecting an argument about that.

But Brian didn't want to talk about his stint on disability any further. The thought made his depression rear its head again, and if he allowed that to creep back in, he'd be visiting the shrink for more than a few sessions.

"Let's talk about the case," he said. "What's new on Wilson?"

"He got clean away," Hal said. "The bastard took a plane with two of his bodyguards. The rest of them were left at the compound, and since they weren't issued severance checks, they were pretty much ready to cut a deal. What they told us was that the two who left with him were the ones who beat you up and terrorized Kaylen. These guys are also trying to pin Tim's death on the pair, but we're still processing evidence."

"Tim's death looks more like retaliation from the cartel," Brian said. "Although the way those two laid into me, I can see they would have been capable of going too far while trying to get information out of Tim."

"He was a big guy," Hal said. "It must have taken a lot to bring him down to where they could beat him to death."

"They were professionals," Brian said. "They knew where to do the most damage, and how to do it quickly. They had me on the ground and unable to fight back with three blows."

"We believe Sam Wilson sent them to warn you to stay out of things," Hal said. "The word on the street is that the cartel was pretty upset with Wilson for taking that initiative. They wanted you to stick with Kaylen, so you would find out where Tim had hidden the journal. There was conflict between Wilson and the cartel about that. Hastings was another issue. He had been using his position in Vice to take bribes for a long while. At least five years, from the statement his wife gave."

"So she did agree to testify," Brian said.

Hal nodded. "After we brought Sean in, she came to the precinct with her attorney. The deposition she gave portrays Hastings as a verbally abusive husband from the start of their marriage. The physical violence came more recently, probably after he started taking the bribes. He treated her like a servant. To him she was invisible, which meant she heard a lot in that home, between phone calls and visits from his associates. She was terrified of him. She's so glad he's dead, she refused to have anything to do with his body. She paid for the cremation and told the funeral home to toss his ashes out in the trash for all she cared. She's completely dedicated to supporting Sean in any way she can."

"Who burned the restaurant?" Brian asked. "Was it done to place the blame on me?"

"We're still working on that, too." Hal hit the intercom. "Coffee," he said. "Bring in two mugs." He leaned his elbows on the desk. "The fire was intentionally set, but not by Wilson or his employees, unless any of them were working for the cartel."

"So you think the cartel burned the place down?" Brian rubbed his hand over his face.

"Mills thinks Hastings had the restaurant burned and killed Sandy as a warning for Sam to keep his mouth shut and stop his meddling. You had already started poking around too much, and then he made you even angrier by having you beaten up because he was jealous of your relationship with Kaylen."

"I didn't even *have* a relationship with her at that point," Brian said. "He had no reason to be jealous. I know one thing…Wilson would never have had me put into her bed. The one person who could sneak up on me, and who had the physical strength to carry me through a parking lot and up a flight of stairs was my brother. He had to be the one who tattooed Kaylen's leg, too."

"And that's another thing both of you kept from me," Hal said as his administrative assistant, Alicia Solis, brought in the coffee and a stack of messages.

A short, Hispanic girl in her mid-thirties, she smiled briefly at Brian before leaving, her two-inch heels clicking rhythmically against the floor.

"Even *she* pities you," Hal said. "What crap. So what's your excuse for withholding that piece of vital information about the tattoo?"

Brian took a sip of the strong coffee. It felt like coming home. "A need to know basis," he said. "No one outside of Kaylen and me needed to know about the tattoo until we found out why it was put there."

"She walked around with a tattoo on her leg for two weeks and she only told *you* about it?" Hal looked incredulous.

"Her doctor knew," Brian said.

"You're skating on very thin ice," Hal warned. "Don't get smart-mouthed with me. Save that for your coworkers."

"Look, I'm only just beginning to understand the way Kaylen thinks. She's always worried about bad publicity ruining her reputation and either taking all the business away from her new club or damaging her deceased husband's name. The first thing she tried to do was get the tattoo removed, but Tim knew she'd do that, so he used colors that wouldn't come out easily. Then she felt like she'd been branded, but she didn't know by whom, or why, so she kept quiet about it."

"But she told you…"

"She didn't have to. I saw it on her leg the day I woke up in her bed. I figured it was Tim's work. His specialty was roses. But I thought it was his way of leaving Kaylen with a permanent reminder of him when we all thought he'd skipped town. Kaylen didn't tell me about being assaulted right after it happened. She didn't trust me because I couldn't be truthful with her. What a mess." He took another mouthful of coffee.

"A lesson for all of us about sharing information," Hal said. "Although I did tell Kaylen that as far as you were concerned, you weren't able to tell her anything related to an open case."

"Yeah, she was pretty mad at me for not telling her I'm a cop. But she did agree it wouldn't have made her feel safer if I'd also told her I was on suspension. God, I dug a hole for myself I thought I'd never climb out of."

"Yep," Hal said. "You did."

They both stayed silent for a moment, sipping coffee.

"This case was never about drugs or the cartel," Hal said. "It was all about corruption."

"How did you come to that conclusion?" Brian was surprised.

"Your brother led everyone to believe he was a bad-ass. He earned that reputation in his teens and used it to his advantage in his early twenties, as you and I both know. But somewhere along the line, it seems like you finally must have gotten through to him, although he was too stubborn and too proud to admit it."

"He went legit?" Brian put down his cup.

Hal nodded. "IAB is still investigating, but they finally tracked down his attorney. Tim always lived in Little Havana, and he apparently started out buying a taco stand from the financially-strapped owner and leasing it back to the guy. He put money into a new façade and furniture, brought in a couple of cooks from another place that had better food and used discount coupons and advertising in the local community to turn it into a profitable place again. Then he sold it back to the guy, offering him a small-business loan with a low percentage rate. Shortly after that, Tim bought another, bigger restaurant, that time on Calle Ocho. From there, he added real estate investments, including the apartment building he lived in. He kept everything low profile, but he was making money and building an influence in the community the whole time."

"Why didn't he tell me?" Brian ran his hand through his hair. "He let me keep on yelling at him, telling him what a shit he was."

"You two got into a pattern. Well-deserved at first, because Tim was hanging out with the wrong crowd. He continued to count cartel members and gangbangers amongst his friends, even as he moved from their circle into a more affluent one. That's probably how he came to meet Sam Wilson, and he already knew Hastings, of course. Later on, he must have enjoyed baiting you, and since he had a big aversion to admitting that your advice could have any merit, he continued to act out by throwing money around with no visible means of support."

"So he kept the journal as some sort of insurance?" Brian asked.

"I wouldn't doubt it," Hal said. "IAB started a comprehensive investigation into the Vice department. Four of those officers are now on suspension with corruption charges against them. They've also agreed to cooperate. Tim wanted out of Miami. He decided to give you a gift by paying off your boat. Hastings found out about that, and the fact that cash had been used, making it untraceable back to Tim. He had one of his men make an anonymous call to IAB to tell them you had accepted bribes. It was an easy way to get you out of the department altogether, because he was never comfortable with you being a step away from his activities. We're surmising he then paid Wilson's bodyguards to beat the location of the journal out of Tim, but as we unfortunately know, that plan backfired in the worst way."

"So how did they know he was at Kaylen's apartment?"

"They went to pick him up at the club, according to Wilson's other employees. They said Wilson's job was to get him into the back lot, where his car was parked, but Tim had already drugged Kaylen and carried her out a side door, where her car had a reserved space. Wilson sent them to Kaylen's condo, but they must have seen you waiting for Tim in the parking lot, and they couldn't risk you seeing them."

Brian rubbed his temples. He was developing a headache, and his arm was letting him know he was overdue for pain medication. "So they must have seen Tim knock me out and take me up there," he said.

"Yes. They probably had no clue why he did it, but after they screwed up and killed him, they panicked and made a 911 call to catch you in Kaylen Roberts' apartment. Maybe in an attempt to blame his death on you, which was ridiculous. Anyone knowing you would dismiss that bullshit in a heartbeat. But you weren't there by the time the patrol officers arrived, anyway."

"I *was,*" Brian said, "but Kaylen didn't tell them that. Any normal woman would have, but after I convinced her it might be some publicity stunt arranged by a rival club owner to wreck her new business, she was so worried, she shut the door in their faces."

"Maybe she had some intuition about you." Hal finally cracked a smile.

"Maybe she did," Brian said, shaking his head. "She's been the most unbelievable gift Tim could ever have left me. It's a goddamned shame he'll never know that."

"The bottom line is what you do in the future with that gift," Hal said.

"Set her free," Brian said. "It's the only logical conclusion. Kaylen and I don't move in the same social circles, and we've got nothing in common except Tim."

"I don't think you really believe that," Hal said. "Give yourself some time. You've got to heal, inside and out. Making snap decisions about anything right now isn't a good idea."

"Yeah, I know." Brian looked down. "Including what's going to happen to me if I don't get the use of this arm back. But avoiding decisions won't help Kaylen move ahead with her life, either."

CHAPTER FIFTY-EIGHT

Kaylen stood on the balcony of her condo and looked at the pool three floors below. The pristine blue water, sparkling in the afternoon sunlight, looked so inviting, she wished she'd bought a swimsuit. The exercise would have done her good, but she couldn't shake off that horrible feeling of vulnerability. In a few days, she told herself. She'd buy the suit and force herself. Tomorrow she planned to go to Bannisters for the first time since Tim's body had been found.

She looked at her watch. Two-thirty. Brian was coming finally, after two days of debriefing, statements and goodness knows what. He'd called her the previous evening to fill her in on some of the details of the case, so she knew many of the people on Tim's list had either been brought in for questioning or arrested. Everything had been done to keep her involvement low-profile, and her fears about hordes of reporters camping outside her door hadn't materialized.

Brian's tone had been matter-of-fact, businesslike, even distant. He told her he was exhausted after 12 hours at the precinct, and that he was staying the night at a hotel. Although Kaylen understood both Brian's need for uninterrupted rest and maybe even solitude after the chaotic hours following Hastings' shooting, she still felt abandoned.

Now, as she waited for him to arrive, she also felt nervous. Brian didn't need any more information from her. And if he and Lieutenant Shaw were to be believed, he also didn't need to protect her any longer. She wondered if Brian was actually coming over to say goodbye. She'd remind him of Tim, she thought despondently, and not in a good way.

The phone rang.

"Hi." His voice was a little hesitant. "It's Brian. Let me in."

She hit the access code and took a quick look in the gilt mirror above the hall table. She looked pale and anxious. Kaylen ran her fingers through her hair. She found a rubber band around some mail and used it to pull her unruly curls off her face. Maybe she should have chosen a better top, she fretted, looking at her fading tan against the turquoise cotton shirt with a sweetheart neckline.

The doorbell rang. She jumped. When would she stop over-reacting to any sudden noise? She took a couple of deep breaths to slow her racing heart before opening the door.

Brian looked incredibly good, dressed in a dark gray suit over a plain white shirt with a gray and black striped tie. Some of the scars were already fading from his face. He gave her a bouquet of summer flowers, pastel and flowing. No red roses done up in neat cellophane wrap and graced with a big ribbon, like Tim had always brought.

"You look great," she said. "I love the suit. How did you find the time to go shopping?"

"I didn't. A tailor delivered it to the marina yesterday afternoon, and Jim brought it to the hotel for me. An early birthday present from Tim." Brian averted his eyes and made a quick circuit of the living room. "Nice. Think you'll stay awhile?"

"Hopefully. I signed a six-month lease. If I like it here, I'll buy. The owner's looking to sell, but I couldn't commit. Not after..." She hugged the bouquet to her chest. "I'm easily spooked." She changed the subject. "Is everything finished?"

"Yeah, just about. I spent most of yesterday in meetings with Hal and Internal Affairs."

Kaylen felt water dripping from the flower stalks. She left him standing on the other side of the breakfast bar and opened kitchen cabinets until she found a white porcelain pitcher. She filled it with water, arranging the flowers to keep her hands busy.

Brian stood contemplating her with his left hand in his pants pocket. "We got Sean a good lawyer and convinced his mother to testify on his behalf," he said. "The deposition she gave about Hastings' activities was pretty revealing. Sean was right, Hastings beat the crap out of her. She lost several teeth and got two black eyes, but she'll recover."

"Poor thing. I feel so sorry for her, and Sean, too." Kaylen sighed. So many lives would never be the same. "What about Sam?" she asked. "Did he really skip town?" She placed the vase on the breakfast bar and put the wrapping paper into the garbage under the sink.

Brian watched, his brow furrowed. "South America, the FBI thinks," he said as she stopped fussing around and came back into the living room. "They're trying to trace his whereabouts. If they find him, they'll seek extradition."

Kaylen wondered if Brian felt as uncomfortable as she did. He was talking about the case when all she really wanted to hear about was what he planned to do with his life, and whether those plans included her.

He walked over to look out the French doors, his back half-turned to her. "If Sam's employees are telling the truth, he botched things and the cartel's after him, too. We're not sure how they found out about Tim's journal, but it sounds like Hastings ordered him beaten, trying to find out where he'd hidden it."

"There's still a lot to learn, then." Kaylen followed him across the room.

They stood side by side, arms almost touching, but she felt as though there was a chasm between them. Gulls circled in the clear blue sky and a warm breeze slid into the room, softly rattling the blinds she had opened to let in the sunlight.

"Yeah. It'll take a while to put everything together." Brian leaned against the doorframe and finally made eye contact. "One piece of information that isn't in dispute is that Sam didn't like the look of me from the start, even though he had no idea that Tim and I were related, much less that I'm a cop."

Kaylen wondered why she hadn't noticed before how incredibly amazing Brian's blue eyes were, the golden streaks shimmering in the sunlight, or how breathless he made her feel with only a look. "That's the truth," she said.

Brian nodded. "Hal feels the cartel's plans were upset when Sam slowed me down. I was the best hope they had of finding Tim's journal. They knew I'd never rest until I figured out why Tim died, as well as who murdered him. Once they had no further use for me, I'm sure they planned to kill me, too."

He stood quiet for a moment, his gaze directed away from her again. Kaylen couldn't think of anything to say. In fact, she doubted she would be capable of speaking, even if he asked her a question. Talking about the day he got shot brought flashbacks of blood, betrayal and panic.

"I think Sam was lying when he told you that bullet was meant for you." Brian looked right at her, and the distant expression faded. "I was the target. If I hadn't seen that car out the corner of my eye and reacted, the bullet would have gone right through my neck. Instead, the surgeon said only fragments went into my shoulder and forensics found the rest of it buried in the seat back."

Kaylen managed a slight smile. Her throat constricted. "For which I'll be eternally grateful," she said, fighting tears. She slipped an arm around him, but he didn't return the gesture. Her stomach churned. She pulled her arm back to her side.

She left him at the window and took a tissue from the box on the coffee table. "So." She quickly dabbed away the tears threatening to spill from her eyes and made a production out of blowing her nose to cover her complete loss of composure. "Who hit you over the head and dumped you in my bed?"

"Tim." Brian took folded papers out of his pocket and thrust them at her. "I finally read this letter last night. You need to read it, too."

Kaylen opened the pages to find Tim's spidery scrawl.

Hi Bro: If you're reading this, then I guess I didn't make it to Rio. How'd you like the clues I left for you? I could have been a pretty good detective myself, if I wasn't more interested in getting rich.

I want you to know I understood that you had my best interests at heart all the time, but you sure were a nag. Worse than Mom…

"This is way too personal." She tried to hand the letter back.

"You've got to read the whole thing to see what he did, and what he wanted," Brian said.

Kaylen fought back another wave of tears. Her emotions were too raw for this.

"Please," Brian said.

> *…I want you to know that Kaylen's the only woman I've ever loved…*

"Oh, God." She started crying openly. "I can't do this."

"Please," he said again. He pulled more tissues from the box and handed them to her.

Kaylen wiped her eyes. Her vision blurred again. Tim had loved her. She'd never known. She'd always thought he was too much of a player to become serious about her.

> *…but I know she'd never agree to leave Miami and go live with me in Rio. I also know she doesn't share my feelings, although I like to think she's enjoyed being my girlfriend. I helped her get out into the social scene again. She needed that. She was still in mourning, and even though Sam Wilson thought he'd help her forget, it would never happen, except in his dreams.*

Kaylen smiled through her tears. "Tim was more astute than I ever imagined," she said. "Poor Sam."

"I'll never feel sorry for that guy, but whatever. Keep reading."

> *…I hope you'll forgive me for hitting you over the head and dumping you in Kaylen's bed. I couldn't think of a better way to get you two together, or to make you treat her as anything more than a witness. All you ever think about is your job, bro, and you've got to start living life. I want you to live it with Kaylen. I'm delivering her to you on a plate, or maybe it's the other way around, but I'm in a hurry, and I can't wait for you to take some goddamned hint. You've always been completely clueless about relationships. For some stupid reason, you*

think no woman will ever accept you the way you are.

I love you, Brian. Always did, even when we were fighting. You protected me and took all the shit Ed handed out. Your brother, Tim.

Kaylen handed the papers back.

"Are you angry with him?" Brian asked.

"No. Thankful." That time, she had no trouble smiling. "You?"

"I would have been, before all this happened. Resentful. Proud. Ready to tell him I could find my own dates, thanks, even though that wasn't true."

"You couldn't find your own dates?"

He half-shrugged, grimacing. "Somehow, they never lasted. Any girl who stuck it out long enough to make it to the bedroom got freaked out by all the scars." He sighed heavily. "I'm not good at relationships. Abused kids can grow up to be abusive adults. I never wanted to go that route, so I've kept my distance."

Kaylen wrapped her arms around him. Despite his outward calm, his heart was galloping. It gave her a spark of hope, and she laid her head against his shoulder. "We can take things slow. No pressure."

He turned to face her. "We already passed 'slow' the day of the storm," he reminded her.

"That was sex, Brian, not love," she said. "It was great…." She paused. "No, not great…fantastic. I've never become aroused that quickly in my life. But I want even more than that with you, and I think you want it with me, too."

"I do."

Finally, he stopped acting as though they were complete strangers and kissed her. Desire rose inside her with the power and velocity of a rip tide.

"Things would never have worked out between Tim and me," she said. "I want you to believe that. But with you…"

She stopped, afraid to reveal her innermost feelings. Afraid she would push him away with her overwhelming need for intimacy. Even more afraid to tell him she already cared for him so much, she couldn't picture her life without him. His emotions were too fragile. His self-image, too damaged. She had to tread softly and hope that time and her loving support would heal him.

"Remember when I told you I want you all the time?" he asked.

She nodded.

"I don't just *want* you," he said. "It's a lot more than that. We've only known each other a short time, but I swear I've never felt anything close to what I feel for you."

"I owe you everything," she said. "You protected me even when you weren't sure whose side I was on. You saved my life."

"And you saved mine. We're even." At last, he smiled. "That's probably the only place we're even."

His expression changed to one of sadness, and her heart contracted painfully.

"The scales are tipped in your favor, princess," he said. "You're successful, popular, and so beautiful. What could I offer you?"

She took his hand and held it to her lips. "Yourself," she said, softly. "That's more than enough for me, as long as you agree to one stipulation, and it's a big one."

His brow furrowed. He pulled his hand away. "I'm not giving up my job. I love what I do."

"I'm not asking you to give up your career. You're too good at it." She ignored his attempt to withdraw from her by running her fingers across his cheek. His quick intake of breath gave her hope.

"Sometimes I'm good," he said. "Not lately. I lost my perspective and almost got us killed. I want a chance to make up for that. Restore Hal's faith in my abilities."

"I don't think he doubts them," she said. "Not from what he's told me."

Brian's frown eased at her words. "I want to go back, but he won't let me. Not until I've got medical clearance."

"Which makes sense, but it'll be really hard on you," Kaylen said. She knew the boat wouldn't be enough for him.

"Yeah, it'll be tough, sitting on the sidelines, but I can still run charters with Jim's help. In return, I'll lend him a hand with his new career. He's gotten bored with retirement, so he's applying for a PI license."

Brian took her hand and rubbed his thumb over the back of it. Kaylen felt a surge of pleasure, but he still looked worried, and it made her anxious, too.

"You'll be getting involved with a guy who may never have the use of more than one arm," he said.

"Is that all that's holding you back?" She let out the breath she'd been holding. "That's more of a problem for you than it is for me. But whatever happens…" She stopped for a moment, trying to find words that would make him less apprehensive about his injury. "Whether you get the use of your arm back or not," she said cautiously, "I know you'll be okay." She slipped her arms around his waist. "*We'll* be okay."

"You're unbelievable," he said. "How could I get so lucky?"

"Because you deserve a break for once in your life," Kaylen said. "Tim knew that, and he tried his best to give it to you." She smiled. "His methods left a lot to be desired, but then, that was Tim."

Brian held her close, his breath tickling her ear in the most delightful way. Kaylen almost relaxed, but reminded herself that one issue still stood between them, and it was a much bigger one than his left arm.

"So what's the stipulation?" Brian asked.

She reluctantly pulled away from him. "I want you to promise that you'll never lie to me again."

His answer came too quickly, too flippantly. "Okay."

"I mean it," she warned, stepping back to increase the distance between them. "I have to know that regardless of what happens, you won't hold anything else back from me, or try to make decisions for me, either."

He stood staring at her for a long moment before shrugging out of his jacket. He placed his gun on the coffee table.

But the tie defeated him. "Help me," he said as he tugged at it. "I told Jim I didn't need to wear this damned thing, but he insisted, and he made the knot too tight."

Kaylen loosened the tie and Brian dragged it over his head. He began to unbutton his shirt.

She brushed his fingers aside and finished the job.

"Get me out of it," he said. He sounded breathless, and she knew it wasn't from exertion.

Kaylen slid the shirt off his shoulders. For the first time since that fateful morning they had first met, he wasn't wearing a t-shirt. Her heart sped up at the feel of his skin beneath her hands. She tried to fight off the heat flowing over her. He still hadn't promised, and it looked like he meant to distract her, which was working far better than he had any right to expect.

But suddenly, he turned his back to her.

"Now. Really look at me," he said.

Kaylen realized he was doing exactly what she had asked, and that realization was almost too much. Through eyes flooded with tears she saw the heavy scarring from the burns. Raised areas and discolored skin covered his shoulders, his upper back and in some areas, dipped almost to his waist.

He slowly turned to face her again. Scars continued down his chest, some small and round, white and faded…reminders of what may have been cigarette burns. Others, larger and deeper, were lingering evidence of a violence so incredibly vicious, Kaylen knew why he had been so difficult to stop.

Brian had survived what must have been far worse cruelty in his childhood than anything he had suffered at the hands of the men sent to beat him. The staples from the surgery marched in neat precision from his left shoulder down his upper arm, the arm that now dangled uselessly at his side. Kaylen swallowed with difficulty.

"Are you still so sure you can handle looking at all this and touching me on a regular basis?" Brian sounded resigned to the fact that she couldn't or wouldn't be able to do so.

The ebb and flow of her emotions stopped. "Why are you so sure I can't?" she asked.

If he thought she was going to be so easily cast aside, he was in for one hell of a shock of his own, she decided. She felt hatred toward Ed Madison for what he had done. The far-reaching effects of his abuse had scarred Brian not only in his childhood, but for his entire life.

When he stayed silent, she pulled off her own top and bra. She wanted nothing between them. No excuses. No doubts. "It's you I care about," she said. "Not your skin."

She pressed herself against him. Felt his rapid intake of breath. Felt his heart pounding.

"No more lies," she said.

"Dear God, Kaylen." His voice was low, unsteady.

She held him close. "No more deciding what I can and can't handle. No more trying to hide things."

They were both shaking. Her heart beat as hard and fast as Brian's.

"I'm not hiding anything from you now." He buried his face in her hair.

"No." Her voice was little more than a whisper.

She had forced him to confront his fears, and she knew he would never have done so if he didn't care for her so much. But if they were going to leave the painful past behind, he had to make a total commitment.

He took a deep, shuddering breath. "I'll never lie to you again," he said. "I promise."

She believed him.

THE END

ABOUT THE AUTHOR

Heather Ames has enjoyed a nomadic life, living in 5 countries and 7 states. Currently, she has pitched her tents in Salem, Oregon, where after a long career in the healthcare industry, she has finally achieved her dream of writing full-time. She is a past finalist in Romance Writers of America's prestigious Golden Heart contest, and while living in Boston and Los Angeles, she took classes in TV production. She wrote, produced, directed and edited two documentaries, one of which was nominated for an award.

She currently moderates a highly successful online critique group that has been exchanging manuscripts for over ten years. She can be found on Facebook, LinkedIn, Goodreads and Pinterest, as well as her website www.heatherames.com and has been affiliated with Sisters in Crime, Mystery Writers, Willamette Writers, EPIC, Alameda Writers Group and Romance Writers of America. She served AWG twice as a board member as well as host and moderator for the Fiction Special Interest Group, and was a coordinator for several of RWA's local and national conferences. She is currently a board member of Portland·Oregon's Harriett Vane Chapter of Sisters in Crime and an active member of both Northwest Independent Writers Association (NIWA) and the Salem chapter of Willamette Writers.

www.ingramcontent.com/pod-product-compliance
Lightning Source LLC
Chambersburg PA
CBHW071207250626
47159CB00001B/238